THE
DANCE
OF
LOVE

THE
DANCE
OF
LOVE

Angela Young

R
buried
river
press

First published in 2014 by Buried River Press, an imprint of
The Crowood Press
The Stable Block
Crowood Lane
Ramsbury
Wiltshire
SN8 2HR

www.crowood.com

This impression 2018

ISBN 978-1-910208-03-8

The development of this novel has been supported by
the National Lottery through Arts Council England

Typeset in Palatino
Printed and bound by CPI Group (UK) Ltd, Croydon CR0 4YY

for Peter
with my love, always

To watch us dance is to hear our hearts speak
The Hopi people

Also by Angela Young

Speaking of Love

Acknowledgements for
The Dance of Love

FIRST AND FOREMOST I would like to thank my agent, Heather Holden-Brown, who suggested the original idea for *The Dance of Love*: it would not exist without her.

Secondly, I would like to thank Gill Jackson at Robert Hale for her enthusiasm for this book, and for publishing it.

Thirdly, I would like to thank Celia Hayley for her thoughtful readings and trenchant questions which made *The Dance of Love* a much better book.

Fourthly, I would like to thank Gillian Stern for her intuitive suggestions on early drafts and also Melissa Marshall, one of the inestimable TLC readers, for making a suggestion that changed the course of the novel.

And last but not least, I would like to thank Arts Council England who awarded me a grant which bought me valuable time to rewrite *The Dance of Love*.

My great-grandmother was the initial inspiration for this novel, but the characters and the situations in which they find themselves are entirely of my own invention.

The following people patiently answered my questions or made suggestions: thank you so much to the late Josie and to her daughter, Jean Barnett, to Pippa Barrett, Randy Bigham, the Caird Library at the National Maritime Museum, Alan Cameron at the Abernethy Ardgour Adventure Centre at Kilmalieu, Alan Tormaid Campbell,

Dr Stephen Cretney, Lee Desty and Sue Hamblin at BBC South, Andrew Duncan, Judith Fairley at the Falkland Palace Gift Shop, my late father, without whom my writing career might never have begun, Jonathan Ferguson at National Museums Scotland, Jonathan Goodman, Tristan Gooley the Natural Navigator, Harriet Granville, Maggie Hamand and Naomi Wood and all who took the CCWC autumn 2012 and spring 2013 courses; Tessa Hardingham, Penny Hatfield at the Eton Archives, Joanna Hitchcock, Mary Clare Horn, Tarka King, for permission to quote from Anita Leslie's book: *Edwardians in Love*, Kirkaldy Central Library, Fiona de Klee, Frank Larkin, Alastair and Rosemary Leslie, Alex Leslie, Graeme McDonald, Vanessa King Macfie, Jean and Robin Mackenzie, the late Eve Mackworth-Young, Lucinda Mackworth-Young, the Monks at Prinknash Abbey, Campbell Morris and Lisa Wood at the Fife Council Archive, William Gray Muir at Sundial Properties, Pat Newlands, Nadine Rennie, Brue Richardson, the Royal Academy Library, Susan Scott at the Savoy Archive, Brian Ticehurst, Sue Tribolini, Charlotte and Michael Wemyss, Amber White, Peter Wise and last, only because you begin with W, the members of the most invaluable writers' group known to woman: Kate Constable, Sarah Jeans, Fatima Martin and the late Rozsika Parker; thank you for all your insights, suggestions and ideas.

And, finally, thank you, dear reader, for reading this book: your engagement with the characters and their stories gives them the means to travel beyond these pages.

Part One

1899

If any couple danced two consecutive waltzes together every chaperone in the room would cock her ears, wag her head and whisper excitedly to right and left, for what could such a daring procedure possibly spell if not that stirring word *Betrothal*?

Anita Leslie, *Edwardians in Love*

ONE

'I'll race you to Hey Tor,' said Natalie, pushing down her bowler hat and steadying her grey mare.

'The ground is too uneven,' said Millie. 'We ... I ... might fall.'

'We'll stay on the grass, Millie.'

The day was bright and the sky cloudless, but a brisk wind rattled the branches of the oaks and hazels that stood behind them.

'But sometimes the grass hides the granite,' said Millie. 'We might not see it until it's too late.'

Natalie leaned forward and ruffled her mare's mane. 'Artemis knows the moor,' she said. 'And so does Jennie.' She straightened up and began to undo the buttons on her skirt. 'And if we take off our safety skirts we'll fall clear. *If* we fall.'

Millie's cheeks grew almost as red as the Devon earth, but Natalie frowned at her for she was wearing the riding habit she always wore, not a new safety skirt. 'I thought you'd been fitted for one,' she said. 'I thought we agreed—'

'Mama thinks this habit perfectly good enough,' said Millie. 'And besides, I do not wear breeches underneath.'

Natalie shifted awkwardly in her saddle. She turned from Millie and stared out across the rising moorland towards the stony folds of Hey Tor. Patches and paths of short grass grew between tussocks of tall sedge, and the still-brown heather clung to spurs of granite, as if it felt safer there. The fluting call of a skylark filled the air above her, but Natalie did not look up. Instead she stared down at her dark-blue Melton safety skirt and felt it inelegant, despite its fashionable cut; felt her new bowler hat vulgar; felt herself diminished beside Lady Millicent Bridewell.

Millie's saddle creaked and Natalie turned to see her stretching out her hand. 'A gentle canter,' she said. 'Or perhaps just a walk.'

But Natalie turned away. Millie had said she would be fitted for a new safety skirt and she had not. It should not matter but, by obeying her mother, she had dismissed Natalie. Impulsively, Natalie urged Artemis away and when she was galloping across the moor towards Hey Tor she shouted out her frustration. The Bridewells had never understood her but she would not care. She would be herself; she would find her own way in the world. She would defy the Bridewells and their restrictive ways. And she would wear breeches just as often as she wished.

The speed of the ride echoed Natalie's defiance. She was at one with her mare and Artemis did not stumble, neither did Natalie fall as the ground rushed away beneath them. If she could have found a way to stand in the stirrup without unbalancing Artemis she would have, just as she stood in two stirrups when she rode alone, astride her mare. When at last they pulled up beneath Hey Tor, Natalie turned to look back towards Bridewell Wood. Both she and Artemis were out of breath so they stood still, gathering themselves under the bright sun, warm despite the cold wind, and then Natalie saw Millie and her mare, half a mile away. They were close to the edge of the wood and the way Millie rode could not have been more different from the way Natalie had just ridden. Even at this distance it was clear Millie rode sedately, her carriage upright and correct.

As Natalie watched them, her defiance began to give way. She had hoped Millie would change her mind and follow her and now she willed her to turn, to raise her hand, to acknowledge her presence. But she did not. When Millie and her bay disappeared into the wood Natalie tried to banish her disappointment. She had imagined galloping across the moor beside Millie. She had pictured them sitting beneath Hey Tor while their mares grazed. She had heard their laughter and imagined what they might talk about: perhaps the dinner at her father's house the night before and the tedious, mundane nature of the conversation.

For as long as she could remember Natalie had imagined encounters and hoped they would translate into real ones. The only person who had ever encouraged her to do so had been her mother and she was no longer alive. Only her mother had speculated about the things people might really be thinking, the meanings that were hidden beneath the things they actually said. Only her mother encouraged her to treat the natural world as if it were capable of responding. Only she told Natalie that despite the restrictions the world imposed upon women, she could do or be anything in her imagination. But Natalie was not quite twelve years old when her mother died and she had never met another who understood her so well. In those twelve years there had only been one subject on which her parents disagreed: her father wanted his daughter to adopt the ways of their neighbours, the Bridewells; her mother said she should discover her true nature and had no need of adopting the ways of anyone, no matter who they were.

On the day Lady Bridewell told Sir Thomas Edwardes she had hired a governess for her children, Natalie overheard her mother say to her father, 'If you send Natalie to be schooled at Waverton Court, Thomas, then please behave as if you were Lady Bridewell's equal. Do not bow so low when she calls and do not agree with her every suggestion. For if you continue to do so, you will become her plaything.'

Even now Natalie did not know that her father had paid Miss Reedle's wages entirely himself, but his loneliness, in his widowhood, was so obviously lightened by their association with the Bridewells that she rarely had the heart to refuse to accompany him to Waverton Court. And so it was that the Bridewells were the only family Natalie really knew, and the only family in whose company she struggled to hold on to her true self.

She rode sedately away from Hey Tor, just as Millie had ridden into Bridewell Wood, her cheeks flushed from the gallop but her expression sober, for she knew if she were not to upset her father unduly she must behave more like Millie and less like herself. By the time she caught up with Millie, on the far side of Bridewell Wood and within sight of the red-tiled roof of Waverton Court, she said, 'I did not mean to cause you embarrassment with my talk of breeches, Millie. And I should not have galloped off without you.'

'We shall forget about it from this moment,' said Millie and she took Natalie's outstretched hand. But when they drank tea in the drawing room with Millie's sister, Gussie, and the Bridewell sisters informed Natalie of their imminent departure for London, for the Season, Natalie could not help envying them their ease and certain knowledge of their place in the world. She felt as unlike them as the common frog who spends her whole life, except for her brief breeding season, alone.

'We shall find ourselves husbands next year, Millie,' said Gussie, although her lisp reduced husbands to timid, insubstantial creatures, not the dashing young men Natalie imagined for herself. Gussie looked sideways at Natalie without moving her head: it had a belittling effect. 'All the eligible young men in the land will be in London, will they not, Millie? We shall have the pick of them.'

'I think we shall find many young women in London too, Gussie. And they, and their chaperones, will be gathered with the same intention. We must not assume we shall have the pick, as you call it.'

'I think you shall not have a London Season, shall you, Natalie?' said Gussie, ignoring her sister.

'Gussie,' said Millie, 'don't be unkind.'

'It is not unkind,' said Gussie. 'It's a fact. No one in Natalie's family has been presented at Court, so she shall not have a Season.'

Even though Natalie had little desire for a Season, Gussie's words hurt. The way young men and women were matched according to bloodline and land acreage was quite without feeling, but to be prohibited from finding out what the balls and the dinners were like, just because she was not high-born, was painful.

'We are higher born than you, Natalie,' Gussie had said once, her blonde curls bobbing over her seventh birthday cake.

'You should never say such things,' said Millie.

'But it's true,' Gussie retorted, with a determined nod. 'And I know you both think so too.' She nodded at her sister and at her brother. She did not look at Natalie.

'Nevertheless it is very ill-mannered,' said her brother. But his *nevertheless* had given him away too.

Gussie breathed out sharply through her nose, a habit acquired from her mother, when Natalie said, 'Gussie is right. I shall not have a Season.'

Gussie looked directly at her and Natalie smiled sweetly.

'But how shall you find a husband?' said Millie.

'Gentlemen also exist in Devon,' said Natalie. 'I shall fall in love with a farmer. We shall have ten children and breed Devon Rubies.'

'You are more likely to attract a man who will give you rubies,' said Millie. 'You are by far the prettiest of us and you ... stand out, for you are different. In the autumn we shall arrange a ball in your honour and you shall dance with all the landowners in Devon. We shall see you installed in South Devon Manor, perhaps, within the year.'

Neither Millie nor Gussie would contemplate marrying the owner of South Devon Manor, and standing out was not approved of in a young woman, at least not in the Bridewell world. But Natalie's pain at Gussie's dismissal quickly transmuted into relief for, when the Bridewells departed for London, she would be free to live without their constant disdain and, on her way home, she imagined that life, a life in which she and her father no longer called at Waverton Court and she found that, apart from missing Millie a little, she was glad to be free to live without her father's desire for her to become someone she was not. She would ask her Aunt Goodwin to introduce her to the farming and professional families her father had signally failed to invite to Hey Tor House, families among whom there must be at least one gentleman who would, as her mother had once said, 'show himself for an honest man and one who will never be dull, for you will need a man with a lively imagination if you are to live with him happily. And if he has no imagination of his own, then he must be a man who will listen to your spirited imaginings and value them as if they were his own.'

Aunt Goodwin, her mother's sister, would be her protecting angel and, once married, Natalie would bring up her children as her mother had brought her up. They would never know the pain of trying to squeeze themselves into a world where they felt unwelcome.

When Natalie arrived back at Hey Tor House her father asked for news of the Bridewells, as he always did, and she said, 'They go to London in April, Papa, for the Season.' She kissed him lightly on the cheek. 'But even you cannot arrange for me to go with them, for we do not belong at Court.'

'What nonsense you talk,' said Sir Thomas. 'It was at St James's that I received my knighthood.'

'No woman in our family has ever been presented to the Queen, so I cannot be presented.' She kissed him again and said, 'Don't look so unhappy, Papa, for I am glad. The kind of gentleman I shall marry will not be the kind who cares for a London Season. He will care for me because I am myself and your daughter, not because I come from a long line of aristocrats. And with Aunt Goodwin's help, I shall find that gentleman close by.'

TWO

AFTER THAT NATALIE would not go with Sir Thomas to
Waverton Court, but when he received a summons from
Lady Bridewell inside an envelope with a black border, he
made a point of showing it to her. He knew she would not
put up any resistance when he said they must pay a call to
show their sympathy, and she did not. She only said, 'Who
was Lord Ansdrie?'

And now he sat with Lady Bridewell and her only son,
the newly designated Lord Ansdrie, in their drawing room.
The intricate plasterwork above their heads, the heavy
tapestry curtains on either side of the stone-mullioned
windows and the dark oak panels on the walls made the
large room appear to close in on Sir Thomas; he preferred
the light, airy rooms of his own house. But he sat as calmly
as he could opposite Lady Bridewell, whose head always
tipped just slightly to the right so that she looked more
interested in those she spoke to than she actually was.
Sir Thomas waited for her to explain the reason for her
summons.

Lord Ansdrie sat at an angle to Sir Thomas, which made
it impossible for him to keep them both in his line of vision;
he had to turn from one to the other. Lord Ansdrie wore
a dark suit, a black armband and a black cravat and his

mother's mourning dress was of the darkest black silk and crepe; she wore no jewellery. Perhaps Sir Thomas should have worn mourning dress. He braved the subject and apologized.

'I thank you, Sir Thomas, but your apology is quite unnecessary,' said Lady Bridewell. 'You did not know my brother.' She sat very straight. 'We were in Scotland for the funeral last week.'

'I am sorry for your loss.'

Lady Bridewell nodded and her dark headdress shook. It looked like a large spider. She clasped her right hand over her left and then her left over her right. The death of her brother was obviously causing uncharacteristic agitation, but she said nothing more.

Through the windows at the north end of the drawing room Sir Thomas saw Lady Bridewell's daughters, the Ladies Millicent and Augustina, walking across the lawn. They wore black silk dresses trimmed with black crepe and dark little hats with short dark veils. Between them walked Natalie, her yellow dress like a shaft of sunlight in a dark wood.

'My brother and I were estranged,' said Lady Bridewell, at last, 'but his management of Ansdrie has proved even worse than I feared.'

So, not his death, then, but his bad management. Astonishing that she was telling him this; she had never related such details before.

'The house has been dreadfully neglected. There is only one manservant left and the *revenue*,' she whispered the word, 'from Ansdrie's coal is quite gone. The mines have faulted and flooded. There are death duties to be paid. Only the sheep remain and they alone will not keep the estate.'

'I'm very sorry to hear it, Lady Bridewell,' said Sir Thomas, his voice pitched higher than he had intended. He tried to control his amazement, but she had never spoken to him before of the one thing upon which every human being depended, the thing he had spent so much of his life successfully accumulating.

Was she about to ask him for a loan?

Or to act as guarantor?

He must, clearly, prepare for more surprises.

'As you know, Sir Thomas,' said Lady Bridewell, half-turning to her son, 'Ansdrie inherits from his uncle.' She called him by his new title as if he had been born to it. 'But until he marries he shall not live in Scotland.'

She stood, so Sir Thomas stood and made a half-bow and then she walked, or rather, stalked, towards the window. Sir Thomas watched her movements and noticed, for the first time, that the vertical edges of the curtains she stood by were ragged; threadbare patches were made cruelly obvious in the sunlight.

Lady Bridewell raised her lorgnette to the young party outside and then, turning back to Sir Thomas, she said, 'I should like to present Miss Edwardes at Court in June. When I present my own daughters.'

Sir Thomas fell into a flurry of exclamation. His daughter would be honoured to be presented. He would be honoured. She would prove most worthy of Lady Bridewell's kind patronage. He spoke too quickly and he tried harder than usual to lengthen his vowels, but he sounded so unlike himself when he said *arsk* instead of *ask* or *take* instead of *tek* that he often ended up speaking in an odd combination of accents. And then, when embarrassment surfaced through the froth of his stream of speech, he stopped, abruptly, and Lady Bridewell said how well Natalie looked and how her childhood friendship with her daughters was bound to strengthen during the Season. And then she said, 'My son must take a wife with him to Ansdrie, Sir Thomas. It will make the transition so much less . . . difficult.'

'Indeed it will, Lady Bridewell,' said Sir Thomas. 'And I wish them well.' He turned to Lord Ansdrie and then back to Lady Bridewell. 'But how will he and his wife live at Ansdrie when it is in the state you say it is in?'

He glanced back at Lord Ansdrie and then looked quickly away. It was very peculiar to discuss him as if he were not in the room. But Lady Bridewell looked directly at Sir Thomas and smiled broadly, a very rare thing in his experience, and then she swooped towards him with a rustle of dark skirts. 'I am quite certain,' she said, 'that between us all we shall reach a very happy arrangement.'

Between us all? Very happy? Could Lady Bridewell be about to suggest what he thought her about to suggest?

She sat down, so Sir Thomas also sat down, but so quickly that he forgot to flick his coat tails away and so he had to lean a little backwards. And then Lord Ansdrie stood up.

'I should like,' he said, walking towards Sir Thomas, 'to become better acquainted with your daughter.'

They'd been neighbours for thirteen years.

'I have been so often away at school and, lately, with the Waterfirth Reservists,' he said, 'that I do not know our neighbours as well as I should.'

Sir Thomas tried to keep his mind from forming conclusions.

'These are, of course, only the preliminaries,' said Lady Bridewell.

'We simply wanted,' said Lord Ansdrie, who was marginally less cryptic than his mother, 'to inform you of our plans, to make our intentions clear.'

'Trawton will assist with Miss Edwardes's gowns,' said Lady Bridewell.

Natalie had a perfectly good lady's maid of her own, but perhaps Trawton would dress her better? In the correct style?

'I shall chaperone her myself,' said Lady Bridewell. 'She will be an Ansdrie *avant la lettre*.'

Sir Thomas folded his lips inward so that his moustache

21

and beard hid his delighted smile. He was glad Lady Bridewell could not see the images that crowded into his mind, for he saw himself again and again at receptions and balls, soirées and dinners, presenting his daughter, the *future Lady Ansdrie*. But he also understood very well that it was Natalie's dowry that prompted Lady Bridewell to consider her a suitable daughter-in-law. But, in time, his daughter would charm them all and Lord Ansdrie would discover what a brilliant choice he had made, in every respect.

'When shall you speak to my daughter?' said Sir Thomas, finding his voice at last and trying to control his lips, which would not be persuaded out of a broad grin.

Lady Bridewell answered, instead of her son. 'I shall inform Miss Edwardes she will have a Season,' she said. 'But otherwise,' she turned to her son, who nodded, 'we think it better not to inform her of any but the most peripheral arrangements at this stage.'

Again Lord Ansdrie elaborated. 'I should like things to take their natural course,' he said. 'I should like to get to know Miss Edwardes and I should like her to get to know me, without the obligation that would accompany her knowledge of our – of my – intention towards her.'

Lady Bridewell stood beneath the red-brick portico while Sir Thomas handed Natalie into his landau, a courtesy she never usually extended to them, and then she said, 'I shall not expect my children to remain in mourning for longer than three months, Sir Thomas. They never knew their uncle and besides he deserves no more.'

Naturally, Natalie questioned him about the short period of mourning as they travelled back up the hill to Hey Tor House, but he only said, 'You shall discover soon enough, my dear.'

When Sir Thomas was alone in his study at Hey Tor House, when he sat at his desk and looked out through the wide

Georgian sash windows towards the wooded hill that led to Waverton Court to the south and out across the moor to Hey Tor to the west, he did his best to control his feelings of gratification. But it was difficult: he was about to become connected to one of the foremost aristocratic families in the land. He, a man who had risen, in one generation, from grocer to owner of a successful tea-planting enterprise.

He shifted in his chair and turned to look up at the portrait of his late wife. She would not have been impressed with his delight. Nor would she have approved of the whoop of triumph he let out when, later that morning, he tramped across the moor. For Lily Ann never wanted Lady Bridewell to think him a gentleman instead of a man who worked for his living. She took pride in the good, honest man of trade that he was, without affectation. Before they married, when Sir Thomas showed her a Change of Name Deed and said, 'See here, Lily Ann. See how refined our name will become with the added *e*,' she only said, 'What a family does and how a family behaves is what matters. Fiddling with a name won't make the slightest difference.'

Sir Thomas turned back from the portrait just in time to catch sight of his daughter riding past the window. She wore a cap, a jacket and breeches and looked for all the world like a stableboy. Sir Thomas stood up and raised his arm to attract her attention, but she did not, or would not, see him. He turned to the west window and watched her open the wooden gate and set off across the moor. He would tell her, at dinner that night, that she must no longer ride alone, and certainly not in those clothes. For she was about to begin a new, elevated life among the very best, and it would not do.

THREE

'NATALIE, DO PLEASE come to luncheon,' said Millie. 'It's weeks since last you were at Waverton Court.'

Millie dismounted and the groom, John Boundy, took Jennie to the stables, her hooves clattering over the cobblestones.

'I thought you were not supposed to receive calls,' said Natalie, walking beside Millie beneath the white-pillared portico of Hey Tor House.

'Mama says we need not observe strict mourning for Uncle Ansdrie, even in these three months. We only met him once and his neglect of Ansdrie House has upset her terribly.'

When the Bridewells wished to break rules it was perfectly acceptable; when others wished to break them it was not.

Natalie led Millie into the large white drawing room and they sat together on a carved mahogany sofa. Sash windows looked out to the west towards Dartmoor and to the north towards Sir Thomas's park. It had rained in the night but now the room was filled with light. White cumulus clouds sailed in a clear blue sky and soon the yellow-green leaves of the oaks would begin to unfurl, and here and there in the long grass wild daffodils bloomed.

'Gussie would like to see you too, Natalie.'

Natalie thought but did not say, 'Then she could have ridden up with you.' She waited for Millie to say what she had come to say: clearly it was something important, although she talked at length about her uncle's funeral before she came to the point. She said only that they and an old manservant had been at the service. 'None of the miners, nor the flax workers came,' she said. 'Nor any neighbours. Uncle Ansdrie made himself very unpopular.' And then, at last, she turned to Natalie and said, 'But there is happier news. Mama sent me up expressly to tell you. She will present you, Natalie. You shall come to London with us. You shall have a Season. Is that not wonderful? Does it not make you happy? Say it does.'

Millie took Natalie's hands and Natalie did her best to look as happy as Millie wanted her to be, but she felt as if she were falling from the top of Hey Tor.

'Did you suggest it to her, Millie?'

Millie shook her head. 'No, I did not.' She let go of Natalie's hands. 'Mama told us she would present you when we travelled down from Scotland. She was going to tell you herself, but you haven't come to Waverton recently.'

'Because you are in mourning,' said Natalie. And then, 'I must speak to Papa,' was all she said, for although she could not imagine how presentation at Court, even to one so lofty as the Queen Empress herself, could possibly alter the fact that she did not belong among the Bridewells and their kind, she was curious about the Season. But she also knew that she and her father would stand out for their ignorance of the correct codes of conduct, and her presentation would only emphasize their difference. That would be humiliating.

'But you will come to luncheon?' said Millie.

In her father's landau on the way down the hill to Waverton Court, Natalie had failed to convince her father against a London Season. He said the Bridewells knew the very best people and they too would come to know those people in their own right. He looked forward to holding receptions and dinners for her and he thanked her for thinking about the cost of it all, but she need not concern herself.

'You shall have a coming-out ball, my dearest girl. Do you not think your mother would be proud?'

Natalie thought perhaps her mother would be proud, even though the way the Bridewells conducted their affairs had never impressed her. And she could not help imagining a ball held in her honour, in London. And yet . . .

After luncheon, Natalie sat with Gussie and Millie on an iron bench in the spring sunshine.

'Our lives shall begin in London,' said Millie. 'I cannot understand why you hesitate to come with us, Natalie.'

'Mama will treat you just as if you were one of her own daughters,' said Gussie. 'There will be no difference between us.'

Natalie stared at the intricate patterns of the box hedges on the parterre in front of her. They had been cropped and pruned until they looked as if they had been carved from bright-green stone, not made from living plants.

'If you stay here it will be worse than being Returned Empty,' lisped Gussie.

Natalie stood and turned to face the sisters. You know as well as I do,' she said, 'that the Season is not meant for people like me.' She looked at them and they both bent their heads. 'I'm afraid I . . . shall lose myself there.'

'All the gentlemen will fall at your feet,' said Millie, looking up. 'And there will be plenty of them to find you, should you get lost. I think,' she turned to Gussie and waited for her to look up, ' – do you not, Gussie? – that you shall find a husband before either of us.'

'My parents married because they loved each other,' said Natalie. 'But my mother was never in London in her life.'

'That is rather . . . unusual,' said Gussie. 'How did her father know your father had the means to provide for her? How did he know where he *came* from?'

'She knew he was the one for her,' said Natalie, putting her hand on her heart. 'It's a feeling, Gussie, an instinct. Something that no amount of land or money can ever provide.'

She turned away and saw Lady Bridewell walking with her father by the stone steps that led up from the river. Lord Ansdrie followed them as they threaded their way along the circular gravel paths between the clipped box hedges.

Millie stood up and took Natalie's arm. She said, 'A suitable gentleman might also be a loving one, Natalie.'

Gussie stood too and walked towards her mother. She said, 'We have tried to persuade her, Mama, but it seems Natalie will not have a Season.'

'It is hardly a matter for debate, Miss Edwardes,' said Lady Bridewell. 'It is a fact of life.'

Sir Thomas studied the curve of a hedge with particular care. Lord Ansdrie stared above the heads of his sisters into the distance and Millie and Gussie looked at their hands. Only Natalie and Lady Bridewell looked directly at each other. And then Lord Ansdrie said, 'We shall introduce you to everyone, Miss E— Natalie. And you shall have partners for all the dances at all the balls.' Now he looked at her. Was there a slight reddening in his cheeks? 'For we know,' he said, 'how very much you like to dance. And you shall find far better dancing partners than I, in London.'

He made the slightest of bows and then Lady Bridewell patted Sir Thomas's arm and her dark silks rustled as she turned towards the house. She took her son's arm and then turned and said, over her shoulder, 'We expect you for dinner tomorrow.'

In the carriage on the way back up the hill Natalie apologized to her father.

'I did not mean to cause you embarrassment, Papa,' she

said. 'But even though I would dearly love to discover what a Season is like, I don't think I can do it.'

She stared out at the green hills that folded in upon themselves: how welcoming they looked, how very content with their lot.

'I feel so very unlike myself when I am with the Bridewells.'

But her father made no answer.

Lord Ansdrie sat in his late father's study with his mother. The afternoon had grown cold and the fire had been lit. They sat in dark leather wing-backed chairs, just as two gentlemen might sit in their club. But they were not reading newspapers or drinking port.

'Do not worry, Mama,' said Ansdrie. 'I find myself rather attracted to the chase. I had thought we should meet with nothing but enthusiastic, even abject, gratitude. I'm glad to find it is not the case. And I am quite certain that Miss E— Natalie . . .' he found it difficult to call her by her first name; his sisters and Natalie were close in age, but he was six years older and he had never known the kinship with her that his sisters knew. But it was different for women; they were better at such things. He began again. 'Miss Edwardes will, in the end, do exactly as we suggest. How could a young woman of her pedigree resist our invitation?'

'I look forward to news of your success,' said Lady Bridewell. 'I do not wish to be kept waiting.'

When his mother had left the study Ansdrie settled back in his chair, closed his eyes and sighed. He looked forward to the company of his fellow officer in the Waterfirth Reservists, Lieutenant Haffie. He would arrive later in the afternoon and it would be good to have another man in the house, for the concerns of women were, at times, enervating.

But while he waited for his friend he occupied himself by assembling the things he knew about the woman who would become his wife, as if he were collecting stones for a drystone wall. And, as he put the wall together he determined he would discover a weak spot; a place where there were too few hearting stones. When he discovered that place he would be able to persuade Miss Edwardes of the necessity of a London Season, for it was the most important event in the life of every young woman he knew.

She had the advantage of looks; she would turn heads and people would pay her attention. Her eyebrows were dark and too close together, yet womanly. Her face was perhaps too long but it was transformed when she smiled. Her eyes were a startling dark blue and her gaze direct. Ansdrie liked that, although he would ask Millie to advise her not to hold a gentleman's gaze for too long. She was physically strong and she had the gait, sometimes, more of a man than a woman, when she was determined upon something. Ansdrie would stop her riding astride, in breeches, but he admired the fearless nature that made her do so. And she was not afraid to say what she thought: she had an honest, if sometimes over-eager temperament. She rode well; she danced superbly; her tendency to laugh too loudly or to deliver an unsolicited opinion could be tamed; and her dowry was exceedingly handsome.

Ansdrie was pleased with his observations. There was much about Miss Edwardes to admire, despite her unsatisfactory pedigree. But he had not yet found a weakness and he must, for he could not marry a young woman who had not been presented, a woman who had not been brought out into society, a woman who had no experience of the world he had been born into.

He pictured her, that afternoon, standing opposite his sisters on the parterre and he remembered how, when they were children, they had played blind man's buff. But when Natalie was blindfolded he and his sisters hid, quite contrary to the rules, behind the tall, triangular box trees. When it was his turn to be blindfolded Gussie whispered that they should all hide again, but Natalie refused. She said it was unfair and she walked determinedly along the gravel so he would hear her as he searched, blindly, for them. And when, at last, his sisters were shamed into leaving their own hiding places he caught one of them, triumphantly. He did not attempt to catch Natalie for she had stood up for him.

That was it. He could count on her to stand up for what was right. It was not a weakness, but a strength. She would do the right thing and it was indisputably right that she should have a London Season before she became his wife. He would persuade her of it and she would see it. He would begin by paying more attention to her; he would court her as his mother had suggested on that bleak, grey, February day, when they walked up from the chapel at Ansdrie House after his uncle's funeral. A chill wind whipped about them as they looked up at the broken stone pediment high above the great oak front doors, at the cracked ashlar, at the peeling paint on the window frames and the sliding slates on the long roof. The dilapidated state of the house shocked Ansdrie; his mother had so loved it that, in his imagination, it had always been a place of great beauty.

His mother said, against the wind that made her eyes water, 'When it became obvious my brother would never marry and I knew you would one day inherit, I promised myself I would do everything in my power to restore the house. When I lived here, as a girl,' she sniffed and Ansdrie realized, with a shock, that it was not the wind that caused the watering in her eyes, 'this house was so very well loved. It shall be again. When you live here.'

She held on to his outstretched hand with both of hers. She took the handkerchief he offered her, turned away from him and the folds of her dark veil fluttered against her shoulders. And then she bent her head and when she turned back to him he, for the first time in his life, gave his mother an awkward hug. She felt frail in his arms and he was conscious of Verrinder, his valet, and his sisters walking to the far side of the station coach; he was grateful for their tact. Throughout his childhood, Ansdrie had longed for a sign of affection from his mother but she had never given it. But now, outside this broken house, a house that had once filled her with such happiness, she clung to him, needing his reassurance and his affection, and the bricks that enclosed his own walled-in heart began to crumble.

'It is a great comfort, Ansdrie,' she said, 'to know you feel as I feel about this house.' She gave him back his handkerchief. 'It will guide you when you begin the restoration.'

'But we have not the wherewithal, Mama,' he said. 'I do not see how we can—'

'I believe you need only look as far as Hey Tor House.'

Now his mother's smile was confident. She stood back from him as if she had never been in the least upset. For a moment, Ansdrie could not think what she meant and then he said, 'I . . . admire Miss Edwardes, Mama. She is forthright and she is good-looking. But do you really think her *suitable*? Her pedigree is not at all what we would wish for.'

'Pedigree need not be the sole consideration,' Lady Bridewell said. 'Especially when there is an urgent need. Those with the right pedigree, Lady Sophia perhaps, or Lady Victoria or even Miss Eldensworth, have not the fortune this dear house so badly needs. But Miss Edwardes's dowry will see Ansdrie restored. Your marriage will allow this house to regain its proper place among the great houses of Fife.'

She nodded briskly and turned from him. She made a great fuss with her gloves and the edges of her cloak, pulling them together against the wind.

Ansdrie had never heard his mother speak so passionately, nor had he ever felt so alive himself. He would do everything he could to save this house, for her sake. He would fulfil his duty to his bloodline and his inheritance through marriage to a young woman whose potential as a wife he had never before considered; for, through that marriage, he would save the house his mother loved and by doing that he might, lonely man that he was, redirect some of her love for the house towards himself.

FOUR

'I SHOULD LIKE to be able to tell Lady Bridewell, when we dine at Waverton tonight, that we shall go to London,' said Sir Thomas.

He stood before Natalie in his dressing gown. He held a candle. It was very early.

'I don't think I can say yes,' said Natalie, sleepily.

'But Lady Bridewell does you a great honour. It is exceedingly discourteous of you to refuse.'

Natalie turned quickly from her father to hide a sudden flash of anger. Surely it was not wrong to know where she did not belong, even if she was not yet certain where she did belong? But she hated the knowledge that she had upset him. She turned back to her father, kissed him quickly and said, 'I shall go for an early ride. I think better when I am riding. I shall give you my answer when I return.'

He thanked her and walked away.

Natalie drew back the curtains. It was not yet dawn but by the time she had dressed, and saddled Artemis, it would be light enough to ride. She pulled on her breeches and wondered what other young women did, women who were not like Millie or Gussie. She thought about it as she saddled Artemis and when John Boundy came running across the stable yard, apologizing for not readying Artemis for her himself, she smiled and said she had not asked him to, and when she was riding fast across Dartmoor she wondered how a man like Boundy would meet his wife. And surely her own father, who had taught her to ride with the same ease and freedom as a man, surely he must allow her to conduct her life with at least something of that same freedom.

She rode beneath racing white clouds and when the thud of Artemis's hooves sent a black grouse skittering her heart jumped and her mare shied. But she kept her seat and rode on towards Hey Tor, which, that morning, looked as if it were a slumbering grey beast that might turn its angry head towards her at any moment. When she pulled Artemis up, she turned away from the Tor and looked out over the down. Dartmoor ponies and sheep grazed between promontories of granite on the wide expanse of the moor. Clumps of long thin leaves promised the haze of bluebells that would soon eclipse the brown of the old year's oak and hazel leaves and, when the clouds slowed their race, the sun shone brightly between them.

Natalie turned back to Hey Tor and now, in the sunlight, its roughcast presence softened. It was no longer a beast. She took off her jacket and slung it over the pommel. She rolled up her sleeves and tucked her hair up under her cap. And then she rode back down into the valley. She crossed the Bridewell where it rippled in a shallow stream over granite, and then she turned north and rode into the wood.

A small clump of primroses held up their sunny heads and she jumped down, picked a few, breathed in their delicate scent and put them through the buttonhole of her jacket. And then she stood very still and put her hand beneath Artemis's neck for she had seen a red deer, a hind, with her fawn. She watched for several moments before the hind turned, looked directly at her and then leapt gracefully away, her fawn stumbling to keep up.

She led Artemis on through the wood and then she

began to sing, as she and her mother had so often sung together. She sang 'The Tree in the Wood'. It had always made her laugh when they sang it, each of them testing the other's memory as they invented more and more lines, but when Natalie could not remember the final lines they had sung her eyes filled with tears. She stopped singing and stood still: her mother's absence could still ambush her. She tried to remember the sound of her voice, but she could not. She tried to conjure the lavender scent she always wore, but she could not. She listened for what her mother used to call *the hum of things* and, in despair that she could not hear it, she sat beneath an oak and wept.

Artemis stood by her, nuzzling her face gently as if she understood, and when, at last, Natalie brushed away her tears and stood up, she did hear that hum, that almost inaudible sound that told her everything was filled with life, even the stones. The earth smelled musky, the leaves of the oaks and the hazels were luminously green and the pale-green bracken fronds, still tightly curled, looked like tiny ammonites. A splash in the river beyond the trees told her an otter swam there and when she looked up at the blue sky through the branches of the trees, she realized she must consult her Aunt Goodwin, her mother's sister, about what she should do. Why had she not thought of it before? She would ride there now.

Her equilibrium restored, Natalie remounted Artemis and rode slowly into the clearing, hoping to see the otter. And then her heart began to beat quickly for, ahead of her in Hero's Pool, so called for a young man who saved a young woman from drowning there, stood the pale figure of a man. A naked man. He stood with his back to her, the water rising to his waist, and when he shook his head drops of water sprayed out. Natalie dared not move. She watched the man scoop handfuls of water and throw them over himself. And then he too became very still, as if he sensed the presence of another being.

Artemis blew air through her nostrils and a black horse tethered on the other side of the clearing gave an answering snort. Natalie recognized Jupiter, Lord Ansdrie's gelding, but the man in the river was not Lord Ansdrie: his hair was much paler. He said, in a soft lilting accent, 'There's no cause to creep up on me, Ansdrie. Throw me my towel, would you?'

He turned towards her and Natalie leapt down from Artemis and attempted to hide behind her forelegs. She struggled to keep her balance.

'My apologies, young man. I thought you were my host. You'll excuse me, will you not, while I dress.'

Natalie could not speak. She looked away while the man splashed out of the river and up onto the bank. She heard the sounds he made as he dried himself. She recognized the tune he hummed, 'Blow the Wind Southerly', but her mind was frozen: it would not tell her what to say or do. At last she put her jacket back on, for it covered her better than her shirt. She buttoned it up and as she did so she thought the man might be Lieutenant Haffie, Lord Ansdrie's fellow officer: he was expected at Waverton Court.

He walked towards Natalie. He had a swinging stride; she saw his riding boots and breeches from behind Artemis. And then she heard him say, in his lilting accent, 'Do you stay near here, young man?'

Natalie's lips began to quiver. The desire to laugh threatened to overwhelm her, but she managed to say, 'Us work fer Maister Edwardes up a' Hey Tor House. Us'm the groom, John Boundy.' She imitated Boundy's Devon accent well, but she failed completely to alter the tone of her voice.

The man's curling wet hair was red, his face was freckled and there were drops of water on his pale eyelashes. 'Sir Thomas and Miss Edwardes come to dine at Waverton Court this evening,' he said. 'Is Miss Edwardes as pretty as they say?' His brown eyes watched her.

'Er's preddy enough,' said Natalie. And then the

laughter that had been welling up inside took hold of her. She turned away, leaned into Artemis's neck and laughed as she had not laughed since her mother had been alive. She laughed with her whole body and although she was conscious that he might think her rude, the feeling was so exquisite that she did not try to stop. When, at last, she heard the man's footsteps behind her she turned back, resolutely, and said, between smaller bursts of laughter, 'I did not mean . . . I do not mean to be rude, truly I do not.' But she saw that he was smiling at her, laughing also, and she pulled off her cap and shook out her dark hair. 'It is a rare pleasure to laugh like that. But I am not John Boundy, as you can see.' She held out her hand, palm downwards, just as if she were in the drawing room at Hey Tor House. 'I am Natalie Edwardes,' she said, 'and I think, perhaps, you are Lieutenant Haffie.'

'I am,' said Haffie. 'But it is I who should apologize.' He took her hand and bowed. He was serious now and so was she. 'I thought this a secluded place.'

'It is,' said Natalie. 'That's why I come here.'

Haffie cleared his throat. 'Then I am doubly sorry for intruding. Let alone for thinking you were someone you clearly are not.'

'And I am sorry,' said Natalie, looking away to hide her blush, 'for surprising you.'

She gathered her hair and pushed it up under her cap. Then she grasped the reins and turned to mount Artemis. But she turned back to Haffie and said, 'I promised Papa never to ride in these clothes if I thought I should meet anyone. So, when we are introduced tonight, would you pretend you do not know me?'

'Most certainly, Miss Edwardes,' said Haffie, putting his hand on his heart and bowing again. He rolled the *r* in her name. 'If it would help.'

'Thank you,' she said, turning back to her horse.

'I came up here,' said Haffie, 'to paint the river.'

Natalie looked beyond him and saw, for the first time, an easel with a watercolour standing on it. It showed the Bridewell beneath a low mist; the greens of the river-bank and the blues of the sky were muted, early dawn colours; the willows were almost black. A chair made of canvas and wood stood by the easel; a rectangular wooden box was on its seat and a brown felt hat hung from one side.

'I want to capture the light on the water as it shifts and changes. If such a thing should not prove outwith my ability.'

Outwith. A word Natalie had never heard before. She said, 'I heard you were an officer with the Waterfirth Reservists. Not a painter.'

'I am an officer,' said Haffie. 'But I am also a painter. I learned to sketch with the Reservists, and then I taught . . . am still teaching . . . myself. Ruskin says the best drawing masters are the woods and the hills.'

How difficult it must be to capture the shimmering river in paint. What a wonderful thing to be able to do.

Artemis nudged Natalie and, indicating to Haffie what she intended to do before she rode away, she led her grey mare to the river. While Artemis drank, Natalie stared at the floating green weed beneath the clear water and watched the gently swaying branches of the willows and then, impulsively, she pushed up the sleeves of her jacket and knelt by the river to drink. But the river was too low and she could not reach the water.

'Allow me,' said Haffie, kneeling beside her.

The sun flared behind his head as he leaned down, scooped up some water and held out his hands. Natalie cupped her own hands to receive it but, by the time he had poured the water from his hands into hers, there was very little left. He leaned down to scoop up some more and then he looked at her. She hesitated, but only for a moment. She took off her cap, held her hair back and bent her head. She drank the cold water straight from his hands. She felt the tips of his fingers beneath her chin and the heels of his hands against her forehead and when she looked up she pushed water from her nose with her fingers and said, 'I should like to drink water like that every day.'

She stood quickly, pushed her hair back beneath her cap and turned to her horse. She did not want Haffie to see her blush, again. But he touched her arm lightly and said, 'That was a beautiful thing to say,' and so she turned back to him, her blush burning her cheeks, and gave him a faltering smile. When he smiled two lines, like crescent moons, appeared on either side of his mouth.

'Thank you,' said Natalie, and then she mounted Artemis and with a quick, 'I look forward to seeing you tonight,' she left the clearing.

When she emerged from the wood she saw the large white cube that was Hey Tor House above her, and the orangery her mother had so loved just below it. As she rode past the orangery she saw her father pacing up and down the drive. Smoke from his pipe drifted up beside his head and he walked with his shoulders hunched. Natalie stopped and watched him and when he turned and gave her a hesitant wave, her heart filled with pity and with love. She knew how much he still missed her mother and she longed to make him happy. She rode towards him and she knew, without consulting her Aunt Goodwin, that she would go to London. She would do it for her father's sake. She urged Artemis on and then she smiled broadly for it occurred to her that Lieutenant Haffie, who was, after all, a friend of Lord Ansdrie's, might also go to London and the thought of such a gentleman being there made the Season a far more appealing affair. They would, perhaps, discover what it was like together.

FIVE

THAT AFTERNOON, FOR the first time in her life, Natalie could not decide what to wear. It had never troubled her before, but now she found nothing suited her. No dress fitted well enough. The colours were wrong. The trimmings too fussy. The cut unflattering.

'What's the matter with me, Hocks?' she said.

But her lady's maid only smiled and persuaded her not to discard a deep-blue silk gown. She said it set off her eyes very well. And when, eventually, Natalie stepped down from her father's carriage and looked up at the familiar Jacobean façade of Waverton Court, she clasped her gloved hands together and said a quick prayer. She prayed Lieutenant Haffie would not think the worse of her for what had happened that morning by the Bridewell; that he would not think her forward, as the Bridewells would. Her hands were still tightly clasped together when her father took her arm and they walked beneath the portico.

Anderson had only just taken their cloaks and her father's hat when Millie hurried to greet them.

'I thought you should like to know,' she said, 'before you meet Lieutenant Haffie, that he is not at all an ordinary officer. He knows about painters and he paints, properly, I mean, not the sketches he must make on manoeuvres. Can you imagine that?'

'Goodness,' said Natalie. 'An officer *and* a painter. What an unexpected combination. I very much look forward to meeting him.'

Her voice was too excited and her words too many.

'I think you will like him,' said Millie, as Sir Thomas escorted the two young women towards the drawing room, 'for he is different.'

They held themselves as straight and tall as their corsets required and by the time Lady Bridewell greeted them and Natalie had taken her outstretched hand and curtsied, she had seen Lieutenant Haffie. He stood with his back to her, beside Gussie.

'A word, Sir Thomas,' said Lady Bridewell, patting the seat beside her.

Natalie turned to her father and smiled, and then she inclined her head in the sign they made to each other when they were in company, to show that all was well. He too inclined his head and took his seat by Lady Bridewell. They would begin their discussions for her London Season before Natalie had reached the other side of the room.

Millie took Natalie's arm and, when they had greeted all those they knew, she said, as they walked towards the man Natalie had met that morning, 'Gussie and I are pleased you will come to London. Mama told us just before you arrived.' She squeezed Natalie's arm. 'You will like it,' she said. 'And I shall like it very much that you will be with us.'

'Thank you, Millie,' said Natalie.

And then Millie presented her to Haffie but she could barely look at him. He said, 'Enchanted, Miss Edwardes.'

'Lieutenant Haffie will make our portraits, Natalie,' said Millie. 'Mama has commissioned him.'

'Oh,' said Natalie. 'Do you paint, Lieutenant Haffie?'

'Of course he does,' said Gussie, 'otherwise how could he make our portraits?'

Glad for a reason to laugh, Natalie laughed too loudly,

and Lord Ansdrie turned towards her as if he would tell her to be quiet. To stop him she asked about his horses and his Widecombe Whiteface sheep, as if she had not asked for a long time, and then she sat with her Aunt Goodwin by the window.

'I hear Lady Bridewell shall present you at Court,' she said.

Lord Ansdrie turned towards them, his expression now benevolent.

'You will be the first from our family to be presented. I think my sister would be proud.'

'Do you truly think so?' said Natalie. 'I really do it for Papa. I know it makes him happy.'

'No doubt you shall return engaged to be married,' said Aunt Goodwin.

'I have heard that those who do not find husbands are called the "Returned Empty". It's very unkind, is it not?'

'It is,' said Lord Ansdrie, who had been standing quietly by them. 'But not a fate that awaits you, Miss Edwardes, I would bet on it.' And then, apparently surprised at himself, he said, 'If I were the sort of a person who made bets.'

Ansdrie bowed and Natalie took his hand and stood, and then Gussie crossed the drawing room on Haffie's arm and said, 'Mama has decided Lieutenant Haffie should take you in to dinner,' although she said it as if she wished he would take *her* in to dinner.

'Miss Edwardes,' he said, and held out his arm.

A little shock ran through Natalie's fingers as she touched Haffie's arm and when the footman pulled out her chair, Haffie's presence beside her made Natalie keenly aware of the way she sat down, of the places where the silk of her dress clung to her corset and the way it rustled where it did not. She was conscious of the confinement of her corset, of her arms encased in their long white gloves, of her petticoats and the hairpins that pulled at her scalp. And then Haffie said, 'I understand Hey Tor House is close by.'

'Two miles north,' said Natalie, 'along the Bridewell.' She kept her expression as neutral as she could. 'Do you know the river, Lieutenant Haffie?'

'I was there this very morning,' he said. The two crescent-moon lines appeared on either side of his mouth. 'I made several paintings.'

Natalie took off her gloves and put them in her lap and when she looked up at him she said, softly, 'What kind of paintings did you make, Lieutenant Haffie?' But she had to turn away to take some salmon from a footman. When she turned back he said, 'I stayed for the best part of the morning. I painted the Bridewell while the light shifted and the look of the river changed and changed again, just as I had hoped.'

He turned to accept some wine from a footman and when he turned back Natalie said, 'Do you ever work in a studio, Lieutenant Haffie?'

'I own an easel, a block and a box of watercolours,' he said. 'Nothing more.' He looked at her and she smiled when he said, 'I should be delighted to show you the paintings I made this morning, if you would care to see them.'

'I should like that very much. I suppose many people see your paintings at exhibitions.'

'Not yet,' said Haffie. 'But three of my watercolours shall hang at the Academy in July.'

'At the Exhibition?' said Natalie, and when Haffie nodded she said, 'Then I think I shall see them too ... I mean, as well as the ones you made this morning. For I think we go to the opening.' She looked at him. 'Is it not very brilliant to have three paintings accepted by the Academy?'

'That is not for me to say.'

'Well, I think it quite magnificent,' said Natalie and she clapped, which had the effect of making the others fall silent and turn towards her. Quickly, she explained what she had just discovered and Ansdrie said, 'I think we have never sat down to dinner with a man whose paintings shall hang at the Academy. It is an unexpected honour.'

But Natalie heard the irritation in his voice and knew her enthusiasm to be its cause. She had never seen him show enthusiasm for anything and she knew he disliked it in others, just as his mother did. She turned back to Haffie and, as the others resumed their conversations, she said, 'Tell me more about your paintings.'

'I should prefer you to see them for yourself, for they never work so well in words.'

Natalie stared at him and then she said, 'Oh! I know just what you mean. I see people as . . . other things, sometimes. Things that describe them better than words, I mean.'

'What kinds of things?'

'I have not told anyone before. I'm afraid they will think it too odd.' She paused, trying to work out whether he would take her seriously. 'I shall only tell you if you promise not to laugh.'

'I'll not laugh, Miss Edwardes,' said Haffie, 'for the things of our inner worlds are fragile. And they can disappear altogether in the face of ridicule.'

'They can,' she said. She had never put it that way to herself, but she knew it to be true. She leaned towards Haffie and spoke softly so she would not be overheard. 'Sometimes,' she said, 'Papa is a white bear, sometimes an oak and occasionally a lonely owl.' She paused. An image of her father's unhappiness that morning filled her mind and she glanced down the table to find him. He smiled happily back at her and, reassured, she turned back to Haffie.

'Lord Ansdrie is a heron for the way his hair stands out at the back of his head.' She hesitated. Were his brown eyes laughing at her? But when he said, 'Tell me more,' she held on to her courage and said, 'Millie is a tall, elegant tulip. Gussie is Honiton lace, lots of it, on sturdy bobbins that you cannot see, and Lady Bridewell . . .' she hesitated again and glanced at Haffie. But he nodded and said, 'Lady Bridewell is. . . ?'

'Lady Bridewell is the Eiffel Tower. I saw a drawing of it once, in the *Western Ariel*.'

Natalie waited anxiously for Haffie to reply. She searched his face for signs of ridicule, but she saw only approval, even, perhaps, admiration.

'I don't know these people nearly as well as you, Miss Edwardes,' he said, 'but already I find your images sit well with them. Do they come quickly?'

'Some are quick. Others never come at all. I think they don't come when I'm trying too hard. But I knew very quickly what you were. It came to me as I rode away this morning.' She looked at Haffie steadily and then she said, 'You are what you did. You are water, in a pair of cupped hands.'

She turned back to her plate. She had said too much and now nervous excitement robbed her of her appetite, but she must at least pretend to be interested in the food set before her. And then Aunt Goodwin spoke to Haffie and he turned to talk to her, before he could say anything else to Natalie.

She looked about her. She had never seen a table so beautifully laid, nor footmen so impeccably dressed. She and her father had been guests at Waverton Court so often and she had taken part in so many dull conversations and eaten so much dull food but, on this evening, when the footman handed her a damask napkin its intricate pattern proved to be a labyrinth. The drops of water on the leaves of the watercress were tiny jewels. The glass was stilled water in the candlelight and the evening light on the lawn was a translucent gold carpet. When Uncle Goodwin began to talk to her, Natalie had little idea of his conversation for her attention never really left Haffie and, when she turned to him once more, the expression in his eyes made her catch her breath. She hoped, very much, that he would not dislike her description of him.

'It will be an honour,' he said, 'to be your water-bearer, Miss Edwardes.'

Natalie blushed.

And then he said, 'This afternoon, when Lady Bridewell asked me to make portraits of the Ladies Millicent and Augustina, she also asked me to make a portrait of you.' He lowered his voice. 'But the image that sprang directly to mind was of one John Boundy.' His brown eyes laughed. 'And I must tell you that I disagree with him profoundly.'

'Why?' said Natalie, her heart beating quickly and the corners of her lips curving upwards into a smile.

'Because his description of you was severely wanting.'

Natalie pressed her hands together beneath the table and managed to still her laughter. She would not draw attention to their conversation again, nor would she have it interrupted. But when Haffie leaned towards her and said, *'Er's preddy enough* indeed,' a shout of laughter burst from her and every head turned to look at her for the second time that evening.

She put her hand to her mouth, turned from Haffie and realized her fingers were quivering.

She looked across the table directly into Ansdrie's dark eyes and could not help thinking him, thinking all of them, quite ordinary beside the man she had met by the Bridewell that morning.

SIX

Sɪʀ Tʜᴏᴍᴀs, ᴡʜᴏ had spent the day in Crediton choosing shoe leather, found his daughter waiting for him by the front door on his return. She followed him to his study and said, almost before he had shut the door, 'A letter has come for you from Waverton Court. It asks—' but he turned to her, and she stopped. She was flushed, excited, the way she had been when she sat beside Lieutenant Haffie at dinner. With difficulty, he dismissed the memory.

An open letter lay on his desk.

'You might as well tell me what he writes,' said Sir Thomas, gesturing towards the letter. Perhaps Lord Ansdrie had asked permission to ride with Natalie, unchaperoned.

'I did not mean to open it, Papa. But you were not here and I could not wait.' She looked at him. 'It does not come from Lord Ansdrie,' she said.

Had she read his thoughts?

A gust of fine, misty rain covered the windows and, for a moment, hid the world outside entirely.

'In that case you should not have opened it.'

'I know. I'm sorry.'

Sir Thomas picked up the letter and read:

Dear Sir Thomas,

It was a great pleasure to meet you and Miss Edwardes last Thursday, and I very much look forward to our next meeting.

I should like to make a start on the portrait of Miss Edwardes, and so I hope you might both come to Waverton Court tomorrow, in the morning, when the light will be at its most favourable.

I look forward to your reply.

Yours respectfully, Lt AW Haffie

Sir Thomas looked up. 'You shall not go, Natalie. It would be quite wrong. You met Lieutenant Haffie for the first time only a few nights ago and, I should have said so immediately, you behaved in an over-familiar fashion. If we accept this invitation it will encourage him to think—'

'Papa!' said Natalie. 'What could possibly be wrong with a portrait?'

Sometimes she would just not see what he meant her to see.

'You know very well I do not refer to the portrait,' said Sir Thomas, 'but to your enthusiasm for the lieutenant. You are altogether too forward.'

'I'm sorry, Papa,' said Natalie.

Could there be tears in her eyes?

'You are naturally quick and your heart is open and these are admirable qualities,' he said, resisting the desire to give her his handkerchief. 'But you are eighteen. You are about to have a London Season. You should cultivate a little circumspection.'

The misty rain became stronger and Sir Thomas's study, which had grown dark, was lit by a flash of white lightning. And then the rain began to hurl itself against the sash windows and a clap of thunder burst above the slate roof of

Hey Tor House. Natalie turned towards the window and, as the thunder echoed away across the moor, Sir Thomas cursed his stupidity. He should have spoken to her; he should have informed her she could expect a proposal from Lord Ansdrie after her presentation at Court. Then she would not think of any other attachment.

She turned back to him just as a pale sun slid from behind a dark cloud and shed its cold light into his study. 'You are right, Papa,' she said. 'I should not have behaved as I did.' She looked directly at him. 'I'm sorry if I caused you any embarrassment. Truly I am.'

He stepped out from behind his desk and took her hands. He would tell her now. He ordered the words in his mind. He reordered them. It would be a great and advantageous match. It would make him very proud. She would become a member of one of the oldest and most aristocratic families in the land. But, in her presence, Sir Thomas's rehearsed words seemed empty. Her forthright nature and her open heart would speak against such advantages if she felt nothing for the man who embodied them. But Sir Thomas had already made over a substantial sum to Lady Bridewell, in trust for her son. It was more than half Natalie's dowry and the restoration of Ansdrie House would begin very soon.

He must speak. He had no choice. But she spoke first.

'Perhaps you don't know,' said Natalie, 'that Lady Bridewell commissioned Lieutenant Haffie to make portraits of Millie and Gussie as well. And they too have only just made his acquaintance.'

He did not know. Why did he not know? But if Lady Bridewell had made the commissions, how could he object?

'And a portrait by Lieutenant Haffie will be a valuable thing one day,' said Natalie. 'His paintings shall hang at the Academy in July.'

He would not, as his daughter seemed so clearly to realize, prevent her from doing as Lady Bridewell's daughters did, and she had cleverly appealed to his sense of the value of the thing.

'We shall go on one condition,' said Sir Thomas.

'Anything, Papa.'

'You owe much to Lady Bridewell. We know no one else who would do us the honour of presenting you at Court. You must curb your enthusiasms and your eagerness in her presence. You must make sure you do not fail her in whatever she might request.'

Natalie smiled up at him. 'Of course, Papa,' she said.

Sir Thomas nodded and when his daughter left his study he rang for Stephens and wrote his reply to Lieutenant Haffie. But he wished they were already in London for, once there, Lady Bridewell would chaperone his daughter. Once there, the Ladies Millicent and Augustina would have a stronger influence over her and she would, surely, wish to do as they did. But he also recognized that the best way to drive his daughter directly towards Lieutenant Haffie would be to make it difficult for her to become better acquainted with him. Once they were in London, Lord Ansdrie would make his proposal and all would be well.

The following day Natalie and Sir Thomas drove down the hill beside Bridewell Wood, in a pony and trap. The sky was newly washed, the air fresh and the puddles in the road were the only indication of the rain from the day before. When they were shown into the drawing room at Waverton Court Lieutenant Haffie stood at his easel in the middle of the room, a dustsheet spread out below him, a long apron over his clothes. Much of the furniture had been pushed to the sides of the room and beyond Haffie, in front of the stone-mullioned windows in the north wall, stood two disembodied evening gowns.

Natalie smiled shyly as she walked towards him. She saw at once that he had been working on the portrait of

Millie and Gussie for some time, for their faces and their hair, their shoulders, their hands and their arms were finished, and it seemed to Natalie that their dresses were almost complete.

'They are very good likenesses, Lieutenant Haffie,' she said. 'Are they pleased?'

'They are,' said Ansdrie, from a chair by the unlit fire.

Natalie turned. She had not noticed him. He folded his newspaper into a neat rectangle and stood up. Sir Thomas held out his hand to greet Ansdrie and then Haffie juggled paintbrush and watercolour box to shake Sir Thomas's hand.

'Are Millie and Gussie in the morning room?' said Natalie. 'Shall I go to them?'

'Haffie works very quickly,' said Ansdrie. 'I should wait here if I were you.'

'I should not mind sitting for w—' she stopped and turned to Haffie. 'What I mean is, if it should take a long time I should not mind.'

Sir Thomas made a disapproving sound and Natalie said no more. But Haffie said, 'If a portrait took me weeks I should have to declare it a failure.'

He turned back to his work and Natalie went to sit by Ansdrie. He told her the servants had gone that morning to open the London house. He said, 'And Lieutenant Haffie shall stay at Eaton Terrace for the Season with us.'

Natalie held her hands tightly together in her lap but she could not control her smile. Without turning round Haffie said it would be his first Season and Ansdrie said that, as the best dancer in the Waterfirth Reservists, he would never be without a partner. Haffie rang for a maid to remove the evening gowns and, as he did so, their owners arrived.

'So much more immediate than oils,' said Millie to Natalie, looking at the portrait. 'Don't you think?' She sat down beside her.

'Less gloomy than old Mr Greaves's,' lisped Gussie.

'Mr Greaves studied with Mr Whistler,' said Haffie. 'I do not find his work gloomy.'

Haffie smiled at Millie and Natalie wanted to be her. She had been sitting for him, she had been in his company for several uninterrupted days. She watched him pick up his easel and move it to the side of the room and, when the maid arrived to take away the gowns, she said to Sir Thomas, 'Her ladyship asks if you would join her in her morning room.'

When her father was gone Natalie said, 'Will you escort us to the galleries, Lieutenant Haffie, when we are in London?'

'I should be delighted,' he said, turning to look directly at her. 'We shall explore them together, for I have yet to visit them myself.'

'How exciting,' said Natalie. She turned to Millie and Gussie and said, 'Is it not?'

Neither sister replied and then, even though she was not looking at Haffie, Natalie stood up.

'I think just there,' he said, acknowledging that she was walking towards exactly the right spot. 'I shall make sketches of you first and then, when I am satisfied, I shall begin the portrait. Did you bring a particular gown?'

'Oh, no,' said Natalie. 'Should I send for one?'

Haffie put a mahogany Hepplewhite chair in the middle of the north end of the room and asked her to sit down. He said, 'It does not matter. In fact I should prefer it if you did not. There is time enough for a portrait. Today, I shall make a drawing of you just as you are.' He moved a small easel a few feet from the chair and put a box of pencils and charcoal pieces on a table beside it. When he had fixed a sheet of paper to the easel he began to look at Natalie.

He said, 'Lift your head a little, would you, Miss Edwardes.' And then he stood beside her and said, softly, 'Would you mind?'

He moved a dark curl away from her forehead in a quick

movement. And then, as he walked back to his easel, he said, 'When you look at me, would you think about something that intrigues you, something you should like to know more about.'

Gussie giggled. 'He said that to us and I thought about Nellie. But she turned out not to be quite as interesting as I thought, so I thought about her foal as well.'

But Natalie saw Haffie's pale back and the spray of water when he shook his head. The way he stood with his arm lifted, when she rode away. His voice when he talked about the fragile nature of the things of the inner world. She looked directly at him and thought about him, boldly, while he worked. She was glad he would make a drawing of her as well as a portrait. She would have to sit for him for longer.

'You should ask Lieutenant Haffie to make a drawing of you, Ansdrie,' said Millie. 'I have yet to see one that does you justice.'

'What a capital idea,' said her brother. 'How about that, Haffie? Would you make a drawing of me in exactly the same proportions as you make that one of Miss Edwardes? A complementary pair, you might say.'

Haffie held up a pencil to gauge the proportions of Natalie's face and then said, 'I should be delighted. It is the least I can do to thank you for introducing me to three such delightful young women.'

While he worked Haffie never took his eyes from Natalie's face: sometimes his expression was amused, mostly it was entirely concentrated and once, when he looked at her, Natalie was transported to her bedroom where she stood with her back to him just as she stood, every morning, without clothes, waiting for Hocks to put her undergarments over her head. She blushed, deeply, but she did not turn from him.

Later that afternoon, when the drawing was almost finished and they all stood in front of it, Gussie said, 'You have not drawn her hat, and yet you painted all my ribbons. And you have made her jacket look like a gentleman's.'

'Sometimes character is conveyed by a pair of eyes,' said Haffie. 'Sometimes by ornaments or clothes. It all depends.'

He moved a thin piece of charcoal between his fingers, as if he were signalling to Natalie behind his back. Then he turned to her and said, 'But should you wish, Miss Edwardes, I'll not mind adding your hat or altering your jacket.'

'Oh no, thank you,' said Natalie. 'I like it just the way it is.'

The expression he had captured in her eyes, which were wide open, was amused and a little shocked. Her mouth showed the beginnings of a smile, at the corners, but hid her long front teeth. And the way he had drawn her jacket subtly suggested the one she had worn that morning by the Bridewell.

'I think it a very good likeness,' said Millie. 'You have even captured the way Natalie's hair grows, yet you never once asked her to remove her hat.'

Afterwards, Ansdrie stood with Haffie on the parterre outside the drawing room; they smoked oval Turkish cigarettes. Millie and Gussie walked with Natalie on the western side of the parterre and the sun, which was just beginning its descent, cast its warm evening glow over the young women and made them look very well together.

Haffie said, 'I think your sisters delightful and . . . if I should paint an impression of Miss Edwardes, I should try to capture something of her enthusiasm.'

Ansdrie bent his head and shifted his weight. Perhaps he should make his proposal to Natalie before she was presented at Court? She clearly was very appealing and Haffie had paid her particular attention that morning; other men would certainly pay her court in London.

He looked up and saw Natalie and his sisters walking

back across the parterre. Natalie was smiling and when she smiled her face took on a different aspect; it made him want to smile with her and, for a moment, he felt confident of her, until he realized she was smiling at Haffie. He too looked at Haffie and said, 'There will be many beautiful young women in London and once your skill in the waltz is discovered they will all ask Mama for an introduction. I have no doubt you will make a strong impression ... in other ways too, Haffie. For it seems painting makes an impression on all young women.'

'I do not paint to impress young women,' said Haffie.

'No, no, of course not,' said Ansdrie.

But when the young women arrived beside them, Ansdrie took Natalie's arm a little more quickly than he meant to and left Haffie with his sisters.

SEVEN

LONDON WAS NOISY. Natalie woke each morning to the sounds of creaking carts and jingling hansom cabs whose drivers called to each other above the constant clatter of horses' hooves. Coal rumbled into coal holes; milk churns clattered and rang on their creaking floats; horses whinnied and stamped. And London smelled. When the day was warm and there was very little breeze, horse manure mingled with petroleum fumes from the spluttering, engine-driven carriages. They gave Gussie headaches.

But London was exciting too. There were so many people and new discoveries to be made every day: new music and new buildings and, most surprisingly of all, London was green. The plane trees were tall, protective substitutes for the oaks and the hazels in Bridewell Wood and their mottled boles were, Haffie suggested, the legs of elephants that had travelled from the outreaches of Empire to discover their capital city. The flower-lined paths in Kensington Gardens and the secret lawns that opened out from them were perfect places for walks with her father, and with Millie and Gussie. They discussed the teas and the dinners, the receptions and the soirées they would attend and the museums and galleries they had visited. Above all, they discussed the balls that would come after their presentation at Court at which, in Natalie's imagination, she always danced in Lieutenant Haffie's arms.

But her early excitement in her discovery of London and her relative freedom had been quickly cauterized. They had not come to London, Lady Bridewell said, to do as they pleased. The structure of their days grew rigid, ordered strictly by invitations to tea or to dine, or by the calls they paid, and Natalie was constantly chaperoned by Lady Bridewell. Only on rare occasions did she have any time to herself and even then her father would not go anywhere Lady Bridewell disapproved of, and she disapproved of much: the West End and all its entertainments; the Savoy Theatre with its electric lighting; the new cinematograph at the Empire Theatre of Varieties. In fact, anything Natalie read about in her father's copies of the *Illustrated Sporting & Dramatic News*.

Lady Bridewell told Natalie that the freedom to do as she chose would come with marriage, but until then she was not a free woman. And her father never disagreed; in fact, he spent much of his time reminding Natalie how very lucky they were. If Natalie spent more than a moment away from the Bridewells, at a tea or a soirée, with a new acquaintance, especially if he were a man and most especially, it seemed, if that man were Lieutenant Haffie, Lady Bridewell appeared at her elbow and ushered her elsewhere. Conversations of any length with Haffie, or anyone of whom Lady Bridewell did not approve, became impossible. On the day that Natalie, Millie, Gussie and Lady Bridewell drove along the Kensington Road to St James's Palace in her father's landau – Lady Bridewell had requested it, her own carriage was too small to carry them all – her father had whispered, proudly, as she kissed him goodbye, 'Look, my dear, at the Ladies Millicent and Augustina. Their headdresses have two plumes. Two *is* the correct number.'

He wanted the best for her and she should not be ashamed. He wanted her to fit in, to wear the correct clothes, to be just like them. But his anxiety and his desperate pride at her presentation at Court showed how different she, and he, really were. The Bridewells and their kind never commented on what was or was not correct, for the knowledge ran in their veins. They had been born into one life and Natalie into another. Their houses were of similar sizes and the Edwardes's household wanted for nothing materially, but Natalie's father was in trade; Lord Bridewell had been a gentleman and an aristocrat. The London Season was turning out to be just as difficult as Natalie had imagined.

She smiled gratefully at Millie when she leaned towards her and said, 'I feel a little nervous. Do you, Natalie?'

'There is nothing to be in the least nervous about,' said Lady Bridewell, briskly, as their carriage rumbled over the uneven setts in the Kensington Road. But when Natalie caught sight of their reflections in the carriage window she saw how the white plumes on their heads nodded as the carriage wheels dipped in and out of the ruts in the road, and she thought of the black plumes horses wore at funerals.

'Presentation at Court is the most important event of the Season,' said Lady Bridewell, reaching forward to straighten one of Gussie's plumes. 'Betrothals will, undoubtedly, follow.'

For days after the Lord Chamberlain's summons arrived Lady Bridewell had schooled them in the correct curtsey and the exact way to walk backwards after their presentation. To cheer herself, Natalie had imagined their arrival on a sunny day. But this day was chilly and grey and they grew cold as they waited in a long line of carriages in St James's. And then they shivered in a corridor in a similarly long line of white-gowned, bare-armed young women.

Why cloaks were not permitted was beyond imagination.

At Millie's and Gussie's coming-out ball at Claridge's, the first ball of the Season, Ansdrie was uneasy. He had not yet spoken to Natalie; he had only managed, together with his mother, to arrange it so that she and Haffie had very little time together. They had discussed waiting until she knew him a little better, waiting until after her own coming-out ball, as was the custom. But now his awkwardness in the simple walking steps of the quadrille embarrassed him; they demonstrated the hopelessness of his suit altogether.

Natalie smiled sweetly and gave his elbow a gentle push: he had continued to face her in the *Chaîne Anglaise* when he should have been facing Millie. His embarrassment was far greater than the small mistake warranted but, as he continued to make the same mistakes throughout the evening it became clear to him that he, unlike his mother, was not possessed of unshakeable certainty. He wanted to believe himself superior to all born beneath him but, at moments like these, he had to admit his inadequacy, had to admit that his superior bloodline was not enough to maintain a consistently superior attitude in all things. In the time since he had considered Natalie his future wife, although he was only yet dimly aware of it, her nature had acted upon him. In her curiosity and enthusiasm he discovered his disdain; in the strange, bold things she said, the awkwardness of his formal reserve. In short, he became increasingly aware of a lack of substance in himself when he was in her presence.

'Lieutenant Haffie taught me to look at the shadows of things,' she said, as they walked one morning in Kensington Gardens. 'Look, there, Ansdrie. Look at the patterns the leaves make on the path. No, not the fallen ones, the shadows of the living ones. Are they not beautiful?'

It was all so very odd. She might as well have said Lieutenant Haffie himself was beautiful. He glanced back and saw Haffie walking between his sisters. He saw his mother and Sir Thomas walking behind them. He wished Haffie as far from London as it was possible for him to be. He should never have invited him.

'It is good to talk to a gentleman who does not insist on treating conversation as if it were mechanical. As if he had swallowed the *Book of Etiquette* whole.'

'I have heard you talk of the way you see people, Natalie,' said Ansdrie, ashamed of his own often-stilted conversation with her. 'How . . . how do you see me?'

'You will be scornful,' she said.

'I will not,' he said, forcing a smile to his downturned lips.

'Well, sometimes, you remind me of a heron, because your hair stands up at the back and you stand so tall and straight.'

'Although not often on one leg,' he said.

She laughed and he, relieved, patted her hand and leaned a little towards her. His mood often lightened in Natalie's company, if he let it. He had taken to walking more quickly when he paid a call at Hyde Park Gate and details of her appearance were by now very easy for him to recall. Should he tell her these things?

Again he missed his cue in the quadrille and again she gently guided him, and when it ended he handed Natalie to Alfred Farrars, her partner for the lancers, and retired to a seat at the edge of the gilded, white-walled ballroom. The complications of the lancers made him particularly aware of his lack of skill, and watching Gussie, at ease with her partner, Edward Fountain, the man his mother already thought likely to ask for her hand, made him wish his own future so easily settled. Haffie made neat crosses, passes and retreats opposite Millie and the dancers' reflections in the candlelit mirrors seemed to mock Ansdrie's own inadequacy. When Haffie stood still, Ansdrie saw that he followed Natalie's movements with his eyes just as he did.

Natalie offered Farrars the same sweet-natured but polite expression she habitually turned upon him, not the animated, changeable expressions that lit her face when she looked at Haffie.

But when it came to it, Ansdrie told himself, Natalie would accept him over Haffie, for she would be as honoured and flattered as her own father had been. He looked forward to her coming-out ball, to the time when she would be properly out in society, for then he would make his proposal. But in the meantime he and his mother must keep Haffie and Natalie apart as much as possible, for even Ansdrie understood she was not his by divine right and she had proved, often enough, that she had a will of her own.

When the lancers ended Ansdrie stepped in quickly to take Natalie for some refreshment but, as they left the ballroom, her shoe came undone and while she bent to do it up a female voice spoke from an alcove close by. It declared that Miss Ashenapper's betrothal to the aristocratic Gerald Snareswell was expected imminently and although she was American and of 'inferior blood, she brings with her a most superior dowry.'

Ansdrie turned and saw his mother nodding in agreement. She sat with Gerald Snareswell's mother beneath a gilt bracket that held two large candles and a trail of ivy. Their heads were turned intently towards each other, their faces partly hidden by the curved wall of the alcove, and he supposed they thought they would not be overheard. But as Natalie straightened up and took Ansdrie's arm her eyes held a startled expression, reminiscent of the look in Jupiter's eyes when he shied.

She said, very quietly as they walked past his mother, 'Perhaps you think as your mama thinks, Ansdrie. For I know that in your circles marriage is not often considered a matter for feeling, but I could not marry under those circumstances. Could you?'

*

The following day, when the Bridewells, Ansdrie, Sir Thomas and Natalie sat together drinking tea in the upstairs drawing room at Hyde Park Gate, Gussie was very excitable. She kept saying, 'Mama, shall we. . . ?' and 'Mama, may we. . . ?' until, at last, Lady Bridewell said, 'We should like to inform you, Sir Thomas,' she nodded at him, 'and Miss Edwardes, that Mr Edward Fountain asked for Augustina's hand this morning.'

She paused and then she said, as if announcing the most momentous event, 'He has been accepted.'

She nodded and actually smiled while Natalie and her father congratulated them and then she said, 'It is come, of course, not quite as I should like. I should prefer to see Ansdrie betrothed,' she glanced up at her son, who looked quickly away, 'followed by Millicent and then Augustina. Nevertheless, it is a most welcome event.'

'I cannot help it if my betrothed,' Gussie smiled triumphantly, 'should wish to declare himself before Mama thinks he should.' She took Natalie's hand in her happiness and Natalie let her hand lie in hers. 'He lives at Marvill House in Wiltshire.' Her lisp made it sound like *Marvill Huth*. 'It is made in the Palladian style and all the rooms are perfect cubes and, Mama told me, he has twenty thousand acres.' She clapped her hands and Natalie's own hand fell away. 'I know Mama says we should not talk of such things, but he is also very rich.'

Lady Bridewell sighed but Natalie felt, not for the first time, that she would never truly understand them. They, who thought it quite vulgar to discuss money, thought it perfectly acceptable, when a betrothal was announced, to talk only about the assets the gentleman possessed and to say nothing at all about the gentleman himself.

'Do you think Mr Fountain a kind man?' said Natalie. 'Does he make you laugh?'

'Of course,' said Gussie. But she gave no example of

these things, only of his lineage as if the latter proved the former.

But Gussie's engagement brought an unexpected gift for Natalie. Lady Bridewell held a dinner in her honour and, just before they walked in, she said to Natalie, 'I hope you will not mind, my dear, but in order to seat the members of Mr Fountain's family correctly among my own, I had, unavoidably, to seat you among the younger ones.'

Natalie did her best to put on an offended expression, but the idea of unaffected children for supper companions so delighted her that she barely registered Ansdrie's agitated expression as he escorted Lady Fountain in to dinner. And when Lieutenant Haffie walked across the room to take Natalie's arm she could hardly contain her happiness.

'I fear we have both been relegated,' he said.

'I could not be happier,' she said and he laughed.

They crossed the hall towards the dining room, the last couple to do so, and then Haffie squeezed her arm and signalled for her to stop. Carefully, he took a white rose from the inside pocket of his dress coat and said, 'This is a Scotch rose and I give it to you in honour of the occasion. I have missed your company.' He put his gloved fingers together and made a cage round the rose, and then he gave it to her.

The rose had five plain white petals, like the dog roses in the hedgerows in Devon, but these petals were larger and rounder and the rose had a stronger scent. At its centre was a large yellow sunburst of stamens. Natalie smiled broadly, pushed the stem into her dark hair and said, 'How did you know we should sit together tonight?'

'I did not.'

'Then why—?'

But at that moment a footman cleared his throat and when they looked up he gestured for them to walk in to dinner. The younger Fountains had already gone ahead and it was not until they were seated that Haffie gave Natalie an answer.

'I was walking in Eaton Square this afternoon,' he said, 'and I saw a cluster of Scotch roses. I had not seen them in London until today, but when I saw them I knew how well one would look in your hair and I took it for a good omen. I picked it and hoped I might find an opportunity to present it to you.'

Natalie blushed and smiled.

'In Scandinavia they call them Midsummer roses, but I always think of them as Scotch roses. I'm very fond of them for they thrive even in inhospitable places.'

The two crescent-moon lines appeared on either side of his mouth.

And when, inevitably, the time came for Natalie to talk to Mr George Fountain, Edward's fifteen-year-old brother, she did so with good grace for now she knew Haffie had missed their conversations just as much as she had. When he had the chance he said, quietly, 'You are particularly beautiful, tonight.'

Natalie felt the blush heat her cheeks as she took some lamb from the footman and then, because of an oddly persistent movement at the corner of her vision, she looked down the length of the table and saw Lady Bridewell pushing her hand against her head. Natalie made exactly the same motion but she let the rose remain where it was. She glanced at her father, who was talking to the Fountains' youngest daughter and, when he looked up, Natalie could not tell whether he approved or disapproved of her rose. She inclined her head to show him all was well and then, together, she and Lieutenant Haffie broke one of Lady Bridewell's cardinal rules: they failed utterly to talk to those who sat either side of them until the women rose to leave the gentlemen to their port. Worse, they failed to realize that they failed.

'I have been surprised by the lack of opportunity for real conversation in London,' said Haffie.

'The Season is convened to make matches, is it not?'

Natalie hesitated. She had not meant to imply a match between herself and Haffie, but when he showed no sign of insult or surprise, she said, 'But those matches are, apparently, to be made between people who know almost nothing about each other.' She lowered her voice to a whisper and said, 'Gussie knows so very little about Fountain. She thinks only of how she will live at *Marvill Huth*.'

Haffie laughed softly and Natalie said, 'At least we know each other, a little, I think.'

'So one of those matches will never be made between us.'

Natalie did not know what to say.

'I meant, one of those matches between people who do not know each other.'

'Oh . . . no,' she said. 'I would hate to marry a man I barely . . . knew.'

Haffie picked up his wine glass. 'I hope we shall see a little more of each other in the coming weeks. Your card filled so quickly at the Bridewells' ball that I missed my opportunity.' He put his hand close to hers on the table. 'But I saw how you waltzed. It was . . . like the wind.'

Natalie did not want to move her hand but the footman held out a dish of salad and she had no choice. When he was gone she said, 'How does the wind dance, Lieutenant Haffie?'

'Outwith the laws of gravity.'

And then Haffie told Natalie about the painters whose work would hang at the Academy, and how honoured he was that his own paintings would hang among them. He told her he would miss the west coast of Scotland when he took up his position in his father's sugar-refining business and she told him, proudly, about Edwardes Tea and her father's success. And by doing so she broke another of Lady Bridewell's diktats, the one that proscribed business as a subject for conversation. But Natalie was too far from

Lady Bridewell for her to hear: she and Lieutenant Haffie inhabited a private island all of their own, at the inferior end of the table.

Natalie's happiness that evening increased her appetite. She asked the footman for three brandy snaps and ate them greedily, just as if she were one of the Fountain children. When she licked her fingers she looked up and saw Ansdrie's cold expression at the far end of the table and, understanding him very well, she exaggerated her movements as if to say, 'They taste better this way, Lord Ansdrie. You should try it.'

That night it took Natalie a long time to fall asleep. The conversation with Haffie repeated itself over and over again in her mind until, at last, she fell asleep just as the sun was waking up. But when she did sleep, a sweet scent filled her dreams for she had put Haffie's Scotch rose beside her pillow.

When all the guests had left and his family were safely in their bedrooms, Ansdrie asked Haffie to stay in the drawing room with him. He dismissed Anderson for the night and made sure the door was properly closed, but when he spoke to his friend he could not turn to face him.

'I shall come directly to the point,' he said, his jaw set and his eyes focused on the oval door handle. 'I must warn you to keep your distance from Miss Edwardes for I intend to ask for her hand.'

Haffie did not reply and his prolonged silence forced Ansdrie to turn to him.

'Have you nothing to say?' he said.

When his friend still failed to speak, Ansdrie could not help wondering whether, in his anxiety to secure Miss Edwardes . . . Natalie . . . for himself, he had read too much into Haffie's attentions towards her. But, at last, when Haffie fumbled for a cigarette, lit it and spoke without looking at him, Ansdrie recognized that he was troubled. He said,

'Does Miss Edwardes think of marrying you?'

'That is, of course, a matter for her,' said Ansdrie. 'But I very much doubt she will refuse me.'

At last Haffie looked up and said, 'It would have been good to know this a little earlier, Ansdrie. But I thank you for saving me from making a fool of myself.'

The two men faced each other, awkwardly, and then Ansdrie put out his hand and Haffie took it. But although their hands touched, their eyes did not meet.

EIGHT

IT WAS, OF course, obvious to Sir Thomas that, on the rare occasions when his daughter was in the company of Lieutenant Haffie, she was far more at ease than when she was in the company of anyone else, including himself. And his own uneasiness in the company of Lady Bridewell and her kind had increased, when he had expected it to decrease as they spent more time together.

But whenever Lady Bridewell presented Sir Thomas and his daughter to another family he sensed their subtly dismissive ways, their, 'He's not quite one of us,' expression, even though their voices made perfectly polite greetings. But after the usual enquiries had been made they would turn back to their own and Sir Thomas was rebuffed. When he could, he retreated to the sanctuary of a coffee house where all men were equal, and sometimes he longed to be back in Devon near his sister-in-law, to escape the aristocratic codes of behaviour which were not only impenetrable, but subtly hostile. It was made clear to him, for instance, that his title, a conferred one, was inferior to their inherited titles, although they never exactly said so. He consulted the pages of *Modern Etiquette* and *The Peerage & Baronetage of the British Empire*. He addressed all those he met correctly, but he could not grasp the intricacies of their behaviour, and he knew he was often too studied in his.

In Devon he understood the difference between his family and the Bridewells but, when he and Lady Bridewell had come to an agreement over his daughter, he had assumed her attitude would shift. It had not and, in London, it seemed he was the only one of his kind who was so often in the company of a family of their kind. He wondered just how much more of Lady Bridewell's patronizing tolerance he could take.

When she told him Edward Fountain's family was one of the foremost in the land he, irritated by the implication that his own family's origins were humble, said, 'We all come from somewhere, Lady Bridewell. The only difference is that families who established their trade, and therefore themselves, long ago, are no longer talked of as being in trade. But it is their trade that gives them their position.'

'Not quite so, Sir Thomas,' said Lady Bridewell. 'Many great families were established in recognition of their faithful service to a monarch.' She paused, apparently waiting for his acknowledgement of the importance of what she had just said. He gave the faintest of nods. 'Although I concede,' she said, 'that the Fountain family origins in . . . cotton . . . are similar to your own. But the point that you fail to grasp, Sir Thomas, is that we simply do not refer to trade whether or not we are connected with it.'

Sir Thomas was out of his depth for he was, at heart, a straightforward man. He was proud of his business and his origins, even if he did not say so, and he did not welcome the idea that those who had risen before him would not accept him, simply because his own rise had been so very recent. If Natalie were to marry into this family she would have to forget or, at best, disguise, her own origins in order to survive among them and Sir Thomas realized, belatedly, that he did not want her to do that. His desire for her to become a countess was precisely the same as Lady Bridewell's desire to pass her off as one of her own.

Between them they had set out to construct a falsity, a lie: they would deny Natalie her very self.

Sir Thomas was sickened by his attempts to persuade his daughter of Ansdrie's qualities: that because Ansdrie was the scion of an aristocratic family he would live an honourable, indeed an estimable life. But what guarantee was there? And how, really, would it benefit his daughter to marry him? Ansdrie had not shown himself capable of much and the estate he had inherited was in desperate need of money. Men like Ansdrie were called gentlemen, a description Sir Thomas longed for for himself but in the sense of honest and trustworthy, not in the sense of a man who never lifted a finger to earn his living.

This new frame of mind, and the sight of his daughter's happiness when she had the rare opportunity of Lieutenant Haffie's company, prompted Sir Thomas to extend the hand of friendship across this sea of polite hostility. He would discover the lieutenant's intentions towards his daughter. He would not allow him to trifle with her affections but, if he should prove sincere, Sir Thomas would listen with attention, for he realized belatedly that he would rather be party to his daughter's happiness than to her unhappiness.

And so, after a dinner hosted by Sir Theophilus Fountain, Sir Thomas put from his mind the consequences of his actions and approached Lieutenant Haffie. He sat smoking a cigarette in a corner of the Fountains' elegant drawing room and they talked, at first, of the weather and then of the rumours of another war in the Transvaal and then Sir Thomas made his first foray. He said, 'Tell me, Lieutenant Haffie, which of the great painters do you admire?'

'Turner,' said Haffie, immediately. 'And Monet. And Whistler's *nocturnes* are miraculous. And I should like to capture Dartmoor with Albert Goodwin's skill.'

The memory of his own father's amazement that Turner, a mere painter, had left a will his family thought worth contesting made Sir Thomas listen with interest.

'But although painting is my chief interest,' said the lieutenant, 'and I will not deny that if I should make a little money from it it would be a source of great delight to me, there are few men privileged enough,' he looked at Sir Thomas directly, 'to earn an income from this work.'

The lieutenant was realistic and humble; good attributes.

'My reservist commission provides a small income,' said Haffie, 'but not enough to provide . . .'

Sir Thomas watched Haffie turn towards his daughter, as if attracted by a magnet. She escorted Lady Bridewell to a chair by one of the large sash windows and he ground his teeth at the thought of the difficult conversation he would have to have with her if their arrangement for his daughter's future should alter. Haffie seemed nervous. He would put him at his ease. Clearly he was in need of encouragement. 'I believe Mr Sargent has done well enough,' said Sir Thomas.

'Yes, he has,' said Haffie.

'So,' said Sir Thomas, 'it is not impossible.'

'No . . .' said Haffie. 'But my father holds a partnership open for me in the family sugar business. I go to Liverpool soon. I hope I shall also find time to paint.'

A man who would work for his living just as Sir Thomas always had. A man who had nothing of the aristocratic impenetrability about him. It was very difficult not to like him. In fact, Sir Thomas realized just how much he did like the lieutenant.

'My late wife always said we should never allow the getting of money to master us,' he said. 'But it is a certainty that those who possess money will always hold the balance of power over those who do not.' As soon as he had spoken Sir Thomas realized he had ascribed a habit of employing money to buy influence to himself and wished he had not. In an attempt to show he had no desire to influence those they sat among in this way he said, smiling in what he hoped was an encouraging manner, 'To be frank with you, our time in London has been a little wearying. I envy you your escape to Liverpool.'

'I should like to remain in London as long as ... you and your daughter remain,' said Haffie. 'I have never met anyone quite like her, Sir Thomas. She thinks for herself and ... she thinks differently. I have discovered this even though it has not been easy in these rather peculiar circumstances.'

These rather peculiar circumstances. A man he could whole-heartedly agree with.

'And I ... think her decidedly the prettiest young woman in London.'

Sir Thomas was satisfied: Lieutenant Haffie's intentions were clear.

Now all that remained was to encourage him, for he was a little hesitant, just as Sir Thomas himself might be were he his age, and surrounded by more socially confident gentlemen.

NINE

CARRIAGES RUMBLED BENEATH the decorated stone archway into the courtyard in front of Burlington House. Rain mizzled down onto the elegantly dressed young men and women, and their chaperones, who left their carriages quickly and hurried up the stone steps to the Academy beneath umbrellas held by their footmen.

'Do not forget, Miss Edwardes,' said Lady Bridewell. 'The point of a private view is not to look at the paintings, it is simply to attend. One must be seen.'

Natalie and her father, Millie and Gussie, Ansdrie and Fountain walked through the crowded galleries greeting those they knew, and being introduced to those they did not by Lady Bridewell. But when they reached the third gallery Natalie had greeted so many people that her head buzzed with names and even Ansdrie looked a little dazed from his mother's litany of Snareswells and Havenhams, Hawkesworths and Farrars, Morvenishes and Gillsboroughs and so many more.

It was then that Natalie said, 'I should like to look at the paintings, Lady Bridewell. I think it rude to those who have made them to ignore them.'

Mr Hawkesworth laughed as if Natalie had told a particularly good joke, but Sir Thomas said, 'That is well said, my dear. I shall accompany you.'

Natalie took his arm gratefully and he said, over his shoulder, 'Don't worry, Lady Bridewell, we shall not be gone long,' and he made the smile he made when he did not want to be seen to be smiling, his lips becoming invisible between his moustache and his beard.

Lady Bridewell did not reply directly to Sir Thomas or to Natalie, but Natalie heard her say, 'This way, Millicent,' as if Millie were about to escape as well and, when she turned back, Millie surprised Natalie by making her laugh when she grimaced at her. And then, in the freedom of her father's company, Natalie began to look at the paintings. She shut out the sounds of the chattering crowds gathered in the middle of each gallery and searched for the paintings Haffie had told her he admired. She found a luminous portrait of a naked boy sitting on a rock by a green lake. She stood in front of the painting and a blush coloured her cheeks when she thought about Haffie's similarly pale skin. She saw a strangely populous painting called *Love the Conqueror* in which love, a young, winged man on a black horse, stood beside a row of red-liveried heralds who summoned people of all nations and all ages to follow the conqueror.

Natalie stared at the people in the painting for some time, and then her father said, 'I see how much you like Lieutenant Haffie, my dear. And in case you were wondering, I am not opposed.'

Without a thought for public etiquette, Natalie hugged him.

'Save your enthusiasm, my dear,' he said. 'We don't want to give the wrong impression.' But he smiled as he disentangled her arms from his neck and then they walked on, keeping to the perimeter of the gallery and looking at the paintings, avoiding the crush of people who stood with their backs to them in the middle of the room.

Natalie stopped before another painting and said, 'I

think it's Dartmoor. Do you, Papa?'

'It is Dartmoor,' said Lieutenant Haffie.

Natalie turned quickly, her hand on her heart.

'Did I not tell you Mr Goodwin was a master?'

'You did,' she said. 'He has made the air so . . . so . . . brightly shining. It's as if you can see the moor *through* it.'

'Just so,' said Haffie. 'But it is difficult, is it not?'

Natalie's dark eyebrows rose in questioning arcs.

'To describe a painting, in words.'

'Oh yes! It is,' she said. 'But this is a happy chance, Lieutenant Haffie. I did not know you would be here.'

'Then I had the advantage,' said Haffie. 'For I knew you would be. Although I had thought to find you with the Bridewell party for you belong among them, do you not? You are so very nearly a daughter to Lady Bridewell.'

There was a coldness in his manner that made Natalie's heart jump. Did he think she considered Lady Bridewell a mother to her? Did he not know her better than that? 'I have never looked to anyone to . . . to replace my own mother,' she said. 'I know no one . . . except perhaps Papa . . .' she glanced up at him but he was looking at Haffie, 'who could ever take her place.'

Haffie did not reply and they stood together for a brief moment, awkwardly silent. And then Sir Thomas said, speaking quickly, 'We should very much like to see your paintings, Lieutenant Haffie. Will you take us to them?'

Natalie took her father's arm and they followed Haffie through the crowd of people and when they stood before Haffie's paintings Natalie felt proud to know a man whose work was so very beautiful. She looked at his paintings for a long time without speaking, and then she heard Lady Bridewell's voice and, before she had a chance to say anything to Haffie, the Bridewells were upon them.

Gussie said, 'For a reservist, your outlines are not very definite, Lieutenant Haffie.' Her hand rested on her beloved Fountain's arm and she smiled up at him. He signalled his agreement with a downward movement of his chin.

'These paintings were not made for military purposes, Lady Augustina,' said Haffie, 'but from a love of light and shadow.'

'They are most unusual, Lieutenant Haffie,' said Sir Thomas.

Natalie realized her father was struggling to understand what he was looking at, but she felt as if she were inside the landscapes of Haffie's paintings. They drew her to them as surely as a flower is drawn towards the sun. What Gussie thought of as indefinite outlines were, to Natalie, intimations and suggestions of trees, rocks and wide skies, shorelines, hillsides and water. She stared at the blues of the water and the skies, at two sunlit paintings and at a rainwashed one, at the limpid greens and purples and greys of a mountain with a wide, flat top and a concave curve that fell away towards blue water. In one painting seabirds became clear and transported her to a shore where she heard their cries. In another she saw a seal basking on a rock and she could smell the salt air. She felt the warmth of the sun or the chill of the rain and the colours glowed as if they had captured light itself. The longer Natalie stood the more she saw. The lines of a whitewashed house with a bay window showed themselves to her, by a waterline. She was enthralled; she had never stood in front of paintings that slowly revealed themselves. But after a while the one with the flat-topped mountain saddened her and she had to turn from it.

She said, 'They are so . . . they are . . . mysteries made of light.'

'That is a great compliment, Miss Edwardes. Thank you.'

'And this one, is it a mountain? Or is it a large wave? It seems to be both.'

'If you see it as both then it is both,' said Haffie.

'I should like to buy one,' said Natalie. 'May we, Papa?'

'Miss Edwardes!' said Lady Bridewell. 'We do not *buy*.

We simply look, if we do anything about the paintings at all.'

'I'm sorry,' said Natalie. She bent her head and then, defiantly, she lifted it and looked at Haffie. 'But I thought your paintings . . . obviously I was mistaken.'

'Most of the paintings in the Exhibition are for sale, Miss Edwardes,' said Haffie. 'And I am delighted you should think of buying one of mine.'

His brown eyes twinkled and his earlier coldness seemed quite gone. When Sir Thomas put his hand on Natalie's shoulder and said, 'I expect we should talk to someone other than you about a sale, Lieutenant Haffie; is that the way of it?' she looked up at her father gratefully. Of course he would know how to go about it for he understood such things.

He gave her shoulder a quick squeeze and said, softly, 'We shall see to it later,' and then he took Lady Bridewell's arm and said he would be glad of introductions to the people he had not met while he looked at the paintings, and he guided her away. The rest of the party stayed by Haffie's paintings but they paid them little attention and talked only to each other. But Natalie asked Haffie if it was a seal she could see in one of the paintings.

'I like to think she is a selkie.'

'What is a selkie?'

'A mythical creature. She is sometimes a seal and sometimes a woman. It is said that when a selkie captures the heart of a man she disappears.'

'How cruel,' said Natalie. 'How very cruel.' And then, 'Where is the house? Your painting makes me want to go there.'

'I made these paintings in the Argyll Highlands, a place I love above all others.'

Natalie's heart beat quickly. She stared at the titles of Haffie's paintings. She read: 'Beinn Iseachan, Sunlight', 'Beinn Iseachan, Clouds' and 'Kilmalieu House, Bright

Day'. And then Ansdrie startled her. He said, 'I prefer the Lowlands.' He sounded angry. 'For they are altogether gentler. Which is fortunate, for I shall live there soon enough.'

Ansdrie was awkward in front of Haffie's paintings and Natalie, to put him at ease, said, 'The water in Lieutenant Haffie's paintings makes me think there might be good fishing there, don't you think?' At which Haffie laughed and Natalie was crushed. 'I only meant,' she said, turning to Haffie, 'that they give me such a sense of the water. They made me think about fishing.'

'I have been asked about my painting technique, or what inspires me,' said Haffie, 'by the few people who have seen my paintings. But if I have rendered the waters of the loch so that you think Ansdrie might fish them, then I am delighted.'

'What I really mean,' said Natalie, 'is that I didn't know it was possible to make paintings that changed when you looked at them.'

Haffie gave her a shy smile and Natalie took a couple of steps towards him. She stood very close to him and she knew she should not, but she could not help herself; and when he put out his hand, she thought he would touch her cheek and she lifted her hand to hold his. She quite forgot where she was and when he leaned down towards her, she thought he would kiss her. And then she heard Ansdrie's voice, very close. He said, 'I think we have had quite enough of painting for one morning.'

Natalie looked at him and her happiness turned abruptly to shame when she saw his shocked expression. He pulled her away from Haffie and through the chattering people, and she did not resist him. She tried to compose herself. She looked back at the watercolour room but she could no longer see Haffie or his paintings. She saw Millie, Gussie and Fountain, Lady Bridewell and her father standing together in the middle of a large gallery but Ansdrie did not take her to them.

He turned to her and said, 'There is something I should like to say to you.'

His pale face and his rigid expression frightened her. His grip on her arm was as strong as steel. 'You were almost . . . you were . . .' A few people turned their heads and he said, through his teeth, 'It is a little airless in here, is it not? We shall go outside.' He steered Natalie towards the door and she said, the tears coming to her eyes, 'But we should not—'

'You are hardly an authority on what is or is not permissible,' he said, smiling a thin, closed smile. 'Besides, most people will think you one of my sisters.'

And so Natalie and Ansdrie walked from the galleries and down the stone stairs without a chaperone. When they stood in the courtyard beneath scurrying white clouds, which made the sunlight itself seem anxious, Ansdrie said, 'What I am about to say may come as a surprise.'

'I don't think it will,' said Natalie. 'I should not have behaved as I did. You are quite right to be angry and I am sorry. I shall . . . take more care.'

'Your behaviour was unseemly,' said Ansdrie. 'Quite wrong, in fact. But I . . . in point of fact I am grateful for it, for it made me realize what I . . . .' He paused and Natalie's heart jumped. 'If there were not so many puddles I should kneel,' he said. 'But I should like—'

'No,' said Natalie. 'No, please, Lord Ansdrie. Do not say it. Please do not say . . .'

Ansdrie stared at his feet for so long that Natalie said, eventually, 'I'm sorry. I didn't mean to presume. But I thought—'

'No. No. You are quite right.' Ansdrie had difficulty holding her gaze. 'I was about to ask you . . . I shall ask you . . . will you do me the honour of becoming my wife?'

Natalie's gloved hand flew to her mouth and covered it, as if to stop words of amazement from flying out.

'Miss Edwardes?'

At last Natalie dropped her hand and said, 'I never thought of this, Lord Ansdrie. I don't know what to say.'

'You need not answer immediately,' said Ansdrie. But his tone was anxious and Natalie knew she must give him a reply, as much for her own sake as for his. She took a deep breath and said, 'I cannot accept your proposal, Lord Ansdrie, because I . . . because I do not think you . . . because there is no love in it. There, I have said it.'

Ansdrie put his hand to his cheek and turned his face away, quickly, just as if she had hit him.

'I'm sorry,' she said. 'But I could not marry a man I . . .' She began again. She would tell him everything. 'I should not have allowed my feelings to show. I know how you disapprove of such things. But my feelings are strong and, sometimes, they make me forget myself. I am not yet certain of Lieutenant Haffie's feelings; he has not declared himself. But I am very sure of my own and if I were to delay answering you I should make you think I might accept you and that would make a lie of all that I feel for . . . Lieutenant Haffie.'

An image of Haffie's tentative, shy smile filled her mind as Ansdrie stared at her, blankly, as if he had not heard her. Surely he would not make her repeat herself?

At last he said, his jaw set, 'I thank you for your courage, Miss Edwardes.' He laughed the short, Bridewell laugh, through his nose. 'It's a quality that will make you a fine wife. And yes, I have noticed how very much you like the company of Lieutenant Haffie. And I have seen how, when you are in his company, you are very much yourself. In fact,' he said, 'you make me wish I knew myself half as well as you know yourself.' The bones of his jaw made a neat rectangle of his pale face. 'It was foolish of me to think I might persuade you.'

'You pay me a very great compliment, Lord Ansdrie,' said Natalie. 'And I thank you for it. I am only sorry I could not give you the answer you wished for.'

They stood so close together by the entrance to the Linnaen Society that anyone watching them, anyone too far away to hear what they said, might think them a young couple in precisely the opposite situation from the one in which they found themselves.

It was some time before either said another word and when Ansdrie did speak it was to say, 'Queer business, painting, is it not?' He turned towards the Academy. 'I would rather a real loch where one might fish, than a painting of a loch where one cannot.'

Natalie saw the way the hair at the back of his head escaped its pomade and then she heard Lady Bridewell's voice and saw Millie and Gussie walking down the steps either side of her, followed by Edward Fountain, and a little way behind them her father and Lieutenant Haffie.

Lady Bridewell gave Natalie a quick nod and said, 'Sir Thomas has informed me you shall not take luncheon at Eaton Terrace today.'

When she and her daughters climbed into Sir Thomas's carriage and Ansdrie and Fountain walked away towards Piccadilly, Natalie was heartily relieved her father had changed his mind; it would have been very difficult to spend the afternoon with Ansdrie, and besides, she wanted to tell her father what had happened before they went again to the Bridewells.

'I am sorry,' she said, to Haffie. 'I didn't mean to leave you, or your paintings, so quickly.'

'It was very crowded,' said Haffie, offering her his arm. And then, while Sir Thomas strode ahead to find a hansom, he said, 'It is I who should apologize, Miss Edwardes. I behaved as if we were quite alone when we were not.'

'No, no,' said Natalie. 'It was I . . . who. . . . Lord Ansdrie was not impressed with my behaviour.'

They stood together in the same part of the courtyard where she and Ansdrie had so recently stood, but Natalie felt as if she were on an entirely different planet. She looked up at him, a little shy herself now, and said, 'I wanted to say ... I think you see beyond the places you paint, Lieutenant Haffie. I think you hear what my mother used to call the "hum of things". I see it in your paintings.'

'That means more to me than I know how to say.' He smiled down at her, his brown eyes fixed on hers. 'Tell me, Miss Edwardes,' he said, 'do you feel that hum when you think about your own life? When you stare ahead into the future and wonder how you will live there?'

The intensity of his expression convinced Natalie he was asking if she imagined him in her future, and his question conjured an image that confirmed her conviction: they sat together on a bench outside the house in his painting and they were turned towards each other. They were alone and so, clearly, they were married.

Natalie waited for Haffie to say something more but when he did not, and when she saw her father walking quickly towards them, she said, 'Since childhood I have hoped the things I imagine will come to pass even though, often, they do not. But I have discovered,' she squeezed Haffie's arm, 'at least in these last few weeks, that what is actually happening is more delightful than anything I could imagine. So I am learning to imagine the future less and to live in the present, just as it is.'

She smiled up at Haffie. She hoped he would understand her as her mother had always understood her. She hoped he would realize that she meant he was better than any man she might conjure from her imagination. She would have liked to describe the image his question had conjured, but she was afraid he really would think her too forward. And then her father stood beside them, they said their goodbyes and Natalie stepped into the hansom that waited on Piccadilly.

TEN

Sir Thomas sat in the drawing room at Hyde Park Gate drinking tea with his daughter. She wore a pale dress of a light material that floated about her so that, even though she sat on a chair, she seemed to defy gravity. She said, when the footman had taken away the tea things, 'There is something I must tell you.'

'Before you do, my dear,' said Sir Thomas, 'although it pains me to have to say it again, I must warn you about your behaviour. You are too forward.'

'I am truly sorry, Papa,' said Natalie. 'It's just so difficult, sometimes, not . . . to show how I feel.'

'I must ask you to promise to curb your enthusiasms, to be more circumspect, until . . .'

'Until?' said Natalie.

'Until you are in a position in which it will not be of such great account.'

She gave him a dazzling smile and then she said, 'I promise, Papa. I shall do my very best.'

She stood and then she cupped her hands together and held them out as if offering him something, a flower perhaps, although he had the peculiar sense she offered him refreshment of some kind. She was more lovely than ever he had seen her and his own foolish desire for their social elevation shamed him. This daughter of his would not consider such things when she thought of marriage; her obvious happiness made his agreement with Lady Bridewell a petty, grasping thing.

He said, without looking up, 'When it comes to it, I advise a long engagement. A year, perhaps, or even two. Then you shall discover the lieutenant and he shall discover you. And if it should not prove to be the match you think it now, it is a simple, if painful, matter to break an engagement. It is well-nigh impossible to end a marriage.'

His daughter sat at his feet. 'He does not speak,' she said, 'in the way so many of the other young men speak. He never talks about the weather or who he has just had dinner with, or who he shall drink tea with. He's so very . . . different. I can tell him things I know other people will think odd and it's perfectly all right. He likes shadows, you know, and I think he understands me better than I understand myself. Or, perhaps, when I'm with him, I understand myself better because he shows me who I am. Just as if he were a human looking-glass.'

Sir Thomas put out his hand to slow her down: he was feeling out of breath himself; but she only took a deep breath and said, 'I like the way he walks. I like the sound of his voice. I like the things he says, most especially the things he says. He never bores me. And when he laughs, two lines, like crescent moons, appear on either side of his mouth. I think about him all the time. I say his name to myself. I imagine my name becoming his. I want to know everything about him and I grow jealous when Millie or Gussie tell me something I did not know about him. And sometimes, when he looks at me, I am quite unable to look away.' She stopped, and then said, 'And he is decidedly handsome, don't you think, Papa?'

Sir Thomas was quite out of breath. He did not answer for a moment but when she threatened to speak again he held up his hand and this time she remained silent and he said, 'I do not think myself a particularly good judge of a gentleman's physical attributes, but you need tell me no more about the lieutenant for you have left me in no doubt about your feelings for him.'

'Are you not pleased, Papa?'

'I am very pleased,' he said. 'Just a little overwhelmed.'

'But you do like him?'

'Yes, I do.'

'Thank you, Papa,' said his daughter, and she stood to kiss him.

'But now,' he said, 'what were you going to tell me? Unless that was it?'

Natalie stood and walked to the window. She no longer looked ethereal. Her shoulders were high against the back of her head when she said, without looking back at him, 'Lord Ansdrie made a proposal to me today.'

Sir Thomas held his breath.

'And I turned him down.'

'Goodness. What did he . . . say?'

'What I suppose any man would say, Papa,' said Natalie, turning back to him. 'He asked me to do him the honour of becoming his wife and I told him I could not. I told him there was no love in his proposal.'

'What a momentous day it has been,' said Sir Thomas, hoping his daughter would never know just how momentous. 'I shall call at Eaton Terrace immediately.'

'Why, Papa?'

'In order to request an interview with Lieutenant Haffie. For I should like to discover and, I very much hope, to confirm, his intentions towards you.'

Natalie took Sir Thomas's hand, kissed it and thanked him for acting so quickly. 'I shall await your return anxiously,' she said.

And he hoped she would never know quite how anxiously he anticipated the conversation he must now have with Lady Bridewell.

*

He walked to Eaton Terrace. He thought better when he walked, and he had much to think about, but he walked quickly for he must say what he had to say just as soon as possible.

The solid rows of new, white stucco houses in Prince's Gate were orderly and neat and he attempted to impose a similar order upon his thoughts. He would speak first to Lieutenant Haffie to confirm his intentions, and then he would conduct the much more difficult conversation with Lady Bridewell. He would be magnanimous for the sake of his daughter's happiness; he would not ask for repayment of the money he had made over to the Ansdrie estate. He should never have anticipated the course of his daughter's life; he could blame no one but himself. He expected Lady Bridewell to refuse to see him thereafter, but he discovered he minded far less than he might have guessed. His daughter's happiness was paramount and the sincerity of her feeling for Haffie gave him courage. He would no longer be party to what amounted to a piece of business, a merger disguised as a marriage.

He crossed the Cromwell Road, threading his way between hansoms, traps and carts. He passed an engine-driven carriage that he could not help admiring. He would ask his driver, Morris, to make enquiries about one when his present difficulties had been negotiated and his daughter was safely married to her lieutenant. He thought about the large sum he would forfeit for his mismanagement of her affairs as he crossed Thurloe Square and turned east along Pelham Street, and he remembered what Lily Ann had said when Edwardes Tea began to bring in the kind of return that altered their expectations for ever: 'I am very proud that your hard work has achieved so much, Thomas. I am very proud to be the wife of such a man. But let us not forget what really matters.'

He had asked if she objected to the comforts money

brought and she said she did not. 'We are more than fortunate, much thanks to your foresight and ingenuity. But your fortune should serve us just as the pony and trap serves us. We shall give away what we do not need.'

At last Sir Thomas arrived at Eaton Terrace. He waited at the end of the street for several moments before summoning the courage to walk up the steps and ring the bell. He did not look forward to his conversation with Lady Bridewell, but he would suffer any insult she might hurl at him in silence, and he would leave with as much dignity as possible.

But in the event Sir Thomas only left his calling card at Eaton Terrace for no one was at home. They were variously at a concert, at a soirée and riding in Hyde Park although, perhaps, Lieutenant Haffie might be found in Eaton Square. Sir Thomas walked quickly to the square but could not find him so he walked on in a north-easterly direction towards a coffee house where he would be distracted by conversation that had nothing to do with his own foolish mismanagement. But when he passed Burlington House he called in, on impulse.

But Lieutenant Haffie was not there, either.

Sir Thomas walked up to the watercolour room and stood in front of Haffie's paintings. He tried to see what his daughter saw in them but he could not; there was too little definition for him. But when he saw that two of the three watercolours had already sold, he went to the clerk's office and bought the third for Natalie.

He would give it to her on her wedding day.

ELEVEN

'I WONDER, ANSDRIE,' said Lady Bridewell, 'that you have not told me that it is done.' She asked the footman to leave. She did not look at him, she simply dismissed him with a sharp flick of her hand. 'I saw you standing with Miss Edwardes, in a most intimate fashion, outside the Academy. I would have remonstrated had I not known what you were about.'

Ansdrie shifted in his chair at the breakfast table, but he did not say anything.

'Your inheritance becomes lawful in August. This is in good time.'

'You make it sound so very businesslike, Mama.'

'Your betrothal shall not be announced immediately, not until after Miss Edwardes's coming-out ball. But it pleases me to know you have secured her.'

'I have not secured Miss Edwardes, Mama.'

'You have not?'

Lady Bridewell leaned towards Ansdrie as if to see inside his mind and ferret out its defects. He waited for one of her coldly furious outbursts but she remained silent and he was grateful to Miss Edwardes for her assistance in this for he rarely managed to silence his mother. But when she had not broken the silence between them for several minutes – if a stare whose fury made the air crackle can be said to be silence – he said, 'I think I may never make her my wife, Mama. And if I do not, we must see to it that Sir Thomas is repaid.'

Lady Bridewell pushed her chair back from the table and stood up. She seemed to expand until Ansdrie thought her purple bombazine would burst. But at last she said, her words propelled from her throat as if on a jet of steam, 'So it is to be an American, is it? I believe there is one left. She goes by the name of Sangster. Her dowry will be more than satisfactory.'

Ansdrie was astounded. He barely knew Miss Sangster, but he had expected far worse from his mother. He thought she might attempt to force a marriage between him and Miss Edwardes, although he could not imagine how for Miss Edwardes would not tolerate it.

'I think perhaps you should not have seated them together, with the younger Fountains, at Gussie's engagement dinner.'

Lady Bridewell towered over her son and said, 'Determination will always eclipse a simple mistake in *placement*.'

Ansdrie watched his mother sweep from the room with a peculiar mixture of relief and consternation. He remained sitting, upright and very still despite his quick heartbeat, until the return of the footman prompted him to leave.

Sir Thomas Edwardes sat at the desk in his study. He rang frequently for Stephens to discuss the arrangements for the evening. He asked him to check, again, that Mr Hirst's generator was safe. He asked about the supplies of wine and champagne from Berry Brothers, the lobsters from Billingsgate and the plovers' eggs from Smithfield. He asked about the flowers from Covent Garden and what time Mr Havenshaw, the pianist, and Mr Peters, the violinist, would arrive.

To each enquiry Stephens replied, without irritation, that

everything was in order until, at last, Sir Thomas was satisfied. Between Stephens's entrances and exits Sir Thomas glanced at the portrait of his late wife. He had brought it to London for company, and now it hung in more or less the same relation to his desk as it had always hung in his study at Hey Tor House. When he rose to take his breakfast he thought, not for the first time, how physically like his wife was his daughter: the blue of her eyes and her dark hair, the low tone of her voice and her quick, confident walk.

'You would be pleased, Lily Ann,' he said, 'with the way things have turned out. There is nothing to shame you now.'

Sir Thomas left his study, took a plate of kidneys and scrambled egg and seated himself at the head of the dining room table. Because Natalie was not yet downstairs, he began to read *The Times*. He turned to the obituaries; it was always interesting to find out how people had spent their lives, and when one obituary in particular caught his attention an idea began to form in his mind. By the time he had read it for a second time he had determined upon a course of action that would surely persuade Lieutenant Haffie the time had come to make his proposal.

He heard the front door open and close and then Stephens came into the dining room at a great pace, followed by Lady Bridewell; she had not even given him her mantelet. Stephens made an infinitesimally helpless shrug but Sir Thomas thanked him as if he had carried out his duties perfectly. When he had gone, Lady Bridewell said, 'You left your card yesterday, Sir Thomas. May we have a word, in private?'

'My study,' said Sir Thomas, standing up.

'My carriage, I think,' said Lady Bridewell, turning and striding towards the door. Her dark purple dress rustled and billowed. Sir Thomas followed her quickly.

Natalie turned the corner on the landing above them just as Stephens handed Sir Thomas his hat, his gloves and his cane, as if nothing were out of the ordinary. Sir Thomas inclined his head in an attempt to reassure his daughter, but she simply stared. Stephens sidled quickly down the stone steps to open the door of Lady Bridewell's singularly small carriage and Sir Thomas stepped in after her. But when they were seated he could not turn towards her for, if he did, his face would be much too close to hers for comfort, or propriety. So they spoke to the wooden carriage wall that stood only a few inches in front of them.

Lady Bridewell smacked the side of the carriage with her hand and when Verrinder ordered the horses to walk on, the carriage jolted over the wooden setts in Hyde Park Gate and out onto the Kensington Road.

'I have instructed Ansdrie to make his proposal to Miss Edwardes tonight,' said Lady Bridewell. 'The way she behaved yesterday, at the *Exhibition*,' she said the word as if she were uttering an obscenity, 'suggests there is no time to waste.'

As Sir Thomas steadied himself with his cane against the jolts and jarring movements of the carriage he realized, with a little shock of pleasure, that Lady Bridewell did not know her son had already made a proposal to his daughter, or that she had turned him down.

'Has Lord Ansdrie agreed?' he said, innocently.

'Ansdrie understands very well what is required of him.'

Lady Bridewell remained absolutely still, apparently entirely unaffected by the erratic movements of the carriage.

'I understand your anxiety, Lady Bridewell,' said Sir Thomas. 'But, by my lights, we must allow our offspring to decide for themselves. This is not Ceylon and, as far as I know, my daughter has not been consulted.' And he found that he believed his own lie.

'We made an agreement, Sir Thomas,' said Lady Bridewell.

It was hot in the carriage but Sir Thomas did not attempt to open the shutters. Instead he stared straight ahead through the slim pane of glass beside the wooden panel. He saw a young married couple walking arm in arm beneath the plane trees. The young man's head was bent towards the young woman's and their obvious empathy gave him courage. In a year or two his own daughter would be in just such a happy state.

'And I have always assumed,' said Lady Bridewell, 'that, to men from your walk of life, a financial transaction signified a binding agreement.'

'You are quite correct,' said Sir Thomas, who was beginning to feel claustrophobic. 'But the parties to the agreement were you and me. My daughter's consent has yet to be given.'

'Your daughter has behaved dishonourably and I do not use the word lightly, Sir Thomas. She is in a *scrape*. This will save her. You must admit that.'

Sir Thomas said, calmly and coldly, 'My daughter has not behaved dishonourably, Lady Bridewell. She has behaved impulsively and not entirely correctly, but I will not allow dishonourably.'

Lady Bridewell cleared her throat. 'Without my patronage Miss Edwardes would never have been presented at Court. In fact, she would not be here at all. Her behaviour at the Exhibition was outrageous. You should have exerted your authority and you did not. Now is the time.'

'I repeat,' said Sir Thomas, 'I will not force my daughter into any . . . arrangement.'

'I should never have troubled myself over her,' said Lady Bridewell. 'Indeed I wish I had not.' She made an impatient guttural sound. 'If you will not cooperate then I shall announce her betrothal tonight, myself. With or without your consent.'

Sir Thomas had become very warm. He said, staring at the bole of a plane tree as they passed, 'I believe my daughter has fallen in love, Lady Bridewell, and love is not governed by any rule.' He breathed in to calm himself.

'What a young woman decides to do when she realizes she has fallen in love is the only thing over which she can have any control. And there, I admit, Natalie has failed to observe the code of behaviour that you . . . and I . . . would expect. But falling in love of itself is not dishonourable.'

'Love!' said Lady Bridewell. 'What has love to do with anything?'

For the first time in their awkward journey he felt her shift beside him, but he did not turn to see if she looked at him.

'If you cannot understand that,' said Sir Thomas, 'then we have nothing more to say to each other.'

Without asking her permission he rapped his cane on the ceiling of the carriage and at once Verrinder called the horses to a halt. He stepped from the landaulet without tipping his hat or turning to bow to Lady Bridewell. He shut the carriage door behind him and when he heard her sharp command and the wheels of the carriage turning in the street, he took a long, deep breath of the warm summer air and even though it was laden with the smells of horse manure and petroleum he thought it the freshest air he had breathed for days. As soon as he arrived home he sent word to Lieutenant Haffie to call upon him.

But Lieutenant Haffie did not call that morning and so Sir Thomas went in search of him. He knew he could not be at Eaton Terrace because he had not replied to his request to call upon him, so he summoned Morris and travelled east along the Kensington Road in his landau, bound for Piccadilly and Burlington House. He would make clear to Lieutenant Haffie all that had happened. He would say that if he intended to, then he must declare himself to his daughter without delay.

But he failed to find Haffie and when he returned to Hyde Park Gate he discovered he had called there and they had missed each other. When he asked Natalie whether she had spoken to him she said she had not known he had called. She had been occupied with Hocks, making preparations for the ball, deciding on finishing touches to her dress, deciding on shoes.

'Besides, Papa,' she said, smiling happily, 'I should not have received him even if he had asked to see me, which I am sure he would not, without you here. For it would be quite wrong until . . .' She kept smiling, but said nothing else.

In a state of agitation Sir Thomas consulted his book of etiquette, particularly the page that explained how many waltzes a young lady and gentleman might dance at a ball, and when Stephens brought in his copy of *The Times*, neatly folded at the last page he had been reading, he felt a sudden surge of energy. This would give Lieutenant Haffie the opportunity he needed. There was no need for a conversation.

He wrote to Lady Bridewell to say he wished their interview had not ended in disagreement and that, on reflection, there was a great deal more to discuss. He said he would call at Eaton Terrace the following afternoon but he would be grateful if she would not say anything until they had spoken again, particularly not that night. And that afternoon, when Natalie asked him what Lady Bridewell had come to discuss, he told her she had been outraged by her forward behaviour at the Exhibition, but he had persuaded her out of her fury. He said all would be well.

That evening, as he dressed for his daughter's coming-out ball, he put away the silver sleevelinks Lady Bridewell had given him. Clearly she meant him to wear them while they were in London, but that night he would not. He would wear the emerald sleevelinks Lily Ann had given him, the ones set in gilded tea leaves. They had been made to celebrate the arrival of the first Edwardes Tea buyer at the Ceylon Auctions, and without Edwardes Tea Sir

Thomas could not have bought Hyde Park Gate, nor could he have given his daughter a London Season, the result of which he now anticipated with more or less uncomplicated happiness.

TWELVE

Natalie sat at her dressing table. She wore her corset and her petticoats and waited for Hocks to arrive with her gown. She looked at herself in the glass. She bent her dark head to a small bowl of white Scotch roses and breathed in their heady scent. Tonight she would dance 'outwith the laws of gravity'. She mimicked Haffie's lilt. She picked up her handglass and stared at her reflection. She tried to breath slowly to calm her excitement but she could not stop smiling.

When Hocks began to brush out her hair Natalie said, 'I've changed my mind. I think this would look very well.' She took a rose from the bowl and handed it to Hocks.

'Very pretty, miss,' said Hocks.

She put the rose carefully onto the dressing table and then rolled hanks of Natalie's hair round cushioned hair-pads and secured them. She held out a yellow bodice and a matching embroidered silk skirt. When Natalie moved the materials rustled softly. Her upright walk made her seem taller than she was and when she stood in front of her cheval glass she was delighted to see the darker yellow appliqued butterflies looking just as she had hoped, as if they were flying upwards to land on the pale tea-coloured silk roses that decorated the top of her bodice. And then, while Hocks straightened the bodice at her waist, Natalie thought about her father, about the necessary parting from him that her marriage would bring and an unexpected sadness filled her.

She said, 'Could you ask Sir Thomas to come to me, please?'

Hocks bobbed and said, 'If you wouldn't mind my saying so, miss, you do look lovely.'

Natalie burst into tears when her father arrived but he said, 'My dearest girl, this is not an occasion for crying.'

'But it is, Papa,' said Natalie. 'For when I marry I shall leave you.'

'But you will come to stay at Hey Tor House,' said Sir Thomas.

Natalie felt her father's arms enfold her as he said, 'This evening marks the beginning of a new life.' He stood back and looked at her. 'But you are right,' he said, and he blinked. 'It is also an ending.' He squeezed Natalie's hand and she did her best to smile. 'There, that's my girl,' he said as she dried her eyes. 'And you be sure to tell me just as soon as Lieutenant Haffie has spoken to you.'

'I think he may speak to you first, Papa,' said Natalie. 'You do think he will . . . speak?'

'I have no doubt of it,' said Sir Thomas. 'If not tonight, then at the very latest tomorrow.' And then he said, as they sat together on small button-back chairs in the middle of the room, 'I have something for you,' and he took a red leather box from his pocket.

Inside was an exquisite little brooch, a primrose, set on a long gold pin. A brooch Natalie had not seen for years. 'Mama's favourite,' she said and she stood to kiss her father. And then she turned to the glass so that he should not see her renewed tears. She said, brightly, 'Shall I wear it here, do you think?' She held the brooch at her shoulder, but it became lost among the roses. 'Or here?' She held it at her waist where it looked very well against the plain yellow bodice. 'How did Mama wear it? I cannot remember.'

She caught sight of her father in the glass. His head was bent and he had taken his handkerchief from his pocket. She waited a moment before she turned back to him, and then she said, 'If only she were here.'

Sir Thomas stood, took Natalie's hands and said, 'She is here, my dear. Through you.' He looked at her. 'It does me good to see you looking so lovely. Your mother would be very proud.'

He bent and kissed the top of her dark head and then they stood for a moment, looking at each other, before Sir Thomas said, 'All will be well.'

A constellation of electroliers and wall brackets, lamps and sconces shone with brilliant electric light inside Hyde Park Gate. The generator hummed in the basement and when the guests began to arrive, guests who were used to the softer light of oil lamps and candles, they turned their heads away from the flood of light in the Edwardes's household. But Natalie thought it magnificent.

'I have never seen them all lit together before, Papa. Will they last the evening?' she said, as they stood together at the top of the stairs.

'Mr Hirst's men assure me it is a most reliable generator,' he said. 'I have every faith in it, even should you dance until dawn.'

Natalie took her father's arm and they walked slowly, regally, down the stairs towards Stephens and the two footmen, who stood by the front door. At that moment Lady Bridewell, Millie, Gussie and Fountain arrived. Lady Bridewell's diamonds flashed in her grey-streaked hair and when Natalie and her father reached the hall they greeted each other, a little more formally than usual, while Stephens and the footmen bowed and took their cloaks. And then, for an uncomfortable moment, the brilliant lights troubled Natalie. She wanted to escape them: she felt as if they were trained upon her, as if Lady Bridewell were about to interrogate her beneath them. But her father tactfully took Lady Bridewell by the arm and Millie, Gussie, Fountain and Natalie walked quickly together into the ballroom where foliage hung in loops from the picture rails between the pier glasses and tall vases were filled with jasmine and trailing vines, lilies and white roses.

Natalie said, 'Is it not magnificent?'

She spread her arms wide and pirouetted. She began to dance the length of the ballroom with one arm stretched out, her wrist through the loop on the train of her skirt, just as if she danced with a partner. Spontaneously the musicians, a violinist and a pianist, struck up a waltz and Edward Fountain bowed to her and took her in his arms. Gussie gasped and very quickly Natalie, who had meant only to dance alone, disentangled herself from Fountain and took the dance card Lady Bridewell held out to her.

The cards were small white paper fans. The names of the dances were printed on the ribs and as Natalie opened her fan and looked at the blank spaces on the leaves above the ribs, she imagined Lieutenant Haffie's name above one of the waltzes.

Lady Bridewell said, 'Do not forget, one dance for each gentleman, two at the very most. And if you should dance more than once with the same gentleman, be sure you take other partners in between. Except, of course,' she turned to Gussie, 'for you, Augustina. It is different for you, now.'

She tapped one of the dance cards against Natalie's gloved hand and Millie said, 'Of course we shall not forget, Mama. We have never forgotten,' and then she smiled at Natalie, opened her own dance card and said, 'These are unusual.'

The young women looped the ribbons of their dance cards round their wrists and then Natalie heard the first carriages arriving and the sounds of the first guests giving their cloaks and hats to the footmen. She stood between her father and Lady Bridewell, as Stephens began to announce them. Sir Thomas received the guests with bows and words of welcome. Natalie smiled and greeted them all, but as she listened to Stephens's voice announcing their names she thought of the long list of begats in the Bible and remembered the things she had learned about these people since she had been in London: Mr and Mrs George Bellinger had a particularly unhappy marriage and the Misses Laetitia and Alice Bellinger were spectacularly silent as a result; the Earl and Countess of Morvenish and their son, Lord Favell, had only accepted their invitation to Natalie's coming-out ball because they considered Lady Bridewell to be giving it; Captain Alexander George and Captain Peter Henderson were honest, ordinary soldiers who danced well and had not an ounce of intrigue in their souls; the Ladies Sophia and Victoria Calderswell were good-looking and clever and talked, privately, about following Millicent Fawcett; and Natalie thought it more than likely that the Havenhams and the Hawkesworths, the Ashenappers, the Sangsters and the Eldensworths all felt much that they would never speak about publicly. But now, beneath their immaculate clothes and jewels, Natalie was certain there lay much more than she had ever allowed before she left Devon. Lord Ansdrie's proposal, despite its want of love, had shown her as much.

But as the sounds of voices rose in the ballroom and the guests gathered and Natalie greeted them, the only name she longed to hear had still not been announced.

Ansdrie and Haffie walked down the wide staircase at Eaton Terrace, side by side. When they reached the hall Ansdrie said, 'Might we have a word, Haffie, before we leave?' And to make sure Haffie would not object Ansdrie put his hand on his shoulder and ushered him into the drawing room in front of the footman, who stood by the front door with their cloaks, hats and walking canes.

'Don't look so worried,' he said as he shut the door behind them and held out his hand. 'For I wish you well.'

But Haffie merely looked at his feet while Ansdrie watched him clasp and unclasp his hands behind him and rock backwards and forwards on his heels.

'You do intend to propose to Miss Edwardes?'

At last Haffie looked up. 'I have been meaning to speak to you since our last . . . conversation on the . . . subject. I am sorry that I have not. But are you telling me you no longer intend. . . ?'

'I can only apologize for misleading you but I have . . . in point of fact I have changed my mind.'

'Damned confusing, Ansdrie, if you'll forgive me. First you tell me you doubt she will refuse you; now you tell me you will not have her.'

'Women are mysterious creatures, are they not? I had thought her enamoured of me, but now I . . . well, suffice to say I misinterpreted the signs. . . .'

Ansdrie would not admit to the humiliating truth of Natalie's refusal, but nor would he continue to lie to the man he wished, despite everything, to remain his friend. And he thought he might learn something of the ways of women by watching Haffie's success.

He was profoundly grateful when Haffie grasped his outstretched hand, shook it and thanked him. The difficult interview was over.

When, at last, Stephens announced, 'Lord Ansdrie,' and then, 'Lieutenant Angus Haffie,' Natalie's heart beat quickly as she smiled at the two men who stood before her. And then her smile transmuted into a straightforward gasp of admiration for they were dressed as she had never seen them dressed before. They wore short scarlet jackets with yellow epaulettes, facings and cuffs. They wore kilts and waistcoats of a kingfisher blue and deep-green tartan inter-sected by fine red and white lines. Their hose was of the same pattern and their shoes were shining black patent and brass-buckled. Their shirts and gloves glowed white against the scarlet of their jackets and their brass buttons shone.

'You are exotic birds,' said Natalie. 'You outshine us all.'

Both men bowed and Lieutenant Haffie said, 'It would be difficult to outshine you, Miss Edwardes.'

Natalie thanked him and said, looking at Ansdrie, 'Why have I never seen you wear a kilt before?'

'Because it is considered incorrect south of the border,' said Lady Bridewell.

Natalie saw her frown at her son but Haffie said, 'We wear the mess dress of the Waterfirth Reservists in your honour, Miss Edwardes.'

'I am deeply honoured,' said Natalie.

The two men bowed again, greeted Lady Bridewell and then, when the last guests had arrived, Natalie stood for a moment beside her father and looked at the great gathering of people. She heard the hum and buzz of their voices beneath the electroliers. She saw the colourful silks and satins of the older women and the paler colours of her own generation. She saw the flash of bright jewels and the clean lines of the men's white ties and dark dress suits. She searched for Haffie and found him at the far end of the ballroom with Millie. She longed for the moment when he would engage her to dance; the moment when his name would be inscribed on her dance card.

'My dearest girl,' said her father, 'shall we dance the first lancers?'

Natalie smiled up at her father and took his arm and as they stood in a set waiting for the musicians to begin he said, 'Make sure Lieutenant Haffie engages you for a waltz, my dear. I have a feeling you shall waltz very well together.'

Natalie replied, very quietly, 'Thank you, dear Papa. For everything.'

When the lancers ended, Lady Bridewell ushered Natalie

towards a group of young men, including Ansdrie, and said, 'Here is Mr Hawkesworth and Mr Farrars. Where is your dance card, Miss Edwardes?'

Natalie handed the little white fan to each man and then Ansdrie stood in front of her and said, 'May I have the pleasure of the next quadrille?'

When he had written his name on the leaf in the little fan Natalie said, 'Should you care to dance a waltz, as well, Lord Ansdrie?'

He looked up. 'You are kind, Miss Edwardes. But, as you know only too well, I have not much of a head, or feet for that matter, for the quicker dances.'

'Two separate dances would be quite acceptable,' said Lady Bridewell. 'You are well enough acquainted.'

'Indeed, Mama,' said Ansdrie, but he took Natalie gently by the elbow and led her away from Lady Bridewell towards a group of people among whom Haffie stood.

'I only meant to show you,' said Natalie, turning to Ansdrie so that no one else would hear, 'that I am sorry for yesterday. I did not mean to be rude, and I did not wish to be unkind.'

'As I said, Miss Edwardes, you showed great courage for you spoke from your heart. It must have been difficult. If we all did so more often, we should know each other a great deal better.'

'Thank you,' said Natalie.

When they turned back to the throng in the middle of the ballroom Haffie was already standing in a set with Miss Sangster for the quadrille. Ansdrie bowed to Natalie and said, 'And I thank you. And I shall accept. I *shall* dance a waltz with you in order to learn how to dance it well.'

'It's quite simple, really,' said Natalie.

'You make it look simple, Miss Edwardes,' said Ansdrie. 'But only because you are so very good at it.'

While he wrote his name against the third waltz Natalie wondered at his softer manner, softer than she had ever witnessed in him, and felt a corresponding softening towards him. She took a glass of lemonade with him after the quadrille and then, when he escorted her back to the ballroom, she was besieged by requests from young men to dance. She accepted because to refuse would have been churlish at her own ball, but she counted the group of men and tried to take her fan back before all the dances were spoken for, because Haffie was not among them. But she did not succeed and when, at last, the little white fan was handed back to her she saw that every single one of the twenty dances had a name written above it and not one of them was Haffie's. Now she and Haffie would not dance like the wind for they would not dance at all.

It was difficult to contain her disappointment when she danced with Edward Fountain in the same set as Ansdrie and Miss Sangster. Indeed, she was so consumed by it that she failed to take Ansdrie's arm. 'Miss Edwardes?' he said. 'It's very unlike you to miss a step.' When she turned to him she saw he was smiling, but she was close to tears.

'I'm sorry, Lord Ansdrie,' she said. 'But I . . . I was thinking . . . Lieutenant Haffie has been so very well mannered. He has not put himself forward to . . . to . . . ask me to dance. And now he has waited too long. We shall not dance together tonight.'

'But you *must* dance with the finest dancer in the regiment,' said Ansdrie as he led Miss Sangster away, 'especially at your own ball.' He glanced back at her, tipped his head in a manner not unlike the way her father tipped his head to her when he wanted to show her all was well and then, when the measured music ended, he bowed to his partner, gave her to her next partner and took Natalie's hand from Fountain's and walked her straight towards Lieutenant Haffie.

'What are you going to do, Lord Ansdrie?' she said, a mixture of alarm and excitement filling her.

'I am going to give you the opportunity to dance with

the one person you want to dance with.'

'But *I* cannot ask *him.*'

'*You* probably could, Miss Edwardes,' said Ansdrie. 'But there will be no need.'

When they reached the group of people among whom Lieutenant Haffie stood, Ansdrie put Natalie's hand on Haffie's arm and said, 'I give you this waltz, Lieutenant Haffie. I have never managed them well.'

There were murmurs of greeting to Natalie from Mr Hawkesworth and Miss Alice Bellinger. She smiled and bowed and then she said, to Haffie, 'Perhaps . . . you are . . . I do hope you are not already engaged for it.'

Haffie looked surprised, but then he said, 'I am not,' and Natalie's heart fluttered as she watched Ansdrie substitute Haffie's name for his own on her dance card.

There was very little space between them: the ribbon of the dance card bound Natalie to Ansdrie but her hand rested on Haffie's arm. She wanted to kiss Ansdrie's cheek to thank him, but of course she did not. She hoped her thank-you properly conveyed her gratitude. Ansdrie inclined his head again and then he led Alice Bellinger away across the ballroom.

Haffie leaned down towards Natalie and she breathed in the honey-scented pomade in his hair. 'The ballroom looks grand and so, if I may say so, do you, Miss Edwardes. Would that be a Scotch rose?'

'It would,' she said, knowing very well he knew that it was.

'I am so sorry,' he said, 'for failing to ask you to dance. But Lady Bridewell suggested it would not be the mark of a gentleman after we spent, as she put it, such an intimate time together at the Exhibition. She said, "I am sure you would not want Miss Edwardes to become the object of speculation," and so, for your sake, I did as she asked. But I have spent the evening badly regretting my promise.'

'Then we owe Lord Ansdrie much,' said Natalie.

'Indeed we do,' said Haffie.

Natalie smiled up at him as they walked to the centre of the ballroom. She put her wrist through the loop on the train of her skirt and when Haffie took her in his arms while they waited for the musicians to strike up the waltz, she looked into his brown eyes and thought, 'This is the moment I shall remember when I am old.'

But the musicians took their time to strike up the waltz and Natalie turned from Haffie to discover the reason. She stood on tiptoe to look over the heads of the other guests. She leaned in towards Haffie as she tried to see what kept them from playing. She very much liked the pressure of his hand on her back and made no attempt to move away. And then she saw her father. He and the violinist were in conversation and then Sir Thomas straightened up and turned to face the waiting pairs of dancers.

'I apologize for the unexpected interruption,' he said. 'But Mr Peters and I have agreed a small change to the programme.'

There was a murmur of voices in the ballroom and then Sir Thomas took a step back and Mr Peters stood up. He held his violin and bow in his left hand. He nodded to the pianist and then he addressed the guests. His voice was thin and reedy and the guests leaned towards him in a gentle rustle of movement, the better to hear what he had to say.

'In memory of Herr Johann Strauss, who, as you will all know, died only a few weeks ago,' he said, 'Sir Thomas has requested two Viennese waltzes. We shall play the *Blue Danube* and then the *Viennese Spirit* and we shall play both waltzes at a quick pace; the second will follow the first without pause.'

For a moment the air was filled with the sound of voices and then several older pairs of dancers left the floor. But Natalie clapped her gloved hands together and a ripple of applause broke out among the couples who remained. And then the opening phrases of the *Blue Danube* flooded the ballroom.

Haffie leaned down and said, 'Do you dance a quick, or a very quick waltz?'

'Very quick,' said Natalie, looking up at him. 'Very quick indeed.'

She felt Haffie's hand press firmly against her back and as soon as they began to move she knew she was in the arms of a man who waltzed musically and exceedingly well.

The pianist's fingers flew over the keys and the violinist played with a soaring energy and grace quite unlike his voice. The music enchanted Natalie and the dance itself became their conversation. She had imagined they would have much to say to each other, but they could not speak for the speed of the waltz and so they communicated through their movements. Natalie's whole being gave itself to the dance, to the way Haffie led her without making her feel in the least propelled or pulled, to the way they turned and turned and turned again. She never once thought where her feet should be. She and the music were one. She and Haffie were one. And as he whirled her round the ballroom she felt as if she were *being* danced. Her body responded instinctively and a delight in the dance and in Haffie coursed through her so that when she turned her smiling face up to his, she felt as if the sole purpose of meeting him had been to dance with him, like the wind.

The reflections of the other dancers in the pier glasses merged and flew by in bright ribbons of light, but Haffie's face remained clear. His sandy moustache that was a little too long, his eyelids with their peculiar droop, his pale eyelashes, his freckled face, all remained constant. And when his brown eyes met hers Natalie was filled with a joy so overwhelming that she was afraid she might cry. When the waltzes ended the ballroom was a smaller place, the lights less bright and Natalie felt the eyes of her guests upon her.

She looked up at Haffie and said, 'That was quite quite . . . wonderful. Thank you.'

'Indeed it was,' said Haffie and when she put her hand on his arm he said quickly, his lips very close to her ear, 'It was like the wind, was it not?' And then he straightened up and said, formally, 'Will you take supper with me, Miss Edwardes?'

Natalie's smile was more brilliant than the jewels that sparkled and flashed from the dresses and the heads of her guests, and as they left the ballroom and crossed the black and white marble floor towards the dining room, she acknowledged her guests but did not really see them. She did not hear Lady Bridewell address her nor did she hear her father. She drank a glass of lemonade and, although she knew it could not be true, it tasted sweeter and sharper than the glass she had drunk earlier, with Ansdrie. Haffie drank a glass of claret and then they took plates of lobster, plovers' eggs and salad and went to sit at a small table by the window. Natalie heard the carriages in the street and saw the gas lamps. She saw clouds moving across the face of the almost-full moon and, beyond the carriages, the glittering, black wrought-iron of the Queen's Gate at the entrance to Kensington Gardens. But all the time she was more conscious of Haffie than of anything or anyone else.

'I have been wondering,' he said and Natalie sat straighter, her heart jumping in her breast, 'but I have not found the opportunity to ask you until now.' Natalie held her breath. 'If I am water in a pair of cupped hands, what are you?'

'I never think about myself in that way,' she said, unable completely to dismiss her disappointment that he had not asked what she thought him about to ask. 'But I love the red deer. I see them often at home and I hope I might be as quick and as graceful, as . . . sensitive as they are.'

'You are,' said Haffie. 'And quite as beautiful.'

Natalie blushed but she held his gaze and when they

had finished eating he asked her if she would mind if he smoked. She shook her head and watched his long fingers take an oval cigarette from a silver case. He lit it with his silver lighter, which – could it really be? – now had an engraving of a simple, five-petalled Scotch rose upon it. Natalie stared at it and then looked at Haffie, who said, before she could ask, 'It is just what you think it is. I collected it yesterday. Now I have something to remind me of you whenever we are apart.'

'Thank you,' said Natalie, softly. And then, breathing in the pungent smoke she said, 'How do you think of me, Lieutenant Haffie? What do you see?'

Haffie drew on his cigarette and looked at her with great tenderness and Natalie's imagination conjured an image of their wedding day. She walked down the aisle beneath St Petroc's barrel-vaulted ceiling on her father's arm and saw, through her mother's Brussels lace, the back of Haffie's head. He stood by the chancel step and she heard the choir singing the Bach cantata she had heard, as a little girl, at her Aunt Goodwin's wedding. When she stood beside him, Haffie whispered, 'Our day of days has come.'

'Miss Edwardes? . . . Miss Edwardes?'

Natalie looked up. 'I am sorry. I was . . .'

'You were somewhere else entirely.'

'I was,' she said, smiling shyly.

'I was saying I think of you as quicksilver. Mercury.'

'Oh,' said Natalie. 'Is that . . . a compliment?'

'Sometimes quicksilver stands quite still,' said Haffie. 'In the moment when it gathers itself before it moves. You have that way about you when you are struck by something, as you were when you looked at my paintings. As you were just now.' He put out his cigarette and said, 'And sometimes quicksilver moves like lightning, just as you did when we waltzed.'

'Then I am glad to be quicksilver,' said Natalie.

'Will you take me into your confidence? Will you tell me

what you were thinking about just now?'

Natalie felt the blush rising but she said, thinking quickly for, yet again, she would not tell him she imagined herself married to him for fear he would think her forward for touching upon the subject before he did, 'Your red jacket put me in mind of Sergeant Troy.'

'Did it?' said Haffie, his expression serious. 'I'm not certain how I should take that.'

'It is a compliment,' said Natalie, leaning towards him. 'He was a gallant and good-looking soldier. He wore scarlet and brass.'

'But he was, as I remember,' said Haffie, 'a man who would speak of love and think of dinner.'

'Oh, no,' said Natalie. 'No, not at all. He married Bathsheba. They were very much in love. It all happened quite quickly.' She glanced at Haffie but his expression was disapproving and she wished she had said what she had really been thinking for now she had talked about a marriage between two fictional characters and it had, somehow, displeased him more than he might have been displeased if she had talked of the possibility of their own, real marriage. She stared at the rose on his lighter. 'I have not finished the book,' she said. 'I left it at home when we came to London. I didn't think I would have time to read it here.'

'I am glad to hear that,' said Haffie, and his disapproving expression transmuted into a smile. 'When you return to it I think you may discover a different story. I look forward to another conversation about it.' He picked up the lighter and put it into the pocket of his scarlet jacket. 'And now there is something else I should like to ask you, Miss Edwardes. Would you and Sir Thomas come boating with me tomorrow? On the Serpentine?'

'I cannot think of anything more delightful,' said Natalie. And then, conscious that her father watched her, she said, 'But now I really think I should return to the ballroom.'

And so Haffie stood and offered her his arm and, as they walked across the hall together, smiling at Sir Thomas as they went, Haffie leaned close to Natalie and said, 'I have never, ever, had the pleasure of dancing with such a fine, quick partner . . . Natalie.'

'You make my name sound beautiful.'

'It *is* beautiful,' said Haffie. 'You do not object to my use of it?'

'I do not object . . . Angus,' said Natalie. 'I do not object in the least.'

They walked towards the ballroom under the blaze of light from the electroliers and Natalie noticed, with a pleasure quite disproportionate to the fact, that their step was of exactly the same length. She said, 'Would three o'clock tomorrow afternoon suit you, A—' but when she saw Lady Bridewell standing by the ballroom door, she said, quickly, 'Lieutenant Haffie?'

'Suit you for what?' said Ansdrie, appearing from behind his mother.

Natalie smiled brilliantly at them and said, 'Lieutenant Haffie and I, and Papa, of course, go boating tomorrow. On the Serpentine.'

Lady Bridewell's expression did not alter but Ansdrie said, 'Capital idea.'

Haffie bowed and said, 'Thank you, Miss Edwardes, for the most delightful evening. I look forward to tomorrow.' And as he left their little group he bowed to Ansdrie as if he were thanking him too.

Natalie watched him walk away across the ballroom and when she caught sight of her father she inclined her head happily. Then, taking Ansdrie's arm, she suggested they sit together before the dancing began again. They walked to the far end of the ballroom and sat beneath a pair of electric sconces, which lit a gilt-framed pier glass. Several pairs of guests stopped to talk to them and so it was, in the end, only just before the first dance after supper that Natalie managed to say, 'I had not realized it was the supper waltz you gave us. Thank you, especially, for that.'

'It is the least I could do for my friend,' said Ansdrie. 'And the least I could do for you.'

He stood and as he handed her to Captain Henderson for a polka, he whispered, 'You are unique, Miss Edwardes.'

When all the guests had left and the footmen had carried away the glasses and the plates; when Stephens began to turn out the lights and the musicians and the servants retired downstairs for some well-earned food, Natalie walked up the stairs, tired and very happy, on her father's arm. When she turned, at the top of the stairs, she saw the morning sky turning pink through the demi-lunette above the door. And then, when she and her father stood outside her bedroom, she thanked him for the evening, and he told her that Haffie had apologized for being unable to call a second time that day: he had been discussing an important commission.

'He has invited us to go boating tomorrow,' said Natalie.

A whole world of possibility existed in those simple words.

'And he would like to draw Mama's brooch. And the Scotch rose in my hair. And he thought me like quicksilver. He said we danced like the wind. I could have danced all the waltzes with him, Papa. Every single one.'

'Waltzes are irresistible, are they not?' said Sir Thomas. 'And what follows when two have been danced together is equally irresistible.'

'But we did not . . .' she looked up at him and saw his broad smile. 'Oh, Papa,' she said, throwing her arms around his neck, 'you dear, dear man.'

THIRTEEN

AFTER MATINS, AT which Natalie said a fervent prayer that Haffie would ask what her heart longed for him to ask, and after luncheon at which she ate very little, Natalie and Sir Thomas walked between the grey stone balustrades on the Serpentine bridge. The sun blazed down and the water glittered and shimmered. Small wooden boats with green hulls were out on the lake. Men wearing boaters rowed, while women held pretty parasols above their heads and leaned forwards from time to time to speak to their companions. It looked like a painting Haffie had shown Natalie in *La Vogue*, a painting of people in a park in Paris.

She squeezed her father's arm and said, 'My heart is beating so fast I feel as if it might fly from me. Hold on to me, Papa, please.'

He said, 'Steady your nerves, my dear. It cannot be long now.'

They turned to walk down the stone steps to the boathouse where pairs of oars stood against the wooden wall and a sign read, 'Boats for hire. One shilling the hour.'

Natalie looked about her but could not see Haffie. She felt her father's fingers grip her arm but, looking at him quizzically, she resisted his attempt to steer her away from the boathouse. And then she followed his gaze and saw

Ansdrie, not Haffie, standing beneath a plane tree several yards from them. He looked up and, very slowly, began to walk towards them. He looked at the ground as he walked and by the time he reached them Natalie's heart was filled with foreboding.

He did not say good afternoon. He did not greet them at all. He only said, 'Lieutenant Haffie has gone from Eaton Terrace. He is gone.'

He spread his hands in a hopeless gesture. Then he took off his hat and smoothed his dark hair with his hand. He looked first at Sir Thomas and then at Natalie. His face was pale. 'I hardly know what to say,' he said. 'Except that I am so very sorry to be the bearer of this news.'

'What can you mean?' said Natalie. 'He cannot have gone far. He will return.'

'He left no word,' said Ansdrie and he looked out across Serpentine water. 'We cannot understand it.'

Natalie took an unsteady step towards Ansdrie and then stopped. 'His family . . . his mother or his father . . . his sister . . . must have been taken ill.'

'We do not know, Miss Edwardes,' said Ansdrie.

'Did he not . . . even . . . leave word for me?'

Ansdrie shook his head. 'No word at all. Not for anyone.'

'We must find out if he . . . what he . . . ' but she could not continue for the tears that overwhelmed her. She turned to her father, away from Ansdrie's helpless expression, but she heard him say, 'I have sent word to his father's house. And to the refinery.'

'Then we shall hear from him soon,' said Sir Thomas. 'I have no doubt of it.'

Natalie allowed her father to walk her away from the Serpentine. She did not look back at Ansdrie and, as they crossed the bridge, she neither saw nor heard the riders, or the families with their children and their dogs. She did not see the young married couples strolling together, nor the chaperoned young women and the sauntering young men. They went about their pleasant and peaceful Sunday-afternoon activities unseen and unheard by Natalie, who only heard the words that kept repeating themselves in her head: 'There will be a letter from him at home. There will be a letter from him at home.'

Part Two

1899–1911

Faint heart ne'er wan
A lady fair;
Wha does the utmost that he can,
Will whyles do mair.

Robert Burns, *Epistle to Dr Blacklock*

FOURTEEN

I<small>N THE WEEKS</small> that followed Haffie's departure the sun shone, but Natalie could not rejoice in it. The trunks of the plane trees still looked like the legs of elephants that had travelled from the outreaches of the Empire, but now they broke her heart for the man who had suggested it might be so was no longer beside her.

She was in what Lady Bridewell and her kind called a *scrape*, which, in plainer language, meant she had been too forward, too swift to show her affections for one particular gentleman *and* she had done so in public. To make matters worse, he had left London, which proved, quite clearly, the guilt of both parties and, as a result, Natalie had ruined her chances of attracting a suitable husband. Every respectable young gentleman now considered her too racy and all the young women, and most especially their mothers, shunned her for her inability to disguise her affections if she could not tame them. Their invitations ceased, but Natalie would have asked her father to refuse them if they had continued to arrive, for she had no heart for conversation, let alone for dancing.

But Millie came to call every day and Ansdrie every other day, even though Natalie would not receive them. She did not regret what she had done, nor was she ashamed of the way she felt but, in her vulnerable, despairing state, she could not bear to hear their lectures, nor could she countenance their disdain or their ridicule. It did not occur to her that Millie or Ansdrie might have come to sympathize.

She spent the days after Haffie left walking endlessly into the hall to stare at the silver tray on the table that held a mounting stack of the Bridewells' calling cards. But all she longed to see there was a letter from Lieutenant Haffie.

She had written to him, passionately.

11 July 1899, Hyde Park Gate, London

Dear Lieutenant Haffie,

I'm sure there are many people in this city who would tell me I should not write this letter. But I must tell you how I feel.

I love you.

There, I have said it.

I should have told you what was really on my mind when you asked me at my coming-out ball: I was imagining our wedding. I was not thinking about Sergeant Troy at all and now, I am mortified. I asked Papa to collect the book from the library and I have finished it. Now I know Troy's careless and cruel nature. You must think me very stupid, or worse. And, when we stood in the courtyard at Burlington House, I imagined us together at the house in your painting, alone. But I did not tell you the truth then, either.

I did not tell you what I imagined because I was afraid I should appear too forward. It was not for me to presume what was in your mind, or your heart. But since you left London I have lived only in the future. I have imagined your return so often that several times, for a moment, I truly believed you stood in front of me. Would you have said you had no desire to marry me if I had admitted what I saw in my imagination?

I hope not. I believe not. Because you have awakened my soul, Lieutenant Haffie, and I cannot believe you do not know that. Without you I am incomplete. You taught my heart to sing. I didn't know that was possible until I met you. You reminded me what it feels like to laugh with my whole being. You are my soul's mate, my other half. But I waited for you to tell me how you felt, as is the custom and, truly, I thought you would.

But now I don't know what to think and so I write this letter to you, so that you can be in no doubt about my own feelings.

I hope with all my heart you will reply in kind. But if you cannot, if you feel nothing of what I feel for you, please write to tell me so for I cannot bear not knowing.

With my most particular love,
Natalie Edwardes

For his part Sir Thomas found his daughter more unkind than he could ever have imagined her and yet, in his own anger with Lieutenant Haffie, he understood hers.

'He decided he could not love me because *your* bloodline is so very inferior,' she said.

A remark so very unlike her: she was grasping at straws.

And on a different day, in a different mood, 'He never cared for me, only your money. Everyone else who comes to this ugly city intends to marry for money, or for lack of money, but of course they do not say so. At least Lieutenant Haffie had the good sense to realize he did not love me and could not marry me for money alone.'

Sir Thomas had also wondered whether Haffie had been chiefly interested in his daughter's great wealth but he reminded himself of their conversation and of Haffie's partnership in his father's firm, and he could not convince himself of it. But nor could he find a satisfactory explanation for Haffie's departure.

On another day Natalie said, 'I wrote to him, Papa. I told him all that I felt and he has not replied. Obviously he does not care for me in the least. He never did, or he would have replied.'

This was particularly dishonourable. His daughter must have had to get up her courage to write to the lieutenant: how could he have failed to reply?

And on another day: 'Only you are honest, Papa. Only you talk about the one thing that makes this world of ours work, and all despise you for it.'

And it was on that day that Sir Thomas said, 'You are too much alone, Natalie. A little company is better than none at all.'

'I have you, Papa. And I should like to leave London. I shall return to Devon, "Empty", and live the life of a spinster, by your side.'

'If you should choose such a life I cannot say it would make me unhappy,' said Sir Thomas, 'but only because it would be a pleasure to have you near me, not because I think it a wise choice. If you do decide upon it, it must not be a measure of last resort; it must be a considered choice. And I think it much too early in your young life to make such a decision.'

He could not tell her how much he blamed himself for all that had happened for, if he did, he would have to tell her what he had done. He was mortified that he had ever thought a title for his daughter such a wonderful thing; mortified that his desire for social elevation had blinded him to what would make her happy. But what more could he do now? Lieutenant Haffie had proved himself damnably unworthy of his daughter, had made her cruel in her unhappiness and, most unforgivably, he had broken her heart.

He said, 'At least take a walk with me, my dearest girl. Or perhaps a ride? Shall I ask Boundy to saddle the horses?'

But this did not cheer Natalie at all; in fact it made her

cry so desperately that Sir Thomas sat beside her and took her in his arms. When he did so she cried all the more and he remembered Lily Ann's words, that tears were better cried than dried. And so, although it seemed to Sir Thomas that his daughter would never stop crying, he stayed with her and did not attempt to suggest she should stem the flow of her tears. He simply held her and told her how precious she was to him, but otherwise he said nothing for he doubted there was anything he could say that would comfort her.

When at last she said, 'I really should like to return to Devon, Papa,' he gave instructions to Stephens to despatch an advance party of servants to Hey Tor House. He said that Hyde Park Gate should be shut up as soon as they left and, although he disliked himself for it, he took a little comfort when he wrote the date on the farewell cards he sent out, for it might reasonably be assumed they had left for the grouse shooting and not because his daughter had been unsuccessful, through his own terrible mismanagement, in her first London Season.

FIFTEEN

WHEN THE BRIDEWELLS arrived back at Waverton Court they continued to leave their cards just as they had in London, and when Natalie finally agreed to see Millie and Gussie, Gussie said, 'We were so certain you should tell us of your engagement, Natalie. We expected it every moment.'

'What Gussie means,' said Millie, 'is that we were very shocked when Lieutenant Haffie left London.'

Sir Thomas suggested Gussie might take a walk with him. He said he would like to hear how her wedding plans progressed and she, with a happy, if surprised, expression, immediately agreed. As soon as they were alone Millie apologized for her sister's insensitivity and said she admired Sir Thomas's tact, and then she said, 'I know you have suffered a terrible shock, Natalie. I have thought about you so often. I have longed to say how much I felt for you.'

'Thank you.'

'I too have been Returned Empty,' said Millie, 'although I never felt for any of the gentlemen we met the way you felt for Lieutenant Haffie.' She looked at Natalie and then they both looked through the drawing room windows that gave onto the park and watched Sir Thomas walking with Gussie beneath the green oaks.

'It's a cruel expression, is it not?' said Millie. 'And I think it wrong.'

'We do not, apparently, exist without husbands,' said Natalie. 'But I'm sorry it has happened to you for I think you shall mind more than I.'

'I prefer to be Empty, than to marry without love, or at least without affection.'

'Love did not help me,' said Natalie. 'But all the gentlemen in London must have been blind not to want to marry you, Millie.'

'I gave them no encouragement. They were all so very . . . ordinary.'

'Do you think Edward Fountain ordinary?'

'Yes,' said Millie. 'But he is landed, and he is rich. And that's what Gussie cares for, more than anything.'

'Did you . . . did you think I deserved what happened to me? I could not help what I felt and it was so very difficult to keep it inside. But you would not have behaved as I did and I know you, all of you, thought me too forward.'

'We all thought Lieutenant Haffie would propose and none of us can understand why he did not. And I admired you for your refusal to pretend you felt as you did not feel.'

'But you did think me too forward?'

'Only in the beginning. Only until I began to think for myself. And then I thought you brave, Natalie. Courageous. And I wished for someone with whom I might be similarly brave.'

'You were lucky not to find anyone. Courage is not what a gentleman wants in a woman.' And then, because she could not help herself, she said, 'Have you, any of you, heard from him?'

'Ansdrie heard, through the regiment, that he sailed for the Sandwich Islands. He's been managing the Haffie sugar plantations for his father ever since his mother was taken ill. She did not live long after they returned to England. We wanted to tell you, but Mama said we should wait until we saw you. Then we should be able to judge whether you wished to hear anything about him.'

'I am glad he is there,' said Natalie. Her heart gave an involuntary twinge of pity for him, for she would never forget the death of her own mother. And then hope surged within her and she dared not look at Millie.

'Why should you be glad?'

'I thought he might have been sent to the Transvaal.'

'If he had, Ansdrie should have been sent with him,' said Millie, putting out her hand to take Natalie's. 'We would have known.'

Natalie looked up. 'It was his mother's illness that took him from London so suddenly,' she said. 'Was it not?'

'We do not know,' said Millie. 'But surely he would have sent word to you by now?' She paused and looked at Natalie so directly that Natalie had to look away and the bright flame of her rekindled hope darkened. 'It is more than three months.' And then, after another silence, Millie said, 'Did you ever discover . . . why?'

'No,' said Natalie. 'I wrote to him. I told him . . .' she looked at Millie and wondered whether she should tell her, but the kindness of her smile encouraged her, and the relief that came as she began to unburden herself persuaded her to tell her friend everything. 'So you see,' she said when she had finished, 'courage makes not the slightest difference. Not in the end.'

Millie and Natalie saw each other almost every day after that and Natalie wondered that they had not become such firm friends before, for Millie was not as different from her as she had always thought. It was only a veneer, a manner adopted because her mother required it. Now Natalie discovered in Millie a young woman very much after her own heart, a woman who had begun to question the things her mother had taught her about the people she should and should not associate with. A woman who understood when Natalie said she had always felt different from the Bridewell family, felt they had little in common, but a woman who thought the Bridewells themselves should take the lion's share of the blame for Natalie's feelings of alienation from them, for they had not understood her, not when it truly mattered.

Millie said, much as Natalie's own mother had often said, that people were people and the important ones were the ones who were important to you. The ones you admired, the ones you liked and could talk with about all manner of things. Nothing else mattered.

'You and I may have different roots, Natalie,' she said, 'but they are swiftly growing towards each other. Our friendship makes them do it.'

'Perhaps we shall become hybrids?'

'We shall be the better for it,' said Millie, laughing. 'Tully told me only this morning that his hybrid apple trees are always stronger than the ones they are cultivated from.'

A natural result of this burgeoning friendship was that Ansdrie and Natalie also saw each other more often. The four rode together across Dartmoor as they had when they were children, although Gussie very often stayed behind with Lady Bridewell to discuss and change, and change again, the arrangements for her wedding. But in all the time Millie, Ansdrie and Natalie spent together, Lady Bridewell said nothing more than a clipped 'Good morning' or 'Good afternoon' to Natalie. But at least she did not scold her for her behaviour in London as Natalie had expected, and for that she thought she had Millie to thank.

Sir Thomas, on the other hand, had long sought an interview alone with Lady Bridewell before she finally agreed. But at last the day came when she called upon him and they sat together in his study at Hey Tor House and looked out through the windows and across the moor. The bare branches of the beeches stood out darkly against the clear blue sky. Rooks cawed and jackdaws piped as they swirled and circled about the branches. The first frost of the year still sparkled on the lawn where the sun had not yet reached it.

Both Sir Thomas and Lady Bridewell began to speak and to give way to each other at the same time. Unused to hesitation in Lady Bridewell, Sir Thomas nodded and waited for her to speak first.

'I owe you an apology,' she said, at last. 'I should, long ago, have come to you to discuss your generosity. You made over a very substantial sum to the Ansdrie estate . . . .' She stopped and searched in her reticule for a handkerchief. Astonished, Sir Thomas realized she was about to cry. 'I am sorry,' she said, turning away. When she turned back she said, 'You were so very generous when we were making arrangements for the marriage. I have come to ask whether I might repay you . . . ' she hesitated and was clearly embarrassed, and then said, very quickly and quietly, 'over a period of months?'

'My dear Lady Bridewell,' said Sir Thomas, 'there will be no need.'

'No need?'

'We both anticipated something we should not have anticipated. We both made mistakes. Some time ago I thought I should write off the money I made over to the Ansdrie estate; thought I should consider it a bad debt. There is nothing to repay. I should have written sooner to let you know what I intended.'

'Oh, Sir Thomas, my dear Sir Thomas, you are a quintessential gentleman.'

Sir Thomas stood and bowed. He walked to the window to give Lady Bridewell time to recover. It was bitterly ironic that she should think him a gentleman now when, according to his lights, he had behaved in the most ungentlemanly fashion towards his daughter.

'I did not behave well and I am sorry for it,' said Lady Bridewell.

Two apologies in as many minutes. Astonishing.

'My affection for Ansdrie,' – it was not clear whether she meant her son or the house – 'caused me to be inexcusably rude to you.'

'Thank you for your apologies,' said Sir Thomas. 'Thank you very much.'

He sat down opposite her.

'I should dearly like to have received an apology from another quarter but it has not come.' In answer to her enquiring expression he said, 'Neither my daughter nor I have heard a word from the lieutenant, despite Natalie's letter.'

'She wrote to him?'

Sir Thomas nodded. 'A heartfelt letter, by her own account. But his failure to reply only serves to illustrate what a bad lot he is. I am truly sorry to think I ever encouraged an attachment between them.'

'I did not think Lieutenant Haffie capable of . . . such unkindness,' said Lady Bridewell. Her surprised expression lent her features an unusual fragility.

'Nor did I,' said Sir Thomas.

Lady Bridewell put away her handkerchief and said, 'Would you and Miss Edwardes care to dine at Waverton Court tonight? The Fountains stay with us, as you no doubt know, but it would be a welcome relief to discuss something other than Augustina's wedding arrangements.'

After dinner that night, Ansdrie sat between Georgiana Fountain and Millie in the drawing room but he rarely joined their conversation for he watched Natalie, who sat opposite him, in conversation with his mother. She sat in the chair Haffie had chosen for her when he made his drawing of her, seven months before. But now Ansdrie knew Natalie so much better than he had then for, after Haffie left London, he had been on an unexpected journey of his own, a journey in which he discovered, through

Natalie's brave refusal to hide her unhappiness, that he had never felt for another person as deeply as she felt for Haffie; that he could not imagine finding the reckless courage to commit those feelings to paper when there was a risk they might be rejected. But now he felt at least something of what she felt for Haffie, for Natalie herself. He had watched her and listened to her. He had looked forward to hearing her low, gentle voice which, unlike his own, seemed made to include those she talked to, whereas his kept them at bay. When she smiled it was with genuine pleasure, whereas he smiled only when it was expected of him.

Unwittingly Natalie had shown Ansdrie that he too could feel and now, when he looked at her, he felt happier just because he could look at her, just because she was in the same room. He no longer recognized the young man who had told her father so matter-of-factly that he wished to become better acquainted with her, as if such acquaintance and subsequent marriage were merely a matter of arrangement. Ansdrie knew now that if she should ever give him the slightest encouragement he would renew his proposal to her, but this time there would be love in it, love that she had so courageously shown him to be quite absent before.

He wanted to make her happy.

He wanted to exorcise the pain Haffie had caused her and above all he wanted to live beside her just as she lived, true to the way he felt and with a proper disregard for those who refused to allow that inside every single human being there beats a heart capable of love and fear, laughter and tears; a heart that is not merely a mechanical organ.

SIXTEEN

G<small>USSIE</small> B<small>RIDEWELL'S</small> <small>WEDDING</small> day dawned cold, windy and bright.

Natalie stood at the window of her bedroom in Hey Tor House and looked out across the garden to the moor beyond. Hocks helped her into an elegant, dark-blue velvet suit while the wind whistled through the bare branches of the trees outside. Beyond them, Hey Tor stood out from the moor, its craggy outline clear against the blue sky. In her head the words of an old story repeated themselves: she had heard John Boundy telling it to the stableboy. 'They say 'er was young and beautiful, but 'er faither, 'ee promises 'er to old squire Tresson. She tells 'er faither she'll be the bride o' death afore she marries 'im, and 'er jumps from 'Ey Tor. But the wind, 'ee whips under 'er skirts, 'ee does, and slows 'er fall. She lands on 'er feet and runs away to 'er lover 'er does. That's what they say.'

The story haunted Natalie and made her think herself a coward for not running away to find Haffie. It would not have been so difficult to discover him in Liverpool. But when she stood beside her father in St Petroc's and watched Ansdrie return to his pew after giving his sister away, his warm smile touched her lonely heart and she knew that even she, even at the height of her distress, would not have risked the ostracism that running away would have caused. She needed her father, she could not have borne his refusal to see her, and the Bridewell family's kindness to her since they had returned from London had been such a comfort, the more so because it was unlooked for. To begin with, Natalie had been certain they would, eventually, withdraw their kindness, but they had not, and her gratefulness to them for their lack of criticism, their friendship and their acceptance of her after all that had happened made her feel safe. For she knew that if this family, particularly Lady Bridewell, did not shun her, no other family would.

The young woman who had drunk water from the hands of a stranger by a shimmering river had disappeared. A young woman who longed for safety, for a cocoon inside which her feelings might be protected from harm, had taken her place.

The decorations for Gussie's wedding breakfast brightened the wintry gloom of Waverton Court. Swags of white silk hung from the stone lintels and from the horseshoe-shaped table in the dining room, which was decorated with pots of white hellebores. The guests congratulated the bride, drank a little wine, ate a piece of cake and admired the wedding presents on the long table in the hall, and then only those who had been invited to the wedding breakfast remained.

Natalie had an opportunity to study Gussie's wedding gown as she watched her greet her guests. It was heavily trimmed with Honiton lace but it was still possible to discern the stern lines beneath it and, painfully, she remembered describing Gussie to Haffie as Honiton lace, lots of it, on sturdy bobbins that could not be seen. But she pushed the memory resolutely from her mind, walked into the dining room on her father's arm and took her place. She put her dark-blue gloves in her lap and turned to George Fountain, who told her he would go to London for the

Season in two summers' time and asked if she had yet had the pleasure. Natalie smiled, glad to think he thought her too young for her first Season and delighted that he obviously had no idea what had happened to her there. She promised to ride with him and Millie on Dartmoor the following day and then they turned to the apex of the horseshoe as a silence descended and the toasts began.

Ansdrie proposed the health of the bride and groom. He welcomed Fountain into the Bridewell family and when Fountain thanked him and proposed the health of the bridesmaids, a lock of his pale hair fell across his forehead and Natalie imagined their blonde children. When Fountain's bridegroomsman talked about Fountain's faithfulness in friendship and his thoughtfulness to his younger brothers and sisters, Natalie's heart was filled with a simple gratitude for faithful friends and kind families.

They ate a variety of gamebirds followed by lemon posset and apple charlotte, Gussie's favourites, and then in no time at all Gussie was rising from the table with Millie and her mother to change into her travelling dress.

Afterwards the guests followed Gussie and Fountain from the hall and out into the cold afternoon air. They watched them climb into their beribboned carriage while the two bridesmaids, Edward Fountain's sisters, handed out white satin slippers and handfuls of rice. When Natalie had thrown her slipper as accurately as she could after the departing pair, she turned away quickly. She did not want to see whether it had hit its mark, but when she sat with Millie by the fire in the drawing room Millie said, 'Yours landed on the roof and so did mine. We shall both have good luck.'

Only then did Natalie acknowledge how much she longed for a sign that good luck would return to her.

She looked up and saw Ansdrie smiling at her. She returned his smile and went to sit beside him. She wanted to tell him how happy she thought he had made Gussie on the day, of all days, when a father would be so very much missed by a daughter.

On Christmas Eve that year Natalie sat with her father in his study and opened his birthday present to her. He always gave her a present the day before her birthday because otherwise, he said, 'Your day is overshadowed by Christmas. It can never be yours alone.'

Natalie held up a pair of sapphire earrings and a matching necklace and thought them exquisite pieces of jewellery. They caught the light from the little candles on the Christmas tree and sparkled. She put them on and immediately felt happier and prettier. She had, since the summer, come to rely on her father's presents to lift her mood. She never admitted that the change in mood did not last more than a week or so, but the memory of his kindness always remained.

'I shall wear them at dinner tonight,' she said, standing to give him a kiss. 'I should like Millie to see them.'

After dinner that evening Natalie sat with Lady Bridewell, Millie and her Aunt Goodwin in the drawing room at Hey Tor House, but only her Uncle Goodwin joined them when all the gentlemen should have come from the dining room.

'Where's Papa?' said Natalie, pouring coffee for her uncle. 'And Ansdrie?'

'The latter,' said her uncle, 'has asked the former for an interview.'

'Uncle Goodwin,' said Natalie, laughing, 'you speak as if they were strangers.'

'They were determined to make a stranger of me,' said Charles Goodwin. 'They decidedly did not wish me to partake of their conversation in your father's study.'

Natalie could not decide whether her uncle teased her or whether he was truly offended. Lady Bridewell tightened her lips and blew air through her nostrils like an impatient horse, and then, at the moment when even Natalie thought her father had been absent for too long and was verging upon inexcusable rudeness to his guests, he walked into the room, his expression betraying a nervousness Natalie rarely saw.

He said, 'I'm sorry not to have joined you sooner.' He nodded particularly towards Lady Bridewell, who, to Natalie's surprise, smiled graciously and said he had not inconvenienced them in the least. And then he said, with an expression that betrayed even more anxiety, 'Natalie, my dearest, Ansdrie waits for you in my study. Will you go to him?'

SEVENTEEN

ANSDRIE SAT WITH his back to the door of Sir Thomas's study. He was nervous. He stood and then sat down again. He walked to the window and looked at the candles that hung in glass bowls from the Christmas tree. If it had been daylight, he would have seen Hey Tor as he had seen it that afternoon, stern and looming, high on the moor. But the glass candle-holders magnified the yellow flames and took his mind from the dark and cold outside: they were so much more imaginative than his mother's paper decorations, so much more welcoming. He took courage from them.

Only once before, as a child, had he been certain that another human being held the key to his happiness, but that woman, his own mother, had badly disappointed him all his life. When he told her he had discovered a genuine affection for Miss Edwardes ... Natalie ... and that he would marry her now if she would have him whether or not she brought a substantial dowry, his mother said, 'It is a happy coincidence that the two have coincided.'

'It is *not* a coincidence, Mama,' he said. 'I do love her.'

'Love for another human being,' she said, as if it were something contemptible, 'is a capricious thing. It can leave without warning.'

He turned when he heard footsteps in the passage.

Natalie opened the door and he put out his hand. When she smilingly shook hands with him he realized he had greeted her as if she were a man. Quickly, he lifted her hand and kissed it.

'Papa said you wanted to see me,' she said, sitting opposite him, beside Sir Thomas's desk. Behind her the Christmas candles glowed and Ansdrie's eyes were fixed on them as he wondered how any man managed to do what he was about to do, if he truly cared for the woman. It had been easy when he did not care for her, but now he needed some kind of sign. If she turned him down for a second time he felt he might never make another proposal in his life. In the months since they had been back in Devon he had come to know her more deeply than he knew any other human being. He no longer thought of her as the saviour of his inheritance; he felt something far nobler. She was an honest, courageous, beautiful young woman for whom he felt a tender affection and a deep sympathy, a feeling he could only call love.

He realized he had not answered her, had not given her any reason for his desire to speak to her. He felt foolish. And then she stretched out her hand towards him in a natural, unaffected gesture and he grasped it. He had never held her hand before, except in greeting, but now he knew it for the sign he had been hoping for.

'You have been wonderfully kind to me, Ansdrie,' she said. 'All of you, including your mother, but especially you and Millie. Far kinder than I deserve. Far kinder than anyone in London thought proper. You have shown me I am not the shameful monster I thought myself when Lieutenant Haffie threw me over and all London thought me beyond the pale.'

She looked up at him. Her dark hair shone in the candle-light and her eyebrows, so dark and a little too thick but so very expressive, lowered over her eyes in the beginnings of a frown.

'I never thought you a monster, Miss Edwardes ... Natalie,' he said, although he had thought her forward behaviour quite shameful until he understood it as a manifestation of her deep love for Haffie. He said, 'Why do you look at me like that?'

'I think you are sad.'

Her miraculous taking of his hand had touched him more than he could have imagined. He said, 'I was thinking about your courage.'

She inclined her head and said, 'My courage has not helped me. I told Millie so.'

'On the contrary,' said Ansdrie. 'You have never tried to hide the way you felt and you have been remarkably courageous since Lieutenant Haffie left. At least that is how it seems to me and I admire you for it.' But he did not want to talk about Haffie. 'When you told me my proposal ...' he had not intended to talk about his first proposal, either. 'When you said there was no love in my proposal I thought you courageous. Not immediately. I didn't understand, at first. But afterwards I did.' He leaned forwards and took her other hand.

'Thank you,' she said. 'But why does that make you sad?'

'Because I know you will never deny the way you feel,' he said. 'And the way you feel may not, perhaps, be in my favour.'

'That makes you the courageous one,' said Natalie. 'But I shall do all I can never to give you reason to be sad.'

Ansdrie felt his heart jump and, letting go of one of her hands, he took a small leather box from his pocket. He opened it, a little awkwardly, and held out a sapphire ring. He said, 'Because of your courage, Miss E ... Natalie, I believe in you. And believing in you has made me realize that I love you.' He let go of her other hand and took the ring from its box. He said, 'Dearest Natalie, will you be my wife?'

He watched the transformation that always happened

to Natalie's long face when she smiled. He looked into her dark-blue eyes and saw her acceptance of him. Her long, oddly muscular fingers took hold of his and held them and the ring and its box in a firm grip and, with a quick and very pleasing shock, he imagined those fingers touching the skin beneath his clothes.

'I will, Ansdrie,' she said simply. 'I will.'

And she held out her left hand and he put the sapphire onto her finger.

Just after first light on Boxing Day Sir Thomas and Natalie strode along the frozen path through the garden and out across the moor towards Hey Tor. Sir Thomas had persuaded his daughter to walk rather than ride, as she suggested, because the ground was so hard. But he wanted to talk to her, and if they had ridden she would have been too quick, too often too far ahead of him for conversation. He said, after she had told him, not for the first time, how glad she was to welcome the Bridewells and Ansdrie to Hey Tor House on Christmas Day, and how delightful it been that they remembered her birthday, 'This is a difficult question, but I must ask it, Natalie. Do you care for him? Or is it his affection for you that makes you think you care for him?'

The wind was bitingly cold and Natalie turned from it so that she stood with her back to Hey Tor when she replied. She pulled the fur-lined hood of her long coat closer to her face and said, 'I shall learn to love him, Papa. He has shown himself capable of a change of heart and that makes me think very well of him. And I am grateful to him, to all of them, for their kindness.'

Sir Thomas looked up at the leaden-white sky and knew snow would come soon: the birds were already flying low. He stamped his feet on the frozen ground and said, 'To be welcomed where you thought you would not be welcomed is comforting and I understand your gratitude. But that is not a reason to marry.'

Her slight frown and her pallor, the signs of sadness that still haunted her, pierced his heart. He caught her up in his arms and she said, into his fur-lined collar, 'When Ansdrie asked me to marry him in London he was jealous, I think. He wanted what Lieutenant Haffie and I had, for himself. He thought he could have it by marrying me. But now he cares for me very much, I can see that he does. And I think I shall make a good wife to him. I think my heart will heal, with him. He is a good man. Besides, who else would have me, after all that has happened? And I dread the spinster's life. At least,' she said, looking up at him, 'I dread the ridicule and the restriction.'

It was shocking to Sir Thomas to realize that the very thing he had once wanted for his daughter, for his own selfish reasons, should now fill him with misgiving. 'I should not like to think,' he said, 'that you married Ansdrie for any reason other than true affection.' He stood back from her and held her gloved hands in his. 'You might give yourself time to think on it, perhaps? A dread of the spinster life is no reason to marry, either. Besides, there'd be no shame in living respectably with your old father.'

Natalie turned her head away. 'The wind is so sharp,' she said. 'It makes my eyes water.' But the quiver in her voice told Sir Thomas her tears were not just the wind's doing. She turned back to him and said, with determined cheerfulness, 'Let's go home. Let's sit by the fire and give out the Christmas boxes and then Stephens can take the servants to their cottages to celebrate. And, Papa,' she said, 'I will ask Ansdrie if we might have a long engagement. If it would make you happy.'

'That's my girl,' said Sir Thomas, his spirits lifting. 'That's my girl.'

As their feet crunched across the hard ground, Sir Thomas said he thought the South Devon would not hunt that day.

'Ansdrie will be disappointed,' said Natalie. 'I wonder

who he shall hunt with when we are in Fife?'

The wind whistled between them and Sir Thomas pulled down the flaps of his fur hat and tied the ribbons behind his beard. 'The Fife Foxhounds, I should think,' he said, his voice muffled by the fur inside his hat.

He meant it facetiously; he did not know the name of the Fife hunt, although, unwittingly, he had stumbled upon the right one. But when his daughter said, 'Of course he will,' so trustingly, so unaware that he had only guessed at the name, he was filled with remorse. He wanted to say, 'I have done you a terrible wrong, Natalie. I made an agreement with Lady Bridewell that I should never have made.'

But he did not. He could not. For if she believed marriage to Ansdrie would heal her broken heart then who was he to urge her against it? If she believed this was her only chance to marry, who was he to tell her otherwise? He was no longer a trustworthy adviser.

'Papa?'

'Yes, my dearest girl?'

'I don't think you heard what I said.'

'No, I did not. This wind,' he said, lifting the earflap of his hat, 'makes it difficult.'

'It's your hat, Papa,' said Natalie, laughing. 'not the wind that stops you hearing. I said it pleases me very much that Ansdrie consulted you about my engagement ring.' She put her gloved hands inside her fur muffler, as if to keep her ring safe. 'That he should think enough of you to ask your advice.'

She took her hands from the muffler and put them to her cheeks against the wind. 'The two most important men in my life chose the same stones, together. Sapphires shall be my favourites from now on.'

EIGHTEEN

NATALIE SHIVERED AS single heavy drops of rain fell from the great dark pines that lined the drive to Ansdrie House onto the roof of the station coach. The day was grey and the grass beneath the pines unkempt. The drive was badly rutted and the coach jolted and swayed while Natalie waited, nervously, for her first glimpse of the house where she would live.

When Ansdrie handed her down from the coach her father and Lady Bridewell were already standing beneath the grey-pillared portico. Natalie looked up beneath the umbrella Ansdrie held over her and saw a tall, classical, rectangular house made of broken grey slabs of stone. Wooden scaffolding stood everywhere about the house and there were indentations on the façade where once windows had been, but now rain-streaked stones walled them in and the few windowpanes that remained were held precariously in dark, peeling frames; they were spattered and streaked with rivulets of rain.

It was a broken, blind building.

When they travelled on the sleeper from King's Cross, Natalie had told Hocks how she imagined Ansdrie, the house her future mother-in-law so loved. She thought it would be a Scottish version of the house she had loved in her own childhood: the Georgian Hey Tor House. But Ansdrie was a cold, grey, forbidding fortress compared with her father's white, warm, well-lit sanctuary. Natalie kept her eyes on the gravel and tried to control her disappointment.

'Restoration has only just begun,' said Lady Bridewell, gesturing upwards beneath the umbrella Sir Thomas held. 'My brother neglected the house terribly and I cannot expect you to see it as I once knew it. But it was magnificent, and it will be again.'

Lady Bridewell was excited, almost girlish, but Natalie's gloom was as difficult to lift as the fallen stones by her feet. She watched Ansdrie take a large iron key from his pocket and open one half of the great oak door. A musty, damp smell rose in the hall and it was colder inside than outside, cold that seeped up from the flagstones through Natalie's feet and into her bones. She tried to persuade herself that it was only because the house had been so ill-treated, so uncared for, that it felt so very unwelcoming, just as a friend made frail by illness might not make a cheerful greeting.

'By the time you are married,' said Sir Thomas, as if he sensed his daughter's despair, 'this house will be unrecognizable.'

'I hope not entirely unrecognizable,' said Lady Bridewell.

Ansdrie picked up a box of matches from a marble table and after several attempts a match flared and he lit three candles that stood in a tarnished candelabra. The candles spluttered but remained alight and he said, 'Come with me, Natalie. Come and see what must be done.'

She followed him along a wide, stone-flagged passage. He opened the shutters at the far end of a small hall, a replica of the larger one they had just left, and they looked out together through wooden scaffolding poles over a wet terrace to a neglected garden beyond. The fallen bowl of a stone fountain leaned awkwardly against its column and a stone cherub's wings lay detached from its body on the ground. Ansdrie put the candlestick onto a speckled dust-sheeted table behind them and then took Natalie's hand.

'Ansdrie is in need of kindness,' he said, as if he spoke of a person not of a house. 'I know you will help the old place find her feet again.'

'I had not thought it would be so . . . so . . .' but Natalie could not finish for the constriction in her throat. She leaned against Ansdrie's arm and when he kissed her forehead she tried valiantly to control her tears.

'I felt as low as you when first I saw the house,' he said. 'But with your . . . spirit and . . . your memories of the airy rooms at Hey Tor House, you will succeed.'

'I have never done anything like this before,' she said. 'I have barely even heard Papa give instructions. He always employed . . . architects . . . and people who know what to do with houses.'

'An architect has already given much advice and Havening, the factor, will find whoever and whatever else we need. We shall do it together, my dearest.'

His faith in her and his endearment restored her optimism, a little. She said, 'The only thing I know about houses is that the ones I love, I love because of the people who live in them and the special places that I made my own.'

'Then we shall do very well, shall we not?' said Ansdrie. 'We shall . . . love . . . Ansdrie and make it our own. Side by side.'

Natalie gave Ansdrie a brave smile and when she heard her father and Lady Bridewell walking along the passage she turned to them. Her father held another candelabra and Lady Bridewell said, with a quick clap of her hands as if to show Natalie that all would be easily achieved, 'Havening was just here. The roof is almost finished. The worst is over. And Trawton has just told me our rooms at the Ansdrie Arms are ready.'

And so, while the new owner of Ansdrie House

stayed in the village and his wife-to-be travelled to and fro from Devon, the real work on the house began. The walled-in windows were replaced with glass panes; the window frames and struts were painted a pale grey-blue, which lifted the grey stone even on the darkest of days, and soon enough the house was flooded with as much light as the often rain-soaked climate allowed. Ansdrie himself oversaw the repair of the broken structures and the repointing of the stonework. Natalie chose white paint and pale yellow wallpapers, powder blue chintzes and light green muslins, linens and silks for the summer and bright, thickly lined quilted chintzes for the winter. They replaced the moth-eaten, blood-dark velvets and purple brocades and whenever Lady Bridewell expressed a desire for a piece of worm-infested furniture or yards of moth-eaten material to be restored, or replaced with identical colours, Ansdrie would take her aside and say, so that Natalie might hear, that they had agreed they were beyond repair and that he and Natalie would live at Ansdrie, while she only came to stay with them. He said they would live among hangings and furniture of their own choosing.

Pier glasses were hung and electricity, powered by a large generator in the coach house, was installed. Natalie asked her father's advice about bathrooms, an idea that incurred Lady Bridewell's disdain until even she was persuaded of the convenience of hot running water. And as her confidence in her future husband and in her abilities grew, Natalie took advice from the experts in Edinburgh who restored the ancestral paintings and furniture, rugs, wall hangings and tapestries. One afternoon, Ansdrie suggested they restore the ballroom to its former glory.

'Dancing is not the only thing that makes me happy,' said Natalie. 'We need not go to the expense.'

'But I wish to learn to dance better so that I might make you a good partner,' said Ansdrie. 'You shall teach me.'

He took her in his arms beneath the shrouded chandelier

and they danced a slow polka across the dusty floor, a polka which became quicker and quicker while Natalie's hummed accompaniment became louder and louder until Anderson had to shout, in so far as he ever shouted, that sandwiches were served in the dining room.

Ansdrie's furniture was restored and polished until it gleamed; tartan druggets and Turkey carpets were brought down from the attic, beaten and cleaned and laid across the newly scoured stone flags and polished wooden floors, and enormous hanging tapestries of flowers and vines, follies and landscapes worked by Ansdrie's ancestors, were restored and hung in the dining room.

Lady Bridewell continually made suggestions, some of which they adopted, but when Natalie failed to persuade her to have the gloomy four-poster, which she so often praised, in her own rooms because she wanted to put her own mother's bed in her bedroom, Ansdrie came to her rescue yet again and pointed out that the bed had been his grandmother's and, if his mother thought about it, she would realize that any woman would prefer to sleep in her own mother's bed. Spontaneously, Natalie kissed him on the cheek and by the time her own cheval glass and her mother's dressing table were installed in her bedroom at Ansdrie, she felt she would soon live in a house that welcomed her, a house in whose rooms she could recreate the special places she craved.

As the work progressed Natalie took more and more pleasure in it and in the restored treasures; she discovered she had an eye for the arrangement of a room and she grew to love certain pieces of furniture and sculpture. She even managed to cheer Lady Bridewell when they opened a trunk full of treasured ornaments and found many of them broken.

'We have managed the restoration of a whole house,' she said. 'It will be a simple matter for one of the experts to put these pieces back together.'

But even so there were, occasionally, things that unsettled Natalie. When Mr Turnbull, the auctioneer from Edinburgh, arrived with some new paintings for her approval, he brought one that so reminded her of Haffie's paintings that she gasped and the auctioneer, mistaking her reaction for admiration, said, 'There is another young painter who works in the impressionist style whom you might like, Miss Edwardes. He has been sending me some very good work from the Sandwich Islands. Will I bring them for you, next time?'

'No,' said Natalie, 'no, thank you. I . . . prefer paintings whose subjects I can recognize. This style – did you call it impressionistic? – is too . . . indefinite. Find me some pretty works that show the countryside just as it looks.'

At that moment Ansdrie walked into the drawing room and, to Natalie's joy, he understood immediately. 'We like to know where we are with a painting, Mr Turnbull,' he said. 'If you remember that, you will not go wrong.'

Turnbull nodded and when he was gone Ansdrie took Natalie in his arms. She said the dust from the scouring of the flagstones was obviously still in the air when he looked into her tear-filled eyes, but she knew he understood her and she was filled with gratitude. When they discussed the restoration of the garden and the park with Hoxash, the head gardener, and he took particular pleasure in showing them where the Scotch roses grew wild and where he had cultivated them, Ansdrie took Natalie's hand as she said, 'I do not wish to offend you, and I am sorry if I sound unfriendly, or . . . English,' she attempted a smile, 'but I prefer more complicated roses. I should like these uprooted. All of them. Please plant different varieties in their place.'

A tender understanding grew between Natalie and Ansdrie as they restored the house and it filled Natalie with confidence: she knew she could look forward to a marriage inside which the pain of the past would be safely left behind.

NINETEEN

ON A WARM summer's day in the second year of the new century, Natalie Ann Edwardes and John Jocelyn Ansdrie were married.

It was a simple service, arranged entirely by Natalie and Millie.

There were no bridesmaids, save Millie, who acted, much to Lady Bridewell's astonishment, as Edward Fountain acted for Ansdrie: she was Natalie's brideswoman and she stood by her just as Fountain stood by Ansdrie.

The small wood and stone interior of St Petroc's was decorated only with tied bunches of yellow furze and only family members filled the pews. Natalie walked down the aisle on her father's arm and caught the honeyed scent of the furze and saw, through her mother's Brussels lace veil, the unruly strands of hair on the back of Ansdrie's dark head as he stood by the chancel step. Her heart filled with gratitude and something very close to love but when she turned towards him, as the service began, she realized he was not going to turn to her but would remain looking straight ahead. She told herself that if he turned to her when she touched his hand it would bode well for their marriage; and then she wished she had not made such a foolish bargain.

But she did touch his hand and he did turn towards her, without hesitation, and when she saw the love in his dark eyes, tears filled her own eyes and she knew she had already begun to discover how she might love this man.

A photograph, taken outside Hey Tor House where Natalie and Ansdrie would live until they moved to Fife, showed Natalie in a simple white silk dress trimmed with her mother's Brussels lace, and Ansdrie in a dark morning coat, light trousers and white waistcoat. They did not face the camera; instead they faced each other, as if all that was important in the world was embodied in the other.

By the autumn of the year of Queen Victoria's death, the Ansdries had been married for five months and had lived in their house in Fife for a few weeks. When Natalie asked her husband if he was happy with the transformation they had brought about, he said it pleased him very much and he thanked her for her patience with his mother, and for her flair. And he said, 'Your father is a remarkable businessman. He has taught me much. In point of fact he is still teaching me and I look forward to learning all I can. Now that this house is back on its feet, I must find a way to keep it there.'

Sir Thomas, who had inspected the Ansdrie coal mines and found them quite beyond repair, who had learned that sales of the flax crop had been undercut for years by imported Indian jute, had nevertheless decided to wait until he was convinced by his daughter's happiness before he discussed the worst of the difficulties with his son-in-law. There were farm workers and miners to rehouse, and when Sir Thomas had seen the ledgers he had decided, without consulting Ansdrie or his mother, that he would fund the restoration of Ansdrie House entirely. It made any discussion of the future unnecessary until he chose to discuss it, and it assuaged his guilt for his mishandling of his daughter's affairs.

But now he judged the time right and so, on a bright November day in 1901 when the generator beneath the office rumbled and hummed and Natalie had gone to call on Marina Robinson, one of their closest neighbours, at Kersley House, Sir Thomas asked his son-in-law and Lady Bridewell to come to the room above the coach house, the room he and Ansdrie had made into an office. When he told them how things stood Lady Bridewell gave him a haughty look but remained silent. But Ansdrie said, 'Then we must sell land. We shall follow the Duke of Fife and become smallholders. Crichton's land marches with mine; he might buy.'

'Indeed he might,' said Sir Thomas. 'And it's a good suggestion. But we must do more. I propose that Eaton Terrace be sold and perhaps even Waverton Court.'

Lady Bridewell gasped but Sir Thomas said, 'I shall sell my villa in the south of France,' to which Lady Bridewell said, without looking at him, 'The girls are out, so the sale of the London house is a possibility. But not Waverton.'

Ansdrie said, 'We might prospect for iron ore. I hear there's some to be had in Fife.'

'I too thought of that,' said Sir Thomas, impressed to discover that Ansdrie really had been thinking about the future.

'And the bicycle does not seem to be much in evidence here,' said Ansdrie. 'Do you think we could, perhaps, get up a franchise for the new safety models?'

'Bicycles?' said Lady Bridewell. 'Have you lost your head? A gentleman does not go into trade.'

'My father always said honest employment made a man a gentleman,' said Sir Thomas.

'And we could turn the remaining land over to a tenant sheep farmer,' said Ansdrie.

Sir Thomas was more impressed with his son-in-law than he could have hoped. He said, 'The land, I am told, is good land for sheep and it'll fetch a fair rent; there are not as many sheep farmers in Fife as I had thought there might be. But,' he said, closing the leather folders that held the Ansdrie ledgers, 'whatever we agree upon, we must begin with a sale. First the land here, I suggest, and then Eaton Terrace. After that,' he said, attempting to make light of their difficulties, 'we only need to find something others have not yet thought to do. A good idea for a successful business, it seems to me, is one that adds something to life, or at least that makes it more convivial. After all, tea is just a way of making hot water more interesting.'

Lady Bridewell stood and Sir Thomas nodded his agreement that their meeting was over. After she had gone Ansdrie said, 'I hardly know how to thank you for all you have done for me, for us. But I do thank you, with all my heart.' He stood and walked to Sir Thomas's side of the desk and took his hand.

'All I wish for is my daughter's happiness,' said Sir Thomas, taking Ansdrie's hand in both of his. 'And it does make me very happy to see how things have turned out. But until these matters are settled I suggest we keep the details from Natalie. I should not want to worry her unnecessarily.'

'Particularly not now,' said Ansdrie and he smiled broadly. 'We have not told Mama yet,' he said, 'but some time in February or March, our first child will be born.'

At this Sir Thomas made no attempt to hide his delight.

TWENTY

Before Natalie's confinement, she and her husband were hardly ever alone at Ansdrie. Sir Thomas was there very often and Lady Bridewell, Millie, Gussie and Edward, and Felicity and Charles Goodwin all came to stay. Those who lived in the nearby houses also came. The restoration of Ansdrie was much admired, Natalie was fêted and her husband told her often that his life would never have become what it had become, without her by his side.

Natalie rejoiced in the opportunity life had given her, to put what she now thought of as her aberration with Haffie behind her. Only in the very beginning had the sight of someone other than her husband in a kilt, or the sound of a west-coast Scottish accent, or the single word *outwith*, a common word in Scotland, disconcerted her. But now she took pride in her house and in the elegant, and expensive, furniture and wall-hangings, the restored Ansdrie heirlooms, the clever redecoration that had converted its gloomy dankness into light, bright airy rooms.

To escape the chaos of restoration they had often fished the Leven from a small boat and Natalie admired her husband's skill at the oars. There were many times when the misty Scottish rain made the land so green that she was reminded, happily, of her native Devon. For a wedding present Sir Thomas had given them a yacht, the *Natalie Ann*, which they sailed to the Isle of Wight for their honeymoon. Captain Hiram Rosewood, Sir Thomas's skipper, had said, as he leaned against the coach roof watching Natalie at the wheel, 'Lady Ansdrie is as good a skipper as I have met.'

'You exaggerate, Captain Rosewood,' said Natalie, but she could help smiling. 'Just because I can tie a bowline does not mean I can skipper a boat. I really understand very little.'

The tail of her white silk scarf, which Hocks had tied turban-fashion to keep her hair from her eyes, flapped gently across her cheek. She pushed it away and wriggled her toes on the rough teak deck beneath the soles of her feet: it was a delightful feeling, for her feet were so rarely free of shoes.

'I do not exaggerate, my lady,' said Captain Rosewood. 'You know how to avoid the Bramble Bank and make good use of the tide. You will see us safely to Cowes.'

It was then that Ansdrie said, 'When we are in less tricky waters I should like to take the wheel.' Natalie stared at him. 'I always knew you could sail,' he said. 'I persuaded your father to teach me the essentials so that I should not shame you.'

It did not occur to Natalie to ask when either had had the time; she was simply glad to find her husband, yet again, so thoughtful. And when she found herself the object of much admiring attention from the gentlemen among their new neighbours, she made a point of talking about her own husband's qualities, sometimes quite pointedly, so that they were left in no doubt where her loyalty lay.

With her Aunt Goodwin's encouragement Natalie discovered the history of Ansdrie's park and gardens from Hoxash. From beneath a magnificent magnolia, which, that spring, would flower despite its neglected state, they looked out towards the beech woods, which would stand protectively over a haze of bluebells the following April and they then fell to talking about the fruit that would or would not grow in Fife and to the restoration of the walls of the old kitchen garden so that every flower, fruit and vegetable that grew there would be protected against the Scottish winters.

Natalie asked Hoxash to arrange for two large orangeries to be built to remind her of the orangery her mother had so loved at Hey Tor House. They would be planted with trees from Seville.

'We shall be positively tropical,' said Ansdrie.

And, in time, the orange flowers would fill the house with their scent in the summer and provide Natalie with a sanctuary among their glossy leaves and bittersweet fruits in the winter months when the warmth from the coal burners made it possible for her to sit and dream, think or read there, for hours.

Hoxash told Natalie there had once been a terraced garden to the west of the house that ran down towards the river Leven, so she asked him if he thought he might restore it and he, with a quick nod, said nothing would give him greater pleasure. He suggested planting the terraces with camellias and azaleas in the lee of the walls, and lavender in rows along the edges. They also talked of making a parterre on the second level. He suggested a Belle Isis rose to replace the Scotch roses, and when Natalie asked him what kind of rose it was, he replied that it was one of the oldest roses ever grown. 'French, pink, hardy, with a magnificent scent.'

She thanked him and said, 'Yes, please, Hoxash. Lots of them.'

Ansdrie hunted with the Fife Foxhounds and Natalie looked forward to joining him the following season and then, as the winter made the days shorter and because of her confinement, they spent peaceful evenings alone by a blazing fire and no longer entertained their neighbours. One grey afternoon snow began to fall and the restored bowl of the Italian stone fountain filled with snowflakes, just as surely as Natalie's womb filled with her child.

*

Six weeks after Natalie's twenty-first birthday the Ansdries' first son was born. The pain of giving birth and the joy of his safe arrival were both beyond anything Natalie could have imagined. In the brief moments when the pains receded and it was possible to think, she resolved, as women through the ages have resolved, never to bear a child again. But after her son had been safely delivered, the sheets had been changed, the midwife had bathed her and helped her into a lavender-scented nightdress, touched her arm and said, 'You were very brave, my lady. You did well,' Natalie burst into tears at her kindness and shuffled back to bed. Her tiny son, all wrapped in white, was handed to her and she marvelled at the miracle of him.

She smoothed his fine black hair and kissed the top of his fragile head where a little pulse beat. She held him at first nervously and then more confidently when she realized that his tiny body would not break. She breathed in his sweet, earthy, newborn smell and when she put her finger into his wrinkled palm his fingers curled tightly round hers and she stared at his nails, which were so small but so unimaginably perfect, like little pieces of sugar. She saw, in her mind's eye, a tiny, tightly curled, green fern and felt an overwhelming desire to protect him. She looked into his grey eyes, eyes that would stay that colour all his life, and felt as if he were pulling her down into them, into his soul, and her own soul responded with a profound recognition, unlike any she had ever known. She began to cry and as her tears fell she hoped she would always find enough love in her soul to protect him, to love him just as he deserved.

She tipped her head back in an attempt to drain away her tears. She reached beneath her pillow for the handkerchief the midwife had put there. At that moment Hocks arrived and asked if she would like her hair brushed, and her kindness brought on Natalie's tears once more.

'I feel as if I shall never stop crying,' she said.

'I've heard it's quite normal, my lady,' said Hocks. 'And isn't he a lovely little boy?'

Natalie and her son slept a little and when she woke she knew something had changed, irrevocably, but, for the briefest of moments, she could not remember what it was. And then she heard a snuffling cry and turned to see her son on the pillow beside her and her heart lurched. While she slept something terrible could have happened to him. She picked him up and promised she would never neglect him again, and when Ansdrie walked in, a bowl of snow-drops in his hands, she told him what she had done as her tears welled up yet again.

'Marina Robinson says Nurse Mackay is the best in all Fife,' he said. 'Remember? You told me so yourself.'

Natalie nodded. 'I know,' she said. 'But . . . he is so tiny . . . so . . .'

'He is our son,' said Ansdrie, sitting on the bed beside her. 'And he will be well loved and well cared for.'

'I hope he won't remember the first sounds he ever heard me make.'

Ansdrie put his hand on her arm and said, 'Even if he does, by the time he can tell you so he'll be able to see how very beautiful you are when you cry.'

'I really am very happy,' said Natalie, as the tears coursed down her cheeks. 'Truly I am.'

Natalie sang to her son.

She had woken one morning with a great longing in her heart for her own mother, the mother who had held her just the way she held her son. She sang *The Tree in the Wood* to him. It was her way of introducing her son to her mother, and when Millie came in she sang with Natalie. When they finished the final roundelay Natalie said, 'I didn't know you knew it.'

'You taught me,' said Millie. 'Years ago.'

'Did I?'

'One day when we were riding in Bridewell Wood,' said Millie.

For a fleeting moment, Natalie saw Haffie standing in the river, and then he was gone. She said, her lips touching the top of her son's head, 'We have decided to call him Duncan. Ansdrie tells me it means dark-haired.'

'My brother would never have troubled himself over such a thing before he fell in love with you,' said Millie.

Natalie gave Duncan to Millie and pushed herself up against the pillows. Through the window she saw the long drive, now wide open to the glens on either side, free of the oppressive pine trees. Now, small, glossy-green rhododendron bushes lined the drive and behind them stood burlap windbreaks to protect them until the beeches grew tall enough.

'Ansdrie is a remarkable man,' said Natalie. 'Beside him I have rediscovered myself.' And then, as she watched Millie put Duncan gently into his cot she said, 'You are looking particularly pretty, Millie. Tell me, has anything happened?'

Millie blushed and said, 'Do you remember I told you I thought all the young men I met in London so very ordinary?' Natalie nodded. 'And I should rather marry for love, or at least for affection than for any other reason? Well, now I shall.'

Natalie swung her legs over the edge of the bed and when Nurse Mackay arrived to take Duncan for his bath, they sat together by the window and Natalie took Millie's hand. 'Who is he?' she said. 'And why have you not told me about him before?'

'Because I did not want to tell you, until I was certain you were as happy as I am.'

'I am happier than I could have imagined,' said Natalie.

Millie sat forward in her chair.

'He is a diplomat. His name is Étienne de la Roche. I am my best self when I am with him, Natalie.' Millie smiled.

'He corrects my French, but kindly. I'm learning to speak it better.' She stopped.

'Go on,' said Natalie.

'Mama disapproves dreadfully that we shall live in Paris. She thinks it a very peculiar idea, as if Paris were the Antarctic.'

They both laughed and then Natalie said, 'I wish you very great happiness. Can you imagine growing old beside him, as I can beside Ansdrie?'

Millie nodded.

'This house brought us together, you know. As it was restored, I too was restored. The love I had before, Millie, was too urgent a thing. It overtook me; it was painful. I grew jealous if I could not keep Haffie's attention and I wanted to die when I knew he did not love me. I hope you do not love your Frenchman like that, for it is a desperate, selfish thing.'

'I did not know I loved him for several months,' said Millie. 'But when he had to return to Paris, I missed the sound of his voice, I missed the way he has of making any conversation interesting. I missed his . . . presence. And as the weeks passed I realized I loved him. It stole up on me slowly, but now I cannot imagine a life without him beside me.'

When Millie, Lady Bridewell and Sir Thomas left, Natalie and Ansdrie indulged in rare days alone. It was not the custom for anyone other than family to pay calls for some time after a birth, so they were without anyone except the servants. They sat in Natalie's morning room by her fire or in Ansdrie's study by his fire. Sometimes they took the key to the newly built orangeries from Ansdrie's desk and surveyed the young saplings. Ansdrie told Natalie about the plans he and Sir Thomas were making, and Natalie asked him to make sure the men and women who had worked the Ansdrie coal mines and flax fields were provided for until other employment could be found. She said perhaps a little of the money might come from the sale of bannocks and butteries, cullen skink and cranachan made by Ansdrie's cook, Mrs MacAlasdair, for the local fairs.

And that summer was the finest since first Natalie saw Ansdrie House. They took to sitting on the southern terrace facing the great sycamores in the park that led to the foothills of the Formonts, the low hills that marked the boundary of the Ansdrie estate. The hills were pale-green in the sunlight and the wide expanse of lawn that flowed down to the park from the terrace glowed emerald. Hoxash's carefully planted and tended herbaceous borders were crowded with colour and life and Natalie's happiness flourished in harmony with her garden.

She said, as she rocked Duncan's pram with one hand, 'Those trees must have seen much.'

'I'm certain they have,' said Ansdrie. 'But I'm also certain it's been a long time since they witnessed such happiness.' He reached for Natalie's hand.

'When the weather is like this,' she said, 'Ansdrie out-shines anywhere on earth.'

'I told you it would not always be dreich,' he said. 'And now,' he stood up, 'I have a surprise for you.'

He picked up his straw boater and, before Natalie could ask what the surprise might be, he strode off towards the kitchen gardens. She turned her face up to the warming sun and pulled the wide brim of her straw hat down to shade her eyes. She looked out from beneath it towards Ansdrie Chapel, which stood in the shade of an ancient yew, the chapel where Duncan had been christened.

When Ansdrie returned, his cheeks were flushed and his hands full. He took a damask tablecloth from the trug he carried and spread it on the wooden table in front of Natalie. He laid the table with two blue earthenware bowls, a small jug of cream, a white plate that held a splint punnet from which red juices seeped and a piece of Ansdrie honeycomb in a dish. Finally, he put a silver vase that held two tall ox-eye daisies in front of her. He poured raspberries from the punnet into the blue bowls, then spread a damask napkin across Natalie's knees and said, 'The first Ansdrie raspberries,' and smiled, like a guileless boy.

There were no spoons so Natalie dipped a raspberry into the dish of honey, and then into the cream and ate it, and several more, with her fingers.

'Once,' said Ansdrie, 'you ate brandy snaps with your fingers and I thought you ill-mannered and . . . and greedy.' He dipped several raspberries into the cream and then into the honey. He ate them from his fingers, too. 'But now I know better,' he said. 'Now I know you were simply more honest than the rest of us.'

There were two more bright, untroubled years, towards the end of which Natalie happily anticipated her second confinement. But on the day she felt a cramping pain in her lower abdomen, a hollow, empty feeling accompanied it, which she could not shift. She had stood, quickly, to rearrange the delphiniums in the vase on the table in her morning room, but the pain made it impossible for her to walk and she gripped the chair with one hand, bent over and put the other hand on her abdomen. She bit her lip until the blood came. She breathed deeply through her nose. And then she gathered her skirts and struggled up the stairs, calling weakly for Hocks as she went.

'My lady,' said Hocks, running into Natalie's bedroom. 'My lady?'

Natalie said, 'I think I'm losing . . . I think I'm having a . . .' but she could not continue for the pain.

'Oh, my lady,' said Hocks.

Natalie felt Hocks's hands helping her into her bathroom, helping her to undress and then wrapping her in warm towels. She walked slowly back to her bedroom where Hocks laid out several more towels on the bed.

'Lie down, my lady,' she said. 'Breathe as deeply and slowly as you can. I'll send Verrinder for Doctor Harrison. I'll be back directly.'

And so Natalie lay, miserably, on her bed, the bed in which Duncan had been born and she had sung to him. The pain was severe and when Hocks returned Natalie gripped her hand as if she were a midwife and Natalie were giving birth. Only this was not a birth and by the time Doctor Harrison arrived it was all over. Natalie lay weakly on her bed and described her symptoms. Doctor Harrison examined her and then Hocks brought her a strong cup of tea and, when Ansdrie arrived back from a day's hunting, his kind concern made it impossible for Natalie to hold back her tears.

'There will be more children,' he said. 'Duncan is strong. There will be other strong ones, just like him.'

'Yes,' said Natalie, through her tears. 'There will. Of course there will.'

But when Ansdrie took her hand and kissed her forehead, when he sat close by her on the sofa in her morning room, his presence could not rid her of the hollow, empty feeling that had arrived with her miscarriage, as if the very centre of her being had been carved out. It was difficult to imagine life growing there ever again.

TWENTY-ONE

ANSDRIE ALLOWED SIR Thomas to persuade him against the bicycle franchise. It had become clear there were no customers in rural Fife for machines that cost twenty pounds when a miner's wage was one pound a week and the paper-mill workers half that. Even a schoolteacher's wage would not allow the luxury of a bicycle, and anyone who was rich enough would travel to Edinburgh to buy one. When iron ore was not found, many hundreds of acres of Ansdrie land were sold to Crichton, and what was left had been let to a tenant sheep farmer. Eaton Terrace and Sir Thomas's villa in France had been sold, but still Ansdrie and his father-in-law had not come up with an idea that would secure the future of Ansdrie House.

On a cold spring day in the year after Edward VII died and Duncan celebrated his ninth birthday, Ansdrie, Sir Thomas and Lady Bridewell sat in the drawing room. The fire had been lit and, as Lady Bridewell worked a tapestry for a fire screen, she said she could not understand Natalie's obsession with her orangeries. 'She has a perfectly good morning room for reading, and it would be warmer.'

'She used to sit in the orangery at Hey Tor House with her mother,' said Sir Thomas. 'Orangeries have a particular meaning for her. Besides, oranges need protection from the cold just as much as we do. She will not suffer.'

And Ansdrie noticed, not for the first time, the difference between his father-in-law's treatment of his wife, and his mother's. Even Gussie no longer thought Natalie beneath them, but his mother had a way of reminding them all that Natalie's behaviour was different, if not exactly inferior.

'Well, I find it peculiar,' she said, 'when this house has more than enough rooms.'

'As it happens,' said Sir Thomas, 'it was Natalie's orangeries that gave me the idea I have been pursuing. An idea that just might secure Ansdrie House for Duncan.'

Ansdrie stood up. 'We must discuss it,' he said. 'In the office.'

When his mother stood to accompany them Ansdrie said, for the first time in their business discussions, 'I think it better that Sir Thomas and I discuss his idea alone.'

If she would not alter her attitude to his wife, the woman without whom Ansdrie House would have been lost altogether, he would no longer allow her to influence its future.

'Am I to be excluded from discussions about my . . . this house?'

'It is not your house, Mama,' said Ansdrie. 'And I shall inform you of any decision we might take.'

Ansdrie was glad of his father-in-law's reassuring hand on his shoulder as his mother sat down and pulled tightly on a thread, and he turned his back. As they walked towards the office across the courtyard, blowing out their cheeks against the chill wind, Sir Thomas said, 'I thought we had exhausted the possibilities for saving Ansdrie. I had, more or less, resigned myself to funding it, alone.'

'You have been the most generous of fathers-in-law. You have given us, you still give us and this house, far too much.'

'Perhaps you do not know what a pleasure it is to give,'

said Sir Thomas. But he sounded weary and Ansdrie hated the idea of relying on his generosity and hard work for ever. His father-in-law had made it possible for Duncan eventually to inherit a proper, well-cared-for, small, estate as long as Ansdrie found a way if not to repay Sir Thomas entirely, then at least to take over financial responsibility for the running of the house.

They walked up the wooden stairs and sat in the office. It was cold but Ansdrie was glad he had suggested they talk there for, without his mother's controlling presence, he spoke freely about money. 'I can only imagine what it must be like to give as you have given,' he said. 'But I should be so very glad of an opportunity to repay you.' The generator beneath them hummed loudly, echoing Ansdrie's renewed hope. When he listened to Sir Thomas's latest idea, he did not at first understand.

'I know a man in sugar,' said Sir Thomas. 'One Edwin Tate by name.' He picked up a letter from his desk. 'He has just agreed to a meeting, in London. He suggests the week before the coronation. I know you will be in London then.'

'We are to go into sugar?' said Ansdrie, wondering how Sir Thomas thought that possible. 'I suppose it would complement your existing business.'

Sir Thomas laughed and shook his head. 'Marmalade, I thought. One hundred years ago the Keiller family began a small business in Dundee. They've had a factory in London these past twenty years and now they ship marmalade all over the world.'

'How could we possibly compete?'

'There's room for more than one successful Scottish marmalade producer and Ansdrie has an immediate advantage over Keiller's for she grows her own oranges. We could, perhaps, expand into other preserves. Once the business is established, the purchase of a Spanish orange grove might be in order. I don't know why I never thought of it before. I think we might give Keiller's a run for their money.'

'Ansdrie Marmalade,' said Ansdrie, smiling. He stood and stretched out his hand. 'I like the sound of that.'

Perhaps this was the idea that would remove their difficulties for ever.

London in the week before the coronation of George V and Queen Mary was unbearably hot. The stink from diesel exhaust and horse manure was worse than Ansdrie had ever known but, this year, it was mitigated a little by the sweet smell of sawdust from the timber for the stands that would hold all those who came to watch the coronation procession. Ansdric's starched collars were limp by mid-morning but Verrinder was always ready with a fresh one whenever he returned to Hyde Park Gate, where he stayed with Sir Thomas.

Natalie had not travelled south with them. She said she would rather stay with Duncan, but Ansdrie knew how much she disliked London now. Even their invitation to the coronation could not persuade her; she would attend the procession in Ansdrie instead. But she had cheered up tremendously when he told her Sir Thomas's idea and he had promised to send her a telegraph as soon as they had had their meeting.

They met Edwin Tate in a coffee house on the Strand. He was very late and arrived full of apologies. He had come from his office above the Henry Tate warehouse in Silvertown and explained, a little breathlessly, that there were men, and, by George, women, attending a meeting that had blocked the road for half an hour. 'There may be strikes among the workers,' he said. 'We may face difficult times.'

There were traces of Lancashire in his voice which, to Ansdrie's ears, sounded not unlike the traces of Yorkshire in his father-in-law's voice.

Sir Thomas put forward their proposal and Tate seemed interested. Ansdrie described the orangeries and their plans to test receipts, and to import Seville oranges or to buy a Seville orange grove when the business began to grow. Sir Thomas said Ansdrie would run the business, but that he would oversee it.

'If you don't mind my asking, Lord Ansdrie, how much business experience have you?'

'Not . . . much,' said Ansdrie. To his horror he felt his cheeks growing warm.

'As I said,' said Sir Thomas, 'I shall oversee the business until it is established. I shall stand surety for Lord Ansdrie.'

'I see,' said Edwin Tate. 'I see.'

But he was clearly doubtful.

'I'm prepared to do whatever it takes to make it work,' said Ansdrie. 'I have a house—an estate—at stake, you see.' But he realized, too late, that his concern for Ansdrie would be unlikely to endear him to Edwin Tate.

'A man has to make a start somewhere,' said Sir Thomas. 'And, as I said, he'll have me to answer to.'

'I know you of old,' said Edwin Tate. 'And I trust you entirely. Your idea is good, very good.' He looked at Ansdrie, who could not hold his penetrating gaze. 'There's plenty of room for another preserve manufacturer and I've no doubt you'll succeed, but I think,' he looked at Ansdrie again, who this time managed to hold his gaze and it was Edwin Tate who looked away, 'I think not with Henry Tate's sugar. I'm sorry to say it but since I agreed to this meeting I've had a positive nod from one of Abram Lyle's sons and, if it turns out the way I hope, Tate won't have any spare capacity.' He spoke his last words very quickly, as if speed would add conviction.

Sir Thomas and Ansdrie were silent.

'Lyle's just got the Royal Warrant. They make that syrup that sells so well. You know it?'

Ansdrie did not know it and he wished he did. He also wished he had thought to consult Sir Thomas about how he should conduct himself at this meeting. It had been foolish to talk of the house and the estate: it had doubly alienated Edwin Tate.

They walked back through St James's Park. The lawns were bare and brown for lack of rain, and the fountains were shut down. They walked beneath the newly erected marble and gilt peace memorial outside Buckingham Palace and when they reached Kensington Gardens they walked between the troops bivouacked there for coronation duty later in the week. They walked in thoughtful and disappointed silence until, at last, Sir Thomas said, 'There are, of course, other sugar refiners. There's Fairries and there's Kerrs. And several others. We shall approach them all.'

'I wish I could do this by myself,' said Ansdrie, 'without troubling you. But I have no credibility in this business. In any business.' He was irritated with himself. He should have foreseen Tate's reaction. 'They'll all say what Edwin Tate said. No one will risk his money or his sugar on a man he's not sure he can trust to make a success.'

'We could buy the sugar,' said Sir Thomas.

'More capital outlay for you,' said Ansdrie.

'You are perfectly capable, Ansdrie,' said Sir Thomas, putting his hand on Ansdrie's back. 'I know you are. We'll convince someone. We'll adopt a different approach next time.'

'But there's no getting round what Edwin Tate meant,' said Ansdrie. 'Even if he didn't directly say it. I lack the necessary experience and the—' He stopped.

'What is it?' said Sir Thomas, but Ansdrie did not hear him.

'Look,' he said. 'Look. Straight ahead. It's Haffie, is it not?'

'By my lights!' said Sir Thomas.

They stood absolutely still on the path between the tents and watched Haffie walking towards them. His face was turned away from them, towards a small, pretty woman whose gloved hand was tucked into the crook of his arm.

Ansdrie's immediate impulse was to confront Haffie, to ask him if he had any idea of the heartache he had caused his wife. But a competing impulse urged him to avoid the man altogether. And then he could not, for Haffie had seen them and it was impossible for either party to turn off the path without stumbling into the troops and their closely packed tents on the grass.

Ansdrie said, through clenched teeth, 'We'll plead a luncheon engagement.'

Sir Thomas nodded and they walked on.

Ansdrie shook Haffie's hand and he and Sir Thomas raised their hats and gave small bows when Haffie introduced the woman, his wife.

There was an awkward silence that Mrs Haffie broke by saying, in a voice with a singing quality, 'We arrived back in London two weeks ago. We are renting a house in De Vere Gardens, but we'll leave for Lancashire soon, after we've seen the coronation procession.' She looked up at her husband. 'Angus is anxious to return to the refineries and I look forward to seeing our new house.'

They exchanged a few remarks about the terrible heat, which Mrs Haffie smilingly said was, 'Quite like the Sandwich Islands. I had expected rain and cold. Is that not how an English summer so often turns out?'

Ansdrie laughed his short laugh, through his nose, and then said they were expected at Hyde Park Gate for luncheon. As they took their leave Haffie held out his card, tentatively, and Ansdrie thanked him for it. He could do little else for he would not be openly rude in front of Mrs Haffie, with whom he had no argument. But as quickly as he could, and with a relieved blowing-out of his cheeks, he and Sir Thomas walked away.

That evening, as they sat drinking port after dinner, Sir Thomas said, 'I think you will not like what I am about to suggest, but . . . we could approach Haffie, you know. Would you consider it, Ansdrie? What do you think?'

Ansdrie was confused. What was Sir Thomas thinking? How could he trust a man who had behaved so reprehensibly? And besides, how would Natalie feel?

'It may seem to you that I've lost my head, but . . . well . . . he knows you. Any other man of business will have to take you on trust and, as we've discovered, your lack of experience goes against you. And in this climate, with strikes threatened every day, you are not – forgive me – the most appealing proposition. But Haffie might feel an obligation towards you. There might be a desire in him to behave decently towards you, and therefore to Natalie, through you. He might wish to make amends.'

'I thought you were an astute businessman, Sir Thomas. How can you think any of those reasons good enough to go into business with Lieutenant Haffie? And why would he want to make amends? It was his idea to leave . . . my wife.'

'There is much at stake here, Ansdrie, and it cannot hurt to claim the moral high ground if it will achieve what we require. If you will not do this for yourself, will you do it for your son? Will you secure his inheritance?'

'I am indebted to you, Sir Thomas,' said Ansdrie, 'but I know you would not force me into a partnership against my will.'

'Not only would I not,' said Sir Thomas. 'I could not. But I do think this an opportunity we would be foolish to dismiss out of hand.'

Ansdrie felt cornered. He knew his father-in-law was right, in theory. But the idea filled him with distaste. The man had behaved unforgivably towards his wife and, in point of fact, to him, for they had once been friends.

'I would do anything to prove I have it in me to secure Ansdrie for my son. And with your guidance I know we shall, eventually, find the right thing. But this idea does not sit well with me. Nor, I think, will it sit well with Natalie.'

'How would it be,' said Sir Thomas, 'if I wrote to suggest the idea to Haffie? If I outlined our proposition? He may turn it down flat and there'll be an end to it. But by the time he replies you'll have had time to think about it. And even if he says he's willing to discuss the idea, we can always pull out. We'll always have the upper hand.'

Sir Thomas pushed the port decanter towards Ansdrie but he shook his head. If only he could think of a better idea. If only he had more land to rent. If only he were good at something, anything, that he could turn to profit. If only.

'I shall write to Natalie,' he said, after some time. 'I shall tell her what has happened and what you ... what we suggest. I shall ask if it would cause her pain, or even the slightest difficulty. We shall not approach Haffie if it would. Her decision will govern us.'

'Haffie Sugar is one of the soundest businesses in the country,' said Sir Thomas. 'But you are right. We shall be governed by Natalie's feeling on the matter. We know she will not dissemble.'

After her first, and even after her third, miscarriage Natalie allowed Ansdrie to persuade her that Duncan's safe delivery meant she would safely deliver another child. And so she allowed herself to imagine each child she carried as he or she would become: a slender daughter with Ansdrie's dark eyes; a second son with their mutual love of the natural world; a child who made them laugh. But each time, when the pains began and the blood came, her optimism failed just a little more and, by the time, just three months earlier, when Doctor Harrison told her that her body was no longer capable of carrying a child to full term, she felt as though she had been flattened beneath one of the great pine trees they had felled when first they came to Ansdrie.

Her body had become an unfit place for a healthy child to grow. The miscarriages were a punishment, a judgement on her capacity as mother, wife and woman.

It was in this state of self-accusation that she read her husband's letter and recognized the reason for her punishment. Clearly, her selfish behaviour in London with Haffie, behaviour she had mistaken for love but that, now, she understood as a kind of madness, a desire to possess another human being entirely, clearly this was the reason for her punishment. She read and reread Ansdrie's letter and knew what she must do. She would agree to this partnership for, if her husband and Haffie were successful, here was her opportunity to free herself for ever from her youthful madness; her opportunity to show herself capable of behaving rationally with the man whose every look had once obsessed her; her opportunity to atone for her youthful selfishness and so end her punishment for it.

When she told Lady Bridewell about the new venture her mother-in-law put up a surprisingly spirited resistance for, as she put it, 'Lieutenant Haffie's character has nothing to recommend it'. But when Natalie told her how successful Ansdrie and her father thought the venture likely to be, but how difficult it might prove to secure a partnership with a sugar merchant other than Haffie; when she told her how sound a business Haffie Sugar was and besides, how long ago it had been since Haffie had behaved as he had, Lady Bridewell's objections subsided. And when Natalie reminded her that Ansdrie House, the house Lady Bridewell loved more than she loved any human being, would be likely to fall to Duncan without any form of debt, indeed with the wherewithal to run smoothly for the foreseeable future if they went ahead with the venture, her objections ceased altogether.

TWENTY-TWO

NATALIE, SIR THOMAS and Duncan stood on the nursery balcony looking up at the night sky. They shivered, but Natalie was determined to stay outside until Duncan had shown his grandfather all he had learned at her knee; things she had learned, in her turn, at his knee.

'There's the Great Bear,' said Duncan, 'and the Little Bear.' He pointed upwards and his jacket lifted away from his kilt. 'There's the Plough and there's Merak and Dubhe. And there,' Natalie watched him measure a line in the night sky with his finger, just as she used to with her father, 'there's the north star, the pole star. There.'

'I never learned as quickly as you, Duncan,' said Natalie.

'Well done,' said Sir Thomas, putting his hand on Duncan's shoulder. And then he leaned down and whispered something into his ear and they both turned back to Natalie.

'Mama,' said Duncan, 'could you stay out here for a little bit longer?' His breath showed white as he spoke. 'I know it's cold but there's something we should like to do before you come back in.'

Natalie pulled her fur coat close and nodded.

'Promise not to look,' he said.

Natalie nodded again and turned away from the French

window to look out over Ansdrie's parkland, towards the Formonts. She saw a shooting star and thought, on this Christmas evening, that it was a good omen for the coming Hogmanay when the Haffies would arrive. Lieutenant Haffie had agreed in principle to a partnership with Ansdrie, but he wanted to see the oranges and to assess, with Ansdrie and Sir Thomas, when and where they should plant, or buy, more. And so—it had been Natalie's idea— they invited the Haffies to stay for Hogmanay when the oranges would be at their best and when, said Natalie, 'Our families will surround us and so diffuse any awkwardness, should it arise.'

But despite all her plans, Natalie could not actually imagine how it would be when the Haffies came to stay. All she thought about, in terms of Haffie, was that his partnership with Ansdrie heralded an independently solvent estate and house that her husband could leave, proudly, to their son. Ansdrie's renewed confidence and enthusiasm touched her deeply and she wholeheartedly supported the venture, for her husband had stood by her through so much more than many another man might have borne, during the dark times of her miscarriages.

After a little while the French window creaked open and Natalie turned, but there, making her heart race in her chest, stood Haffie, not Duncan. Natalie gasped. He wore his scarlet jacket and his mess kilt. He held out his hand. She took a step towards him and he took a step towards her but, when he emerged from the shadows, she saw that it was her own husband, not Haffie at all. In a maddened moment, she had mistaken him.

'Duncan is ready,' he said. 'He hopes you have not been too cold.'

Natalie shook her head, took her husband's outstretched hand and quickly kissed his cheek. She said, 'I am touched that you wear your mess dress.'

'I wanted to mark the transition,' he said. 'Otherwise

your birthday and Christmas day are never separated.'

'That's what Papa always used to say, before we married. But I have never had better birthday celebrations than those I have had with you, Ansdrie.'

'Duncan tells me you must close your eyes,' he said, and when Natalie was inside, sitting between her husband and her father, she heard her son's footsteps coming towards her. He put something, a book perhaps, into her hands. She felt paper and ribbon. And then three male voices in their different registers sang *Happy Birthday*. Duncan's voice, at times, reminded Natalie forcibly of her mother's voice as he sang out boldly.

'If you can,' said Duncan, 'open your present without opening your eyes.'

'If you will help me,' said Natalie.

She felt Duncan's fingers guide her to some ribbon and she undid a bow. She felt for the edges of the paper and slid her fingers beneath it. When she held a box, or a book, in her hands Duncan guided her until she found a lid. She lifted it and felt, inside the box, an uneven surface, small indentations beneath her fingers.

'Lift it, Mama,' said Duncan. 'Hold it in front of you and then open your eyes.'

She did as he asked and, at first, all she saw were little points of light directly in front of her. And then she realized she was looking at a constellation. She saw Ursa Major in miniature, on a card pricked with little star-shaped holes. It was lit from behind by a bank of candles and, when she looked round, she saw there were candles everywhere.

Natalie stared and stared. It was quite beautiful. And when Duncan knelt beside her and gave her another card from the box, Natalie made out Ursa Minor and Polaris. She studied the star-shaped holes in the cards. They were outlined in silver against a midnight-blue sky and the hand that had written the names beneath the stars was Duncan's.

'Happy birthday, Mama,' he said.

Natalie looked first at him, then at her husband and then at her father, and when she turned back to her son she said, 'You could not have given me anything better in all the world.'

Duncan began to tell her how he and his tutor, Mr Brown, had made the cards and then, even though he protested that he was much too old, Natalie gave her son a tight, tight hug and the smell of Wright's coal-tar soap filled her nostrils.

TWENTY-THREE

ANSDRIE STATION'S MOTORTAXI gleamed in the courtyard. Two Ansdrie carriages stood nearby in the snow, with grooms standing at their horses' heads, and a large, canvas-covered station wagon shook and rumbled away along the drive between the rows of snow-covered rhododendrons, empty now of its luggage. Snow fell from a grey sky onto the horses' manes, the grooms' caps and onto Ansdrie's grey stone portico, which was strewn with branches of rowan, hazel and yew for good luck and protection. But the guests barely noticed as they hurried inside, anxious for warmth.

A fire blazed in the hall and footmen took coats and hats, gloves and walking canes, while Nurse Mackay ushered the excited children up to the nursery. And then Anderson escorted the guests to the drawing room. Lady Bridewell, Gussie and Edward, Millie and Étienne and Lieutenant and Mrs Haffie followed him along the passage. They crossed the Turkey carpets and passed the blue and ivory wall hangings. They walked beneath ancient Ansdrie swords and past gleaming silver urns. They admired tall glass vases filled with red-berried holly and trailing ivy, and Millie laughed and Lady Bridewell made a disapproving sound when they saw Hogmanay circlets of mistletoe on the wrists and the heads of the Italian stone statues.

Natalie waited for them all in the drawing room, picturing exactly what they would see as they walked towards her, hoping they would like her redding for Hogmanay. Every ornament gleamed. Every pane of glass sparkled. Every floorboard shone and in less time than it would take her to count to twelve they would be with her.

She turned towards her father and her husband. They stood by the crackling fire. Sprigs of holly decorated the miniatures that hung on either side of the fireplace and newly dried potpourri filled the room with the scent of roses, cinnamon and orange peel. Natalie stood by the bay window at the west end of the room. She turned back and stared out at the snow-covered terraced garden and the icicles on the alders by the banks of the River Leven far below, but she did not really see them. She pushed a silver pot of potpourri to the centre of the table and away again to the side, without knowing what she did. Round the delicate cream lace of her high collar, she wore her birthday present from her father: a tiered sapphire and diamond necklace with a saltire for its clasp. She touched it, and then her hands fluttered, apparently independent of her will so that, at last, when she heard her guests' footsteps outside the drawing room door, she clasped one hand inside the other as if she were capturing a frightened bird. And then Anderson knocked on the door and Natalie whirled round.

'Your guests, my lady,' he said.

Lieutenant Haffie was the last to enter the room but the first Natalie really saw. And to her great relief he looked quite ordinary. Older, obviously and, perhaps, a little tired. But he was just an ordinary man following his small, pretty wife into the room. Instantly, Natalie's confidence surged. She caught her husband's eye, smiled and strode across the room towards him so that they might greet their guests together.

'It makes me very happy to see you all here,' she said.

She kissed her mother- and sisters-in-law, and then Sir

Thomas led Lady Bridewell to a seat by the fire. Étienne de la Roche took Natalie's hand and kissed it and she heard his unmistakably French accent. Ansdrie asked him about Paris while Millie and Natalie embraced. Gussie said, 'The house looks so elegant,' and Natalie thanked her. Edward Fountain took Gussie to greet Sir Thomas and then Ansdrie put his hand on Natalie's waist as they greeted the Haffies.

Mrs Haffie said, 'It is a great pleasure to meet you.' She smiled, and long dimples appeared in her cheeks. She had beautiful grey eyes, many freckles and a singing quality to her voice. Natalie took her hands and said, 'I have heard you were born in the western Highlands, Mrs Haffie. I hope you will feel equally at home here.'

'Please call me Edwina,' she said. 'And I'm quite sure I shall, thank you.' She stressed every syllable equally. 'It's a very long time since I celebrated Hogmanay in Scotland. I have missed this country.'

'We have been looking forward to celebrating with you,' said Natalie. She turned to her husband. 'Have we not?'

'We have,' said Ansdrie, kissing Edwina's hand and then shaking Haffie's.

Haffie bowed and said, 'Thank you for inviting us.'

Natalie held out her hand and when Haffie bent to kiss it she said, 'The oranges grow very well. You shall see them at the first opportunity.'

'I am impressed, for they are far outwith their natural habitat.'

He glanced up at her. He sounded uncertain. Natalie looked at Ansdrie and when she saw his worried expression she said, as if she were defending a maligned child, 'Ansdrie's oranges are well tended, and protected from the frost just as they should be. You must not worry. In fact,' she said, with a quick turn of her head towards the windows beyond which the orangeries stood, 'I think you'll find them quite the best oranges you have ever had the pleasure of inspecting.'

Ansdrie gave his short laugh and squeezed Natalie's waist.

'I didn't mean to criticize your husbandry, Lady Ansdrie,' said Haffie. 'I only thought the Scottish climate might prove unkind to a fruit that needs much sunshine.'

And then Edwina said, as she turned to face the garden, 'Snow always makes me feel safe. I could forget the rumours of invasion, here.'

'The rumours have no substance,' said Ansdrie. 'We would do well to ignore them.'

'Then I shall,' said Edwina and she smiled over her shoulder and the two long dimples appeared again. And then, as if she and Natalie had been friends for years, she held out her hand and Natalie took it and led her away. 'Come, sit by my father,' she said. 'He will tell you about Ansdrie and you can tell him about the Sandwich Islands.'

And then Natalie busied herself with her guests. She ushered Millie to sit by Ansdrie, opposite Edwina and her father, and she took Gussie to talk to Étienne by the bay window beyond the round table. She took Lieutenant Haffie to sit by Lady Bridewell, and Edward Fountain to sit with her by the south-facing windows. This separation of the married couples was no more than was expected of a competent hostess and Natalie did it automatically, but on this particular afternoon she was conscious of taking pleasure in her actions, conscious of her pride that Haffie should see her so at ease in her house, so well settled with her husband.

Anderson and Arthur, the head footman, poured tea and offered Mrs MacAlasdair's potted shrimp sandwiches and fruitcake to the guests, and then Natalie signalled for Arthur to draw the curtains, for the light had all but gone. When she stood for a moment by Lady Bridewell to make sure she had all she wanted, her mother-in-law patted the arm of a chair and asked her to sit down.

'Lieutenant Haffie professes himself surprised to

discover I grew up here,' she said.

'I made an inaccurate assumption,' said Haffie. He glanced at Natalie and then turned back to Lady Bridewell. 'I thought your roots were in Devon.'

'I was born in this house,' said Lady Bridewell. 'And it gives me great pleasure to see my daughter-in-law thriving here.'

Lady Bridewell never paid such compliments and for a moment Natalie was lost for words. Haffie filled the silence by saying, to Lady Bridewell, 'Do you find it rains more in Fife than it does in Devon?'

'There is, perhaps, too much rain in both places,' said Lady Bridewell. 'But in the Lowlands the rain is a kind, mist-filled rain. It makes me feel at home.'

More compliments. Was Lady Bridewell trying to upstage Haffie with her knowledge of his own country?

Natalie asked about their journey north and they talked of it for some time, and as she listened to Haffie she realized she had never heard him discuss such mundane matters. It was very reassuring. He had changed beyond recognition and she had no need to rid herself of her youthful madness, for she knew now it would never return. It would not be difficult to behave rationally with the man whose every look had once obsessed her, for there was nothing to capture her in this man, and nothing to fear. Her atonement for her punishing miscarriages was going to be easier than she had imagined. And then Haffie looked at her and asked if she would mind if he smoked. She inclined her head and felt delightfully composed. He took a pipe from the pocket of his Norfolk jacket and a lighter from another and Natalie rose to fetch an ashtray.

But when she returned, her confidence and composure disintegrated for she saw, on the table where she put the ashtray, the silver lighter he had said he kept to remind him of her: the lighter engraved with a single Scotch rose. She must have made a sound for Haffie looked up at her, and then, on seeing what she was staring it, he picked up the lighter and put it quickly into his pocket. He did not look at her when he said, to her mother-in-law, 'Fife, with or without its rain, holds little attraction for me.' Natalie was astonished.

'I cannot tell a lie,' said Haffie. 'My heart stays in the Highlands. Its wild beauty is unmatched. I shall return often, now that we shall not go back to the Sandwich Islands.' He pulled on his pipe and said, 'I find the Lowlands altogether lacking in character.'

Lady Bridewell drew herself up and looked away. She did not reply but merely put out her hand to Natalie to help her from her chair, to take her to another part of the drawing room. Automatically, Natalie helped her mother-in-law, but one hand remained on her solar plexus for Haffie's words had had a visceral effect. She was sure he directed his unkind remarks at Lady Bridewell, not at Fife itself, and she could not understand him.

When she had seated her mother-in-law with Edward Fountain and Étienne she said, 'Come, Millie, Gussie. Let us make sure the children settle well together.'

She did not look at Haffie as she walked across the drawing room, but she knew he watched her and she was glad she had so quickly found a reason to rid herself of his disquieting gaze.

TWENTY-FOUR

At DINNER THAT night, Natalie sat between her father and Edward Fountain.

While she was changing, Ansdrie came to her bedroom and gave her a sapphire and diamond parure that had once belonged to his father's mother. He said he had asked his mother to bring it up from Devon, to thank her for agreeing to invite the Haffies to Ansdrie. But as she sat at the head of her table she felt she wore the jewellery as a knight might wear his gorget rather than as beautiful decoration, and when she saw Edwina's simple jade necklace she wished she had worn the freshwater pearls Ansdrie had given her for her twenty-third birthday.

The porcelain and glass gleamed and the silver shone in the candlelight, but these things, which so often filled Natalie with pride, barely held her attention. She was glad only that she had put Haffie far enough away from her so that she would not be tempted to ask the question that had worried at her since he had arrived: why did he keep the lighter that reminded him of her? She put her finger to the hollow above her upper lip, a trick Millie had taught her to stop herself feeling faint, and pressed hard.

After dinner, when the women sat in the drawing room before the gentlemen joined them, Edwina said, 'Angus told me that you love dancing, so I thought you might like these.' She handed Natalie a small square parcel wrapped in linen and tied with red ribbon. 'We danced to them on Kaua'i.'

'Thank you,' said Natalie. She did not say she thought it a peculiar remark for Haffie to make to his wife.

'I think you'll find the music difficult to resist,' said Edwina and she moved her feet in quick, jerky steps.

Natalie opened the present, for it would have been rude to ignore it, but she would have preferred to leave it unopened. She saw two squares of coloured cardboard which held two records. She said, 'Does the music come from the Sandwich Islands?'

'I don't think their music has been recorded,' said Edwina. 'This is Brazilian.' She made it sound exotic.

Natalie looked at one of the records and read: '*Atraente* [Attractive].'

'But, perhaps,' said Edwina, 'there is no phonograph at Ansdrie.'

'It's in the ballroom.'

'There is a ballroom here?'

Natalie nodded. 'We do not often use it.'

When the gentlemen rejoined the women, Étienne said, looking at one of the records, 'In Paris zey love Le Maxixe.' He pronounced it *macheech* and he took Millie's hand. They danced a few quick steps just as Edwina had done and then Étienne said, 'Natalie? Would you like me to show you how zey dance?'

Natalie shook her head for she thought she would not be able to master the peculiar fitful steps. She looked up and saw Haffie looking directly at her. She stood, to avoid his gaze, and then Millie said, holding out one of the records, 'Chiquinha Gonzaga's music is heavenly. You'll love it, Natalie. Do let's dance.'

Ansdrie said, walking across the drawing room to stand at Natalie's side, 'I'd rather digest my supper.'

She was as grateful to him as if he had saved her from falling over a precipice. But Millie, who would not, or could not, grasp Natalie's reluctance to dance, said, 'You can be such a stuffed shirt at times, Ansdrie.' She said it gently and she smiled, but then she turned to Natalie and said, 'You will love it, Natalie, I promise. The rhythms are infectious. Quite unlike anything else. Come. It'll make you laugh.'

Afterwards, Natalie wished with all her heart she had refused, but when she glanced up and saw Haffie looking at her with his peculiarly disconcerting gaze, she decided she would show him just how well she and her husband could master a dance together. So she said, 'You have persuaded me, Millie. Why don't we see what we can make of Le Maxixe, Ansdrie?'

'I'll give it my best shot,' he said, and offered her his arm.

As they led their guests upstairs to the ballroom, Lady Bridewell said, 'I shall not partake.'

But now Natalie was filled with a fierce desire to conquer the strange, jerky steps with her husband. If Edwina and Millie could dance Le Maxixe with their husbands, so she could with Ansdrie. The man she had chosen to live her life beside, the man she had taught to waltz in the early days of their marriage, that man would not be bettered at this dance by anyone.

The shrouds on the chandeliers in the ballroom diffused the light and the shapes at the edges of the room only gradually resolved themselves into chairs and chaises longues covered with protective sheets. Dust motes danced in the pale light when Natalie crossed the room to lift the cover from the phonograph. She wound the machine and put a record onto the turntable. When a saxophone, a flute, a tambourine, drums and perhaps a cello or a violin began to play a rhythm that was quite unlike anything she had heard before, Natalie stared at the phonograph as if it were emitting sounds from an alien planet.

At last she said, 'How *does* anyone dance to this?'

She watched Haffie and Edwina, Millie and Étienne begin a swinging, exuberant dance.

Lady Bridewell said, 'It is indecent. I shall not watch,' and she turned her head away, but Natalie saw the amused expression on her father's face when he said, 'It's not so very long ago, my dear Lady Bridewell, that people thought the waltz shocking. We lose our curiosity at our peril.'

Lady Bridewell made a low grunt of disapproval, but she did not leave her dust-sheeted chair beside Sir Thomas and when the music stopped and the dancers stood still, Étienne and Edwina offered to show the steps to the others. Before Natalie knew what had happened, Lieutenant Haffie was standing in front of her, asking her to dance.

Ansdrie said, 'I'm not at all sure I shall manage this,' but Natalie saw Millie take his hand and reassure him.

'Let them teach us, Ansdrie,' said Natalie. 'And then we'll show them what we can do.'

'I'll do my best,' said Ansdrie.

Étienne took Gussie's hand and Edwina took Edward's and so, hoping very much that she and her husband would master the dance quickly, Natalie said, 'I don't think I understand the steps or the rhythm either, Ansdrie.' She looked at Haffie, who said, 'The music will tell you what to do.' And then, when he stood close to her he said, softly, 'You'll find it steals its way into you.'

Natalie glanced up at him and looked away quickly.

Edwina set the needle on the turning record and Natalie hesitantly followed the steps Haffie showed her. But she stumbled more than once and wondered, when she looked at him, if he wished to make a spectacle of her for the rhythm was unfamiliar and she found it difficult to follow him. But she said, to her husband, 'We shall learn the way of it, Ansdrie.'

And then Haffie said, 'This is the Castle Step. Some call it the Castle Walk. Follow me. Just so.'

Natalie copied him once more, but this time she recognized what her feet were doing and she said, so that Ansdrie should hear, 'It's just a simple one-step. Not as complicated as we thought.' She looked up and stretched her hand out towards her husband. 'Not anything like as difficult as it looks,' she said.

But although he smiled he shook his head, despite Millie's encouragement, and by the time Edwina had put the second record on the turntable and said, 'This is the *Corta jaca*; it's a bit faster,' Ansdrie had persuaded his sister to stop teaching him. Natalie said she would stop too but Ansdrie encouraged her to continue. 'You're quick at such things,' he said. And when a complicated guitar melody crackled out beneath a soaring flute and Haffie continued to dance the Castle Step Natalie said, 'You're teaching me simpler steps than the ones you danced with Edwina, Lieutenant Haffie. Show me those steps.'

'As you wish,' said Haffie.

He walked behind her and, automatically, Natalie turned towards him. He said, walking behind her once more, 'At the beginning of the dance I stand behind you and you put your hands here, just so.'

Even though Natalie heard Edwina telling Edward she would make exactly the same movements, still she wondered if Haffie wanted to disorient her. But when she turned to him his eyes showed her he was perfectly serious and, when she saw Edwina continue to make the same movements, she turned back and put her hands on her breastbones. She felt self-conscious, but she *would* learn this dance. She would not let it defeat her. And then she would teach it to her husband.

'Now,' said Haffie, 'I put my hands over yours, just so. And I guide your hands. Just so.'

And then he began to dance behind her. She had to follow the rhythm of his movements, for she could not see his feet. He guided her hands down the front of her body, then out to the side and up over her head. She blushed.

He said, 'That's it. You're following very well.'

But Natalie, who thought she was not following but being led, said, in order to exert a little control, 'Quicker, please. Just as you danced with Edwina.'

'As you wish,' said Haffie.

Edwina put the *Atraente* on the turntable again and this time, when the music crackled out from the phonograph, its jumping syncopation made sense to Natalie. Haffie turned her towards him and put her left hand behind her back, a movement she instinctively resisted until she saw Étienne make the same movement with Gussie and then, when they began to dance a syncopated two-step, Natalie's refusal to be defeated by these strange new steps transmuted into an absolute understanding. The music had stolen its way into her just as Haffie had said it would.

It was wilder music than any Natalie had ever heard but, despite its complicated rhythms, its melodies were simple and she gave herself to it and urged Haffie to dance faster and faster, as if she were challenging him to a duel. They whirled past the shrouded pier glasses but when, at last, she dared look up into his eyes she saw a deep tenderness there that surprised her so much she caught her breath. In that moment her brittle determination fell away and she was filled with a joy so overwhelming she was afraid she might cry. And he looked different. He was no longer tired and no longer ordinary, but animated, as if he had just come to life. Here was the Haffie she remembered, the man whose eyes were alive when he looked at her, when he talked to her. He said, his lips very close to her ear and his voice pitched so that only she would hear, 'Oh, Natalie.'

That was all, just two little words, but Natalie's whole being responded as if he had declared he would love her until he died.

Now she danced with him as if her body was an inextricable part of his body, as if a part of her that she had long ago lost had been found. She was no longer aware of anyone but him. The years disappeared and she was a girl again, with all her life, a life full of hope and promise and laughter, before her. She felt the pressure of Haffie's hand against her back and heard him laugh, and she too tipped her head back and laughed and, as they whirled beneath the shrouded chandeliers, Natalie discovered that to dance to this music was to laugh with her whole body.

The skirts of her long, black velvet dress flew about her ankles. Two sapphires from her bodice rattled across the floor but she did not notice, nor did she notice when Edwina stopped showing Edward the steps and Étienne stopped showing Gussie. She did not realize that Étienne played the record again, and then again, nor did she hear him when he said, 'Brava, Natalie! Brava!' She did not see Ansdrie walk the length of the ballroom and gently lift the needle from the record. All she knew was the exhilaration, the freedom, the sheer delight of dancing with Haffie.

It was only when the wild music stopped and she and Haffie stood still, when Natalie's heart raced and her breath came in short bursts, that she saw the expressions on the faces of those who sat or stood at the edges of the ballroom. Ansdrie, Gussie and Edward, her father, her mother-in-law and Edwina all looked at her with awkward or disapproving expressions. Only Millie and Étienne laughed.

And then a movement at the edge of her vision made Natalie turn her head. She saw Duncan, in his pyjamas, his hair ruffled and his eyes half-closed, standing on the threshold. She wondered if he had seen her dancing. As Ansdrie took her arm, kindly, and walked her towards their son she very much hoped he had not.

Ansdrie whispered, 'See him back to bed, Natalie. I'll take our guests downstairs.'

Before she left the ballroom Natalie said, her throat aching, 'I think I . . . I don't like the . . . Le Maxixe. It's really quite unrefined.'

She saw Haffie hold a white handkerchief to Edwina's face; she realized Edwina must be crying. She turned to her son. She heard Haffie ask for ice. Instinctively, Natalie said she would ring for Anderson, but Ansdrie said he would do it and gently reminded her to look after Duncan. As she walked across the hall towards the nursery wing Duncan gazed up at her and said, 'I've never seen you dance before, Mama. It was excellent. I should like to learn that dance. You looked like a jack-in-a-box.' He waggled his arms and his head and he laughed, but Natalie said, 'It is not a dance for a gentleman, Duncan. And I shall never dance it again.'

She touched his soft cheek with her hand and, holding back her tears, she allowed him to persuade her to read him a story, as much to distract herself as to send him back to sleep. She read his favourite, 'The Cat that Walked by Himself', but the story of a man, a woman and their contented life with their child upset her terribly. Before the end of the story Duncan fell asleep and Natalie realized, with relief, that all her guests had gone to their rooms. She took a fur-lined velvet cloak from her bedroom and hurried down the stairs. The only thought in her head was to go to her sanctuary, the orangeries, for her heart felt as if it would burst with the confused feelings that fought each other there. Among her orange trees she would be able to calm herself and to think. She prayed that Ansdrie would not be in his study as she hurried along the passage, already imagining herself taking the key from the drawer in his desk. But when she reached the small hall on the south side of the house, the sound of raised voices made her stop on the flagstones outside her husband's study. She heard Lady Bridewell's voice, at its most imperious.

'You *must* control her, Ansdrie. Your wife can*not* be allowed to disgrace you in this fashion. You must rein her in. And if you will not, I shall.'

Natalie stood stock still, afraid to make a sound. She held her breath.

'You must make her understand the enormity of her selfish, thoughtless behaviour. She must curb her . . . desires. I will not have the noble name of Ansdrie tarnished.'

'The noble name of Ansdrie, as you put it,' said Ansdrie, his voice as icy as the winter night, 'has suffered far worse than a chaotic Brazilian dance.'

'Open your eyes, Ansdrie!' roared Lady Bridewell. 'That was not a dance. That was a declaration of . . . of . . . It was a thoroughly degrading display. Your wife should be *hobbled*!'

Natalie's hand flew to her mouth.

She heard the sound of liquid pouring into a glass and then the creak of Ansdrie's chair. She heard the sound of silk rustling and Lady Bridewell's footsteps as she paced up and down. She heard the smack of a fan into a gloved hand.

'Speak, damn you!' said Lady Bridewell. 'Speak, Ansdrie!'

And then Natalie heard her husband say, very clearly, 'I love Natalie more than my own life, Mama. And it is because I love her so very much, and because I trust her, that I know we shall find a way . . . to deal with what happened. But not in the manner you suggest.'

Despite her fur-lined cloak Natalie's body began to shake uncontrollably and tears slid down her cheeks. She saw the star-filled sky and the pale, waning moon through the French window. She saw the bare black boles of the trees against the night sky. But, through the unsteady lens of her tear-filled eyes, what she saw was a distorted, frightening landscape. She tried to take in what her husband and her mother-in-law were saying. Her mind raced.

'You had no choice but to make her your wife, for the sake of the Ansdrie estate. We knew her background was not suitable but if you had schooled her properly she would have learned how to behave, by now.'

Another silence followed and then another slap of a fan into a gloved hand. 'If not for this house and this land how should you hold your head up, Ansdrie?'

'I did not *have* to make Natalie my wife, Mama. And I should still be quite myself without this house.'

'You would be *nothing*,' said Lady Bridewell.

And then there was a silence that lasted for so long Natalie was afraid her heartbeart, which was loud in her own ears, might be heard in Ansdrie's study.

At last her husband said, 'You and I differ greatly, Mama. Ownership of Ansdrie has not changed my character and it never will; although, in case you have forgotten, I am doing my level best for the old place and I should very much like to be able to leave my son a proper inheritance. But your obsession with our position borders on madness. For all your insistence on correct form, you fail to understand that I am a custodian of Ansdrie. It is not ownership of this house that is important, it is its preservation for future generations. And if I cannot serve my inheritance well, I shall relinquish it. It is the state in which I leave it for Duncan that matters. Your possessive attitude is quite against any principle I understand. I belong to Ansdrie. Ansdrie does not belong to me.'

There was another silence, and then Ansdrie said, 'When Natalie agreed to marry me, it was because she wanted to. She knew that when first I asked her I did not love her and I admit that, then, I was only thinking of how to preserve this house, for your sake. But it was she who, so courageously, told me there was no love in my proposal. I thought then she would marry Lieutenant Haffie. But when he left London, and when she and I did finally agree to marry, there was no coercion on either side, although I have always known that if Haffie had behaved better, if he had proved himself a suitable husband, she would have married him and not me.'

'He was *not* suitable!' said Lady Bridewell. 'I cannot understand you! I brought you up to believe in duty and selflessness above all else, yet still you have no *idea* how to behave.' There was another rustle of silk. 'But happily for you,' she said, 'and, more importantly, happily for this house, *my* actions have always been governed by a sense of duty. If they had not been, Ansdrie would have been lost.'

'I have not the slightest idea what you are talking about, Mama. For if my love for Natalie is not selfless, I don't know what is.'

But as the meaning of Lady Bridewell's words dawned on her, Natalie heard a sound like a slap and her husband said, 'By God, Mother! You *sent* Haffie away!'

There was another long silence and then Lady Bridewell said, her voice lacking its usual hauteur, 'I did it for the good of this house, this estate, Ansdrie. I could not allow it to slip from my . . . your grasp.'

'What did you say to him?' said Ansdrie, icily.

When Lady Bridewell did not reply, Ansdrie repeated the question and this time, in Natalie's imagination, he towered over his mother when he said, *'What did you say to him?'*

Natalie took a deep breath and walked in to her husband's study. She walked slowly, but determinedly. Tears streamed down her face as she crossed the Turkey carpet and she was afraid she might stumble for her legs shook very much, but she kept her eyes on her husband, refused to acknowledge her mother-in-law and, when she reached him, she touched his arm and said, as levelly as she could, 'I came for the key to the orangeries. I . . . I heard . . . everything.'

She looked into Ansdrie's startled dark eyes.

'But I don't think either of us wish to hear one more word. Do we, dearest?'

TWENTY-FIVE

Natalie leaned against the side of her high bed and cried. Ansdrie walked about the room. When he stopped and turned to her, he said, 'How could I have been so blind?'

'I never imagined it either,' said Natalie. 'But now I think she would have done anything to save this house. She loves it with an unnatural tenacity.'

'Don't forgive her.'

'I'm not forgiving her. I'm trying to understand what made her do what she did. I'm trying to understand . . . why I did what I did, tonight. Why this feeling . . .' her tears began to fall again and she put her hand on her heart, 'why after so many years I still . . . This is terrible, Ansdrie. Terrible. I shall return to Devon and live with Papa. I shall become a nun. I shall—'

'Ssshhh,' said Ansdrie. 'Ssshhh.' He sat beside her and held her. 'This is madness. Think of our son.'

'Don't forgive me.'

'I love you, Natalie,' said Ansdrie, simply. 'You were captured by Haffie tonight. Neither of you really knew what you were doing.'

'Please don't, Ansdrie. I don't deserve your forgiveness.'

At last, when they agreed to try to sleep and Ansdrie left Natalie's room for his own, she sat shivering in a chair.

But it was not the cold that caused her to shiver; it was a sense that she, like the earth itself, was slowly spinning in a huge void, a place where she recognized nothing and where nothing was safe.

When eventually she rang for Hocks she had very little idea of the time, but Hocks arrived dutifully, sleepy-eyed, in her dressing gown and nightcap.

'How thoughtless of me,' said Natalie. 'I'll make myself ready for bed.'

'If you don't mind me in my nightclothes, my lady,' said Hocks, 'I'd like to help you.' She looked at Natalie as if she knew exactly what kind of help she needed and the tears Natalie kept fighting to keep at bay overwhelmed her once again.

'Oh, my lady,' said Hocks, 'shall I call for your husband? Shall I make you a hot drink?'

Natalie shook her head and sat at her dressing table. She stared at her mother's perfume bottle. She thought how very ashamed she would be of her behaviour. She picked up the bottle but it shattered.

Natalie could not understand why it had broken.

Hocks said, 'Give me your hand, my lady.'

Natalie saw the blood, but did not think it hers.

'I'll fetch a bandage and some carbolic,' said Hocks. 'Hold your hand up, my lady. Keep it up until I get back.'

Natalie watched drops of perfume slide from the edge of her dressing table onto the black velvet of her dress. She opened her hand and her mother's broken bottle fell to the floor.

Pieces of glass landed on the Persian carpet.

Pieces of glass skittered across the wooden floorboards beneath the window, and the scent of lavender filled the room as if it were the very air itself.

When Natalie woke she found an envelope on the pillow next to her. She read:

My dearest Natalie,

Mama has left.

Verrinder took her to the station early this morning and I think it best if we tell our guests she has been called back to Waverton on urgent estate business. No one will believe us, but they'll have the good grace not to ask questions.

I intend to sever all connection with her, at least until I know what else to do. And, my dearest Natalie, we shall discuss what we must do when all our guests have gone.

Your loving husband, Ansdrie.

Natalie stared at the still-drawn curtains. She slid from her bed when Hocks knocked at her door, but she did not come in, so Natalie opened the door and was surprised to see Millie standing there, dressed in a riding habit. She said, 'Come, Natalie. I think you need fresh air. To blow the cobwebs away.'

'I really don't think . . .' She held up her hand.

'You can ride one-handed,' said Millie. 'Ring for Hocks, Natalie, do.'

And so they rode through the park towards the Formonts, but they did not ride to blow the cobwebs away because the ground beneath the snow was too hard for their horses' feet. So they walked slowly through the clear air beneath a bright blue sky and then, when Natalie's tears would not be held in any longer, they stopped beneath a sycamore and she said, 'What am I to do, Millie?'

'If he feels . . .' Millie reached for Natalie's injured hand and said, 'Look at me, Natalie.' And when she lifted her tear-stained face Millie said, 'If Haffie loves you, why on earth did he leave London? It does not make sense.'

And so, despite what Ansdrie had written, Natalie told Millie all that she and he discovered the night before, and Millie cried bitter tears.

'We were so shocked when he left we could only think

we'd badly misjudged him,' she said, at last. 'Even Mama was shocked.' She corrected herself. 'Seemed shocked.' She kissed Natalie's injured hand. 'Did you discover what she said to him?'

'No,' said Natalie.

When they walked into the dining room for a late breakfast, their boots and the hems of their riding habits damp from the snow, Natalie stopped on the threshold, for Haffie sat at the table. She had not expected anyone to be there; it was past ten o'clock. He glanced up and then looked away. He put down his knife and fork, picked up Edwina's brightly coloured shawl from the chair beside him and left while Natalie stood, as still as a statue, staring after him. She felt as if he had reached into her breast, wrenched out her heart and taken it with him.

Later, when Natalie sat at her desk in her morning room, she watched Edwina and Gussie making a snowman with the children on the terraced lawn below her window. She took a piece of writing paper from a pigeon hole and wrote, 'I discovered something terrible last night. Please come to the southern orangery if you possibly can, this afternoon. Natalie. P.S: You can say, if anyone asks, that you wish to inspect the oranges.'

She put the note into an envelope and asked Arthur to give it to Lieutenant Haffie. And then she discussed, without any enthusiasm, the final preparations for the evening's celebrations with Mrs MacAlasdair. She watched her son playing in the snow with his cousins with a mixture of anxiety, confusion and sorrow in her heart. All she knew, clearly, was that she must speak to Haffie. She must apologize to him and she must discover what Lady Bridewell had said. And then, she told herself, when she knew, she would be able to say goodbye to him. What she did not admit, because it was too complicated and too dangerous, was how very much she wanted to hear Haffie tell her what she knew she'd seen in his eyes the night before.

That morning was one of the longest Natalie had ever known and, by the time she walked to the orangery, she felt as if she had lived through several days and nights. She sat on a wrought-iron bench between two trees at the far end. She breathed in the bittersweet scent of the oranges and warmed her feet by a coal-burner. She watched the sun begin to sink towards the western horizon and then she heard the door open. She stood and, when he saw her, Haffie quickened his pace until they stood opposite each other, muffled in winter coats, hats and scarves.

'I'll not stay for long,' he said.

'No . . . no,' said Natalie.

'I should not have danced with you the way I did last night. I am a married man—'

'Yes . . . yes . . .'

They looked at each other, helplessly, and then Natalie gestured for Haffie to sit down.

'What is the terrible thing you have discovered?'

'I . . . I thought you left London of your own accord,' said Natalie. 'But last night I discovered Lady Bridewell sent you away.'

Haffie stood abruptly and walked away from her. He did not turn back when he said, 'Do you people never speak to each other? How could you not know what she did?' His voice was very angry and when he did turn back to her, his brown eyes blazed. 'Lady Bridewell told me you were betrothed to Ansdrie, which, at first, I could not believe. But when she told me your father had signed over five thousand pounds for the restoration of the house where you would live,' he flung his arm out towards it, 'when she showed me his signature on the promissory note, I . . . well, you can imagine what I thought. You led me a pretty dance, all of you. And all because you could not stand the truth. You could not face the fact that your betrothal was a matter of money alone. You wanted to show yourself as a woman of . . . feeling . . . and Ansdrie wanted me to think him an honourable man. Your father was the only honest one, in his way, for at least he admitted that money buys influence. But you all used me for your own ends. I was a pawn in your elaborate game.'

Natalie let out a cry that sounded as if she were being tortured. Her breathing was quick and shallow. She tried to press her finger to the place above her upper lip to stop herself feeling faint, but her hands shook so much she could only clasp them together. The blood roared in her ears and she bent over as if she were in great pain. She fought for words but they would not come. She saw a small clump of snow melt away from the side of one of Haffie's brown leather boots. And when his boots began to move towards her, she heard his voice again. He said, 'How can you be so very upset by all this? You knew what you were doing.' And then, his pace quickening, he said, 'You did know, didn't you? Natalie?'

She did her best to shake her head.

She felt him reaching for her hands and, very slowly, she sat up. But when she looked at him, when she saw the puzzled, questioning expression in his eyes, her body convulsed again. She bent over and a great sob burst from her. The bones of her corset dug into her but, more keenly than the pain they caused, she felt Haffie's arms holding her and she thought her tears would never stop. She crushed the handkerchief he gave her in her gloved hand.

Betrothed to Ansdrie. Five thousand pounds. Promissory note. An elaborate game.

The words repeated themselves over and over again in her mind while he said, over and over again, 'Oh, Natalie, oh, my dearest, dearest Natalie. How could you not have known?'

At last she took a deep, broken breath and pulled away from him. She dashed at her face with his handkerchief and said, her voice exhausted and devoid of expression, 'Ansdrie did propose. But I told him I could not marry him.

You . . . were the only one in my heart.'

'Oh, my dearest.'

'And I did not know . . . I cannot believe . . . what my father did.'

They sat together, hidden from the world outside by the orange trees. The sun sank lower and lower in the sky until its red-gold rays were level with the leaden planters that held the trees, until the only light in the orangery was the glow from the coal burners.

At last Natalie said, 'But I wrote to you. Surely my letter would have shown you I had not taken part in any . . . game.'

'I hardly know how to tell you this,' said Haffie. 'But I didn't read your letter until . . . this summer. And then I didn't know what to do about it. It confused me. I thought it part of the . . . game. But your courage rang true and I . . . when your father and your husband wanted to talk to me about. . . .' He looked up at the orange trees. 'If I had not read your letter I should never have agreed to talk to them. And I hoped with all my heart I should have an opportunity to talk to you.'

'Why did you wait so long to read it?'

'It arrived after I left for the Sandwich Islands. I can only think my mother was too ill to forward it. I found it in a box with some other letters, in her desk, when I returned this summer.'

Haffie stopped.

Natalie waited. And then Haffie took a crumpled envelope from his pocket and said, 'I have kept it with me since I found it.'

He handed Natalie the envelope and she stared at it. And then they sat for another few moments without speaking until Haffie took Natalie's hand and said, very tenderly, 'I held back, that summer in London. I . . . I wanted to be entirely certain of you, and of myself. But because I didn't act, because I defied my own heart and . . . and yours . . . I lost everything. *Faint heart ne'er wan a lady fair.* I should have asked for your hand when first I wanted to. In Devon.'

Still Natalie could not speak.

'Last night the way you danced with me told me you . . .' he hesitated, 'told me you had not forgotten how once you felt. Just as I have not.'

'Last night,' said Natalie, at last, the tears brimming in her eyes and her throat constricting, 'my heart remembered where first it loved. And I realized it had never truly forgotten.' She looked at him. 'I should have travelled to Liverpool. It would not have been difficult to find the refineries. But I thought you . . . I thought you didn't . . . You once said you understood how fragile the things of the inner world are. So when you didn't reply I could only think . . . I. . . . But you keep the lighter with you. . . .'

'I have kept it with me since I read your letter. I should have believed in you, Natalie. I should never have left London. I should have defied Lady Bridewell and known you would never behave as I convinced myself you had behaved.'

Haffie took Natalie's hand. His face was very close to hers. And then the orangery door opened and the leaves on the trees rustled, as if in sympathy with the lovers' predicament. Natalie wished she had thought to lock the door.

A light came steadily towards them through the long avenue of trees, accompanied by the light-holder's footsteps. Natalie gestured for Haffie to lean back between the trees, but she knew it was hopeless for the boles of the orange trees were thin.

'Natalie?'

It was Ansdrie's voice.

Natalie sat frozen, staring at the wooden boards beneath her feet. And then, as the footsteps came closer, she took Haffie's arm and they stood and turned towards her husband. 'I thought it was time Lieutenant Haffie . . . saw the oranges,' she said.

The lantern Ansdrie held cast a white glow over them; it made their faces pale.

'And what did you think?' he said. 'Will they . . . do?'

'I cannot imagine any better,' said Haffie.

TWENTY-SIX

'PAPA!' SAID NATALIE, walking quickly into Sir Thomas's bedroom without knocking. 'I have to speak to you. Now.'

Sir Thomas dismissed Chapman, his valet, and waited apprehensively. His daughter was not yet changed for dinner. She still wore a coat, her scarf was barely unwound and when she wrenched off her hat strands of hair fell about her face, so very unlike her usual neat arrangement. Her cheeks were pale and her hands, when he took them, were cold. He had been, as they all had, very unsettled by the events of the night before, and by Lady Bridewell's departure and he had been expecting his daughter to come to him all day. She had not been at breakfast, she had avoided his eye at luncheon but now, here she was and he was frightened of . . . he knew not what. Was she about to tell him she would divorce Ansdrie?

Natalie pulled her hands away from his, turned and fell into a chair by the fire.

Sir Thomas stood, waiting, unaware that his white tie and the buttons of his white waistcoat remained undone.

Natalie stood again.

'You betrayed me, Papa,' she said, at last, and her dark-blue eyes flashed. 'You made a bargain with Lady Bridewell. You *bought* my . . . my marriage and you treated my soul, my heart, as if it were nothing more than one of your consignments of tea. You cut me off from the man I love . . . loved . . . love,' she said. And then she fell back into the chair.

Sir Thomas expected her to cry, but her pale fury and now, as she sat upright, her still watchfulness were far more troubling. One hand remained in her coat pocket and it struck him, implausibly, that she might be holding a gun.

By contrast with his daughter's stillness, Sir Thomas shook in every part of his body. His lips shook so much he could not speak. When he tried to raise his hand in an attempt at a calming gesture his arm would not be lifted. He walked, unsteadily, towards the chair opposite his daughter and lowered himself into it, in an ungainly manner. He had begun to sweat.

'Well?' she said, turning to face him. 'What have you to say?'

Sir Thomas made several attempts to speak before he managed, 'I never . . . I did not cut you off from . . . Haffie. I did not – by my lights I did not make the best of it, I know that, and I have always been sorry for it. But my intentions were good. I knew how you felt for Haffie. B-besides,' he said, grasping at a memory that floated at the edges of his mind, 'he never replied to your letter. Your heartfelt letter.'

'It arrived after he left,' she said, and then she was on her feet shouting down at him. 'Your *money* is the reason I am not wed to him and living peacefully. You and Lady Bridewell are shameful. Shameful! You paid her! And she sent him away.'

'Sent him away?'

'Oh please, Papa,' said Natalie, turning from him in her fury. 'Don't pretend you didn't know.'

'I didn't know she . . . sent him away, you say?'

'Stop it, Papa!'

Sir Thomas put his shaking hand to his forehead and realized, with horrible certainty, what Lady Bridewell must have done.

He tried to stand.

He pleaded with his daughter to listen to him, but she would not.

He realized his sonorous voice had risen and he was speaking in the high, feeble tones of a querulous old man.

And then Natalie stood and Sir Thomas stared at his daughter's back. He did not know that his mouth hung open. He wanted to tell her what he had done and yet he did not know how to begin. He felt her anger as if it were a piece of hot steel inside his chest. And then Natalie began to sob great, heart-rending, body-wracking sobs.

Sir Thomas tried to stand once more but he could not leave his chair. He watched his daughter fling open the bedroom door and stared after her, at the emptiness she left behind, at the door that, very slowly, swung shut.

When they were all gathered in the drawing room before dinner Anderson approached Natalie and said, in a low voice, 'My lady, Sir Thomas will not be down for dinner. I have removed his place. Mrs MacAlasdair will send something up to him.'

Natalie thanked him and when he had gone she said, to each of her guests, 'My father is not well. He will not join us tonight.' She said the words through almost immobile lips, as if she were repeating a prayer. And then she added, 'But we shall still celebrate Hogmanay, for the children's sake, I think?'

They all agreed but, at the Hogmanay dinner, Natalie wondered if she would be able to talk to any of them, especially to Haffie. Anderson had made the *placement* – she had forgotten to talk to him about it – and, too late, she realized he had put Haffie on her right. But, in her guests' determination to behave as if nothing out of the ordinary had happened, they talked only of mundane things and both she and Haffie joined the conversation, for it required very little of them. No one mentioned Lady Bridewell's departure or Sir Thomas's absence, although the air crackled with unspoken supposition. And everyone quickly agreed when Natalie suggested they watch the children dance reels, without joining in themselves.

Étienne and Edward talked of their ride in the foothills of the Formonts. Haffie said the Ansdrie oranges were finer than he could have hoped and Ansdrie told them the first marmalade would be ready to taste by the end of January. Natalie felt as exhausted as if she had not slept for a week and Haffie was ashen. Millie and Gussie talked of the snowman they had made with their children and Edwina said she had spent a pleasant afternoon telling the children stories from the Sandwich Islands, but she looked drawn. Only Ansdrie gave a clear outward sign that the equilibrium of their party had been upset, for he drank too much wine. But Natalie trusted the sturdy vessel of her guests' good manners to see them safely through Hogmanay. After that, she dared not imagine what might happen.

The cakes and kebbuck, the shortbread and apples, the black bun and silver bowls of sugared almonds stood ready on the sideboard. A decanter of whisky and a wassail bowl also stood there, and Natalie asked Anderson to prepare the het pint because she wanted to protect her husband in case he made it badly, or burned himself. When, finally, she spoke once more she said, 'We shall eat the Hogmanay sweetmeats in the drawing room with the children. Gentlemen, please join us.'

She stood and as she, Millie, Edwina and Gussie walked along the passage to the drawing room, the servants' children spilled out into the hall behind them, followed by Hoxash with his bagpipes. And then Duncan ran from the drawing room towards his mother, looking very fine in his Ansdrie kilt, his Montrose jacket and lace jabot. 'We're ready for you, Mama,' he said. His hands were behind his back and Natalie was about to tell him to put them by his sides when she remembered what he would be hiding from her.

'We're all here,' she said, stretching out her hand.

'Where's Papa?' said Duncan.

A rush of icy air flew along the passage as the great oak front door was pulled open and Ansdrie said, loudly, 'Do not trouble yourshelf, Hoxash. I shall collect the Hogmanay *onges.*'

'There he is,' said Natalie, unnecessarily.

As she turned towards the hall, she thought her husband should not collect the oranges in his intoxicated state. But, then again, the cold air might sober him. Natalie hovered indecisively, understanding very well why he had drunk so much, and when her indecision threatened to tip her into another flood of tears, she said nothing and let her husband go. She gave her guests a faltering smile as they walked up the passage, and then she turned back to her son, put her hand on his shoulder and together they walked into the drawing room. She pretended not to notice his swift move-ment of the bouquet from behind his back to his side.

The fire had been built up for good luck and the furni-ture and carpets put aside so that the children could dance. Amelia and Louise, Gussie's daughters, stood by the fire in white dresses with sashes of their grandmother's Ansdrie tartan round their waists. Their brother, Edward, wore a kilt as did Millie's sons, Jock and Hubert, and all the grown men. Nurse Mackay stood behind the little girls, a silk sash of Mackay tartan across her bosom. Natalie thanked her for her kindness and care of the children and then Duncan presented Natalie with her Hogmanay bouquet.

'For protection and good luck, Mama. For health and happiness.'

Natalie bent her face to the sprigs of holly and mistletoe, rowan and hazel, yew and rosemary. She could not look up for the tears that filled her eyes. 'Rosemary's for remem-brance,' said Duncan.

'Thank you, my darling boy,' she said.

She was saved from having to say anything else, and

from betraying her tears, when the servants' children came into the drawing room followed by her husband, and Duncan ran to him. Ansdrie held a basket of oranges. There was snow on his head and shoulders. He handed an orange to each adult and each child and when he reached Haffie he said, 'A little handful of gold.'

The air in the drawing room filled with a bittersweet smell and when the oranges had been wished upon and the children had handed out sugared almonds and kissed the adults, for luck; when all the other sweetmeats, except the bitter oranges, had been eaten and Anderson had brought in the wassail bowl, the sound of the pipes warming up outside filled their ears and then Hoxash arrived, resplendent in his belted plaid. He played an eightsome reel for the children, and then 'Strip the Willow'. The adults watched and applauded, and then the children danced a very fast 'Gay Gordons' until, at a signal from Natalie, they stopped and all eyes turned to the grandfather clock with its brass sun, moon and stars floating in an indigo sky above the white clock face.

Natalie watched the filigree minute hand climb up towards the twelve and heard the children softly counting down the numbers. And then, when the great grandfather clock began to chime they all waited in silence until, at the final stroke of the twelve, Ansdrie walked to the French windows in the small hall opposite his study and opened them onto the south terrace to let the old year out. Then he closed them and walked, alone, to the front door to let the New Year in.

Natalie heard him pull the great oak doors open and say, as she had heard him say every Hogmanay for ten years, 'Welcome in, New Year, and when ye come, bring good cheer.' But she wondered what good cheer the New Year could possibly bring to them: she had never greeted one with such sorrow in her heart.

The great hall door boomed shut and Hoxash began to

play *Auld Lang Syne*. The group in the drawing room stood in a circle and joined hands and the tears that were never far from Natalie's eyes that evening filled them once more as they sang together. It struck her, as she tried to sing, that a stranger would think them a harmonious group and yet such unhappiness filled at least four of their hearts.

Hoxash turned and piped himself away and, when they could no longer hear the pipes, they broke their circle and Anderson ladled out the het pint from the wassail bowl into glasses in openwork silver holders.

'Will we wait in the hall for the first-footer?' said Duncan. 'Will he bring good luck or bad?'

'We shall wait here,' said Natalie, putting one hand on his dark head. 'We won't go into the hall until we hear the bell. And you know very well,' she said, gently, 'that we never talk of bad luck on Hogmanay.'

At twenty past twelve on the morning of Ne'er Day, the bell sounded and the children ran from the drawing room after Ansdrie. The adults followed and joined the servants beneath the vaulted ceiling of the great hall. Natalie glanced over her shoulder and saw Haffie take Edwina's arm, and then Ansdrie flung open the great wooden doors and the servants moved forward to see who it was who came to first-foot.

But instead of hearing the greeting they all expected, 'A Gude New Year to ane an' a', An' many may ye see'; instead of welcoming a man they knew or, perhaps, a man they did not; instead of seeing a piece of coal, an orange and a cask of whisky clasped in his hands, all those who stood in the great hall at Ansdrie in that first hour of the year 1912 saw Hoxash with his bagpipes still tucked under his arm and a stricken expression on his face.

He held out his large, empty hands and said, 'Come quickly, my lord. Come quickly all. Bring water. For the orangeries are afire.'

Part Three

1912

Courage is resistance to fear, mastery of fear,
not absence of fear.

Mark Twain

TWENTY-SEVEN

NATALIE STOOD IN the ruins of her orangeries. The cracked and broken foundations had been cleaned of pieces of terracotta, of molten lead and scattered earth, of shards of glass and burned trees and now, on this cold March day, the blackened ironwork stood out starkly against the blue sky. Natalie could not look at the spot where she and Haffie had sat. She felt in her pocket for the note he had left her. It read, 'I should dearly love to see you. Perhaps in Liverpool. Or in Edinburgh. But if you do not reply I shall understand.' He had written the address of the Haffie Refineries in Liverpool at the bottom of the page.

She had replied, but only to say she could not meet him. She had imagined many different replies. She had even imagined marrying Haffie and living somewhere remote, perhaps in the house he had painted. But every time she imagined this paradise, the hell of parting with Duncan engulfed her, for she was sure Ansdrie would insist Duncan stayed with him: he was his heir and, as a divorced woman, she would not be granted custody. So she could not meet Haffie for fear that her feelings would overwhelm her and cause her to lose her son. But she never stopped thinking about him, never stopped imagining a different life, with him.

Ansdrie, naturally, withdrew entirely. He spoke to her only to tell her he must have knocked over a coal-burner. He said no words would ever be able to express his sorrow. He became the man he had been when first he asked her to marry him: a man who spoke without feeling, if he spoke at all. And she had been so overwhelmed by sorrow, anger and disappointment, and her desperate imaginings of a possible life with Haffie, that she had little to say to her husband. They had spent the months since Hogmanay enclosed in their own unhappy worlds, worlds so far apart that even the dark shadows they cast never met.

Her father had left a letter for her. He told her that making over the money to Lady Bridewell had been the most foolish, thoughtless, wrong-headed action of his life. He regretted it more than she would ever know; he would regret it for the rest of his life. But he never thought Lady Bridewell capable of putting his money to such venal use for he had written the promissory note in the spring of the year Natalie met Lieutenant Haffie and, by that summer when he realized how things stood, he had told her he would not force his daughter to be party to their agreement and he planned to write off the money – as he had done much later that year – for he knew Lady Bridewell would never be able to repay it.

He told Natalie he knew she might never be able to forgive him and he signed his letter, 'Your foolish, foolish Papa.'

Natalie read the letter with a mixture of anger that he should have attempted to arrange a marriage for her without consulting her; incredulity at his naïve belief that Lady Bridewell would not put his money to any use she thought might further her cause and sorrow that he felt ashamed of their status and had taken such desperate steps to improve it.

She had not replied to him but, on this spring morning as she watched Duncan standing beneath a large beech tree whistling and calling in imitation of a starling beyond the blackened ironwork of her orangeries, she knew that, despite her feelings, she must at least acknowledge her father's letter, for she no longer wished to hurt him. She only wished to keep her distance until she could be civil towards him, until she could find it in her heart to stop blaming him for all that had happened.

The starling had begun to respond to Duncan's fluting, innocent calls and as Natalie listened to the sounds her well of sorrow filled to the brim and she had to look away. And then she felt something brush against her hand. She turned to see her husband. Was that a tear on his cheek, sparkling in the spring sunshine?

'I need to talk to you,' he said. 'A letter from your father has come.'

When she did not reply he turned from her and she stood, listening to her son and the songbird, saddened by his innocent joy.

'I . . . I thought,' said Ansdrie, at last, 'before I found you, here, at Hogmanay . . . I thought you had run away with him.'

At this Natalie turned and her husband put his hand, tentatively, on her arm. She asked what her father had written.

'He has found Seville orange groves, in California. He sails to inspect them in April. He would like me to sail with him if . . . I can tolerate his company.'

'Oh,' said Natalie. 'He must have been very lonely these last months.'

'He wants to try to put things right,' said Ansdrie. 'At least the things he can put right. He will buy the orange groves for us; they'll give Ansdrie Preserves a new beginning. And Haffie has agreed to provide the sugar, if the groves prove suitable.'

'How can Haffie possibly want to have anything to do with . . . any of us?'

'I don't know. But apparently he is willing.'

Natalie looked at her husband. It was the most he had said since Hogmanay. He took off his hat and ran his hand over his head, but the hair that so often would not be per-suaded to stay against his head stayed there obediently. He was no longer a proud heron. Natalie put her hand on his arm and said, 'If anything can be rescued from the ashes, it may be this. When shall you sail?'

'On 10 April, from Southampton.'

At that moment Duncan ran to them, calling, 'Did you like it? Did you like the song?' His cheeks glowed. 'I thought it would make you happy.'

'It was beautiful, Duncan,' said Natalie. 'So beautiful it made me cry.'

Duncan looked at her uncertainly, and then, when she rubbed her hands together in the cold air he said, 'Put them like this, Mama, under your arms. Mr Brown says it's the warmest part of the body.'

She copied him to humour him, but when she discov-ered he was right she thanked him. And when they were back inside, handing their coats and hats to Arthur, Duncan said, 'Oranges grow all over the world, don't they, Papa? Mr Brown told me.'

'In point of fact you are absolutely right,' said Ansdrie. 'I sail to inspect some Spanish oranges in America, next month.'

'Can I come too?' said Duncan.

'We shall be gone for more than two months,' said Ansdrie, doubtfully. But when Duncan pleaded he said, 'If Mr Brown will prepare your schoolwork,' he looked at Natalie, who nodded, 'and you promise to work hard while we are away, perhaps you might.'

'Hooray!'

'But we must also ask your grandfather,' said Ansdrie.

'Will you come too, Mama?' said Duncan.

'No,' said Natalie, thinking, desperately, that she would

see Haffie while they were gone. They would never know and it could not hurt. She put her hand on Duncan's head. 'I think your papa is the best person to decide whether the orange groves are suitable. After all, it is his business.'

That afternoon Natalie wrote to her father. She began the letter many times, cried many times and tore up many versions. Sometimes she became too angry to continue. But eventually she wrote, simply,

29 March, Ansdrie House

My dear Papa,

When you return from America please come to Ansdrie and we shall talk, sensibly. I promise I shall not shout. And, despite everything, please know that I do not hate you, and I thank you for your continuing efforts on behalf of Ansdrie Preserves. I know my husband will do everything in his power to make this new venture a success.

And if you have no objection, Duncan will accompany Ansdrie to London in April and sail with you. He deserves to enjoy himself, away from here. We have been very gloomy since Hogmanay.

With my love,
Natalie

She sealed the letter and rang for Anderson before she could change her mind, again.

'I shall write,' said Ansdrie.
'And so shall I,' said Duncan.
They stood on the platform at Ansdrie Station. Nurse Mackay and Verrinder had instructed the porters and taken their own seats, and then the whistle blew.
'Have a happy Easter with Grandfather,' said Natalie

as she hugged her son. Then she watched them board the train but when Ansdrie turned back and mouthed, over Duncan's head, 'Wish me luck,' she reached for his hand and squeezed it.

The whistle blew, steam puffed from the chimney, the coupling rods lifted and the wheels began to turn. And then Duncan was at the window, pulling it down and waving a piece of paper at her. 'I almost forgot,' he said. 'I made this for you.'

'Thank you,' said Natalie, taking the paper.

As the train pulled out of the station she waved until she could see nothing more than a smoking dot in the distance. When she turned away she saw she held a drawing of a large, many-decked steamship with four funnels. Duncan had drawn it carefully: his grandfather in his Homburg, his father in a boater and himself waving his cap from the ship's rail on a forward deck.

His grandfather and his father were almost as tall as the funnels and he was twice the height of the ship's rail.

Birds flew above the ship and waves rippled beneath it and among the waves Duncan had written, in his neat hand, 'She has a rudder as big as a giant elm and propellers the size of a windmill. She is the largest moving object in the world.'

TWENTY-EIGHT

NATALIE WROTE TO Haffie, in care of the Haffie Refineries in James Street, Liverpool. It was a short, non-committal letter. She simply asked if they might meet, after Easter, and would he recommend a hotel where she and Hocks might stay. She marked the envelope *Private* and posted it herself so that no one would discover she had written to him. She told Hocks they would spend two or three days in Liverpool because, she said, she wanted to be certain of the best hotel for Lord Ansdrie and Sir Thomas when they arrived home from America.

'And I am sorry, Hocks,' she said, 'that the date of your wedding has had to be changed. But it was necessary for Verrinder to travel with Lord Ansdrie.'

'We can wait a little longer, my lady,' said Hocks. 'It's no trouble.'

'Perhaps you'll have a summer wedding.'

Hocks smiled. 'That would be most welcome, my lady.'

Haffie replied by telegraph, perhaps so that his hand-writing would not be identified. He recommended Trials Hotel in Castle Street and said he would meet Natalie in the restaurant there on Friday 19 April. Natalie's hands shook as she read the telegraph. She would have to think of something to tell Hocks. Or perhaps she would send her out on a shopping errand with so many things to buy that she would be away until late. She imagined what the hotel might look like; what the restaurant might look like; how it would be to enter a restaurant on her own; where they would sit and most of all, what they would say to each other.

She spent the intervening days doing her best to distract herself. She discussed the greenhouses that would replace the orangeries with Hoxash, a task she had been putting off because she found the blackened ironwork so terrible to look at. But now she was feverish with ideas and enthusiasm and she wanted the work to begin just as soon as possible. She rode Artemis across the park and up into the Formonts. She did not push her hard the way she had when they were both much younger, for Artemis's joints were not as supple as once they had been. But riding proved not to be the distraction she hoped for: her mind flew back to the man she had surprised in the river when they had been so much younger, and she imagined and re-imagined their meeting in Liverpool. So, instead of riding, she kept herself busy in the kitchen, overseeing Mrs MacAlasdair's preparations for the Ansdrie Fair. She took her turn kneading the dough for the bannocks and she read detailed letters from Marina Robinson, whose advice she had asked about the stocking of her greenhouses.

On the first morning of the week she was to travel to Liverpool she woke, troubled, from a dream. Duncan swam in a wide river, or perhaps it was a large lake, but she, knowing that he could not swim, called desperately to him to come out of the water, to come back to her. But he would not pay her any attention. He splashed and dived and frightened her by not surfacing for minutes on end, and then he would resurface with a gasp, a smile and a shake of his head that sprayed drops of water all round him. But she knew, with absolute certainty, that he must come out of the water if he were not to drown and so, when he refused to heed her, she waded in.

Her skirts grew heavy and impeded her progress and then, in her desperation, she plunged forwards into the cold water. Her hat floated away and immediately she was beneath the surface, beneath Duncan's small, agile, naked body, knowing he could not swim, knowing she could not swim, and yet they were in the water.

The water was translucent and had a peculiarly curving quality: it supported them. Natalie could see and speak easily through it and she pleaded with her son to come back to the shore. She caught hold of his leg, and then one of his kicking feet, and always her body was just beneath his, even though she made no movement to keep it there. She pleaded with him over and over again to come out of the water, to come back to the shore. And then, when she thought her lungs would burst, he looked down at her through the water, his dark hair flowing like seaweed around his head, and said, 'Why should I come in, Mama, when you are here?'

And it was then she knew she must not tell him he could not swim. As long as he did not know, he would be safe. But her lungs began to hurt too much to allow her to stay beneath him. She knew there was a way to let water flow in and out of her lungs, but she could not remember it. And then she woke, gasping and frightened. She sat up and tried to slow her breathing. She coughed and spluttered just as if she had been underwater, and then switched on the lamp and stared at the photograph of Duncan that stood beneath it. She put on her dressing gown but just as she was tying the sash she remembered she could not reassure herself he was safe in bed, because he was not there. He was on board ship.

'Keep him, safe, Ansdrie,' she whispered, without really knowing what she was saying. 'Keep our son safe.'

The dream was so vivid that it came back to her several

times. Twice it made her cry when she thought about Duncan's innocent confidence in her, his belief that as long as she was with him he would be safe, and on the day before she planned to go to Liverpool the dream haunted her terribly. She would tell Haffie about it, about her fears that she might not see her son if they . . . He would know what to do. He would think for them both.

Later that morning, when Natalie stared out at her terraced garden and beyond it to the daffodils in the park, she shuddered. She had not been able to shake the cold her dream had brought on. She put her head into her hands and shivered. She stood to ring for Anna, one of the housemaids, to ask her to light the fire and, as she did so, Anderson brought in the newspaper. He put it on the table as he always did, but then he said, 'My lady . . . will I stay with you while you read *The Scotsman*?'

'I can read it perfectly well on my own, thank you, Anderson,' she said, startled into unintentional rudeness by his strange question.

'I apologize, my lady,' he said. 'But the newspaper boy told me there has been an . . . accident. The ship Lord Ansdrie sailed in has . . . it has been in a collision. There are reports, in the second-edition pages, that it has . . . sunk and—'

But Natalie had already rushed past him and torn open the newspaper. 'Where, Anderson?' she said. 'Where are the reports?'

She rubbed her arms as he found the pages for her and then she scanned the headlines so quickly that the words swirled chaotically together: SURVIVORS' TERROR; HOPE ABANDONED; TITANIC DISASTER; WHEN THE LINER WENT DOWN; A FAINT HOPE; LISTS OF SURVIVORS . . . lists of survivors. She must concentrate. Where were they? She could not find any Ansdries, nor could she find Edwardes on the list. Where *were* they?

An additional list of passengers was received by the White

Star Company last night.

But their names weren't there either.

'Anderson,' said Natalie, 'Anderson, what else do you know?' She held on to his sleeve without knowing that she did. 'What did the newspaper boy say? What's happened, Anderson?'

'The ship was in collision with an iceberg, my lady, late at night, on Sunday. It's still uncertain how many are saved. But several hundred souls are on board a rescue ship bound for New York.'

'Where can we find out more? How can I find out if . . . Duncan, the Master of Ansdrie, is safe? How can I find out . . . ' she tried to hold back her tears, 'if my . . . if Lord Ansdrie . . . if my son . . . if my f-father are saved?'

She held out the newspaper to Anderson as if, within its pages, he would be able to find their names where she had not. She walked up and down the room while he carefully read the small columns of newsprint but at last he straightened up and said, 'They are not here, my lady. Their names are not on the lists.'

He put the newspaper down on the table and Natalie put her cold hands beneath her arms, just as Duncan had shown her. And then she read the lists hectically as if her chaotic method would find the names of the men in her family where Anderson's methodical reading had failed.

At last she said, 'We must go to Liverpool.'

'We can send a telegraph to the offices of the White Star Line, my lady.'

'I must go there,' said Natalie. 'I must find out directly from the company what has happened. I cannot wait here.'

'Oh, my lady,' said Anderson. He raised his arms as if to comfort her and then dropped them as he said, simply, 'Shall I send for Hocks?'

'Yes, yes, please.' And then she turned back to the lists. 'Verrinder,' she said, 'and Nurse Mackay, and Stephens. We must look for them.' She shivered.

Anderson picked up the newspaper again and said, 'There are some sixty souls on this list, my lady. And another seventy-five on the other one. But there's a report that says more than eight hundred have been saved. Lord Ansdrie, the Master and Sir Thomas, and all the others, will surely be among them.'

When Hocks came in and Natalie asked her to pack, she said, 'But first you must look at the lists.' Anderson explained and Natalie said, 'You must see if the man you are to marry,' – Natalie stretched out her hand towards her lady's maid – 'you must see if his name is among the saved.'

She stood with her arm round her lady's maid's shaking shoulders as together they tried, in vain, to find Verrinder's name. Natalie felt a wave of sympathy for Hocks: she knew only too well what it felt like to wonder whether she might never see the man she loved again.

'We are going to Liverpool, Hocks,' she said decisively. 'And there we shall find them all, I know we shall.'

TWENTY-NINE

AT WAVERLEY, THE stationmaster told Hocks the next train south might not run for lack of coal. But when she tearfully explained why she and her mistress were travelling, he found them two seats on the next train to Glasgow, asked if they would mind travelling together and when Natalie said of course they would not, he sent a telegraph ahead for seats on whatever train had enough coal to travel south.

Natalie thanked him, her own tears hidden by the veil on her hat, and when they were safely Liverpool-bound Hocks said, 'If you wouldn't mind my saying, my lady, it's as if you knew about it, somehow. With us going to Liverpool already and the hotel booked.'

'It was very lucky, was it not?' she said.

Incredibly, she had not thought about Haffie since Anderson brought her *The Scotsman*. But now she saw his dear face so clearly in her mind he could have been sitting opposite her in the carriage, and it confused her. How was it possible to see his face so very clearly at a time like this?

'I don't know what I shall do if they are not saved,' she said. 'I keep imagining Duncan in the water, cold and frightened. And my father ... neither of them can swim, Hocks. They don't know how to swim.'

Hocks reached across the carriage and held out a

handkerchief, but Natalie took her hand instead and held it tightly. 'I keep thinking of my husband. And Mr Verrinder and . . . all those poor, frightened people.'

'We'll be there soon enough, my lady,' she said. 'Let us pray the White Star Company keeps open tonight. It'd be cruel if you had to wait until morning for news.'

'And for you too, Hocks,' said Natalie. 'It would be cruel for you too.'

The train pulled into Liverpool Exchange Station at five o'clock. Hocks found a porter, who hurried them into a horse-drawn hansom, gave the driver the address of their hotel and hailed a second hansom for their luggage. The hansom slowed down behind a group of women marching along the middle of the road. They held placards that read, VOTES for WOMEN, NOW! and at any other time in her life Natalie would have asked the driver to stop and let the women have the freedom of the road. But in her desperation to find out whether her son, her husband and her father were alive – as she said their names to herself she gripped the edge of the wooden door in front of her – she simply asked him to take another route. When they arrived in James Street he called down, 'The road's blocked here, too. You'd be better off on your feet.'

So Natalie and Hocks stepped out of the cab and onto the cobbled street. There were crowds of people ahead of them, but none of these were suffragettes.

'We'll find a way through, my lady,' said Hocks.

Natalie saw that the people, men and women, all stood outside the same building and all were leaning forwards, looking in the same direction. It must be the White Star Company's office.

'Not through them, Hocks,' she said. 'With them. We'll take our turn. They are looking at the lists of the saved, I'm certain of it.'

The crowd was sombre and many women held large

white handkerchiefs to their faces when they turned away from the lists towards a husband or a friend. When Natalie and Hocks reached the front of the crowd Natalie could barely look, but Hocks repeated the names to herself as she read them and then, with feverish speed, Natalie read and reread the names but she could not find her father or her husband and, most terrifyingly, she could not find her son. Her throat constricted and her mind became incapable of thought. All she could do was repeat the names of the men and the boy who made up her whole family, her life, as if, by invoking them, their names would appear in front of her on the lists.

She put her hand on her heart. She felt faint. She kept repeating their names and then Hocks said, 'Here, my lady. Here is Margaret Mackay.' She was staring straight in front of her. 'She will not have left the Master's side, you can be sure of that.'

Natalie watched Hocks's forefinger underlining the handwritten names and then she looked up quickly and tugged at a drawing pin that hid the first part of a name at the very top of the list. 'Look, look, my lady! He is here,' she said and her hands reached for Natalie's. 'Look. Up here. He is here. The Master of Ansdrie is here.'

Natalie looked up and saw her son's name imprinted with the circular shape of the drawing pin that had almost covered it. She touched his name. She stared at it. And then a wave of dizziness engulfed her, her legs gave way and she swooned.

She did not know that Hocks caught her, nor that there was a disturbance at the top of the steps that led to the White Star Company's offices as several men tried to make their way down through the crowd with more lists of survivors. She did not know that they lost their position in front of the lists nor that Haffie was one of the men at the top of the steps, nor that he now stood in front of her. But when she regained consciousness she found that she was sitting on a wooden bench several feet from the White Star Company's offices, beside Hocks.

'What happened?' she said.

'You fainted, my lady,' said Hocks. 'But here is Lieutenant Haffie. He has found out everything.'

Natalie stared up at Haffie. She could not believe she had not conjured him from her fevered imagination. But he was there: Hocks had said she could see him.

He said, 'Lady Ansdrie, I am so very glad to find you. I telegraphed Anderson. He said you would be here. I asked after Ansdrie and your son and Nurse Mackay. I asked after your father and Stephens and Verrinder. I . . . but perhaps you have seen the lists?'

'We have only found Margaret Mackay and the Master,' said Hocks. 'Is there more news?'

'There is,' said Haffie, and Natalie held her breath.

'Lord Ansdrie is saved,' he said, 'and Verrinder. They are on board the rescue ship.'

'Oh,' said Natalie, 'oh . . .' And then she twisted her hands together and began to cry again. And when Hocks touched her the two women cried in each other's arms as they had never done in all the years they had known each other.

'You shall be married, Hocks,' said Natalie, through her tears. 'Your Verrinder is saved.'

'And you, my lady, shall see Lord Ansdrie and Master Duncan returned to Fife.'

When Natalie turned back to Haffie she did not see him but instead, through the swimming film of her tears, she saw the face of her husband looking down at her. He smiled tentatively, just as he had smiled when he said, 'Wish me luck,' at Ansdrie Station. She stretched out her hand towards him and then she blinked and when she blinked again she realized she was standing up and Lieutenant Haffie was holding her outstretched hand. She let go and said, 'And my father. Is there any news of . . . h-him? And Stephens?'

Hocks also stood up and the steadily sinking sun spread its orange-red glow along James Street from the Mersey.

'I am very sorry for it,' said Haffie, 'but I have not found any news of them.' He took off his hat and held it in both his hands. 'But they may still be saved. The rescue ship arrives at New York tomorrow. Ansdrie will surely send news just as soon as he can.'

'Yes, yes he will,' said Natalie.

But her heart was in turmoil now and she said to Hocks, 'Do you think you could find our hotel and unpack our bags? There are arrangements I must discuss with Lieutenant Haffie. I shall follow you very soon.'

'Castle Street is just a little way up,' said Haffie, lifting his walking cane and pointing beyond the White Star Company building. 'Through the crowd; turn left at the top.'

If Hocks was surprised that Haffie knew where they were staying, she did not show it. All she said was, 'Thank you, sir,' and turned in the direction he indicated.

When she had gone Natalie asked Haffie to walk with her to the little square that opened out on the other side of James Street, away from the crowds. And then, as the sun sank slowly behind the Mersey, she said, 'I was coming to Liverpool to tell you,' she looked down at her feet, 'before the sinking . . . I. . . .' She made herself look up at him. 'I was coming to tell you that I . . . cannot love you, Angus Haffie. I hoped, at Hogmanay, that I could. I have hoped for the last three months that I could find a way to love you without causing terrible heartache to my – to our – families. But I know now that I cannot. I . . . cannot.'

The mournful hooting of a steamship's whistle echoed up James Street as Natalie walked a few steps away from Haffie. She stopped by a young ash tree and, when Haffie stood beside her, he put his hand gently on her arm. She turned back to him.

'Cannot because you must not?' he said, looking down

at her. She could feel his breath on her cheek, so close was he to her. 'Or cannot because you do not?'

Natalie turned away from him and as she did so the image of Ansdrie as he waved to her from the train returned to her mind. His expression, so full of hope that this venture might save their house and so their marriage, filled Natalie with a tender, sorrow-laden affection. It was not the passionate love of kindred souls, not the deep, heart-rending love she felt for the man who stood beside her, but a love that acknowledged the hurt she had caused and wished she had not. A love that understood her own weakness and her husband's vulnerability. An accepting, loyal love for the man who had loved her and made it possible for her to hold her head up in the world when she thought she never would again. A gentle, sympathetic love for the man with whom she had rebuilt a house and to whom she had borne a son; a grateful love for the man who had stood by her no matter what.

Natalie took a deep breath, and looked back up at Haffie. 'Cannot,' she said, 'because I do not.'

Natalie and Hocks left Liverpool as soon as they could.

Natalie could not bear to remain near Haffie, but neither could she face returning to Ansdrie House until she had absolute proof that her son and her husband were alive. She would only return when she could see her son in his bedroom, safely tucked into his bed, or in his schoolroom with his books and his constant questions to Mr Brown; when she could see her husband's kind face.

She sent a telegraph to Ansdrie care of the White Star Company offices in New York. She said she was so very thankful to hear they were safe. She said she would stay at Hey Tor House and wait for more news. She wanted to be in her father's house, in his rooms, in the rooms where they had laughed together, talked together and read together, the rooms she had known since childhood. She had an idea that if she were in his house she would be able to communicate with him, somehow, and she so desperately wanted to communicate with him for she had discovered her letter, unopened. It must have arrived after he left for London and now all she could think about was the cruelty of the last things she had said to him.

She sat in her father's study and imagined the door opening, imagined herself flying to him and telling him how sorry she was for everything she had said, and how very much she loved him. And he replied, 'There you are.' And, 'That's my girl.' And, 'By my lights, it does me good to see you.'

The following morning Hocks brought Natalie a telegraph. She had slept in her old bedroom at Hey Tor House and, for a moment when she woke, she knew there was something she longed to tell her father, and then she remembered, with a thudding heart, what had happened.

The telegraph read:

Thank you yours darling N + STOP + Duncan, Mackay, Verrinder and I all safe. Sir Thomas and Stephens may be lost + STOP + So sorry + STOP + Duncan very courageous + STOP + Will write when more news Sir T and S + STOP + With my love Ansdrie + STOP +

'The telegraph boy is waiting downstairs, my lady,' said Hocks. 'Will you reply?'

'First you must look at this, Hocks,' said Natalie. 'See, there, his name. Verrinder is safe.'

'Oh, my lady,' said Hocks. 'How lucky we are. I have heard so many were not saved.'

'I think perhaps my father is among them,' said Natalie. 'And Stephens. Please ask Mrs Stephens to come up. I must tell her.'

'And what shall I tell the telegraph boy?'

'Say, "Hug Duncan tightly." And, "It will be wonderful to see you." And send something to Verrinder, Hocks, please do.'

In the days while Natalie waited for news of her father she walked in his park and on the moor and once, on a fine spring day, she climbed Hey Tor. She did not have the heart to ride any of her father's horses, but always she spoke to him and told him how sorry she was for the things she had said, for not giving him a chance to speak. On the third day there was another telegraph from Ansdrie. It confirmed what she had dreaded: only those who had been in the lifeboats had survived the night in the freezing north Atlantic. The bodies of Sir Thomas and Stephens had not yet been recovered.

Two weeks later letters came. Natalie read hers in her father's study and the tears poured down her face. Duncan's letter had been written by a serious young man, not the ten-year-old who had left Ansdrie. He talked of pulling on a large oar with his father in the lifeboat. He wrote, *I suggested we should sing. I thought it would keep us in good spirits.* He described his relief when he found Dubhe in the night sky, *the star that points to the guiding star.* The same words her father had used when he taught her, the words she had used when she taught her son. He wrote, *It was a comfort to know where we were. The able seaman said a rescue ship would come from the south and once I'd found Dubhe I knew we rowed south. There were hundreds of stars, Mama. Some of them were almost in the water. I knew only a few of their names.* He said he thought of her and talked to her in his head. And Natalie remembered her dream: she knew now, from the newspaper reports, that the night she dreamed of her son was the night *Titanic* sank, the night Duncan spent in the lifeboat.

She held the letter to her breast and tipped her head back to drain away her tears. She longed for him to be home. She longed to hug him tightly, to feel his warm, small body against hers. She cried again when she read,

The worst part was the people we had to leave behind. We had to leave Grandfather. He said he wanted to help as many women and children as possible into the boats. Stephens said he would stay with him. They wore their evening dress, Mama. They looked excellent.

The officers said women and children had to go first. Papa was allowed to come in our boat because he knows about boats and he told the captain that Verrinder knew how to row too, even though he does not. When Titanic *went down I could not look, but I heard the screams, Mama. And I can still hear them. Papa says they will go out of my head soon. But we could not go back. The other people in our boat said they would not go back, even though the people in the water were screaming and crying.*

We are safe now. Papa keeps saying that. And we'll be on board the Mauretania *before this reaches you. I want to see you very very much and I am so glad you didn't have to suffer it, Mama. Papa says that often, too. I shiver if I think about it. It was very cold. But I hope I shall not think about it too much when we sail for home.*

Your very loving son, Duncan.

There were none of the drawings that so often accompanied his letters. This was the letter of a child who had seen and heard things children should never have to see or hear. Natalie longed to cover his eyes, his ears, to hold him and shut it all out.

Ansdrie's letter told her how proud she must be of her son, how he never showed the fear he must have felt and how he rowed until he was exhausted. *I tried to stop him, but he would not be stopped.* He wrote that there were not enough lifeboats for all those on board, and that he had been reluctant to board a boat himself, but there were not enough crew for the boats either so he let Sir Thomas persuade him, for the sake of the other passengers. He promised to look after Duncan with his life and then he wrote about her father's selflessness and his care for the women and children. How he was calm and kind and ushered the frightened people to the boats. How he persuaded them their husbands would be on later boats. *Although,* he wrote, *when we saw her sink I knew they would not. But Sir Thomas did all he could, with never a thought for himself. He was kind and he had reassuring words for them all.*

Natalie's eyes swam with tears.

Ansdrie wrote that the last he saw of her father, he and Stephens were calling, with the officers, for more women and children to come forward. And then he turned and raised his hand to them as their lifeboat was lowered, and he never saw him again.

The last thing he said to me, dearest Natalie, was how very much he loved you. And he asked to be forgiven. So, I hope I did the right thing by you, my dear: I said I knew you would forgive him.

Natalie could not read any more.

She stood and stared through the window towards Hey Tor. It was a clear spring day. The moor was green and Hey Tor was a friendly grey. Small white clouds hung in the sky and wild daffodils stood in clumps of bright yellow in the park. Her father would have thought it a good day for a walk, or a ride, but she could only stare through her tears and wish he stood beside her.

And then she heard the high-pitched, laughing call of a woodpecker. She bent to lift the lid of the window-seat to find her father's field glasses, just as he so often did, but she never saw the woodpecker, for in the cavity beneath the window seat was a large, rectangular parcel wrapped in creased brown paper and addressed, in her father's bold hand, to her. Should she open it? Why had he never given it to her?

She sat with the parcel beside her for a long time, the field glasses and the woodpecker quite forgotten. And then, at last, she opened it. The paper was dry and broke easily. The string left dusty marks on her fingers. It must have been under the window seat for a long time. And then, under her hands, was one of Haffie's watercolours and painted neatly onto the frame beneath it, was its name, 'Kilmalieu House, Bright Day.' It was the house in the place he said he loved above all others; the house she had seen on the day she thought he would kiss her, the day Ansdrie had marched her from the Academy and proposed to her.

With shaking hands Natalie picked up the wrapping paper and began to fold it, but it was stiffened with age and unwieldy. She let it fall to the floor and, as it did, an envelope slid out from between its folds. She picked it up and saw her name on it. She put it down behind her and then, apprehensively, picked it up again. She was not sure she could bear to know what this letter might tell her, for clearly it would be connected with Haffie. But if she did not open it, how would she tolerate knowing it existed without knowing what her father had written?

At last she broke her father's seal and opened the envelope. She spread the letter out carefully for its creases were deeply cut into the paper. She read, wide-eyed, the date, 5 July 1899, and then:

For you, my dearest daughter, on your betrothal. The house you loved, even before you saw it. May you be very happy when you stay there with your lieutenant and, more importantly, may I wish you a long marriage filled with love, happiness and children.

Your very affectionate, Papa.

PS: Haffie does not know I bought this painting, but I thought he would not mind having one of his own to hang on your walls.

Natalie stared, dry-eyed and shocked, at her father's letter, and then she looked back at Haffie's painting. She looked up at the door to her father's study and once more imagined him walking into the room; once more imagined telling him how sorry she was for her unkind words.

And then she said, quietly, but as if he really could hear her, 'On your dear life, Papa, I promise I shall never say anything in haste again. I shall not, ever, imagine I know all there is to know.'

THIRTY

Natalie waited under the white stucco portico of Hey Tor House. The rain poured down but she leaned out from under it, paying the rain no attention. She was listening for the sound of the station taxi. She heard the grandfather clock behind her chime twice, and then she heard wheels on the drive and erratic explosions from an exhaust pipe and, despite the rain, she picked up her skirts and ran. One of the footmen, who had been standing by with an umbrella, began to follow her but she was too quick for him and he gave up.

Natalie had waited three weeks for this moment, but it could have been three years. The taxi rounded the corner sooner than she expected and she jumped sideways. Her feet landed in the muddy grass beside the drive but she did not notice. The taxi skidded to a halt between her and Hey Tor House and the door opened. Ansdrie stepped out, his tall figure slightly stooped against the rain, and then Duncan was out of the car and Natalie ran towards him, tears streaming down her face.

'I am so glad to see you, *so* glad to see you,' she said as she took her son in her arms. 'I have not stopped thinking about you.'

She stood back and looked down at him. She saw that

he too was crying. He dashed his hands under his eyes and then he began to shake. She looked up at her husband, who inclined his head and indicated that he would get back into the taxi. And then Natalie caught her son up in her arms and held his shaking body in hers. She did not know that the taxi drove the last few yards until it stood in front of her father's white house. She did not know that Verrinder had run, quite uncharacteristically, in front of Ansdrie into the house to ask where he might find Miss Hocks, nor that her husband and Nurse Mackay stood in the hall for a good fifteen minutes among all those who wished them well and were so heartily relieved to see them saved. She did not hear Ansdrie seeking out Ada Stephens to tell her of her husband's courage, nor did she hear Chapman, her father's valet, say how it grieved him that he had let Stephens take his place on board *Titanic*, for his love of steamships. She only held her son as if to let him go would be to let him die. At last, he looked up at her, his cheeks wet with tears and his hair wet with rain, and he said, 'You were with me in the lifeboat, Mama. You came with me and you helped me.'

She hugged him tightly again and then, slowly, despite the teeming rain, they walked together, her hand on his shoulder, towards the house. When they stood beneath the portico Duncan said, stamping his feet on the ground, 'This is what I've been thinking of, Mama. Standing on the ground. Like this.' He stamped and stamped again. 'It does not move.'

When Ansdrie came outside and stood with them, Natalie took his hand and kissed it. And then she said, 'I think perhaps I have never been so glad to see you.'

In the week that followed, Natalie and Ansdrie planned a service for her father, but Natalie could only concentrate if Duncan was within eyesight or earshot, and preferably in the same room. But, very quickly, she realized she had no need to worry for he was as reluctant to stray far from her as she was to be apart from him. They had many conversations, usually at night when she sat by his bed. And one night she said, 'Many people live all their lives without having to go through what you have been through. They never have to be so brave, nor will they ever be so frightened.'

'I hear them sometimes, Mama. The people in the water. And I get cold when it's not cold. I dream about them. Does Papa have nightmares? I have not asked him.'

'Yes,' said Natalie. 'He does. Perhaps you could talk about it, together,' she said. 'Perhaps it would help you both.'

The day of Sir Thomas's funeral dawned bright and cold.

Ansdrie suggested they plant an oak tree in his memory, because there could be no grave. Natalie chose the place, not far from the wooden fence that separated the garden from the moor. It was sixty-five feet from Sir Thomas's study window, the height *Titanic* had stood above the water; the age her father had reached when he died. Withers, Sir Thomas's gardener, promised to collect acorns in the autumn and keep them cool in leaf mould. He would grow seedlings in the spring; he said they should come south when the plants were hardened off the following winter, or in the spring of 1914. Then they could plant the hardiest seedling together.

Natalie was walking back from the place she had chosen when she heard the sounds of cars and carriages arriving. She heard Millie and Étienne, Gussie and Edward and their children. They had come to Devon as soon as they heard, but whenever Natalie saw them it had always been at Hey Tor House for she had no desire to see Lady Bridewell. She heard Ansdrie and Duncan greeting them and then she walked round the side of the house herself, lifting her long black veil to greet them.

They had decided to walk down the hill to St Petroc's, for Sir Thomas loved walking. Natalie, Duncan and Ansdrie led the procession, Natalie carrying seven white arum lilies from her father's garden, one for each decade of his life. Her Aunt and Uncle Goodwin followed. Then came Millie and her family and Gussie and hers, then friends, acquaintances and colleagues from Edwardes Tea and, finally, all Sir Thomas's servants from Hey Tor House and those from Ansdrie, including Anderson and Mrs MacAlasdair, who had travelled south for the purpose. They made a sober procession beneath the clear blue sky.

The moorland granite of St Petroc's gave it a forbidding appearance but inside, beneath the pale-oak barrel-vaulted ceiling, by the intricately carved wooden arches that lined the nave, Natalie felt at home. She put the lilies in a vase by the pulpit and the vicar led them in prayers for those lost at sea, and for Sir Thomas's soul. They sang *The Day Thou Gavest, Lord, is Ended* and, after a reading, they stood to sing *On Ilkley Moor Baht 'at*, which only the choir, who had practised, and Natalie, who knew it from her father, could sing. And then she stood to read the piece she had chosen for him, a piece by Henry van Dyke that suggested a ship was death itself transporting her passengers to a happier shore. But when she reached the last part, when the ship was about to disappear over the horizon and:

> *Someone at my side says, 'She is gone.'*
> *But others watch her coming.*
> *Other voices take up a glad shout:*
> *'There she comes!'*
> *And that is dying.*

her voice faltered and only by force of will did she manage to speak the last words.

And then Duncan, his dark hair shining, walked to the chancel step quite alone. He turned, lifted his chin and sang *For Those in Peril on the Sea* a capella and solo, as he had insisted he would. He had sung it beside his grandfather on the last Sunday on board *Titanic*. Natalie looked at Ansdrie through tear-filled eyes and silently thanked him for the gift of their son. He reached for her hand and squeezed it, and then he stood to read his tribute.

'Sir Thomas Edwardes was a modest, straightforward and selfless man,' he said. 'Not only in his conduct in the last terrible hours aboard RMS *Titanic*, but all his life. He was also, I think, quite unaware of the effect he had on the people he met. I discovered, through my father-in-law, that the divisions between us mean very little. It was he who showed me that trade, let alone the taking up of a trade myself, was a thing to be celebrated. "How," he once asked me, "do people like you think the things you love to have about you would ever end up in your houses without trade?"

'At the time I thought him vulgar, but I was quite wrong. In point of fact Sir Thomas Edwardes was a man ahead of his time, a man ahead of our time. When his grandson, our son, is sixty-five, a time when many of us will be where Sir Thomas, God rest his soul, is now, the barriers that divide our society will have fallen. Sir Thomas showed me the truth of that through his gentle good sense. He also showed me that to admit a mistake was a courageous and not a shameful thing.

'I salute him for his good sense, and for his courage. I salute him for his selflessness on the night RMS *Titanic* sank. And I salute him for making Edwardes Tea the success it has been for the past thirty years. And there is a corollary: if not for the success of Edwardes Tea, Sir Thomas would never have bought Hey Tor House whose land, as most of you here will know, marches with that of Waverton Court. If we had not become neighbours, I should never have met my wife.

'Thank you, Sir Thomas, for all you meant to each and every one of us, and most especially to your daughter, Natalie Ann. May God rest your soul.'

They knelt to pray and then Ansdrie took Natalie's arm and she took Duncan's hand and they walked down the aisle while the organist did his best with Elgar's *Nimrod Variation*. When they were almost at the low, arched west door Natalie turned towards the last pew. She had seen a figure she recognized. And then she saw, clearly, an elderly woman in a long dark veil, who stood and turned quickly away, but not before Natalie recognized the angle of her head, tipped just slightly to the right.

'Your mother,' she whispered.

Ansdrie walked towards Lady Bridewell, quickly. He took her arm although she tried to resist and when they stood together outside in the bright sunlight, Natalie said, 'Thank you for coming.'

'It was the least I could do,' said Lady Bridewell. Her voice held none of its old command, indeed it sounded as if she had been crying. 'He was a good, kind, honest gentleman,' she said.

'Will you come back to Hey Tor House?' said Natalie.

She heard an intake of breath behind her. It was Millie. She turned to smile at her.

'I would be ... very grateful,' said Lady Bridewell. 'Thank you.'

Despite their state of mourning Natalie and Ansdrie insisted Verrinder and Hocks should make arrangements for their wedding, for, as Ansdrie said to Verrinder when all four of them stood in the drawing room at Hey Tor House, 'We must grasp every opportunity. We can never know what lies ahead and we must hold on to those we love.' He shook hands with Verrinder and congratulated Hocks. 'We shall expect you at Ansdrie when we arrive, in ten days' time.'

Natalie added her encouragement. 'Sir Thomas would not think it wrong,' she said. 'In fact I think he would positively insist upon it.'

It did not occur to Natalie not to change for dinner, but she struggled without Hocks. She opened the door to the bathroom to call out to Ansdrie, and he emerged from the other side with his sleevelinks and shirt studs in his hand.

'I cannot,' she looked away, feeling foolish, 'I cannot do up my dress.'

'Nor I my shirt,' said Ansdrie. 'Should we send for one of your father's servants?'

'That's not how you described my father's vision of the future,' said Natalie. 'I'll help you with your shirt and you shall help me with my dress.'

Ansdrie put the sleevelinks and the shirt studs on Natalie's bed and stood beside her. 'What should I do?' he said.

'You put the buttons through the loops and then you hand me the ends of the sash.'

'Almost as tricky as tying a fly,' he said.

Natalie turned back to him. 'Now,' she said. 'What should I do?'

'The longer stud is for the collar, the shorter one for the shirt.'

'Ansdrie,' said Natalie, as he handed her the silver studs and she fumbled with them and his collar, 'I think you blame yourself for Papa's death. And you think I blame you, but I do not. No one could have known what would happen.'

'That is kind, my dear,' said Ansdrie. 'But you are right. I shall never stop blaming myself.'

'Will you try not to?' said Natalie. 'Please?'

When she took her husband's sleevelinks from his hands she realized they were the ones she had had made for him on their engagement. She looked at the Ansdrie buckled belt and the Edwardes fleur de lys nestled inside it. She put the sleevelinks through the holes in the white cuffs of Ansdrie's shirt and then, glancing at his unhappy face and smiling in an attempt to reassure him, she turned back to look at herself in the glass. She decided all she could do with her hair, since she had let it down, was to leave it down. She would not attempt the complicated arrangements Hocks made. She brushed her hair and tied it at the nape of her neck with a piece of black velvet ribbon.

When they were ready she said, 'It is a little ridiculous that we never do these simple things for ourselves. It is no more than my own mother did for my father before Edwardes Tea became such a success.'

'We shall learn,' said Ansdrie.

After dinner Natalie went to say goodnight to Duncan. She told him how proud his grandfather would have been of his singing and he said, 'I'm looking forward to going home now.'

'So am I,' she said, as she kissed him. 'So am I.'

When Natalie and Ansdrie sat together in the large airy drawing room, Ansdrie, who had expected every day since he had arrived back in England that his wife would tell him she wished to leave him, said, 'Your father would have been proud of you today, and of his grandson.'

'And he would have been very proud of you, my dear,' she said.

She crossed the room and sat beside him. He took her hand and resolved to tell her what he must tell her before he asked her about Haffie, for he must ask her if she continued to say nothing.

'I must tell you about your father's will.'

'There is no need,' she said, 'if you are tired.'

'I think I should tell you,' said Ansdrie. 'For it is not what you might expect.'

'Then tell me,' said Natalie.

'There is nothing except Hey Tor House and Hyde Park Gate in your father's estate.'

'Nothing else at all?' said Natalie.

'Nothing,' said Ansdrie. 'He told me, one evening while

we sailed, that he had emptied his bank account, sold all his stocks and shares, including those in Edwardes Tea, and put the proceeds, in cash, in the ship's safe.'

Ansdrie watched his wife, but her expression betrayed no anxiety.

'But that safe now lies on the seabed.'

Natalie was silent for some time, and then she said, 'Did he tell you why he sold it all?'

'For your sake. He said he might be a good business-man but he was a very bad judge of character. He told me he was ashamed of his behaviour. He planned not only to buy the orange groves, but to build a house for himself in California. He said he would begin a new business. He was thinking of a Marconi franchise. He said he would make a new start and leave whatever he made to you.'

Ansdrie took a sip of brandy. 'But when I saw your Uncle Goodwin, he told me there was no insurance on your father's life or possessions. Goodwin thinks he must have had complete faith in the safety of the ship.'

'So,' said Natalie, after another silence, 'what should we do?'

'If you can tolerate it,' said Ansdrie, 'Goodwin advises us to sell this house and Hyde Park Gate, and if we cannot make a go of Ansdrie we may have to sell it too.'

'I can tolerate it,' said Natalie. 'And we shall teach Duncan to tolerate it, if necessary. The only important thing is that you and our beloved son have survived. We shall live well without the money and the houses for they do not breathe or speak or sing or . . . love.'

Ansdrie took a swig of brandy to steady his nerves. Then he took his wife's hand in his and looked at her. When her dark blue eyes focused on his he took a deep breath and said, 'I had much time to think, in the lifeboat, and I resolved that, should I survive, I would release you from our marriage. For when tumultuous things happen we find out what it is we truly feel.' He looked away. He had not meant to but he could not face her when he said, 'And you may have found out that you no longer wish to remain married to me.' He swallowed. 'As long as you allow me to see Duncan from time to time, I would not trouble you.'

Natalie remained silent for so long that Ansdrie had time to imagine, not for the first time, what his life would be like without her and he could hardly bear the idea. When she stood up he turned back to her and saw the tears filling her beautiful eyes. She had obviously decided.

'You are a kind and courageous man to say such things, Ansdrie. But I have . . . ' she turned away from him and he saw a few strands of grey in her pretty dark hair. He stood and stretched out his hand towards her, tentatively, then withdrew it. 'I have also been thinking about us,' she said, 'about our marriage. Very much.'

She turned to face him.

'And I should like, if you . . . could, if you would . . . if you think it possible, to stay at Ansdrie, or wherever we may live. I should like to stay with you, my husband. I should like . . . to begin again.'

That night Natalie had a dream.

A metal safe plummeted through water. Air bubbles streamed from behind its door but when the safe hit a rock on the seabed and the door flew open, hundreds of large, white five-pound notes swam out, their edges flowing up and down as if they were flat rectangular fish. The safe held an infinite number of notes, which streamed into the dark water for a long time. But when, at last, the supply was exhausted, Sir Thomas's desk floated without difficulty through the small door of the safe, and then his barometer, and the piano Lily Ann used to play, and the generator at Hyde Park Gate, and then sacks and sacks and sacks of tea stamped with the Edwardes Tea insignia.

And Natalie knew, in her dream, that these things would remain lost at the bottom of the sea for ever. But instead of wishing them back, instead of wanting her father's fortune for herself, she felt light, happy and relieved as she floated easily back up to the surface without any of those valuable things to hold her down.

THIRTY-ONE

ON THE TRAIN on the way back up to Scotland, Natalie planned what she would write to Edwina Haffie. She would tell her she wished she had written sooner. She would write:

> *'I shall never be able to apologize adequately for the way I behaved at Hogmanay. It was unforgivable and I do not ask for your forgiveness. I only want you to know that I am more sorry than I have ever been for anything I have ever done. I hurt you and I wish with all my heart I had not.*
>
> *Natalie Ansdrie.'*

Several days later a letter from Edwina arrived. She was staying at the Ansdrie Arms; she asked if she might come to Ansdrie.

Natalie could hardly refuse for she was so very close; she had obviously made a particular journey. But when they both sat in her morning room, she was convinced that the words she spoke were transparent and would never hide the feelings that filled her. They drank tea. They talked of the unusually dry spring weather. Neither woman mentioned her husband or asked about the other's. They drank more tea and Edwina said she was sorry to hear about Sir Thomas. She said, 'But it must have been a great relief when you heard Duncan was saved.'

'It was. But the waiting was terrible.'

But the way she felt for Haffie was behind every word Natalie spoke. Her guilt, her confusion at the eruption of her love for him and a sense of loss now that she faced Edwina – to whom Haffie rightfully belonged – for the life she might once have lived. She blushed to think Edwina could see it all.

They fell silent, and then they both spoke at the same time.

'I am so very—'

'I should like to tell you—'

Both women rose from their chairs, and then each faced the other, awkwardly. Natalie waited for Edwina to speak; Edwina waited for her. Then Natalie took a step towards Edwina and said, 'I am so very sorry for everything that happened. I admire you for coming here. You are . . .' but she could not continue, for, quite unexpectedly, she began to cry. She turned away and then she felt Edwina's hand on her arm. She made herself look at her but she could not control the tears that slid down her cheeks.

Edwina seemed to hesitate and then she lifted her arms and Natalie saw that she too had tears in her eyes. They faced each other for a moment and then Natalie took another hesitant step forwards, lifted her own arms and the two women embraced.

'I should never have danced with your husband the way I did,' said Natalie. 'It was selfish and thoughtless and very unkind.' She breathed in Edwina's lemon verbena scent.

'Ssshhh,' said Edwina, and Natalie felt like a child in her arms. 'Ssshhh.'

'I should have stopped.'

'I saw that you could not. I know how that feels.'

They stood back from each other. 'You are remarkable,

247

Edwina,' said Natalie. 'I'm sure I could not say such a thing if . . . if—'

'I think you could,' said Edwina. 'For you are strong, and your heart is kind.'

At this Natalie cried again and then they turned towards the large bay window where Natalie's desk stood, the window that overlooked the terraced garden and the parterre below it.

'Would you like to walk a little?' she said. 'Perhaps fresh air would be . . .'

She turned to Edwina and saw her staring at something. She followed her gaze to the drawing Haffie had made of her. She should have put it away. She hated herself for her carelessness. She had fetched it from a trunk in the attic, after Hogmanay. She meant to put it back when they returned from Devon, but she had not.

Edwina picked up the drawing and said, 'You were very young.'

'Eighteen,' said Natalie.

Edwina held the drawing towards the light. At any moment she would see the miniature pair of cupped hands Haffie had drawn, for his signature. Perhaps, because her husband had not signed his name, Edwina would not know his work. Natalie put out her hand to take the drawing from Edwina, to put it into a drawer away from them both, but Edwina said, 'Do you wear a gentleman's jacket?'

'I was not wearing one that day,' said Natalie, but she would not lie. 'I wore one on the day we met.'

'Angus made a drawing of me when we were at Puako. But this is . . . is . . . kinder. It's very touching, very . . . beautiful.'

'Please, Edwina,' said Natalie, 'let me put it away.'

But Edwina held the drawing close to her and said, 'I'm glad I have seen it, for now I know how he saw you. Now I know how he felt, for you.' Her sing-song tone gave a poignant emphasis to her words. 'You did not dance alone at Hogmanay, Natalie. My husband danced with you.'

Edwina held out the drawing again and then she put it carefully back on Natalie's desk. She said, looking steadily at Natalie, 'When Angus came to Puako it was clear he had a broken heart. And I knew, even when I married him, that if we came back to this country I should meet the woman, one day. Only I did not think . . . I could not have known . . . how strong the feeling would remain, between you.'

'I did not know, either,' said Natalie.

'But you see,' said Edwina, 'the only reason my heart beats is because he is in the world.'

'Edwina,' said Natalie. 'Please, Edwina. . . .' She gestured for them to sit down, but still they did not. 'Please believe me when I say that since . . .' She stopped and began again. 'I intend to be as true to my own husband as I am sure you have always been to yours.'

Edwina looked at Natalie, and then she nodded. 'I do believe you,' she said. 'And from my heart I thank you.' She reached for Natalie's hand and they faced each other, calmer now, and eventually they did go outside. They walked through the terraced garden and Edwina rubbed a lavender flower between her fingers. 'We had a neighbour on Kaua'i who farmed lavender,' she said. 'Every time I caught the scent of it I thought of my mother's garden.'

'Did you miss Scotland?'

'Sometimes. But we left when I was very young so my memories were few.'

As they became less uneasy with each other Edwina began to tell Natalie about her life in the Sandwich Islands, about her parents, who had taught at the missionary school, and how she followed in their footsteps.

'I loved the children. They called me *malihini ehe ene.*'

The words sang.

'It means "the visitor who laughs",' said Edwina. 'They were happy times. The children made me laugh because they laughed, all the time. And they treated me as if I were one of their own.'

They walked on through the park and into the beech wood, whose floor was a brilliant carpet of green bluebell leaves.

'We hunted for the *pu*,' said Edwina, 'the shells that hold particular meaning for the people who live on Kaua'i. And we cut down the *mailé* vines. They made the best *leis*.' She looked at Natalie. 'I didn't stop teaching when I married Angus, but I have not looked for teaching work since we came home. Although I think, if I . . . if we do not . . . I think perhaps I shall look for teaching work again.'

'If you do not . . . ?'

'Have children,' said Edwina. 'Have you never thought of giving Duncan a sister or a brother? Is he not lonely?'

'Since Duncan was born,' said Natalie, staring at the bluebell leaves, 'I have never been able to hold on to a child.'

'Oh,' said Edwina, quickly putting out her hand to take Natalie's. 'I am so very sorry.' The expression in her grey eyes was full of compassion. 'I should not have asked. But I assumed, because of Duncan . . . but that is thoughtless. I too have not been able. . . . ' she took a deep breath, 'I cannot hold on to my children either. And I suffer from the bleeding disease, the royal disease some call it, and that makes it all the more complicated.'

'No woman can understand what it is to miscarry,' said Natalie, 'unless she has miscarried herself. I felt utterly bereft. And I was certain my miscarriages were a punishment.'

'All those lost little children,' said Edwina.

The two women looked at each other with sympathy and something bordering on affection. Natalie was astonished by the transformation in her feelings since Edwina had arrived. She said, gently, 'I thought only men suffered the royal disease.'

'It seems I'm a rarity,' said Edwina. 'My father was a

haemophiliac, so the doctors think I must have inherited it. I sometimes have nosebleeds. My blood vessels are weak.'

For a moment, Natalie was transported to the ballroom on that terrible night. She heard Haffie asking for ice. With an effort she forced her attention back to Edwina, who was saying, 'If I should ever give birth I might lose too much blood,' she said. 'So it is, perhaps, a blessing that I have not.'

'Even so, nothing can make up for the loss,' said Natalie. And then, as they walked by the Leven, she said, 'When we were in my morning room, you said, "I should like to tell you . . ." but I never gave you the chance to say what it was.'

'I have said everything,' said Edwina. 'You made it possible.'

The river flowed fat and lazy where they stopped to watch it and Natalie knew it would soon be the mayfly season and Duncan and Ansdrie would fish there, but she did not say so to Edwina. She would not speak of Duncan when Edwina had no children at all. And then Ansdrie rode upriver towards them. He tipped his hat to Edwina and greeted her, but it was clear he was surprised to find her still at Ansdrie.

The two women turned and walked up through the park and into the gardens, stopping now and then to admire a plant or a tree. When they reached the blackened ground where Natalie's orangeries had been she said, 'Ansdrie had an idea we should plant an oak in memory of my father. We were going to plant it at Hey Tor House, but now we shall sell my father's house so I brought some of his acorns here. I thought an oak would look very well overlooking the place where once my orangeries stood. I hope we shall be granted the time to see it grow.'

Edwina gave Natalie a quizzical look.

'It may be that we have to sell Ansdrie, too.'

'Should you mind?'

'Not for myself. But for Ansdrie and for Duncan I should. It would mean so much to my husband if he could make a success of something that would support this house. It would restore his confidence and justify everything my father taught him. He very much wants to leave Duncan a proper inheritance but if it should not prove possible, we shall not starve. We are lucky. We have a house to sell.'

'You are very sanguine,' said Edwina.

'The loss of Duncan would have been far worse,' said Natalie. And then, 'Oh, Edwina, I'm sorry.'

'Don't be. It's true. And I'm glad you said it. I'm tired of people trying to remember not to talk about their children in front of me.'

They crossed the southern terrace and walked into the house through the French windows that led onto the small hall where once Ansdrie had said the house needed kindness. Perhaps the kindest thing would be to sell it to someone who could afford to take care of it.

'Will you stay?' said Natalie. 'I should very much like it . . . if you would.'

'Yes,' said Edwina, 'I should like to,' and so her bags were sent for and when the three of them sat in the drawing room after dinner that night Edwina said, 'I have heard that, among fighting men, the most unlikely people become friends.' She smiled and the two long dimples appeared in her cheeks. 'Do you think it might prove the same for us?'

Two weeks after Edwina left, when Natalie and Ansdrie were reading their letters at breakfast, Ansdrie looked up and said, 'Millie writes that Mama is wasting away. She will not eat or drink anything, except water. Millie thinks, if we could bear it, that a visit to Ansdrie would cheer her. She says Mama's only conversation is of the house. She talks endlessly of the loss if it should be sold, as if, Millie says, she talked of a lover.' Ansdrie looked up. 'Millie thinks if she sees us still living here she might rally.'

'But we know we may have to sell,' said Natalie.

'The house means more than anything or anyone has ever meant to my mother,' said Ansdrie. 'If it would restore her strength, would it not be kind?'

'Yes,' said Natalie, 'it would. But she has done terrible things in the name of—' She looked up and Ansdrie saw her irritated frown, her dark eyebrows lowering over her fine eyes. And then he saw the frown clear from her face when she said, 'Oh, let her come if you think it would help. She cannot do any more harm.'

'Thank you,' said Ansdrie. 'I'll do my best to keep her out of your way.'

But Lady Bridewell never did see Ansdrie House again.

A week after Millie's letter, Millie herself arrived from the station with her lady's maid, her mother's lady's maid and all their luggage, but without her mother.

'She died of a heart attack on the train,' said Millie. 'I found a doctor, who said he thought it had been quick, but I think she was in great pain. The expression on her face told me so. I wish I had been with her when she was in the grip of the attack.'

'I think your mother was in great pain often,' said Natalie, as she took Millie in her arms. 'But it was not the kind of pain any doctor could have taken away.'

A month later Ansdrie burst into Natalie's morning room and said, 'It seems our fortunes have turned, again.'

'How?' said Natalie, turning to face him.

'I have just had a letter from your Uncle Goodwin. He writes . . .' Ansdrie sat down in a chair by Natalie's desk and held out a letter. 'It's almost unbelievable, my dear. He writes that a gentleman wants to put money into Ansdrie Preserves. He will put up funds to buy orange groves and to cover the costs of re-establishing the business. You see? I told you it was almost unbelievable.'

'Someone is making fun of us.'

'I don't think so. Your Uncle Goodwin has looked into it all most thoroughly.'

Ansdrie waved the letter, as if it were proof of the integrity of the gentleman.

'There are a few stipulations: one, that Haffie and I must resurrect our partnership.' He looked at Natalie but her expression did not alter. 'Two, that the business should be run along co-operative lines so that all those who work in the company are given shares commensurate with their contribution; three, that the benefactor must remain anonymous and, four, that half a per cent of the net profits be paid to him when the business begins to make a return, which, he suggests, should be within five years.' Ansdrie looked up. 'What can we have done to deserve this?'

'I cannot think,' said Natalie. 'Will you do it?'

'If you should not mind me approaching Haffie. And if he will agree. And if we can make it all make sense.'

'I don't mind,' said Natalie. 'But you must make sure Edwina does not mind either, before you do anything.'

'I'll ask her. Or perhaps *you* should ask her; she is sure to tell you the truth.'

Ansdrie realized that in his excitement he had almost forgotten to breathe. He stood and walked the length of Natalie's morning room and back, breathing deeply, and then he sat down again. 'Your Uncle Goodwin writes that he was approached by the benefactor's solicitors. He says he should like to see Ansdrie Preserves give Keiller's a run for their money.' Ansdrie put the letter down on Natalie's desk. 'That's what your father said.'

'Perhaps the benefactor *is* my father,' said Natalie. 'Perhaps he always planned this but never wanted us to know.'

And so it was that Californian orange groves were secured and Haffie Sugar was shipped directly to them from the Sandwich Islands. Receipts were tried and tested in

Mrs MacAlasdair's kitchens at Ansdrie and sent out to the Californian manufacturers and, despite several set-backs and disappointments, the first shipment of Ansdrie Preserves marmalade arrived on the Clyde in the spring of the year 1914 and Ansdrie was able to arrange delivery to one hundred Scottish groceries.

In the intervening two years Ansdrie had seen how very much at ease Edwina and Natalie were becoming and he followed their lead and found an equilibrium with Haffie that he had not known since first they trained at Fort Humberston at the end of the century before. The four of them spent many a Saturday-to-Monday together, occasionally talking of the business that Haffie and Ansdrie ran from the Haffie Refinery offices in Liverpool, but mostly they talked of the things that interested them. They heard the news of Captain Scott's failed Polar expedition and agreed that, despite the failure, Scott was a true hero and, in the summer of 1913, Natalie and Edwina drove the Haffies' new four-seater French touring car from Carlisle to London to help the exhausted suffragettes on their long pilgrimage.

But there were people in other parts of the world whose sights were set upon something that would have far greater consequences than the burgeoning friendship between these four people for, on 28 July 1914, the Austro–Hungarian Empire declared war on Serbia.

Part Four

1916–1918

The year 1914 broke up the Edwardian world, but
in the agony of losing husbands and sons, no one
realized that it had gone for ever.

Anita Leslie, *Edwardians in Love*

Round me at twilight come stealing,
Shadows of days that are gone.
Dreams of the old days revealing
Memories of love's golden dawn.

Memories, memories . . .

recorded by John Barnes Wells, in 1916
lyrics by Gus Kahn (1915)

THIRTY-TWO

ANSDRIE HOUSE HAD been a quiet place since the end of 1915.

Ansdrie himself, and Haffie, had boarded a troop ship bound for France with the Waterfirth Reservists towards the end of the year. Verrinder joined up and became servant to both Ansdrie and Haffie, and all the male servants at Ansdrie, of fighting age, had obeyed Kitchener's call and volunteered. Natalie wished with all her heart there was something useful she could do, apart from limiting the amount of work her women servants did on her behalf and encouraging them to join Ansdrie Preserves, for it offered them better wages and a share in the business.

On a dreich February morning she opened a letter from the Fife Director of the Red Cross. He wrote that there was a great need for auxiliary hospital accommodation for convalescing soldiers, and might he come to talk to her about Ansdrie House becoming such a hospital? She only wished she had thought of offering the house to the Red Cross herself and, by the summer of 1916, the dining room, the drawing room and the ballroom had all been converted into large wards. Some of the bedrooms were converted into smaller wards and Natalie and Hocks trained as VADs. Edwina also trained, but her much longed-for pregnancy meant she would not nurse any returning soldiers until the following year.

To Natalie's great surprise and even greater pleasure, Edwina's confinement had progressed without difficulty, but she had written to ask Natalie if she might come to live at Ansdrie. 'I would feel safer if I were in a hospital,' she wrote.

'Of course you must come,' Natalie replied. 'I shall see if I cannot discover something of midwifery before your time comes.'

The first convoys of soldiers arrived in August. Matron James told her nurses and VADs they would not see the worst of the wounded this far north. 'But,' she said, her black eyes boring into the women who stood before her, 'you'll not be idle.'

Natalie was touched by the meek, uncertain way the men looked about them when they climbed down, or were brought down on stretchers from the transports. So many of them were so young; only four or five years older than Duncan. She wanted to comfort them all, as if they were her own sons, and she was moved by those with haunted eyes and those who jumped at the slightest sound. There was one young officer, who was no more than twenty-five, whose head jerked repeatedly as if he relived a surprise attack every few minutes.

Natalie and Hocks, the sisters, the nurses and the order-lies who came with the transports escorted the men to their wards. Several were amputees and some of their wounds needed fresh dressings. Quickly and efficiently they recorded the names and conditions of the patients, settled them in their wards and began to treat them. But Natalie knew Edwina's enforced idleness gave her time to worry about her husband so, whenever she could, she sat with her and they read and reread their husband's letters to each other and talked of happier times when the war would be over.

Natalie, Edwina and Hocks knew their husbands were

forbidden to tell them when they would move up the lines but each time their letters confirmed they remained behind the lines, they breathed private sighs of relief. But then, in the middle of July, they began to read reports of the casualties in a valley called the Somme, and when they read the lists and found the names of officers and men of the Waterfirth Reservists there, Natalie forbade Edwina to read any more. She said she would read the lists for her and put a note under her door while she took her afternoon rest. She would write 'All's well,' and only if all was not well would she wake her.

Duncan proved himself a capable assistant to Hoxash in the vegetable garden when he was not away at school, but Natalie watched them with sadness in her heart: the young boy and the old man left behind to grow the food they needed, together, reminded her of the generations between them who were no longer at home but fighting and dying for the sake of that home.

By October, Edwina was heavy with her child.

'You must not lift the coal scuttle,' said Natalie, walking into her morning room and hurrying towards the fire.

'I'm carrying a child,' said Edwina, 'not an infirmity.' But she laughed, and gave in and Natalie put the coal on the fire.

'Shall I fetch you another cup of raspberry-leaf tea?'

Edwina laughed, again. 'If you must,' she said. 'But I think I've drunk enough to keep this child safe for a century.'

'You would be quite large by the end of the century,' said Natalie.

She went downstairs to the kitchen and put the kettle on the stove. She breathed in the sweet smell of yet another of Mrs MacAlasdair's preserve receipts and hoped the German U-boat blockades would not put an end to the business, although she and Edwina had already decided to sell Ansdrie Preserves only on the American continent if the time came when ships could no longer cross the Atlantic.

On her way back across the hall with a plate of drop scones and Edwina's tea, Natalie met Doctor Harrison. He had just finished his ward rounds.

'All seems to be going very well, my lady,' he said.

'Matron James is a wonder.'

'But . . . have you, ehm, been in the coalhouse, my lady?'

'No,' said Natalie.

'Then may I suggest you keep your fingernails hidden from Matron James?'

Natalie looked at her hands, saw the coal dust beneath her nails and blushed at her incompetence. 'I will,' she said. And then, 'You are prepared to attend Mrs Haffie when her time comes?'

'Indeed I am. I'll take blood from her just beforehand and Mrs MacAlasdair will store it in the ice house.'

'And you'll take blood from me, if necessary?'

'I have promised Lieutenant Haffie that I will,' said Doctor Harrison. 'And now I promise you that I will.'

Natalie took the plate of drop scones, which were strewn with cream and honey, into her morning room. It was the only room – apart from Ansdrie's study, which had become their dining room – that they used now. She gave Edwina her cup of raspberry-leaf tea and they ate the drop scones with their fingers. And when Natalie looked at Edwina, who had blossomed like one of her Belle Isis roses, she felt a rush of protective affection. She would see her safely through the birth of her child.

Natalie loved the night shifts. The men often needed little more than kind words, water and, in some cases, morphine so, in the early hours, she had time to read. But more than that, the warm, womb-like nature of the ballroom ward, the red-shaded lamp on the table where she sat and the sleeping sounds of the men made her feel safe, even though she was surrounded by evidence of a very great lack of safety.

She put her feet up on the only other chair and reread a letter from her husband. She heard a man in a bed at the far end of the ward calling to her. His voice was distorted by the terrible burns he had suffered. She stood and walked the length of the ward beneath the shrouded chandeliers. She knelt by the soldier's bed and saw his tears sliding towards his ear. He beckoned her to come close and when she did he whispered, 'When I'm discharged, nurse, and the wife sees me,' he moved his hand above his disfigured nose and the hollow where one of his eyes had been, 'she won't want to look at me. She'll never . . . want to look at me again.'

Natalie looked at him steadily. 'Well, Private McConnachie,' she said, 'I'm looking at you. I'm not turning away.' She sat down by his bed, keeping her eyes fixed upon his face. Private McConnachie grimaced, but Natalie knew it for a smile, the best his poor, ravaged face could manage.

'I'm still looking at you, Private McConnachie,' she said. 'And I will look at you for as long as it takes to convince you that your wife will do the same.'

Eventually, when he slept, she walked back along the ward. And then Captain Monteith began his haunting, repetitive refrain. 'They need me. I must go back for them.' And then, 'The men need my help. I must help them.'

A movement on the threshold of the ballroom ward made Natalie look up. Duncan stood there, listening. He was in his pyjamas and dressing gown. He had surprised them all by managing to find himself a seat on a hospital troop train. He wanted to spend his half-term at Ansdrie.

He walked into the ward and whispered, 'Couldn't sleep, so I came to keep you company.'

'Thank you,' whispered Natalie.

They sat at her table but Captain Monteith's voice grew louder and more and more distressed. At last Duncan said, 'Do you think I might be able to calm him?'

How could a fourteen-year-old boy comfort a soldier of twenty-three?

'I no longer know what to say to him,' whispered Natalie. 'I have tried, but he has seen things that are quite beyond my experience. How could you...?' And then she smiled and whispered, 'Yes, why don't you try?'

The officers' beds were screened off from the men's beds but Natalie heard what her son said to Captain Monteith.

'I think I understand,' he said, but his newly baritone voice was tentative. 'No, no, please don't leave your bed. What you see is in your mind, Captain Monteith. But I know how vivid that can be.'

'You are too young,' said Captain Monteith, echoing Natalie's own feeling. 'You have not seen what I have seen.'

'I have not,' said Duncan. 'But when I was younger, I was in a lifeboat. Our ship sank and people were drowning in the water behind us. They called out for us to save them, but we dared not go back. We would have risked the lives of everyone in the lifeboat if we had.'

While Duncan spoke Captain Monteith kept saying, 'They need me. I should have gone back,' but his voice was growing less agitated.

'I still hear those people sometimes,' said Duncan, 'in my mind. And the only way I can square my conscience with them is by remembering what my father said. "We shall endanger more lives if we return. We must not go back."'

There was silence in Captain Monteith's cubicle for a long time, and then Duncan said, 'You might have endangered more lives if you had returned for your men, Captain Monteith.'

There was another, blessed silence, and then Duncan said, 'You faced an impossible choice. I know how difficult it is to forgive yourself for the decision you took. My father suffers still. And, sometimes, so do I, even though it was not my decision.'

'You mean well,' said Captain Monteith, 'and I thank you. But you can never know what it is I see.'

'No, I cannot,' said Duncan. 'But there must have been men whose lives were saved because of what you did.'

'There were.'

'That's how I tell myself to think about it now.'

After a few more moments of silence Natalie heard a sob, and then Duncan said, 'I cry sometimes, too.'

Natalie's eyes filled with tears at her son's kindness, at his maturity, at her sadness that she had not thought his terrible experience might live on in him. When he emerged from Captain Monteith's cubicle Duncan avoided his mother's eyes, but she stood and whispered, 'That was brave, Duncan. You should do my work.'

He nodded, gave a tired smile and sat down by the night table.

Natalie began to read Ansdrie's letter. Duncan did not speak. Ansdrie wrote that most of the shrapnel had been removed from his leg. He said the whole company was resting behind the lines for a few days. He said it had been so cold that everything, even their kilts, had frozen, but lice hated ice and the ever-resourceful Verrinder had found some foie gras and brioche to celebrate the taking of Beaumont Hamel. He asked to be remembered to Hocks and he asked Natalie to tell her what a stalwart and imaginative servant Verrinder was. He wrote, and this part of the letter Natalie read over and over again with a smile of pride on her lips and a shudder of fear in her heart:

The Hun have given us a nickname. They say, die Damen aus der Hölle *took Beaumont Hamel. My dearest Natalie, the Fifty-First Highland Division has become a (female!) force to be reckoned with and your very own husband in his capacity as Lieutenant commanding First Platoon, A Company the Waterfirths has, apparently, undergone a transformation that could not have been anticipated.*

I have written to Duncan also. I have told him all about it. —She looked up at her son, who was lost in thought— *One good thing about a stint in a field hospital is it gives me time to write letters.*

I'll write again soon. I think of you often. And I see I'm not the only one to have undergone a transformation. The photograph you sent, in your VAD uniform, was with me in the German trench when we surged along towards Beaumont Hamel. It was with me when I felt the punch in my thigh. It was with me when they brought me to the field hospital. It will remain with me, always.

With my very fondest love, Ansdrie.

Duncan stood up and yawned, then bent towards Natalie and kissed her lightly on the forehead. Natalie squeezed his hand. 'Papa is away from the front, for now at least. But he's been in the thick of it.' She prayed that the war would be over before Duncan, who was clearly so proud of his father, had to follow in his footsteps.

After Duncan had left, Natalie dozed fitfully, until a voice woke her.

'Ansdrie,' said Sister Maclean, from the threshold of the ward. 'Mrs Haffie is calling for you. I'll take over here.'

Natalie stood up. 'What is it?' she said.

'Get a move on, Ansdrie,' said Sister Maclean. 'Haffie's baby is coming.'

THIRTY-THREE

P ALE WINTRY SUNLIGHT streamed through the windows and lit Edwina's contorted face. Natalie ran to her and said, to Doctor Harrison, 'How close?'

'Not long now,' he said.

Edwina dug her nails into Natalie's forearm and her body arched upwards. When the pains let go she said, breathlessly, 'I didn't expect . . . this amount of pain. Was it the same for you?'

'Duncan didn't make it easy,' said Natalie. 'Breathe as deeply as you can.'

Edwina grimaced and gripped Natalie's arm again.

'Only a few more pushes, Mrs Haffie,' said Sister Macready. 'You are almost there.'

And then, miraculously quickly, Edwina gave birth to a little girl.

Sister Macready clamped and cut the umbilical cord and cleaned the child. She wrapped her in a flannel sheet and a soft white blanket and when she handed her to Edwina, Natalie realized that Edwina's tears were not the only ones in the room; she was crying too. She unwrapped the child's sheet and blanket for a moment and said, 'Look, Edwina. Look at your perfect little daughter. All ten toes, all ten fingers and such beautiful grey eyes. She is the most perfect little girl in all the world.'

Edwina leaned back against the pillows and kissed the top of her daughter's head. Natalie held a handkerchief to the tears of relief and exhaustion that ran down Edwina's cheeks. She wiped her own tears away with the back of her hand while Doctor Harrison asked Sister Macready to fetch Edwina's stored blood. But Natalie was so absorbed in the newborn child that she did not take in what he said.

'Thank you for letting me stay here, Ansdrie,' said Edwina, her long dimples making deep creases in her cheeks. 'I have felt safe.' She reached for Natalie's hand. 'But it's difficult to believe she's really here, is it not? I don't want to let her out of my sight. Ever.'

Natalie laughed and said that would be difficult, when she was older. And then she said, 'Why am I crying?'

'Because it's exhausting,' said Edwina, 'this giving birth.'

'For you,' said Natalie.

'For all of us,' said Edwina. 'And it's exhausting trying not to think about our husbands all the time.'

'Congratulations, Mrs Haffie,' said Doctor Harrison, cleaning his hands on a disinfected cloth and taking a large wooden box from Sister Macready. 'You did very well.'

'You were brave,' said Natalie. 'Braver than I remember being.'

'Our daughter is healthy and well,' said Edwina. 'Nothing else matters.'

'But now,' said Doctor Harrison, 'I need to give you some blood.'

Doctor Harrison took the lid off the large box and Natalie said, 'Shall I take her, Edwina? Will you trust her to another pair of hands?'

Edwina laughed and handed her child to Natalie, who walked round to the other side of the bed and sat by the window.

Sister Macready said, 'If you will allow me, Mrs Haffie, I'll give you a massage. It will be a little painful but it'll slow the flow of blood.'

'The midwife did that,' said Edwina, 'when I . . . before, in the times when I miscarried. It always helped.'

'That's the spirit, Mrs Haffie,' said Doctor Harrison.

'Everything is all right, isn't it, Doctor Harrison?' said Edwina.

'Nothing to worry yourself about,' he said, as he attached a rubber tube to the top of a small glass cylinder full of blood. The cylinder stood in a wooden compartment inside the large box, beside another identical cylinder; both were packed in ice. Doctor Harrison attached a syringe to the end of the tube and said, 'I should look away, if I were you,' and he put the needle into a vein in Edwina's arm. As her own blood began to replace the blood she had lost giving birth, she turned and said to Natalie, just as if they were sitting in the morning room, 'We agreed to call her Holly for the bright red berries on the trees when Angus was last on leave. And I shall call her Hope for . . . for now. For the time she's been born into.'

'Beautiful names,' said Natalie.

'I'll write to Angus just as soon as I can,' said Edwina.

They looked at the sleeping child and talked about when Haffie might first see her and then Edwina said, 'I'm the luckiest woman alive.'

When the second cylinder was empty, Doctor Harrison said, 'Lady Ansdrie, would you . . . ?' He indicated what he wanted her to do and, with a happy smile, Natalie put Holly into the little cot beside Edwina and walked to the end of the bed. But when she looked she had to work hard to control her expression for, despite Sister Macready's massage and Edwina's new blood, the dressings were soaked. Natalie frowned at Doctor Harrison and he asked Sister Macready to remove the syringe and the equipment, and came to look.

'Is there much blood?' said Edwina.

'Only a little,' said Natalie, valiantly.

But the 'little' blood was seeping out from the sides of the dressings and, when Doctor Harrison looked beneath them, Natalie saw Edwina's blood pumping out in slow, regular spurts. For a moment she was too frightened to think, but then she said, quietly, 'Doctor Harrison, can we give Edwina my blood?'

'Yes,' said Doctor Harrison, in a low voice. 'Wash your arm with carbolic, my lady.'

Natalie did as he asked and then she sat on the chair by Edwina. Doctor Harrison inserted another needle attached to another rubber tube into the vein in her arm, and she watched as her blood began to cling to the sides of another small glass cylinder. When it was almost full he inserted a second needle into Edwina's arm. It took him several moments to find another vein but all the time Natalie smiled at her and reassured her.

'Breathe deeply,' said Doctor Harrison, 'both of you. And count your breaths. It will distract you.'

Sister Macready sat at the end of Edwina's bed and, from time to time, she looked up at Doctor Harrison and shook her head. But then, at last, she smiled and nodded and he said, 'It's beginning to work, Mrs Haffie. It's beginning to work.'

'Thank you, Ansdrie,' whispered Edwina, and then she laughed, softly. 'Why does it always make me laugh?'

'Because it's funny, Haffie.'

After almost two hours, when Sister Macready had changed Edwina's dressings and reported that the blood flow had almost stopped, Natalie let out a whoop of joy.

'You can add lifesaver to your list of accomplishments, Ansdrie,' said Edwina.

'A very successful procedure,' said Doctor Harrison and he withdrew the needles from their arms. But when he had packed his bag, and the wooden box, and instructed Edwina to remain in bed for at least a week, she said, 'I feel very cold, Doctor Harrison. Is that because,' she shivered, 'because of the new blood?'

'Put some more bedclothes over Mrs Haffie, would you please?' said Doctor Harrison, and while Sister Macready and Natalie covered Edwina, he put his hand on her forehead and then he took her pulse. Edwina continued to shiver despite the blankets and the eiderdown, and Natalie saw Doctor Harrison's anxious expression.

'I . . . I think I know what's happening,' said Edwina. 'I feel numb. Is it. . . ? I can't feel my hands.'

'Doctor Harrison!' said Natalie, in an urgent whisper. 'Please. Tell us what's happening.'

'The transfer of blood may not have worked,' he said, simply.

Holly Hope moved in her cot and Natalie saw her tiny mouth open. She lifted her out. She turned to Edwina, who tried to hold out her arms, but they shook too much and she could not. Gently, Natalie put Holly Hope beside her mother. She wriggled a little but she remained asleep. Edwina held out her hand and Natalie grasped it. She said, with many shivering pauses between her words, 'I think it has not . . .' She stopped and then she said, 'Will you look after Holly? As if she were your own?'

'Ssshhh,' said Natalie, but her heart was beating wildly. 'Don't say such things. Remember what Haffie said. He's seen blood transfers in the field hospitals.'

'Field hospitals,' said Edwina. 'Yes.' And then her eyes lost their focus and she began to murmur words Natalie could not understand. And then she said, clearly, 'Among fighting men . . . the most unlikely people become friends.'

Edwina's shivering grew worse and worse and her hand, in Natalie's, was so cold that, instinctively, Natalie blew her own warm breath onto it. Edwina's lips began to turn blue and, as she mumbled and murmured, Doctor Harrison said, very quietly, to Natalie, 'We don't know why this happens, my lady. But sometimes it works and sometimes it does not.'

'Why . . . didn't you tell us?'

'Mrs Haffie knew.'

And then Edwina said, very clearly, 'Tell Holly how much I longed for her. Tell her about me.'

Her songbird intonation was unbearably poignant now that her voice was so weak. She gave Natalie a faint smile but her long dimples looked like wounds and Natalie bent down to hold her as her breathing became uneven.

Doctor Harrison felt Edwina's pulse and listened to her heart. He signalled to Sister Macready to help him and between them they lifted Edwina and moved her down the bed. Doctor Harrison took Edwina's wrists in his hands, pulled her arms behind her head and then he folded her arms and pressed them down onto her chest. He did this several times but Edwina's breathing remained very uneven and when, at last, he looked up he said, 'Your bloods have reacted badly together, my lady. I am so very sorry. There is nothing more I can do.'

Natalie touched Edwina's face.

She could not take it in.

Sister Macready stood by Doctor Harrison, ready to take over from him, but he turned to her and shook his head and together they moved Edwina back up the bed.

Holly began to cry and, automatically, Natalie picked her up and put her on her shoulder. Edwina had stopped murmuring, but now she did not seem to be breathing at all and, as Natalie soothed Holly, she stared down at the pale face of the woman who, from such unlikely beginnings, had become a dear friend.

'There must be *something* you can do, Doctor Harrison,' said Natalie.

But he just shook his head and now Edwina lay on her bed, very peacefully, and, when she failed to take another breath, a stillness filled the room, which even Holly seemed to feel, for she stopped whimpering and lay, quite motionless, on Natalie's shoulder.

'I'm . . . so very sorry, my lady,' said Doctor Harrison.

'I wish I had known this might happen. I wish . . .' Natalie looked down at Edwina. Doctor Harrison felt one last time for Edwina's pulse, shook his head and gently closed her eyes. But Natalie willed her to open them. She had been alive only a moment before. She had a daughter to live for. And a husband.

'We should not have done this,' said Natalie.

'It was her only chance,' said Doctor Harrison.

Natalie steadied Holly Hope's little body against her shoulder. She rubbed her back with her hand. She watched Sister Macready put a rolled towel beneath Edwina's chin and talk to her as she washed her, calling her Mrs Haffie as if she were still alive. And then she motioned to Natalie, but Natalie could not bear to pull the sheet over Edwina's face. She stared down at her friend as Holly Hope's crying grew loud once more. And then she turned and took Holly from her mother's room.

On her way down the stairs she met Hoxash. He climbed the stairs slowly. He held two china cachepots and said, 'The bulbs you asked for, my lady. They'll be beautiful in the spring.'

But he stopped when Natalie shook her head.

'Put them in my morning room, please,' she said. 'Mrs Haffie . . . is not . . . is. . . .' She tried to stop the quivering in her lips. 'Mrs Haffie will never see them now.'

A wet nurse arrived for Holly Hope and Natalie tried to compose a letter to Haffie. She began several times but she could not think how to tell him the joyful and the terrible news. She began a letter to Ansdrie but could not finish it, either. And then she realized it would be kinder to tell Haffie face to face. She began a new letter to Ansdrie and asked him to tell Haffie what had happened when next he saw him.

The squeak of a bicycle made her stop writing.

She hoped, as she always hoped, that the boy brought only the newspapers and not a telegraph. She walked into the hall, thanked him when he handed her the newspapers and, without waiting to watch him pedal away, she turned to the casualty lists. She ran her finger down the names of the officers and the names listed under other ranks. She stopped holding her breath when she was sure that her husband, Lieutenant Haffie, Private Albert Verrinder and the Ansdrie servants were not listed. She returned to her morning room and, automatically, took a piece of paper from a pigeonhole in her desk.

She wrote, '*All's well,*' picked up the note and pushed her chair back, but halfway across her morning room she stopped and stared at the words she had written.

She dropped the note and a wracking sob tore itself from her breast.

THIRTY-FOUR

DUNCAN WHEELED CAPTAIN Monteith along the drive. His mother wheeled another officer beside him while several more officers and men, some in bandages and slings, some on crutches, walked nearby, their feet making crunching sounds on the frozen ground. Matron James ordered fresh air every day and no one dared disobey her, whatever the weather.

Hoar frost clung to the branches of the beeches and the leaves of the rhododendrons drooped darkly. Robins sang and Duncan shivered. He put his hand on his mother's arm. He knew how desolate she had been since Mrs Haffie's death and he longed to take her sadness away but he felt powerless to do so. She told him he helped immeasurably but he wondered if it was true. Their Christmas and his mother's birthday had been quiet, sad affairs; the only lights in her darkness, she said, had been him and little Holly Hope.

Duncan looked up and saw a man at the far end of the drive, an officer whose kilt swung as he walked. He was followed by a porter from Ansdrie Station pulling a cart with two bags on it. The officer's appearance filled Duncan with admiration and envy. He harboured a terrible guilt that he was not yet fighting: his only comfort was the

Officer Training Corps at school. At least he was preparing himself.

He turned when he heard his mother gasp.

'It's Lieutenant Haffie,' she said.

He looked at her and saw the tears on her cheeks. He said, 'I'll stay here with the officers, Mama. You go to him.' He felt ashamed that he did not know what to say to a man whose wife had died. He watched his mother take a handkerchief from her uniform pocket. She blew her nose and then walked quickly towards Lieutenant Haffie. He asked Captain Monteith and his fellow officer to help him take them back to their wards. They complied willingly, propelling themselves faster than he knew they could. Obviously they longed for the comparative warmth of the house, just as he did.

That afternoon Duncan, his mother and Lieutenant Haffie stood by Mrs Haffie's grave. His mother laid a branch of holly on the snow-covered mound of earth, its bright red berries and shining green leaves cheering the desolate corner beneath the yew.

She said, turning to Lieutenant Haffie, 'We did not know how soon you would be able to come. So we decided we must bury her.'

The fine white streaks in her hair were the same colour as the snow.

'You did the right thing,' said Lieutenant Haffie. 'Thank you.'

He put his arm round her and she put her head on his shoulder and they stood for some time, looking at the grave, looking at the holly, looking at the wall of the chapel. Duncan heard the Corrie Burn rushing away beyond the chapel. He stood just behind them. He thought they had forgotten him.

'I wish with all my heart my blood could have saved her.'

'It was a brave thing to do,' said Lieutenant Haffie. 'But

it does not always work.' He breathed out. 'Even so, we thought it worth the risk; Edwina longed for this child.'

'Why didn't you tell me?'

'We didn't want the burden of . . . what might happen, the possibility that it might not work, to be yours.'

Duncan took a step towards them and his mother turned and held out her hand. They stood together for some time in silence and then Duncan said, 'If you'd known, you would have worried, Mama, just the way you're worrying now. But because you didn't know, you didn't have to worry.'

'Just so,' said Lieutenant Haffie.

'We thought we were blessed every time we read the casualty lists,' said Natalie. 'We . . . I . . . never thought of . . . this.'

And then she began to cry. The sounds she made were terrible, as if her heart were breaking.

'I'll not forget your friendship to Edwina,' said Lieutenant Haffie. 'She said, often, how happy it made her.'

And then a terrible sound came from him. He groaned the way a mighty stag groans and Duncan watched, petrified, as his body bent with grief. He watched his mother put her hand on his back, still crying herself, and then, after a little while, she said, 'A pretty sight Edwina would think us,' and Duncan laughed. Lieutenant Haffie laughed too and said, through his tears, 'A pretty sight, indeed.' He took a large handkerchief from his greatcoat and offered it to Natalie and then the three of them walked slowly back across the terrace and into the house.

That evening, after dinner in his father's study, Duncan was proud to stay behind with Lieutenant Haffie. It was the first time he had drunk port. He said, 'If velvet were liquid, it would be port, don't you think? Excellent drink.'

The port had gone to his head but he did not mind; in fact he liked the feeling, for it made him a man. He asked Lieutenant Haffie about the campaign at Beaumont Hamel.

He heard how his father had attacked a German soldier who would have killed Verrinder. He burst with pride. And when they walked towards his mother's morning room he said, conspiratorially, 'Be prepared, Lieutenant Haffie. Mama gives presents away on her birthday these days. Even I am not allowed to give her anything. I must give something to someone in need instead.'

Duncan opened the door and saw his mother sitting on the floor with Hocks. They were surrounded by pieces of material, balls of string and loops of coloured ribbon. They were wrapping presents for the men on the wards, for the children of the Ansdrie paper-mill workers and for the Southampton children whose fathers died when *Titanic* went down. He and Lieutenant Haffie walked carefully between the presents and sat in chairs on either side of the fire. Lieutenant Haffie lit a pipe and asked Duncan if he thought he might smoke, one day.

'Oh, yes,' said Duncan, and a picture of the way he would look appeared in his mind. And then he realized he had put up his hand just as if he were holding a pipe. He was glad Lieutenant Haffie was not looking at him.

Mrs MacAlasdair bustled in and asked his mother how many plum puddings she would like for the men.

'As many as you have made,' said Natalie. 'And please bring the shortbread and the glacé fruits for the children. And of course, the marmalade.'

'Goodness me,' said Mrs MacAlasdair, 'you'll be here all night, my lady.'

'There are plenty of hands to help.'

Duncan knelt on the floor and began to wrap jars of Ansdrie marmalade, a little clumsily, in lengths of black velvet which he thought must have come from an old dress of his mother's for it smelled, faintly, of her lavender scent. He watched Lieutenant Haffie tie the men's presents with string while Hocks tied the children's with ribbon. And then he said, sitting on his haunches, 'Papa was a hero in France, Mama. Lieutenant Haffie told me. And he says Verrinder is grand. He keeps him supplied with sketching paper and charcoal all the time.'

Hocks looked as if she might cry and his mother looked as if she wanted him to stop talking. He suddenly realized he was very tired. His mother said, 'It's been a long day. We'll decorate the tree and finish these tomorrow.'

Duncan kissed his mother goodnight and shook Lieutenant Haffie's hand. But when he walked up the stairs he stumbled. He stared behind him at the offending step and then he blushed and hoped Coffie, his valet, had not heard him. He walked quickly into the night nursery and stopped. He had forgotten it was Holly Hope's room now, not his. A night light flickered on the table by her cot and Nurse Mackay slept in a bed beside her. He felt a stab of pity for the little girl and hoped she would not miss her mother too terribly when she was old enough to know what had happened.

He turned away towards his own bedroom. He did his best to stand without swaying while Coffie helped him undress and then he said, 'I'll teeth my brush myself,' and dismissed his valet. He walked a little crookedly to the bathroom. He brushed his teeth and stared at the shadow on his upper lip. He imagined himself with a neat, dark moustache like his father's. He would ask Lieutenant Haffie when he should begin to shave. He left the bathroom and walked back along the passage. He heard his mother's voice and began to walk quickly towards the sound for he realized she was crying. He would comfort her as he had tried to do, so often, since Mrs Haffie's death. And then he heard his mother say, 'Of course we shall keep Holly Hope here. I would do anything for dear, sweet Edwina.'

Their next few words were muffled, but then she said, clearly, 'The only reason my heart beats is because you are in the world.'

Duncan crouched by the banister and held his breath.

He remembered the way his mother had put her head on Lieutenant Haffie's shoulder when they stood by Mrs Haffie's grave, and the blood roared in his ears.

And then his mother let out a terrible, gasping sob and Duncan doubled over, as if her sob had come from inside him.

THIRTY-FIVE

On a small dance floor at the far end of the Winter Garden, Murray's Savoy Quartette played Dixieland jazz. Most of the tables were occupied and all the diners were in evening dress. Natalie wore a dress of dark green silk decorated with silver thread. Ansdrie wore his mess dress, the colours of his kilt and scarlet jacket contrasting sharply with the black dress suits of the other diners.

A waiter led them to their table and when Natalie picked up the menu the long, transparent green wing panels of her dress slid back along her arms. A notice at the top of the menu read: 'Red stars indicate items in short supply.'

She said, 'If I have lamb and you have beef we could have two courses.'

'How so?' said Ansdrie.

'By each eating some of the other's.'

Ansdrie smiled, but the nervous blink he had developed grew worse when he smiled. And he was thin, as were so many of the men in uniform.

'I'm so very happy to see you,' said Natalie. 'I only wish it were for longer.'

'All the leave I could get,' said Ansdrie. 'But now that I have seen our son, I shall spend the rest of my leave with you.'

'It's difficult to believe he's fifteen,' said Natalie. 'How was he?'

'He doesn't think digging up the fields of Eton is proper war work. I told him it was essential.' Ansdrie studied the menu and then he said, 'But he seemed unsettled. He kept starting sentences and not finishing them. Quite unlike him.'

Ansdrie's hand shook. He put the menu down and signalled to the waiter. He asked for whisky. Natalie put her hand on his to still its shaking and when the waiter returned with the whisky, Ansdrie swallowed it immediately and asked for another.

'It helps, you know,' he said. 'Stops the . . .' he moved his hand in circles by the side of his head, '. . . memories.'

'Duncan worries about you.'

'Yes,' said Ansdrie. 'I know. And I'm glad he's still too young. I don't think I could stand the idea. . . .'

Natalie waited.

'I know I should not say this, but Fountain's lucky. He may have lost a leg but he's safe in the War Office now.'

'Gussie's letters are full of her relief that he's no longer at the Front,' said Natalie. And then, 'I'm sorry, I should not have said that.'

'It's true,' said Ansdrie. 'We never admit it, but we all think it.'

Natalie squeezed her husband's hand and thought how many thousands of others suffered as he did, bravely and in silence. She was touched by his tenderness for their son. She said, 'Would you like to talk about . . . any of it?'

Ansdrie shook his head. 'Just got to get on with it,' he said. And then, 'How are my sisters?'

'Matron James is very strict about our leave,' said Natalie. 'Just as she should be. So we write to each other, and at least they're all together. But Millie's letters are heartbreaking. She seems to think if she had not left France, Étienne would still be alive. She's very brave about him; I can hardly bear to read what she writes. She says he died valiantly at Verdun and she feels only pride. And I'm sure she is proud, but I know how much I miss Edwina. The loss of Étienne must be terrible.'

'Poor Millie,' said Ansdrie. And then, 'Poor Haffie. Poor man.'

They looked at each other for a long moment and then Natalie said, 'I think perhaps I should like a glass of wine.'

'I should have asked if you would,' said Ansdrie. 'I'm sorry.'

And then, when the leader of Murray's Savoy Quartette announced a tune called 'Memories', Ansdrie held out his hand. Natalie took it and wondered how best to comfort him. It must be so very odd for him to sit in this glass-ceilinged room with its jasmine- and ivy-entwined pillars, its ornate plasterwork, its bright chandeliers and gaily dressed women, when he had lived and fought in conditions she could barely imagine. No wonder his eyelid twitched and his hand shook; no wonder he was so pale and the terrible memories plagued him.

'Well?' said Ansdrie. 'Would you?'

Natalie stared at him, uncomprehending.

'Would you care to dance?'

'Oh,' said Natalie, 'Oh, yes. Very much.'

When Ansdrie took Natalie in his arms he danced with a determination and concentration that touched her to the core. She followed him as if he danced like an angel and when he said, leaning in close to her, 'I believe this is a foxtrot,' she said, 'I believe it is, my dear. I didn't know—'

'In point of fact it seems to me,' said Ansdrie, looking down to correct his step, 'that it's just a simple combination of a long step and . . . some quicker ones.'

They danced a few circuits of the small floor to the melancholy melody of 'Memories' and then Ansdrie said, 'I brought you here because . . . should I die . . .' He cleared his throat and Natalie put her fingers to his mouth and gently shook her head. But he took her hand away.

'Should I buy it in the next big push,' he said, 'I should like my last memory to be of my wife, in my arms, dancing.'

THIRTY-SIX

IT WAS MORE than a year before Ansdrie returned to England.

He was wounded in the Battle of Arras and not discharged from Queen Mary's Hospital in Kent until October 1918. His face had healed, but even Harold Gillies's miraculous reconstruction could not hide the disfigurement. Holly Hope was the only human being to whom Ansdrie spoke with ease and the only one who was completely at ease with him. She had never known him before his injuries and when he returned to Ansdrie she mistook him for her own father.

'This is not your papa,' Natalie said, lifting her up and pulling down her white dress. 'This is your . . . ' she looked at Ansdrie for a suggestion, but he was mesmerized by Holly. He said, 'She's a little cherub,' in the lisping, hollow tone his injuries caused.

They were the first clear words Natalie had heard him speak since his return.

Hesitantly, Ansdrie stroked Holly's curling, red-gold hair and said, 'What are you carrying, little one?'

Holly held out a drawing Haffie had made for her just after she was born. It was a self-portrait, in regimental uniform.

'She will not be parted from it,' said Natalie.

'Papa,' Holly said, holding up the drawing. She stood before Ansdrie now, but still at a distance from him. 'Papa,' she said again, as if by saying 'Papa' Ansdrie would become her Papa.

He leaned down towards her and said, 'I'm wearing the same uniform, but I'm not your papa. He is in France.'

Holly looked up at him, puzzled. 'Papa. Fwance,' she said, but her disappointment was palpable and Ansdrie said, 'But, if you'd like, I'll be your proxy papa.' He smiled his lopsided smile, but Holly did not understand.

'Your second Papa.'

She stared at him.

'Your Papa Two, until your real papa comes home.'

'Papatoo!' she said. And very quickly she shortened it to Patoo, and Patoo he remained.

Ansdrie's gentleness with Holly touched Natalie. Her sunny presence soothed all the recovering officers and men at Ansdrie, but after the miracle she had worked on her own husband Natalie asked Nurse Mackay to bring her to him at least twice a day.

On a bright autumn day Natalie wheeled her husband along the drive. The beech trees she had planted shortly after they married stood at almost twenty feet, the copper and yellow of their leaves glowing against the blue sky. The glossy dark green of the rhododendron leaves set off the blazing scarlets and whites of their flowers, and Holly Hope ran and chattered among the officers and men. She paid no attention to Nurse Mackay's calls to her not to wet her coat when she sat on the grass.

'Let her play,' said Ansdrie.

Holly looked up at the sound of his voice. She stood and smiled. She stretched out her arms, her little fists clenched tightly round several yellow and copper leaves, her hair a red-gold halo in the sunlight.

'Come, Holly,' said Ansdrie, holding out his shaking arms. 'Sit with Patoo.'

Natalie stopped the chair so that Holly could clamber onto his knee. Gently Holly touched the eyepatch over his left eye and kissed what she called the *new* of his face. She said, 'Patoo, Patoo,' and Natalie's heart ached for her husband's tenderness, for his courage in the face of all he had been through, and for Holly's loss of her mother.

Duncan had a less easy time with his father. He had tried to tell him, when last he was on leave, something he badly wanted him to know. Instinctively, he knew he should not write it down but now, two years on, the urge to tell his father was still strong. He had been back from Eton for two days and yet he had still not found the right words, just as he had not when his father had been on leave. On this particular afternoon his father sat in his bath chair in his mother's morning room and Duncan drank tea with him. He would tell him now.

His father asked him to pour him a glass of whisky.

'Your mama does not approve,' he said, smiling his lop-sided smile. 'At least not in the day. But it helps with the . . .' he made a swirling movement with his hand, '. . . memories.'

Duncan poured the whisky and asked his father, for the first time, if he wanted to talk about the memories. He made the same swirling movement with his hand. He said, 'I think it might be a little like when we had to leave all those people behind in the water.'

His father looked at him and Duncan thought a tear shone in his one good eye.

'It is, Duncan,' he said. 'It is.' His lisping, hollow voice made Duncan wish the war had not injured him so badly.

'But I expect it's much worse.'

'I'm glad you shall never have to witness it,' said his father.

A log slipped and the fire blazed up behind him. Duncan stood to put another log on the fire and as he did so his father said, 'Now that the Australians and the Americans have made their great advances along the Western Front and the Hindenburg Line has been breached,' he raised his glass as Duncan turned back to him, 'it will be all over before you are seventeen.' He handed Duncan his glass. 'Pour me another, would you?' he said.

'You know how much I should like to do my bit,' said Duncan.

'Too many young men have given their lives, Duncan. I understand very well that you want to do what you can for your country, but you can do it through the business. You can do your bit to help put the country back on its feet when the time comes.'

Duncan handed the refilled glass to his father, took a deep breath and said, 'Men like you have given so much for your country. For all of us. You deserve everything good . . . everything. You have a right to absolute loyalty.'

'Duncan?' said his father. 'What's the matter?'

If he did not say it now, he never would.

'Papa,' he said, 'when Colonel Haffie was here, on compassionate leave, I heard Mama say . . . something to him. It was . . . well, I . . . I think you should know what she said.'

He had to tell him. He must tell him. He could not bear the idea that his father might be left alone in his frailty but he knew, in a small corner of his mind, that he was not making sense, for his mother had shown no sign of leaving. But the fear that she might had never left him.

But it proved far more difficult than he could have imagined to repeat what his mother had said and for the first time he questioned his desire to tell his father what he had heard. He had thought he would give him a weapon with which to kill his mother's love for another man and to reunite their family, but now he realized that weapon might actually hurt his father, might even cause a rift between his parents.

'What did she say?' said his father, after Duncan had

remained silent, alternately repeating what his mother had said in his mind and telling himself it would be better, for his family's sake, if he did not. But then he spoke very quickly, as if to speak quickly would rid him for ever of the terrible knowledge he had carried inside him. 'She said, "The only reason my heart beats is because you are in the world."'

His father's hand began to shake and the whisky swilled in the glass. He put it down unsteadily on the table beside him and said, 'Are you certain?'

'Yes.'

'Were you trying to tell me this when I was last on leave?'

'Yes.'

'But how ... did you hear your mother? Were you ... with them?'

'I was on the landing, above them. I ... I didn't see anything. I just heard what she said.'

Neither man spoke for a few moments, and then Duncan's father said, 'Your mama is a very sympathetic woman.'

But Duncan realized his father was struggling for words and he knew he had made a terrible mistake. He had hurt him through his own desire to relieve himself of the lonely burden of what he knew, what he thought his father should know, what he dreaded happening.

'You ... would not expect ... your mama to remain without feeling,' said his father. 'And especially not after Mrs Haffie died, would you?'

'No. Of course not. But this ... had nothing to do with Mrs Haffie.' Duncan chewed nervously at his thumb.

'You cannot know that, Duncan.'

His father's voice was more resonant now, stronger than his hollow lisp usually allowed. He picked up his glass and did not spill any whisky.

'It might be,' he said, 'that your mama was telling

Colonel Haffie something Mrs Haffie herself said. She and your mama were very good friends, you know. They confided in each other, the way women do.'

His father was making excuses for his mother; he was defending her. Duncan watched him turn his head and stare through the morning room window towards the terrace. He said, 'The men I see sometimes, Duncan, out there, the men I hear,' he lifted his arm and pointed his whisky glass towards the window, 'I think I know what they mean. I think I can make sense of them.' He turned his disfigured face back to Duncan. 'You hear your mama and Colonel Haffie talking, and you think you know what they mean. You think you can make sense of what they say. But you cannot know, you can only guess.'

'I know what I heard,' said Duncan.

'But you do *not* know its meaning,' said his father. 'And in the two years since you heard what your mother said . . . nothing has happened. Is that not proof enough?'

Duncan could not look at his father.

'Mrs Haffie died while your mother did everything she could to save her. Everything humanly possible, Duncan.' He put his empty glass down on the table. 'And I should have died on a hill in the middle of hell but for Colonel Haffie. He came back for me, Duncan. He saved my life when Verrinder and . . . all the others . . . died.' He stopped and his head dropped forwards. Duncan hurried to him and knelt by his bath chair. He put his hand on his father's arm. He wondered if he was having some kind of attack.

'Verrinder shielded me with his own body, Duncan,' said his father, turning to him and looking at him through his one good eye. 'He gave his life for mine. And then Haffie came back for me, through the carnage. He could only carry one man; he had to leave the others to die where they lay.'

Duncan took his father's glass and filled it with whisky. His own hands were shaking now. He poured some whisky for himself and when his father had taken a long swallow, he said, 'Neither your mama nor Colonel Haffie know what a treacherous heart is, Duncan.' He held his whisky glass to his own heart. 'They were not made that way.'

THIRTY-SEVEN

DESPITE THE WAR, Ansdrie Preserves flourished. Perhaps because people welcomed a little sweetness in their lives in the dark and sorrow-filled times they were living through.

Mrs MacAlasdair had perfected a quince jelly and a raspberry and mint preserve receipt which the Ansdrie factory in California had been making for three years, and the warehouse on the Clyde, which Ansdrie had so presciently stocked in August 1914 with all the Ansdrie marmalade the Californians could send, had received subsequent shipments despite the German U-boat blockade. Now Natalie held in her hands a notification of shipment for a further fifty cases that would arrive at the beginning of December. Groceries and hotels across Scotland continued to order Ansdrie Preserves; Natalie's Uncle Goodwin told her that orders were coming in from as far away as Australia and India and she had just received a letter from him telling her that he would soon transfer the third half per cent annual payment to the anonymous benefactor's solicitors. It would, he judged, be twenty-five pounds.

When Natalie told Ansdrie the good news he said, 'We must send Haffie a telegraph. Perhaps you would do that, my dear? It will cheer him to hear good news from home while he demobilizes his battalion.' And then he said, 'Is it not ironic that the business that finally rescued this house is one I had so little to do with?'

'You made all the original arrangements,' said Natalie. 'You undertook much before the war, and you fought to keep the business alive in its first two years.'

'But your dear father paid for it with his life,' said Ansdrie. 'It was my incompetence that caused him to sail to America.'

'It was his idea to sail,' said Natalie, 'and we agreed long ago that you must not blame yourself. So please don't, dear Jocelyn.'

Natalie rarely called him by his given name, but her heart went out to her husband when he smiled his disfigured smile, for it was, as with so many men, no longer an accurate reflection of the way he felt.

'I regret that your father will never know how successful the business has become.'

'So do I,' said Natalie. 'But we shall see Duncan inherit the house and the business one day. And perhaps, who knows, little Holly Hope will have a hand in the business, too. So many of the people who served us now have good employment with the company and that makes up for much, does it not? Even your mother might be . . . ' she hesitated.

'She would be glad,' said Ansdrie and he stretched out his hand.

'And you, my dear, have given much for your country,' said Natalie, kissing her husband's hand. 'For all of us, in ways we could never have foreseen.'

Natalie, Hocks, Duncan and Holly Hope decorated the wards for Christmas. The men talked about when they would go home and Holly Hope made them laugh when she put all the decorations on the lower branches of the trees, the only ones she could reach, and tied coloured ribbons to the metal rails at the ends of their beds. And those with disfigured faces thanked her, silently, when she tied paper decorations to their bedheads and did not flinch, when she looked at them as if there was nothing wrong with them, just as they hoped their own children would when first they saw their fathers' misshapen faces.

Duncan's own father had weakened since October. The wound in his thigh, from Beaumont Hamel, had reopened and he was bedridden. Natalie, Duncan and Holly decorated the Christmas tree in his bedroom and Natalie insisted they hang some delicate glass bowls that held candles from the branches. They were quite unlike the strings of large enamelled lightbulbs they used for the trees in the men's wards and Duncan had great difficulty persuading Holly to let him hang them, and to let him light the candles. He worried she would tie them haphazardly and they would topple and set fire to the tree. But he could not persuade her so, when she had gone, he rehung them all and made sure they were safe.

When they finished the decoration of the wards and had sung carols with the men, Duncan went to sit with his father. He had done his best to follow his line about his mother and Colonel Haffie for, if his father was determined that there was nothing in what he had overheard, then he too should not be concerned. But it was difficult. The words sometimes came back to him when he looked at his mother but she had said he must be kind and patient with his father, for he was weakened by all he had endured. And so Duncan did not talk about it again to his father, and they all did their best to distract him, to read to him, to make him laugh if they could, to be gentle with him while he regained his strength.

He poured his father a glass of whisky and held it to his lips, and then he began to read to him from the book he had asked for, *The Fair Maid of Perth*. After a little while Duncan realized his father was speaking to him, but in a tone so low he had to put his ear to his mouth to hear him. He asked him to repeat what he had said.

'Those glass candle holders,' he said, his voice hoarse and weak, 'they were on the tree in the room where I proposed to your mother.' He pointed with a shaking arm towards the tree and shifted his head to look beyond Duncan. And then, with a great effort, he said, 'There's something I must say.'

Duncan leaned very close and listened.

'If I should die—'

'Papa, please don't say such things. '

'If I should not make it through . . . I want you . . . to tell your mother . . .'

Duncan waited while his father took uneven breaths.

'If your mama should ever wish to marry again . . . tell her . . . I never wanted her to remain on her own. Not for my sake or for anyone else's.' He looked at Duncan through his dark eye. 'Tell her she has my blessing . . . promise me, Duncan.'

His father had struggled and fought to speak and now Duncan waited while his breathing calmed before he answered him. When he spoke he could not look at him, for the expression in his eye was one of such desperation, such pleading, that he knew if he looked at him he would have no choice but to give him the answer he wanted to hear.

'I . . . I . . . find it very difficult to think of her with anyone but you, Papa,' he said, hoping with all his heart his father would recover and he would never have to fulfill this dreadful duty.

He helped his father to sit up and then he held the glass of whisky to his lips once more and his father whispered, hoarsely, 'Do it . . . for my sake.'

But Duncan could not answer.

Later that evening, when his mother came in to change his father's dressing, his shaking became very pronounced and she discussed with Doctor Harrison, outside the bedroom, what to do about a rash of small, angry spots that had appeared by his thigh wound.

'Septicaemia, I suspect,' said Doctor Harrison, in a whisper. 'I'll give him a serum injection. And I'll return in the morning.'

That night, the night of 23 December, Duncan and his mother sat up with his father. He seemed to sleep soundly but when, early on Christmas Eve, his skin shone with sweat even though his forehead was cold, his mother brought hot-water bottles and covered him with blankets.

His good eye did not focus when she said, 'Try to sleep now, my dear,' and he said, 'Good man, Verrinder. Good man. That'll thaw the kilt. That'll do it.'

In the evening Doctor Harrison said, 'Keep him comfortable. I'll come again tomorrow.'

'But tomorrow is Christmas Day,' his mother said.

'A working day in Scotland,' said Doctor Harrison. 'I'll be here.' And then, as he walked towards the door, he bent down and said, 'Well, hello, wee one. What brings you here?'

Duncan turned to see Holly Hope standing in the doorway, in her nightdress, holding her favourite knitted doll. He touched his mother's arm.

'Holly!' she said, jumping up. 'You should be in bed.'

Holly stood on tiptoe and said, 'Patoo?'

'Yes,' said Duncan, 'it is Patoo. He's . . . not very well.'

He looked at his mother, who hesitated and then she nodded, and Duncan stood and took Holly by the hand. He sat her on his knee and then she clambered onto his father's bed and folded her little body into the crook of his arm. He tried to hug her and murmured something Duncan could not understand. Holly kissed the *new* of his face and said, 'Night-night, Patoo.'

Duncan saw the tears in his mother's eyes and when he lifted Holly from his father's bed and carried her towards the door, she turned back and said, 'Night-night, Patoo,' again.

His mother blew Holly a kiss and then she turned back to his father and kissed him just where Holly had kissed him.

Duncan stayed by his father, with his mother, all night. They slept and woke by turns, but neither of them slept for very long. And on Christmas Day, very early in the morning, Duncan watched his mother offer plum pudding and whisky butter to his father. But he could not manage it, so they ate it together. From time to time his father spoke single words, and sometimes several words, but the only word that was possible to understand was, 'Holly.'

And then, after Natalie had opened the curtains and her husband stretched out his shaking arm to her, she bent over him and told him she loved him. She called him Jocelyn, which Duncan had never heard her do before. And then she picked up a square of lint from the bedside table. She stood by him and held the lint against his forehead. When it was soaked with sweat she replaced it with another piece and, after a moment or two, Duncan's father closed his eye. Then his mother soaked another piece of lint in water and held it to his father's lips. His thin body sank so low beneath the covers he might not have been there at all.

His mother said, turning to Duncan and then back to his father, 'We shall stay with you, my dear. We shall not leave you.'

She leaned down to kiss him and when her pearls fell forward and touched his mouth he said something that sounded like, 'Ay.'

His mother said, 'There's no need to speak, my dear. I know how it exhausts you. You and I have said all we shall ever need to say.'

But his father did speak again and, this time, his mother understood what he was saying.

'Almost, my dear,' she said. 'It is almost day.'

His father became agitated and struggled beneath the covers. His mother tried to calm him but he shook his right arm free and pointed at her. Duncan stood and hurried to the other side of his father's bed. He put his hands beneath his shoulders to help him sit up. And then his father said, on a long exhaling breath, 'Burrday.'

His mother began to cry.

She looked up at Duncan and then turned back to his father and stretched her hand across the bed to her son and all three held hands. She said, 'Oh, my dear, how wonderful of you to remember. It *is* my birthday.'

And their arms made a triangle, the strongest shape known to man.

THIRTY-EIGHT

IN A DAZED and unhappy state, just two weeks before her husband died, Natalie Ansdrie voted for the first time in her life. And now she asked Hocks to cut her hair short, the way the woman who had stood in front of her at the ballot box had worn her hair. She told herself she did it so that she would be able to manage her own hair while Hocks ran the Ansdrie Preserves office but, deep in her heart, Natalie knew her short hair marked the death of the man she had lived beside, for the most part harmoniously, for seventeen years. The man who had stood by her and loved her more deeply than she had ever been able to love him. The day after Hocks cut her hair, on Hogmanay, the last day of 1918, Natalie received a letter in a hand she did not recognize.

She stood in her morning room and stared at it. She did not open the letter until she had opened every other envelope that arrived that morning, including confirmation from her Uncle Goodwin of orders for Ansdrie Preserves from Sydney, Brisbane, Canberra and Perth. When at last she did open the letter she found a second envelope inside addressed to Ansdrie, in Haffie's handwriting. And when she looked to see who her letter was from she saw Haffie's sister's name: Sarah.

Natalie's heart began to beat quickly. She read Haffie's

letter to her husband first. It told him Charles Goodwin would confirm he was the man who had put money into Ansdrie Preserves, in 1912, and that, in the event of his death, there was no need to continue to pay the interest. He wrote, 'If I had not told Edwina how much your wife liked dancing, she would not have bought the Maxixe recordings and all that happened would not have happened. Your orangeries would still be flourishing and you, your father-in-law and your son would not have sailed for New York. But you will only read this if I—'

Natalie dropped Haffie's letter and, with shaking hands, began to read the one from his sister:

29 December 1918, Highfields

Dear Lady Ansdrie,

I write this with a heavy heart.

I leave it to you to decide when Holly Hope should be told, but I had a letter this morning, from the War Office, to say that Angus is missing, believed killed. They apologized for the delay. They said it had taken longer in some parts of France to account properly for all officers and men.

I thought perhaps Holly might come to live here, with my father and me. We are her blood relations and I would do my best for her, as her aunt-mother, but my father is frail now and your family is the only family Holly has known, poor little thing. I think it might be less upsetting for her if she stayed with you, if you can manage to keep her.

I look forward to hearing what you should like to do. If you have a telephone you can telephone to us at Broughton 3.

With my heartfelt good wishes,

Sarah Haffie

PS: This letter to Lord Ansdrie was sent to me by Angus's commanding officer.

Natalie stared at the words. And then, as if a tidal wave had surged and broken inside her, a deep sadness overwhelmed her. Her throat ached, her body began to shudder and she was blinded by tears. She stumbled towards the chair by her desk, searched hopelessly for a handkerchief and then she gave in utterly to her grief.

She cried for her father, whose body had never been found. She cried for Duncan and his terrible ordeal in the North Atlantic. She cried for Ansdrie and her guilt that she had not loved him enough, that she had almost broken their marriage. She cried for his disfigured face. She cried for Étienne and she cried for Verrinder and the hundreds of thousands of women and children who would never see their loved ones again.

She cried for Edwina and she cried for their miscarried children.

She cried for her own mother.

And she cried for a life lived without the passionate love she had so confidently believed would be hers, once: a love that had begun one fine spring morning when a stranger had hummed 'Blow the Wind Southerly' by the Bridewell River.

Part Five

1919

Iseachan:

that which is past

THIRTY-NINE

I T WAS IN a dreich spring that the Allied powers met to draw up treaties to agree the end of the most destructive war mankind had ever known, and all those at Ansdrie did their best to come to terms with the loss of the men they had loved so much.

Duncan often found his mother in tears and he tried to resist his own. He wished he could do something to alleviate her burden of unhappiness but every time he attempted to comfort her his own tears threatened to overwhelm him and he did not want her to see him cry, so he remained uncomfortably aloof when she said, 'So many thousands dead, Duncan; we should consider ourselves lucky. But your father, Edwina, Colonel Haffie, Verrinder, Arthur and the two young undergardeners: it's very hard,' and her tears would fall once more.

Sometimes his mother included her own father when she spoke of the dead and her particular grief for him prompted his own private grief for his father. At those times he would saddle his mother's horse, Artemis, the only horse the army had never commandeered because she was too old, and he would ride alone in the Formonts, barely seeing the fresh new growth on the ashes and the sycamores for his tears. Despite the proximity of his mother and Holly, he felt very much alone.

That spring also saw the end of a fatally infectious influenza epidemic, which, mercifully, had never found its way into the Ansdrie Auxiliary Hospital thanks to Doctor Harrison's and Matron James's stringent hygiene precautions. Anyone who had no purpose at Ansdrie was refused entry at the gates, a good mile along the drive. Those who had legitimate business were issued with anti-germ gauze masks and instructed not to touch anyone or to talk to them, unless absolutely necessary. And those who had to come and go were instructed to make as little contact with other people outside the hospital as possible. Cutlery, crockery and glasses were disinfected as if they were pieces of surgical equipment, and the last soldiers who were brought to Ansdrie to convalesce were given disinfectant bed baths before any other treatment was administered.

Mr Emmanuel Shinwell, Chairman of the Glasgow Trades Council, had a hand in settling the strike that might have prevented the unloading of the latest shipment of Ansdrie Preserves on the Clyde when he said, 'There were no plans for revolution, simply a wish to make life in Britain a semblance of the Land Fit For Heroes so glibly promised by Lloyd George.' And, as the officers and men recovered and began to leave Ansdrie for home, Natalie, and the remaining servants who were not gainfully employed by Ansdrie Preserves, set about dismantling the wards and restoring the house as best they could to its former, pre-war self.

Natalie had not the heart to tell Holly Hope her father had died. Every time she saw the happy little child she remembered Edwina and thought she would have delayed telling her daughter until she was older, so she delayed. She had decided to keep Holly at Ansdrie so that her life remained as undisturbed as possible. And in this way she kept Haffie alive in her own heart too, although she was barely conscious that she did so. But the idea of Holly growing up without either of her parents was so painful that Natalie could not, yet, tell her, or do anything to show her that it would be so.

Natalie actively encouraged Holly when she called her Matoo, just as she had called Ansdrie Patoo, and when she telephoned Sarah Haffie from the Ansdrie Post Office, she accepted her invitation to stay at Kilmalieu House for Easter week so that, as Sarah said, Holly would have a chance to see the house her father had so loved, before it was sold.

When the time came Natalie contemplated sending Duncan and Holly with Nurse Mackay, without going herself, for she was not certain she could bear to stay in the house she had once thought she would see for the first time with her lieutenant beside her. It would be easier to leave it all in the past. But Holly clung to her, as if she had intuited her father's death through Natalie's evasive answers to her questions. She would not allow Natalie out of her sight; she behaved just as Duncan had when he returned from America. So they travelled northwest together, Natalie, Duncan, Holly and Nurse Mackay; and Holly proved a merciful distraction for Duncan, who had not set foot on a boat since 1912 and who obviously found the ferry's battle with the surging current in the Corran Narrows alarming.

'We're almost there,' Natalie shouted to him, while Holly kept asking him about the birds they could see circling above.

'You can see the jetty if you look behind you,' said Natalie.

But Duncan clung to the ship's rail and stared at the churning water, his face pale.

'Say, Duncan, say,' said Holly, pointing upwards while the wind whipped her red-gold hair round her face beneath her beret.

Duncan looked up and said, 'It's a golden eagle.'

He picked her up and held her tightly. She had an uncanny knack of knowing what to do when a person was frightened, or worried. Perhaps because she had witnessed such distress on the Ansdrie Hospital wards, perhaps because she had unconsciously absorbed her mother's distress when she was born, but Natalie watched her distract her son and loved her for it.

The ferry struggled to keep its course against a strong southerly current but the spring air was clear, calm and shot through with sunlight. Holly pointed towards the snow-capped mountains to the north and asked if that was where they were going and when Duncan shook his head she clapped her hands against his cheeks and squeezed them until he had to laugh. And then the engine's roar became a watery rumble, the ferry slowed beside a narrow stone jetty and the ferryman jumped down, holding a mooring line.

Sarah Haffie said, 'Welcome to Ardgour. You brought the good weather with you.' Her mourning clothes fitted her short, stout body closely; but she had Haffie's sandy, curling hair and the same crescent-moon lines appeared on either side of her mouth when she smiled.

They shook hands, and Natalie introduced Duncan, Nurse Mackay and finally Holly to her aunt. Holly stayed very close to Natalie when Sarah Haffie said, 'I thought we should have an Easter egg hunt. Would you like that, Holly?'

Holly smiled, shyly, and asked what an Easter egg hunt was, and as her aunt told her she took tentative steps towards her and then, after much conversation about Easter eggs and, among the adults, about how clever Sarah had been to find any chocolate at all, Holly put her small hand into her aunt's and said, 'Long way Papa house?'

'A couple of miles as the crow flies,' said Sarah. 'A little more by car.'

The little group, all dressed in mourning except for

Holly, walked towards a green Belsize and a pony and cart that stood above the stone jetty. When a flight of swallows darted above them Duncan mimicked their excited chatter and laughed when Holly copied him. They clambered into the car while a man called Kennedy loaded their bags into his cart. Sarah Haffie took the wheel of the Belsize and they bumped along a narrow lane bordered by beeches. Holly sat on Natalie's knee beside Sarah. Duncan and Nurse Mackay sat in the back and Kennedy followed in the cart.

They drove through open moorland and crossed shallow burns. When they were high above the loch they turned west and away from it. The land sloped down to the east and Natalie saw a wide bay with a shingle beach. Several tall Scots pines grew by the bay and shaggy highland cattle grazed in a field behind it. A little to the south of the bay, at the base of the moorland incline, stood a whitewashed house. It had its back to them.

'That's Kilmalieu,' Sarah shouted above the noise of the car.

They drove downhill across the moorland and Natalie saw, on the other side of the loch, the concave mountain Haffie had painted. They drove further downhill across the moor and then along a narrow lane between drystone walls where bright green moss clung to the stones. And then they turned off the lane and drove through a wooden gate. Sarah stopped the Belsize in front of the slate-roofed, whitewashed stone house. The window frames were painted green and the wide lawn that ran down to the loch was bordered on either side with bright azaleas and rhododendrons.

Natalie looked up at the house she had seen, so long ago, in a gallery in London. Holly said, 'Papa house,' and Natalie realized she should not have brought her for she would think her father would be here too. She explained, as gently as she could, that her father was not at the house, but Holly simply said, 'Papa come,' and no one had the heart to contradict her.

'There is much to do, as you may imagine,' said Sarah. 'I have made a start. But you must choose what you should like to keep for Holly. There are so many paintings.'

A burn rushed over stones nearby and, as the sun came out from behind a large white cloud and made the loch shimmer, Sarah said, 'You must look. It is such a sight.' And they all turned and looked out across the loch and watched the way the sunlight made the water sparkle and glint; watched the water lapping against grey rocks covered with yellow lichen and brown bladderwrack; looked at the flat-topped mountain with its concave curve on the opposite shore.

'It's called the Isle of Iseachan,' said Sarah. 'And the mountain is Beinn Iseachan.'

Natalie stared at the island and at the mountain, wordlessly, and for longer than any of the others. She was very grateful to Duncan when he said, to Holly, 'See? There? It's a seal,' for he gave her a reason to look at something else, but then she remembered how Haffie had spoken of the selkies, the creatures who captured the hearts of men and disappeared, and she could not join in when her son told Holly what a seal was.

At last, Sarah said, 'Goodness, I'm quite forgetting my manners. Come inside. Take off your coats. Cook has made some soup.'

And Natalie followed quickly, staring only at the rough grass she walked across.

The walls in the hall were hung with Haffie's paintings. The bright, sunlit ones Natalie could look at without difficulty, but the ones of the Bridewell were very hard for her to look at, particularly the one where the mist still lay above the river and the branches of the willows looked almost black in the pale morning light. But Natalie asked Sarah, one evening when Holly was already in bed, whether she might take the sunlit paintings for her.

'He made them in the Sandwich Islands,' said Sarah. 'It would be most fitting. Her mother and father were both so very happy there, poor little mite.'

If Sarah knew about Natalie's love for Haffie she gave no sign and for that Natalie was grateful, for what was there to say? To her, his paintings were poignant reminders of a life she might once have lived with a man she had once loved with all her heart and soul, and she took to walking quickly through the hall with her eyes focused straight ahead.

The walls in the sitting-room were easier for they were lined with bookshelves that held the poetry of Robert Burns and James Macpherson, the novels of Robert Louis Stevenson and Walter Scott. There were histories of the Argyll clans, who fought over the ancient Highland lands, and there was a pamphlet about the Clearances that Natalie read with horror.

She read to Holly Hope from the legends and folk tales of Argyll but when, one evening, she turned the page to find a selkie story she asked Duncan to read it to Holly for she did not trust herself not to betray her sadness. But as she listened to her son reading she discovered the story was not unbearable. She realized she was glad to be here, glad to think she could lay the ghost of her love for Haffie here, in the place he had loved above all others.

Sarah encouraged Duncan to take the boat out to fish the loch, but he discovered he was, embarrassingly, reluctant. He had no desire to repeat the frightening experience on the ferry; he was already dreading their journey home. But one morning his mother said, 'I should like to fish. Will anyone come with me?'

Holly wanted to, but Natalie said she could not look after her and fish and manage the boat. Sarah said, if no one objected, she would carry on sorting things out. She was not specific about exactly what she would sort out because they had told Holly they were merely deciding which things they would take south and which they would leave in the house. They had not told her that this was the only time she would see her father's house, but they made sure she saw every part of it and heard stories about it so that, when she was older, she would have at least a few memories of the house and the land, the mountain and the loch her father had loved.

And then a day came when the loch was as calm as a looking glass and Duncan allowed his mother to persuade him to fish with her. But when they were out on the loch he remembered how calm the sea had been on the night he spent in the lifeboat, and his anxiety returned. His mother took the oars and Holly, without knowing she did, distracted him with her constant 'Whys' and 'Whats'. He pointed out the mountain, Beinn Iseachan, and told her that puffins and gannets would return every year to nest there. He imitated the chattering and the strange *hmmm* sounds of the fulmars and Holly copied him but, all the time, he was afraid the terrible sights and sounds he had witnessed the last time he had been in a small boat on calm water would make it impossible for him to row, let alone to speak sensibly; and he did not want to disgrace himself.

His mother said, 'I should like to cast here, Duncan. Will you take the oars?'

Reluctantly, he changed places with his mother. But when Holly insisted on sitting beside him, which made rowing difficult, he discovered he was grateful for her distracting presence. All his mother wanted was for him to keep the boat steady while she cast, and he managed to do that. And then, when she asked him to row further up the loch he managed to do that too, with Holly perched sideways on his knee. And, without immediately realizing what was happening to him, Duncan began to enjoy himself. And then, after a little more time, he realized he had taken up a pair of oars and nothing bad had happened. He had heard no screams or cries for help. He had not become colder than the brisk spring weather would naturally make him. And most of all he had not disgraced himself; he had not been uncontrollably afraid.

He looked behind him to see where his mother wanted him to stop and when she smiled and said, 'Just here, thank you,' he felt a rush of love for her. Her simple desire to go fishing had shown him that being in a boat would not always remind him of what had once happened. He smiled at her and hoped she would understand how grateful he was.

He looked across the loch at the mountain, whose flanks were grey and green in the sunlight, whose shadows were purple and blue. Granite rocks and ledges jutted out above the trees and the burns gleamed and flashed silver when the sunlight caught them. In places, where the burns spilled over the granite ledges or down ravines, they burst into clouds of white foam and the air was just as it always was at Ansdrie, so clear that it seemed to sparkle and, just as at Ansdrie at this time of year, yellow furze bloomed everywhere.

When they arrived back at the house, Duncan and his mother pulled the wooden boat out of the water and left it above the tide line, and then they walked back behind the rhododendrons up the path to the house. By the gate, Duncan saw a weathered signpost that pointed towards the loch. He had not noticed it before.

'Loch Dubhe,' he said, pronouncing it as they had heard it spoken: *Dooie*. 'Did you know that was how it was spelled?'

'No,' said his mother. She paused, looked at him and then, as if she had made a decision, she said, 'A long time ago, before you were born, a man I knew told me about this part of the world. But I only ever heard him talk of it. I never saw the loch's name written down.'

Holly skipped ahead of them, a purple rhododendron

flower in her hand, and Duncan took his mother's arm as they turned towards the house.

'It's written just the way the star that points to the guiding star is written,' he said.

'The star I taught you to look for,' said his mother and she gave Duncan a quick kiss. 'The star my father taught me to look for.'

Although the man she spoke of was obviously Colonel Haffie – for who else would have told his mother he loved this particular part of the world? – to his great surprise Duncan found that he did not mind. He had seen the sadness in his mother's eyes and heard the loneliness in her voice for several months. He knew how much she missed all those who had died and now, in his own grief for his father, he felt his mother's grief and her loneliness just as if it were his own.

He stood beside her, gazing across the loch that had been named for a star that had shown him where he was on the most terrible night of his life. He felt the comforting solidity of the earth beneath his feet and, when he turned to his mother and thanked her for asking him to take the oars while she fished, he realized that if Colonel Haffie had lived he would, now, have done what his father had asked, if his mother had shown any sign that she wished it. For her kindness to him, her thoughtful, loving generosity, had banished his fear of small boats, perhaps for ever, and he longed to be able to do something equally loving, equally generous, for her sake.

In the brisk spring days that followed they walked by the loch or on the moor; they read or were read to, and every evening, after Holly had gone to bed, Sarah, Natalie, Nurse Mackay and Duncan sorted out Haffie's possessions.

On Easter Sunday they went to the little church by the loch, just south of Kilmalieu House, and then Sarah hid Easter eggs for Holly. By the end of the week, they were ready to leave. Boxes of Haffie's possessions were stacked in the back hall and his guests went to bed with their own bags packed.

But the following morning they woke to find the world about them unusually quiet. When Natalie drew back her bedroom curtains she saw it had snowed heavily. Beinn Iseachan was white right down to the edge of Loch Dubhe and Holly was already busy, with Duncan's help, making a snowman on the lawn between the snow-laden azaleas and rhododendrons.

At breakfast, Natalie and Sarah agreed the Belsize was unlikely to make it across the moorland and Sarah said, 'Even Kennedy might not make it here in this snow.'

As the day wore on and more snow fell from the white-grey sky, they prepared to stay at least one more night on the shores of Loch Dubhe. The wind sent white flakes flurrying and eddying round the house and they put the winter cloaks and coats they found in the porch over their light spring clothes, and lit the fire. They wondered when exactly they would leave. Late in the afternoon when the light had almost gone, Holly Hope went upstairs to fetch her knitted doll, 'Because she's cold,' she said.

Natalie, Sarah and Duncan sat by the roaring fire puzzling over a wooden jigsaw while Nurse Mackay knitted a green hat for Holly. When they heard Holly running down the wooden stairs they glanced at each other, and when she burst into the room, clutching her doll and said, breathlessly, 'Soldier coming,' they all stood up.

Holly insisted they come to her attic bedroom to look, but when they did they could not see what she had seen.

'It's very difficult to see anything in this snow, darling,' said Natalie.

'Soldier,' said Holly, determinedly, and she would not move. So they waited by the window under the eaves while the snow flew about the house, to humour her. They peered out often but no one saw anything or anyone, and at last they persuaded Holly to leave the window. But as she was turning away she dropped her doll and when she turned back to pick it up she said, 'There!' and pointed. And, through a gap in the eddying snow, Natalie saw what Holly had seen: it was a soldier. He walked with a swinging stride and his kilt swayed from side to side. His kitbag was slung over his shoulder and he was heading across the moorland and down the hill towards the house.

'Patoo!' said Holly.

'It's not Patoo,' said Natalie, putting her hands gently on Holly's shoulders and drawing her back from the window. 'You know he has gone to heaven.'

But Natalie's heart beat wildly now, for she knew just who the soldier was.

She covered Holly's ears with her hands, turned to her son and whispered, 'Tell me I'm not imagining it. Tell me I can see Holly's father out there in the snow.'

'You're not imagining it, Mama,' said Duncan, and he gave Natalie a shy smile. 'It is Colonel Haffie.' And then he took her arm, turned her from the window and said, 'Why don't you go out to welcome him? If . . . if my wife had died and I'd been fighting for as long as he has . . . I'd want to see someone who . . . who knew me very well. Just as soon as I could.'

FORTY

NATALIE RAN DOWN the stairs and out into the porch. She took off her shoes, laced up her boots and reached for the nearest hat and coat. She opened the front door and walked outside into the swirling snow. She tucked her short hair up beneath the hat, pulled up the collar of the coat and put her hands into its pockets as she began to run. The cold air caught in her throat and in her lungs, but she lifted her face to the falling snow and thanked it with all her heart for making it impossible for them to leave Kilmalieu House on the day they had planned to leave.

She ran through the gate and out into the lane. The wind blew against her back and pushed her along, but it was difficult to see anything clearly through the thickly falling snow. She knew Haffie had been walking diagonally across the moor and if she went too far along the lane she would miss him.

She stopped and braced herself against the wind. She turned and leaned against the drystone wall and tried to see through the swirling snowflakes. And then she heard footsteps crunching across the snow. She saw him, or at least she saw a figure on the other side of the wall a little way below her, a figure which would, surely, turn out to be Haffie. She ran back down the lane and arrived just as the figure jumped down from the wall.

It was Haffie, but when he looked at her he did not seem to recognize her.

He said, 'I think I've lost my bearings. Do you know Kilmalieu House?'

'Yes,' she said. 'I'm . . . staying there. I could take you there.'

He stood very still, and then he gave a shout of laughter, dropped his kitbag and held out his arms. The two crescent-moon lines stood out clearly on either side of his mouth and snowflakes clung to his glengarry and to his pale eyelashes as he said, 'That wouldn't be John Boundy, would it?'

As Natalie walked into his arms she reached up to take off the hat and, shaking out her short, grey-speckled hair, she said, 'It is, Angus Haffie. It is.'

A short bibliography:

Lawrence Beesley, *The Loss of the Titanic* Houghton Mifflin, 1912

Alan Bishop and Mark Bostridge (editors), *Letters from a Lost Generation, First World War Letters of Vera Brittain and Four Friends* Abacus, 1999

Nancy Bradfield, *Costume in Detail 1720-1930* Eric Dobby Publishing, 1968

Vera Brittain, *Testament of Youth* Virago Press, 2008

Anita Leslie, *Edwardians in Love* Hutchinson, 1972

Juliet Nicolson, *The Perfect Summer* John Murray, 2007

JoAnne Olian (editor), *Victorian and Edwardian Fashions from 'La Mode Illustrée'* Dover Publications, 1998

John Peacock, *Men's Fashion, The Complete Sourcebook* Thames and Hudson, 1996

J.B. Priestley, *The Edwardians* Harper & Row, 1970

Len Smith, *A Finger in the Pie, A War Artist's Diary 1914-1918* downloaded from Forgotten Titles: http://www.forgottentitles.com/index.html

Warne's Modern Manuals, *Modern Etiquette, in Private and Public* Frederick Warne & Co., 1900

And, of course, the internet.